The Last Victim

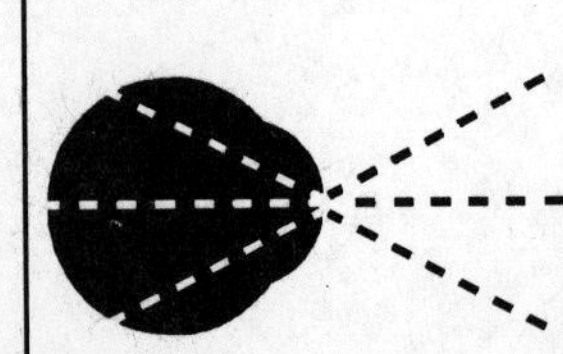

This Large Print Book carries the
Seal of Approval of N.A.V.H.

The Last Victim

Karen Robards

WHEELER PUBLISHING
A part of Gale, Cengage Learning

Detroit • New York • San Francisco • New Haven, Conn • Waterville, Maine • London

The Last Victim is a work of fiction. Names, characters, places, and incidents either are the product of the author's imagination or are used fictitiously, and any resemblance to actual persons, living or dead, business establishments, events, or locales is entirely coincidental.

Wheeler Publishing Large Print Hardcover.
The text of this Large Print edition is unabridged.
Other aspects of the book may vary from the original edition.
Set in 16 pt. Plantin.

LIBRARY OF CONGRESS CATALOGING-IN-PUBLICATION DATA

Robards, Karen.
The last victim / by Karen Robards.
pages ; cm.
ISBN 978-1-4104-5028-9 (hardcover) — ISBN 1-4104-5028-7 (hardcover)
1. Women forensic scientists—Fiction. 2. Women psychiatrists—Fiction.
3. Serial murderers—Fiction. 4. Serial murder investigation—Fiction.
5. Virginia Beach (Va.)—Fiction. 6. Large type books. I. Title.
PS3568.O196L37 2012b
813'.54—dc22 2012026197

Published in 2012 by arrangement with The Ballantine Publishing Group, a division of Random House, Inc.

Printed in the United States of America
1 2 3 4 5 6 7 16 15 14 13 12

This book is dedicated to
Dr. Randal S. Weber.
The words *thank you* are way too small
to express my profound gratitude.
You not only saved Peter's life,
you gave it back to him.

I also want to thank
Dr. Patrick Garvey,
Dr. David Rosenthal,
Dr. Merrill Kies,
and the entire staff at
M.D. Anderson Cancer Center in
Houston, Texas.
These wonderful people make miracles
every day.

ACKNOWLEDGMENTS

No author works in a vacuum, and I certainly don't. Without my husband, Doug, and sons, Peter, Christopher, and Jack, I'd have far fewer things to write about, believe me. Love you guys!

I also want to thank my wonderful editor, Linda Marrow, and the entire staff at Ballantine Books for all your help and support.

Chapter One

If Charlie Stone hadn't drunk the Kool-Aid, she would have died.

But in the random way the world sometimes works, the seventeen-year-old did drink several big tumblers full of Goofy Grape generously mixed with vodka, courtesy of her new best friend Holly Palmer. As a result, she just happened to be in the utilitarian bathroom off the Palmers' basement rec room, hugging the porcelain throne when the first scream penetrated her consciousness.

Even muffled by floors and walls and who knew what else, it was loud and shrill and urgent enough to penetrate the haze of misery she was lost in.

"Holly?" Charlie called, lifting her head, which felt like it weighed a ton and pounded unmercifully.

No answer.

Okay, her voice was weak. Probably Holly

hadn't heard her. Probably the scream was nothing, Holly's little brothers fighting or something. Seeing that it was around two a.m., though, shouldn't the eleven- and thirteen-year-olds have been asleep? Charlie had no idea: she knew nothing about tweenie boys. God, she should have followed her instinct and just said no to the booze. But as the new girl in Hampton High School's senior class, Charlie hadn't felt like she was in a position to refuse. From the first day of school, when they'd found out they were sharing a locker, sweet, popular Holly had taken Charlie under her wing, introduced her around. For that, Charlie was grateful. The veteran of seven high schools in just over three years, Charlie knew from bitter experience that there were a lot more mean girls out there than nice ones.

A late August Friday night in this small North Carolina beach town meant the movies. Four of them had gone together. The other two had moms who were reliable about picking their daughters up after. When Charlie's mom hadn't shown (typical), Holly had invited her to spend the night. They'd wound up sneaking out to meet Holly's boyfriend, Garrett — a total hottie, who had to work till midnight, which was past Holly's curfew — and go for a ride in his car. Since he'd had a friend with him — James, not quite as hot as Garrett, but *still* — it had actually worked out pretty well, except for the whole toxic Kool-Aid thing.

They'd driven to the shore, plopped down in the sand, and shared the concoction Garrett had mixed for them while they talked and watched the waves.

The good news was, Charlie might actually have gotten a bead on landing her own boyfriend. The bad news was, as soon as Garrett had dropped them off and they'd crept back down to the basement where supposedly they'd been watching TV all along, Charlie had had to rush straight to the bathroom. She'd been in there for what felt like forever, being sick as a parrot.

She'd be lucky if Holly ever invited her over again.

The second scream definitely did not come from one of the boys. High-pitched and shattering, it smashed through the ordinary sounds of the babbling TV and humming air-conditioning and thumping dryer in the next room like an axe through Jell-O. The fear in it was enough to make the hair stand up on the back of Charlie's neck. Until it abruptly cut off, she forgot to breathe. The ensuing silence pulsated with . . . something. Tension, maybe. An electric kind of heaviness. Shooting to her feet, she swiped her long brown hair back from her face with one hand and headed for the door. Knees weak, battling a disorienting attack of the woozies along with the worst taste ever in her mouth, she grabbed the cold-from-the-air-conditioning brass knob.

"Teach you to ignore me . . ." The words were followed by the sharp sound of a blow. It was a man's voice, low and deep. Mr. Palmer? Had he found out they'd snuck out?

Charlie froze, her hand still on the knob. She could see herself in the mirror over the sink. Average height, maybe a little too plump. Her face, cute, round, currently rosy from her mostly futile attempts to tan, had gone utterly white. Her blue eyes were the approximate size and shape of golf balls. The yellow T-shirt she wore with jeans looked neon bright in the drab space. Tonight there would be no blending in to the background for her. Earlier, standing out was what she had wanted. Her yet-to-be-proven theory was that, unlike birds, brilliant plumage on girls helped to attract boys. Whatever, James had seemed to like her.

"Don't go anywhere," the man said. At

the ugly note in his voice, Charlie let go of the knob and took a step back. Pulse pounding, she stared at the raw wood panel. The tiny bathroom with its plain white toilet and sink and unpainted concrete block walls seemed to shrink as she stood there. There was no window, no way out except through that door.

Her heart thudded so hard she could feel it knocking in her chest.

A moment later the unmistakable creak of the door to the rec room told her it was being opened. She didn't hear it shut, but then she didn't hear anything after that. No footsteps, no voices. What was happening? Was he gone? Where was Holly?

All Charlie knew for sure was that she wasn't about to just open that door.

Instead she dropped to her knees and tried looking beneath it, through the crack between door and floor.

The overhead light was still on, just like it was when she'd run for the bathroom. She could see the rug, a tan kind of Aztec print laid down over the concrete. She could see two legs of the coffee table, and a sliver of the tan leather couch. And Holly's feet. Yes, definitely Holly's feet, bare like her own. Slim and tanned, toenails painted bubblegum pink, poking out from beneath the fashionably raggedy hems of her jeans.

Judging from their position, Holly was lying on her side on the floor between the coffee table and the couch.

Charlie wet her lips. Something bad had happened. Something was really wrong.

Even as Charlie watched, Holly's toes curled, straightened, curled again. Then Charlie heard a moan, low and drawn out. Her stomach bunched into a big knot. The moan came from Holly, no mistake about that. Whatever had gone down, Holly was hurt. She needed help. Had her dad beaten her up?

Mr. Palmer — Ben, all Holly's friends called him, although Charlie, who'd only met him twice, hadn't quite gotten there yet — was a lawyer. He seemed nice, not like the type who'd hit his daughter, but in Charlie's experience of men, you just never knew.

The door to the rec room was open, she could see that much. There was no sign of the man, no sound from him. In her gut Charlie felt he was gone.

Standing up, Charlie took a deep breath. Then slowly, carefully, she eased open the door.

Just a crack. Just enough to see.

As she had thought, Holly lay on the floor,

on her side. Her taut, tanned, cheerleader-worthy midriff was visible from the top of her hip bones to halfway up her rib cage because her hot pink tee was pulled way up. It was pulled way up because her arms were raised above her head in the most awkward-looking position ever. Charlie's heart stuttered as she took in the silver bracelets circling Holly's wrists, recognized them as handcuffs, and registered that Holly was handcuffed to the black plumbing pipe that rose along the room's concrete block outer wall.

Oh, my God.

Holly's dad hadn't done *that.*

A swift glance around assured Charlie there was no one else in the room. So nervous she almost vibrated with it, Charlie hesitated. But what else could she do? Pulse racing, she flew to her friend's side, nudging the coffee table out of the way, careful not to make a sound. Holly's eyes were closed, she saw as she crouched beside her. Blood trickled from a cut just above her temple. The thread of bright scarlet sliding along Holly's cheekbone horrified Charlie almost as much as the two strips of gray duct tape plastered over her friend's mouth.

Oh, God. Oh, no. What do I do?

Panic tightened her throat, but she did

her best to force it back. Cold sweat prickled to life around her hairline, beaded her upper lip.

"Holly." Charlie's whisper was urgent. She grabbed Holly's arm, shook her. Whatever had happened, this was something way outside her experience. Way outside her ability to deal with. Casting terrified glances over her shoulder, she frantically felt the smooth metal handcuffs, felt the cool strength of the chain linking them, felt the solidity of the iron pipe they were wrapped around. No way were they coming off without the key. Her friend's hands felt warm, but they were limp and almost colorless except for the pink of her nail polish. *"Holly, wake up."*

Holly's eyes opened. The pupils were enormously dilated, making her blue eyes look almost black. For a moment she blinked, unfocused. Then she saw Charlie and seemed to regain awareness.

"Mmm." Holly moved in agitation. She turned her head, twisting, struggling to get free. The handcuffs clanked against the pipe. She kicked the coffee table, the sound of her feet hitting the wood loud as a clap to Charlie's suddenly hypersensitive ears. Charlie's heart leaped. She cast another of those terrified glances at the door.

If the man should come back . . .

Fear twisted inside her like a knife.

Grabbing Holly's arm again, Charlie shook her head in an emphatic *no.*

"Shh," she warned. Holly's eyes met hers and clung, begging her. Fingers trembling, Charlie reached for the edge of the duct tape. Scrabbling at the edges, she managed to pull it off. The sticky side clung to her fingers. She had to pull the doubled strips off with her other hand, then stuck the tape on the wall.

"Do something. Get me out of here. He just walked in. He hit me." The words spilled so fast out of Holly's mouth they tumbled over one another. Her face was shiny with sweat. Her eyes were huge and glassy, her mouth blurry and smashed-looking from the tape.

"Who?" Grabbing one of the metal rings with both hands, Charlie tried yanking the cuff open.

"I don't know. A stranger. *Hurry.*"

The cuff didn't give by so much as a millimeter. Neither did the other. Upstairs, another scream split the night. This one was loud, guttural, animal-like. Charlie's hands dropped away from the chain she was attempting to separate from the metal bracelets as a chill raced down her spine. Holl

went completely still.

"Mom," Holly whimpered. Her eyes darted around the room. "Oh, God, what's happening? Help me."

"*Shh.* I'm trying." Desperately Charlie yanked at the pipe. Solidly set into the wall, it didn't budge. Rolling onto her knees, Holly started yanking at the pipe, too. *Clank, clank, clank,* went the handcuffs.

"You have to be quiet." Charlie's voice was low but sharp. "If he hears you . . ."

"He's got my mother. Oh, my God, what if he comes back to the basement?" Frantic, panting, Holly grabbed the pipe and tried to break it free of the wall. *Thud, thud. Clank, clank. "You have to help me get out of here."*

Terror sent goose bumps racing over Charlie's skin. She shot another frightened look at the door.

"Holly. Stop it. Be quiet."

"You have to help me."

"Shut up."

Charlie's palms were damp with sweat. She let go of the pipe. Holly wasn't the only one at risk here. If the man came back, if he caught her, if he found out she was here, whatever this terrible thing was could happen to her, too. The knowledge dried Charlie's mouth, sent her pulse into overdrive.

She stood up abruptly. "I can't get you

loose. I have to go for help."

"Don't leave me." Holly's eyes blazed with fear. Strands of her long blond hair hit Charlie's face as Holly whipped her head around so that she was facing the wall. Scrambling into a crouch, Holly yanked desperately at the pipe, trying to free her trapped hands. Even as she was backing away, Charlie smelled the citrus-y scent of her friend's perfume. Holly was sweating bullets, Charlie realized. Just like she was herself.

"I have to. I have to go." Anguish made Charlie's voice break as she continued to back away.

"You can't." The handcuffs clanked as Holly kept trying to free herself. Her head turned to track Charlie's progress. Her eyes clung desperately to Charlie's. "You can't just leave me."

"Be quiet, he'll hear you. I'll be as quick as I can."

"Please. Please." Holly started to sob as Charlie, able to take no more, turned her back on her and ran from the room. Charlie's throat went tight. Her heart hung heavy as a bowling ball in her chest. Leaving her friend behind was one of the hardest things Charlie had ever had to do in her life. But getting help was the only smart thing to do, she told herself. She could use the phone, or run to a neighbor. What she couldn't do was free Holly herself. And if the man caught her . . .

She couldn't finish the thought. Fear washed over her in a cold wave.

The stairs were in the unfinished part of the basement, the part that held the washer and dryer and furnace and water heater. Out the rec room door, turn left, and there they were.

Charlie hesitated at the foot, looking up. Her heart pounded. Her pulse raced. The door at the top of the stairs was closed. It opened, she knew, into the kitchen. Concentrating hard as she crept up the stairs, hanging on to the handrail, moving as quietly as it was possible to move, Charlie tried to picture the Palmers' kitchen. Big and modern, it had an island in the center where she and Holly and the other girls had chowed down on pizza earlier. And yes, in the far corner, beside the refrigerator, was the back door. All she had to do was make it to that door, then race across the backyard to the next house just yards away. Forget trying to call for help: she was better off getting out of the house and running to the next-door neighbor as fast as she could go.

I can't let him catch me. Even forming the

words in her mind made shivers race over her skin.

Pausing on the top step, listening intently at the closed door, she heard nothing beyond the normal sounds of the house. But she knew people were up there, in the main part of the house: for one thing, Holly's family had to be there. And the man — where was he? *Who* was he?

Oh, God, if he decides to come into the basement now . . .

The thought was so horrifying Charlie felt faint.

Holding her breath, she turned the knob with infinite care, then pushed the door open the merest sliver.

And found herself meeting Holly's mom's eyes as the man cut her throat. The silver blade of the black-handled butcher knife gleamed in the warm light of the kitchen's recessed lighting as it sliced through the tender flesh. Diane Palmer's hands were behind her back, presumably bound. Like Holly's, Diane's mouth was sealed with duct tape. Her hair was blond like Holly's. The man's fist was wrapped in the short strands, holding her head back so that her throat was exposed. Her eyes were blue like Holly's. As they locked with Charlie's, they radiated the ultimate in terror. But it was too late, it was done, there was nothing anyone, not Charlie, not anyone, could do. The knife left the flesh with a *whoosh,* flinging blood in its wake. Blood poured like a red Niagara from the gaping wound in Diane's tanned throat. Her apple green nightgown was instantly swallowed up by the flood of red. Her arms, her legs, the kitchen floor — everything was splattered with blood, puddled with blood, smeared with blood.

Every tiny hair on Charlie's body shot to instant attention. A scream tore out of her lungs, but she managed to swallow it just in time. Her heart jackhammered. Her breathing stopped.

The man's thin lips slowly curved into a spine-chilling smile. Rooted to the spot with horror, Charlie watched as Diane blinked once, twice, before her legs folded beneath her and she sagged toward the floor. For a moment her killer held her up by his fist in her hair. In that split second, Charlie looked at him: military-cut dark brown hair; a ruddy-complexioned face with a meaty nose and full cheeks; over six feet tall, with a thick-chested, stocky build. He wore a forest green button-up shirt and dark jeans.

Then he let go of Diane's hair, watching as she collapsed like a rag doll. The thud as she hit the floor galvanized Charlie.

The killer had no idea she was there. He hadn't seen her. He couldn't be allowed to see her.

Or she would die.

Heart in throat, Charlie turned and fled back down into the basement.

Chapter Two

Fifteen years later, Dr. Charlotte "Charlie" Stone sat across the table from a devilishly handsome man with prison-cropped dirty blond hair, taking notes as he studied the cardboard rectangle she had just placed in front of him. *Devilishly* was the appropriate adjective, too: from all accounts, this guy was as evil as he was hot, and he used his outrageous good looks as bait to lure his unsuspecting victims to him.

"A magician holding up two knives. That's this here figure in the middle." Michael Allen Garland tapped a blunt forefinger on the hourglass-shaped image that was a central component of the first card in the Rorschach inkblot test. The chain shackling his wrists clinked as he moved. His ankles were also shackled, and a chain around his waist was secured to a sturdy metal ring set into the wall. His short-sleeved orange prison jumpsuit was the only spot of color amidst the unrelenting gray of the walls and the poured concrete furniture, which consisted of the table and the stools on which they both sat. "These two things on the sides are closer looks at his fists clutching the knives. Right there is blood dripping off his hands."

"Um-hmm." Charlie's murmur was designed to be both noncommittal and validating, a reward to Garland for participating in the evaluation without signifying any type of judgment of his description on her part. Historically some ninety-five percent of test subjects identified inkblot Number One as a bat, a butterfly, or a moth. Garland's atypical response was not unexpected, however. In the way her life tended to work, the best-looking guy she'd come into contact with in a long time was a convicted serial killer, and serial killers almost universally saw the world in terms of violence and aggression.

"This here magician done killed somebody," Garland concluded, looking up as he said it, his southern drawl pronounced, his sky blue eyes slyly gauging her reaction to his words. With his square jaw, broad cheekbones and forehead, straight nose and well cut mouth, the muscular, six-foot-three-inch, thirty-six-year-old Garland would have had no trouble picking up women in any bar in the country. Which he had done, at least seven times that the Commonwealth of Virginia knew of. He had slashed each of those women to death before being caught four years previously. Having been sentenced to death, he was now in the process of winding his way through the legal system. For the foreseeable future, however, he was an inmate at Wallens Ridge State Prison, the federal maximum security facility in Big Stone Gap, Virginia, with a Special Housing Unit (SHU) dedicated to some of the country's most notorious criminals, of which he was one. A psychiatrist who was rapidly gaining national renown for her work studying serial killers, Charlie was conducting a forensic assessment of him and seven other serial killers housed in the facility. At the moment she was closeted with Garland in one of the cheerless cinder-block rooms in which such inmates typically met with their lawyers. Equipped with a panic button built into her side of the table as well as a security camera that was continually monitored set high up in a corner, the room was freezing cold even on this sultry August day and small enough to awaken her tendency toward claustrophobia. On a positive note, her office, grudgingly granted to her by the warden at the behest of the Department of Justice, which was funding her research, was right next door.

"What about this one?" Keeping her face carefully expressionless, Charlie replaced card Number One with card Number Two. It was just after four p.m., and she would leave the prison at five-thirty. Dealing with Garland in particular always left her drained, and today was no exception. She was really, really looking forward to the run along the wooded mountain trail that led up to the top of the Ridge and back with which she typically unwound. After that, she would go home, make dinner, do a little yard work, a little housework, maybe watch some TV. After the grim surroundings in which she spent her workday, her house in Big Stone Gap was a cozy refuge.

"Hell, it's a heart," Garland said after a cursory glance down. "A bloody one. Fresh harvested. Plucked right out of somebody's chest. Probably still beating."

Once again he tried to gauge her reaction, which for the sake of her research Charlie was doing her best to conceal. The typical response was two humans, or an animal such as an elephant or bear. His deviation from the norm was interesting, to say the least. She would have been downright excited, and gotten busy hypothesizing that the administration of inkblot tests to at-risk youth might identify the potential deviants among them, if she hadn't halfway suspected that Garland was coming up with his bloody interpretations at least partly to mess with her. Without commenting, she wrote down Garland's interpretation.

Resting his powerful forearms on the table, Garland leaned closer. "You married, Doc? Got any kids?"

She met his eyes at that. From the glint in them, she knew she wasn't mistaken about the enjoyment he was deriving from their interview. As one of maybe half-a-dozen women in the facility, she was accustomed to being the object of the all male inmates' intense interest, with wolf whistles, catcalls, and lewd suggestions routinely following her progress whenever she was within view of the cells. Ordinarily she was able to tune it out, but this was a little different because Garland was not behind bars, was close enough despite his restraints to reach out and touch her if he'd wanted to, and exuded a raw kind of masculine magnetism that, if she hadn't known precisely who and what he was, she might even have succumbed to, thus proving that despite everything she knew she was potentially as vulnerable as anyone else to a predator of this type. The answer to both his questions was no, but she wasn't about to tell him so. This was her third meeting with Garland, and each time he had tried to charm her, to flirt with her, to make her aware of him as a man. Like many serial killers, he was outwardly charismatic, with a friendly, engaging personality that he could turn on and off when he chose. Add his looks to the mix, and it was a deadly combination. *Stone cold killer* was the last thing any unsuspecting woman would think if he started coming on to her. *Dream lover* was more like it. One of the things that made most serial killers so dangerous was their ability to appear normal, to blend in to the fabric of society, to seem just as well intentioned and harmless as the vast, clueless majority. It was almost like protective coloring, akin to the aptitude of a chameleon for taking on the hue of its surroundings to keep from being spotted. She had realized already that Garland was a master of it.

"You know the rules, Mr. Garland." Her tone was deliberately untroubled. Inside, where he couldn't see, her heartbeat quickened and her pulse started to pick up the pace. It was the same kind of reaction, she imagined, that a snake handler might experience when confronting a spitting cobra. Instinctive respect for the creature's deadly potential was felt on a bodily level. "We stick strictly to the test. Otherwise I end the session and have you escorted back to your cell."

Which was a six-by-eight windowless cube in which he was kept in solitary lockup for twenty-three hours a day. The days when he had an appointment with her were exceptions, allowing him out for the time they spent together, which was about two hours, plus the half hour or so it took him to be processed in and out of his cell, as well as his allotted exercise hour. Add to that the fact that she was a woman, and their meetings were a rare treat in what was for him a bleak existence, she knew.

His broad shoulders shrugged. "Didn't you ever just once want to break the rules, Doc? Say to hell with it and go for what you want?"

He was studying her, testing her, trying to provoke her into a more rewarding response than the cool professionalism she had maintained so far.

Not gonna happen. I know what you are. She had seen the autopsy photos of his victims, knew what he was capable of. She

gave him a level look.

"Last chance, Mr. Garland. We're on inkblot Number Three." Charlie replaced the card in front of him with another. "What do you see?"

He glanced down, then up again to meet her gaze. "Whatever you want me to see, darlin'."

Charlie couldn't help it. Her lips thinned and her eyes flashed with annoyance. Although Garland was sitting perfectly still, she could feel the pickup in his interest as her expression changed. Not a surprise. From the beginning she had sensed the intensity of his need for her to become flustered, or angry, or responsive in any way that went beyond the parameters of the doctor/subject relationship. Having spent much of her residency and the three years since immersed in the thought processes and emotions and worldview of serial killers, she knew what he wanted: a connection. She also knew how to react to deny it to him and did so calmly.

"I can see we're finished here." Plucking the card from in front of him, she restored it to the stack on her side of the table and stood up, something that his restraints prevented him from doing, although he sat up a little straighter, watching her. His sheer physical size made him seem to take up way more than his fair share of the space in the room. As she closed her notebook, he slid a swift, comprehensive glance down the length of her body in a classic male once-over. When his eyes came back up, they gleamed at her. Charlie could feel the sexual energy he gave off, and was reminded once again that he was a dangerous man. "I'll have Johnson" — the guard waiting outside the door, who as a security precaution every now and then glanced in at them through the tiny, mesh-lined glass window in the steel panel — "take you back to your cell."

"Ah, Doc, come on. I was just —"

A knock on the door caused Garland to break off in mid-sentence. Charlie glanced around in surprise. Such an interruption had never happened before; the session ended when she opened the door to let Johnson in, as Johnson and everyone else who had any reason to be interested knew. But Johnson's face was framed in the window even as he knocked again, more urgently. Raising her eyebrows at him, Charlie stepped away from the table to open the door.

"Yes?"

"Hey, Johnson, you really miss me so much you just couldn't wait for Doc here to finish up?" Garland drawled before Johnson could reply. Tall, burly, and bald-headed, the forty-something guard cast Garland a look of loathing before focusing on Charlie.

"Sorry, Dr. Stone, but there's two feds here to see you. Warden just took 'em into your office. He told me to tell you you should join 'em and it's urgent."

"Feds?" Charlie asked with a frown even as Johnson stepped inside the room. The heavy door closed and locked automatically behind him as she turned back to the table to gather up her belongings. Maybe someone from the Justice Department checking up on her? Although it had never happened before, given the state of the federal budget it was always possible. At the thought that her grant might be at risk, she felt a quiver of alarm.

"Uh-oh, you been a bad girl, Doc?"

It was all Charlie could do not to shoot Garland a withering glance, but she caught herself in the nick of time and managed to ignore him. Johnson, however, showed no such restraint.

"Shut up, you," he snapped at Garland, who replied with a onefingered salute, which made Johnson's face redden.

"What kind of 'feds'?" Charlie asked, as

much to create a distraction as because she thought Johnson might actually know.

"They're from the FBI," Johnson clarified, surprising her. That nullified her alarm about the grant — the FBI had nothing to do with that — but Charlie's surprise ratcheted up a level.

"If you want, I can wait here till you're done and we can go on," Garland said, smirking at her across the table. "I got to tell you, I'm really starting to feel them inkblots. No tellin' what you might get outta me if we keep at it. Probably some real kinky stuff."

At that Charlie's eyes collided with his, but she managed to refrain from replying. Maintaining the doctor/subject relationship was vital to her research, and it required that she keep control of the interview — and interviewee — at all times. Not always an easy task, considering that her size — five foot six, one hundred eighteen pounds, taut and fit but lacking any intimidation factor, even to a man far less imposing than Garland — and gender put her at a physical disadvantage, at least in the eyes of her subjects, whom she was pretty sure saw her as potential prey to their predator. To maintain control, what she mainly fell back on were classic conditioning techniques

such as reward/punishment. Garland, she knew, considered their interviews to be prime entertainment. Ergo, cutting them short was punishment.

"You can take Mr. Garland back to his cell," Charlie told Johnson. Her choice not to reply to Garland directly was deliberate: more punishment. Garland's eyes narrowed, his face tightened, and for an instant Charlie thought she caught a glimpse of the monster concealed beneath the good looks. A shiver of disquiet slid along her nerve endings. Once again her pulse quickened, although she made sure her reaction didn't show. *This guy feeds off fear,* she reminded herself. She felt the barely contained violence in him instinctively, all the way through to the marrow of her bones. Caged and chained, he posed no threat, but if he should ever get loose — well, he was the kind of guy she wouldn't want to find herself alone with in a dark alley.

He'll never get out of prison alive.

Surprisingly, the thought didn't make her feel any happier. With her notebooks and the inkblots now nestled in the crook of her arm, Charlie turned her back on Garland in a gesture calculated to demonstrate her lack of fear of him, and headed for the door.

"Bye, now, Doc," Garland called after her.

His tone was pure insolence. Brows snapping together, Charlie opened the door and walked on through it as if she hadn't heard.

"You better shut your damn —" Johnson growled at Garland. The solid click of the door closing behind Charlie cut off the rest of Johnson's words. With a little frisson of relief she put Garland out of her mind.

Despite the fitful glow of the overhead fluorescents, the windowless hallway was as gloomy as a tunnel. The faint smell of mildew from the air-conditioning mixed unpleasantly with the odors of ammonia and sweat, and the usual prison sounds — the metallic clang of doors sliding open and shut, angry male voices calling out, shuffling footsteps — formed a constant, nerve-fraying backdrop. At the end of the corridor, the heavy mesh airlock-type double doors that kept this administrative area separate from the cell blocks were manned by a pair of guards. Her office was just a few steps away. Its door, which she always kept closed, was ajar. About twice the size of the interview room she had just left, her office was still just big enough for an L-shaped metal desk that held her laptop as well as various other tools of her trade, plus a tall black filing cabinet and two molded plastic chairs for visitors. The wall behind the desk was enlivened by a photograph of the sun rising over the Blue Ridge Mountains. In one corner stood an easel-style chalkboard with the names and MO's of the murderers she was studying scrawled on it. Two men in dark suits stood with Warden Bill Pugh in front of her desk. One was studying her diplomas, which were mounted on the wall to the right of the door. The other was talking to the warden.

"Dr. Stone," Pugh greeted her. Although she knew he wasn't happy about her presence in his prison — she guessed it was because she was just one more set of eyes to observe practices that would have had the country up in arms if they'd been carried out, say, on animals in a dog pound — he was, as always, polite. Charlie nodded in reply. In his fifties, average height, paunchy and balding, Pugh had a beaky nose and a small mouth. His eyes, which were the approximate color of his rumpled gray suit, were cold and watchful behind rimless spectacles. "You have visitors. They're from the FBI."

"Gentlemen." Charlie looked from one newcomer to the other in turn.

"Special Agent Tony Bartoli." The man studying her diplomas had turned as she entered. Now he smiled and held out his hand to her. He was tall, maybe six-one, lean, not quite as hunky as Garland but certainly handsome enough to make her take notice. On the plus side, he was probably not a serial killer, so maybe her life was looking up. Mid-to-late thirties, with well-groomed black hair, brown eyes, and a healthy tan, which she registered because such a thing was a rarity around the prison. He wore a red power tie with his white shirt. His grip was strong and warm as they shook hands.

"Special Agent Buzz Crane." The other agent shook hands in turn. This guy, who looked a little younger, was about five-ten and slightly built, with a thin, sharp-featured face set off by a pair of black-framed glasses. His hair was a Brillo Pad of short brown curls. Behind the glasses, his eyes were the same bright blue as his tie. Together, the agents made the classic hottie/geek combination with which every female who'd ever spent a couple of hours in a bar or nightclub checking out the wares was familiar. Even as she released Crane's hand she saw, from the corner of her eye, Garland shuffling past her office, his gait made awkward by the chain linking his ankles. Several inches shorter, a whole lot pudgier, and grim-faced, Johnson gripped Garland's arm just above the elbow as he escorted him back to his cell. The clanking of Garland's shackles caused the agents to glance toward the hall. With his wrists secured to the chain around his waist, Garland nevertheless managed to wave his fingers jauntily at them while his eyes sought and found Charlie.

A little rattled by the intensity of that look, she glanced away without acknowledging him.

"So what can I do for you?" she asked the agents, stepping past them to set the notebooks and inkblot squares down on her desk. When she turned back around, it was to find Garland nowhere in sight and both agents studying her. She knew what they saw: a slender thirty-two-year-old woman, dressed for the highly charged, all-male environment in which she worked. Her "uniform" was made up of black sneakers, black slacks, and a pale blue shirt, an outfit she had deliberately chosen to play down her femininity. Her white lab coat was buttoned up the front, and was loose enough to conceal the finer points of her shape. Her shoulder-length chestnut brown hair was twisted up in back and held in place with a large silver barrette. Small, silver hoop earrings and a man's black watch were her only accessories. Her features were even, her mouth wide, her complexion fair, her eyes the deep blue of denim. The men she occasionally dated told her she was beautiful. Usually when they were trying to get in her pants, so she tended to disregard it.

"If you wouldn't mind, Mr. Pugh, we need to speak to Dr. Stone alone." Bartoli's tone was polite but adamant. Pugh looked a little put out, but he nodded.

"Certainly. I understand. Um, if you'll have Dr. Stone call down to my office when you're ready to leave, someone will come to escort you out."

"Will do. Thank you." Nodding affably, Bartoli escorted Pugh to the door and closed it behind him. Left alone with the agents, Charlie leaned back against her desk and waited. Something told her that whatever she was getting ready to hear, she wasn't going to like.

"Maybe she ought to sit down for this." Crane shot Bartoli a nervous look as Bartoli rejoined them.

"She's right here in front of us. She can hear you." Bartoli's response was dry.

"What is it?" Anxiety quickened Charlie's pulse as she looked from one man to the other. "And no, I don't want to sit down."

"We're from the Special Circumstances

division, out of FBI headquarters in Quantico, and we're here because we need your help," Bartoli told her. "We've got a serial killer on our hands, and we've come to ask you to assist with the investigation."

Charlie felt her stomach tighten. Although her life was dedicated to figuring out everything there was to know about serial killers, who they were, what triggered them, if the urge to commit multiple murders was biological or psychological, if there was a marker or common characteristic that could possibly be used to identify them before they killed, etc., her work was purely academic. Objectifying the source of fear (i.e., serial killers) and learning all there was to know about it while keeping it at a safe psychological and physical distance was a classic post-traumatic stress disorder defense mechanism, she knew, but that was how she dealt with her past. The uncomfortable truth was that being confronted with the reality of a serial killer loose in a community of innocent people still made her feel as helpless and terrified as she had as that seventeen-year-old who had failed Holly Palmer.

"I'm happy to help in any way I can." She crossed her arms over her chest. The creeping coldness that was stealing over her was a result of the out-of-control air-conditioning, of course, and nothing else. "If you want me to put together a profile of the perpetrator, I'll need some basic information. The number of known victims, their age and gender, along with any other characteristics they have in common, how they were killed, where the bodies were discovered —"

"We don't have a lot of time," Bartoli interrupted, holding up his hand to stop her in mid-spiel, and Crane nodded agreement. "Last night a seventeen-year-old girl was snatched from her home in Kill Devil Hills, North Carolina. Her family — mother, stepfather, a younger brother — was murdered. This is the third family to be hit like this in less than two months. In both previous cases, the missing girls were found dead approximately one week after their families' bodies were discovered. Evidence suggests that they were kept alive during the period of time between their abduction and when we found their bodies. This girl — her name is Bayley Evans — I figure we have five to six days left to maybe recover her alive."

Listening, Charlie felt her palms grow damp. Her stomach began to churn. Her ears started to ring. Impossible as it seemed, the scenario he described sounded just like . . .

"Is this some sort of joke?" she demanded.

Chapter Three

Charlie's voice sounded hoarse to her own ears. She would have straightened away from the desk if she hadn't suddenly needed it for support.

"I wish it were," Bartoli said, while Crane shook his head. Bartoli continued, "We want you to come with us to Kill Devil Hills, look at the crime scene, see what you can come up with. Give us whatever insights you can."

"No." Charlie's chest felt tight. The floor seemed to heave beneath her feet. Crane had been right, she should have been sitting down for this. But how could she have imagined . . . ?

Bartoli's expression softened fractionally.

"Look, we know what happened to you," he said. Moving closer, he rested a hip against the desk beside her and folded his arms over his chest in rough approximation of her posture. Mirroring: that's what he

(mirroring again? Charlie wondered as she became aware of her own posture; if so, it was more subtle this time), Bartoli leaned in, held her gaze. The intensity in his eyes made Charlie want to close her own. Anxiety tightened her stomach, dried her mouth. "Aside from your personal history, you're the foremost expert on serial killers in this part of the country. Your assistance with this case was requested by the Bureau, and has been cleared through official channels all the way up to the top dog in the Justice Department. Bottom line is, you've been assigned to us for as long as we need you. And you're the best hope Bayley Evans has."

"I've been assigned to you? Without anyone asking me?" Charlie's voice sharpened with welcome indignation even as the image of Holly as she had last seen her rose in her mind's eye. *Oh, God. Another girl's life might depend on what I do next.* She was suddenly bathed in cold sweat.

I'm not strong enough.

"Temporarily. Until this case is over. Technically, I guess you're free to decline."

"I want to help." Even while she said it, she shook her head in dogged refusal, because she couldn't, just could not, expose herself to that kind of life-destroying horror again. She was doing her part in the war against evil by learning all there was to know about the enemy, with the intention of sharing that knowledge with the world so it could be forewarned and, thus, forearmed. She should not be expected to go to battle in the trenches, too. Charlie had to force the next words around the lump forming in her throat. "I'll do a profile. I'll —"

An eruption of shouts out in the hallway was punctuated by a man's bloodcurdling scream. Even muffled by walls and a steel door, the disturbance cut through her words, riveting the attention of everyone in the office, making Charlie's heart jump.

"What the hell?" Bartoli straightened from the desk abruptly. Clanging metal, running footsteps, and more shouts were followed seconds later by a frenzied pounding on Charlie's closed office door.

"Dr. Stone! Dr. Stone!" a man yelled through the panel. "Come quick!"

Such a summons was unprecedented. Alarm flooding her veins, Charlie rushed to jerk open her door. A guard — Parnell, according to his name tag — jiggled from foot to foot with nervous excitement, pointing down the hall the second he set eyes on her. Looking in the direction in which he pointed, Charlie saw that, just on the other side of the mesh double doors, a cadre of jostling guards had congregated, while more hustled a chain-linked contingent of inmates away. Obviously agitated, the remaining guards seemed to be focused on something on the ground.

"What's hap— ?" she began, only to have her question cut off as Parnell grabbed her arm and physically pulled her from her office.

"Warden says you should come *now!*" He was already in motion, breaking into a run, towing her down the hall with him.

"Hey, wait a minute!" It was Bartoli, yelling after her from her office, sounding alarmed on her behalf. As if he thought Parnell was kidnapping her or something.

"It's all right," Charlie called back to him, even as she ran with the guard.

"Dr. Stone! We've got a man severely injured here! You're a medical doctor, you know something about emergency care, right?" Looking around at her as she reached the closed mesh gates, Pugh crouched beside what Charlie realized, from his orange uniform, was an inmate lying on the floor.

"Yes," she replied, her eyes on the injured man. As one of the guards hurried to open the double doors to let her through, she was peripherally aware of Bartoli and Crane running up behind her, flashing their badges to get past the guard, negotiating the complicated procedure of passing through the clanging metal cage right along with her. Charlie stayed focused on the scene unfolding in front of her: a little distance beyond the fallen man, guards were dragging another inmate, this one apparently unconscious, toward the intersecting corridor that led to the main part of the building, where the cells, among other things, were located.

"What happened?" Breathless, she asked the question Parnell had interrupted earlier as she rushed through the last door and dropped to her knees beside Pugh. Adrenaline surged like a double shot of speed as she assessed the victim with the triage mentality of a first responder. With a sense of shock she recognized the injured man as Garland. He lay motionless, sprawled on his back on the concrete floor, blood pumping from his chest. The front of his jumpsuit was already wet, shiny, saturated scarlet. His eyes were closed. His skin was ashen.

"Mr. Garland," Charlie called to him urgently even as she pressed two fingers to the pulse beneath his ear, while Pugh said, "One of the other inmates stabbed him. *Do something.*"

Charlie could feel only a faint, irregular

pulse, but it at least meant Garland was still alive. Moving fast, she unzipped his jump-suit to the chain around his waist and yanked it open to reveal the wound. A muscular, supremely fit man with an inch-long slit just above his left nipple, which was probably going to kill him, was her lightning-quick assessment. The rhythmic way the blood gushed from his chest was ominous, but it told her that his heart was still beating. Although it had been hard to tell at first glance, she saw that he was breathing on his own as well.

"It was Nash who done it. They're taking him to the hole," one of the guards — Johnson, she saw with an upward flick of her eyes — said to Pugh. The way he grimaced told Charlie that he thought he was in big trouble for letting the attack happen. She guessed the warden had been on this side of the gate, on his way to his office in the first of the five buildings that made up the huge prison complex, when the assault had gone down, and that the commotion had drawn him back to the scene.

"Nash was with the group we was taking to the library," another guard added. The library was on the same side of the mesh doors as Charlie's office and the interview rooms, so clearly the attack had happened as Garland was coming out and the library group was going in. "He jumped at Garland so fast, wasn't nothing nobody could do. Just, boom, like that, and it was done."

"We got the shiv," a third guard volunteered. "About six inches long, sharp as a razor blade."

"Goddamn it. Find out where it came from." Pugh's face was suffused with anger as he looked at the guards. Spotting the feds looming behind Charlie, his complexion went from dark rose to magenta in about half a second. His eyes bulged and his jaw worked. Charlie saw all this in passing even as she slapped her hand flat against Garland's wound and laid the other one on top of it, putting her weight into it, applying as much pressure as she could in an attempt to stop the bleeding. His chest was wide, warm, firm with muscle — and slippery with blood. So much blood.

"Put the whole damned place on lockdown," Pugh snapped, and one of the guards started barking the necessary orders into a handheld radio.

It was no wonder Pugh was upset: a violent death inside the prison meant an outside investigation, Charlie knew, and knew, too, that such an investigation was the last thing the warden wanted. Just a month before she had arrived at Wallens Ridge in June, the Bureau of Prisons had concluded an investigation into the death of an inmate who had supposedly committed suicide in his cell. The inquiry had been ugly, and the final report was still pending.

With the FBI agents observing, there would be no hiding this.

"Move back," somebody said above her. The voice was authoritative: she thought it belonged to Bartoli, and that he was talking to the nervous guards, but she was concentrating too hard on Garland to glance up and make sure. "Give her some room to work."

"Uhh," Garland moaned. His head moved slightly. His wrists were shackled and fastened to the chain around his waist. His hands, resting on his abdomen, twitched. His chest heaved as he suddenly began to fight for air. He gasped and coughed and choked. Bloody froth rose to lips.

Not good. Charlie's heart beat faster.

"It's bad," she told Pugh, reluctant to be more specific on the off chance Garland was still capable of understanding what she was saying. She could feel his heart beating against her palm, feel its desperate attempt to function. His skin was still warm, hot even, but she saw with a sinking feeling that his lips were starting to turn blue.

"Mr. Garland, it's Dr. Stone." She spoke as calmly as she could. "I know it hurts. Keep trying to breathe."

"Just keep him alive." Pugh's face was a study in furious dismay. "Dr. Creason" — the prison doctor — "is on his way. There's a stretcher coming, too. My God, we can't let something like this happen again."

"Tell them to bring oxygen." Charlie's voice was tight as Garland gasped again. "Mr. Garland, take shallow breaths. In and out, as easy as you can."

She was almost sure he couldn't hear her. His chest continued to shudder as he fought for air just as violently as before. His blood felt thick and slimy beneath her palm. From the way it was spurting and the location of the wound, Charlie guessed that the aorta had been nicked. Attempting CPR or chest compressions with such an injury would only make the patient worse, as it would force more blood from his body, which was the last thing he needed. Without any kind of medical equipment, she was doing all she could. But she felt woefully inadequate. Helpless in the face of what she recognized, even as she hated to admit it, was encroaching death.

"He needs to be inside an operating room

stat," she looked up from her patient to tell Pugh urgently, although she already knew Garland's chances of survival were almost nil. His only hope — and that it would work was a million-to-one long shot, in any case — was a top-notch surgeon and an immediate operation to open the chest and suture the aorta, which just wasn't going to happen at Wallens Ridge. While the prison's medical facilities included a rudimentary operating room for emergencies, it wasn't equipped or staffed for something like this. And as for getting Garland to an outside hospital, there simply wouldn't be enough time.

Pugh stood up abruptly, saying something to one of the guards, who started yelling into his radio again. Charlie wasn't listening anymore. Every ounce of her concentration was focused on doing what she could to save Garland's life. He was a convicted serial killer with a death sentence hanging over his head, yes, which should have made the loss of his life by brutal murder more a case of justice being served early than a tragedy, but he was also a human being. To have him die like this, under her hands, when just moments before he had been alive and well and full of insolence as he passed her office, was horrifying.

His legs moved, and a fresh fountain of blood coated her hands.

"Keep still," she told him, although she doubted that her words were getting through. Swiftly stripping off her coat, she wadded it up and pressed it down on top of the wound, holding it in place with all of her strength, only to watch the white cotton soak up the blood with terrifying speed. As she worked, she could tell from the way the blood was gushing that nothing was going to help. It was already too late. He was bleeding out even as she tried her best to hold off the inevitable. A scarlet pool of blood spread out around them, creeping across the floor, soaking through her pants from the knees down. She knelt in the warm, wet puddle of it, and the knowledge of what she was kneeling in made her ill. The raw meat smell of fresh blood hung in the air. Garland's wheezing breaths were becoming more widely spaced, more erratic, and with a sinking heart she realized he was going.

"Where the hell is that oxygen?" she bit out, glaring at Pugh, at the guards, even at the two FBI agents who hovered uselessly with the rest, galvanized with the need to try something else, anything.

"Mmm," Garland groaned, coughed up a

bright red dribble of blood, and opened his eyes.

Charlie found herself looking into them. Their normal sky blue had turned almost colorless. The pupils were dilating even as she met his gaze. Death, she knew from experience, was just a few heartbeats away. The baddest of bad men, black heart, merciless and evil: all those descriptions of him and more were written down in his file, and she had no doubt that they were true. Still, she worked feverishly to keep the life-giving blood in his veins.

"Stay with me. Do you hear?" Her voice was fierce, her pressure on the wound relentless.

"Doc," he said. Or at least his lips moved to form the word: her pulse was beating so hard against her eardrums by then that she couldn't be sure she actually heard it.

"I'm here," she said. "Don't try to talk."

Reaching up, he wrapped his fingers around her wrist. They were still surprisingly strong. For a moment their gazes locked.

Then he died.

Chapter Four

Charlie knew the instant death occurred. Garland's chest quit rising and falling, and the sound of his breathing ceased between one breath and the next. His grip on her wrist slackened, and then his hand dropped away. The blood stopped spurting from his wound. Instead what was left from the last pump of his heart oozed out in a warm gush that she could feel soaking through the cotton of her lab coat. His lips quivered once, and then remained motionless. His eyes, which had been focused on her face, fixed and began to glaze.

"Mr. Garland." Refusing to accept the truth, she leaned in, pressing harder on his chest, her voice urgent.

Then it happened. The thing she dreaded, that she went to extraordinary lengths to avoid, that she had never come to terms with and never would.

Garland's soul left his body. Frozen in

place, leaning over him, her hands, which were drenched in his blood, still pressed to his wound, Charlie saw it begin. Her heart started thumping as she watched what looked like tendrils of white mist gather above the whole long length of him. The mist engulfed her wrists in a surge of electric energy. The tingle of it was tangible. She snatched her hands away, out of the force field, sinking back on her heels as the shimmering miasma gathered and seemed to hang like fog in the air just inches above Garland's body. In the next instant she felt a cold rush of wind that went past her with a *whoosh.* The fog blew away, swirling upward, seeming to rise and solidify until Garland himself stood there. Or, rather, until what Garland had now become stood there.

Charlie sucked in air.

Garland's body lay limp and unmoving on the concrete floor beside her, framed in a growing pool of his own blood. His soul, his essence, his being, his *ghost* — Charlie was never sure how best to describe the apparitions she saw — stood near the body's head, not quite solid, not quite as substantial as a living, breathing human being, but undeniably there. His feet appeared to be planted on the concrete floor. His ankles and wrists were shackled just as they had been at the moment of his death. His jumpsuit was unzipped to the waist. His bloody chest was exposed. But no blood pumped from the wound, which was visible as a small black slit, and he appeared as hale and hearty as it was possible for anyone to be, *except for the fact that he was dead.*

Charlie's gut clenched.

Dear God, don't let this be happening again, was the half thought, half prayer that sprang instantly to her mind.

But it *was* happening, and she was the unwilling witness. Garland looked down at his dead body, the apparition taking in the corpse lying on the floor at its feet. Charlie saw a long shiver run through the shade. Then it — or *he,* rather, for the corpse was no more Garland now than discarded wrappings were the gift they had once adorned — raised his head and met her gaze.

Charlie's heart lurched. Her breath caught. His eyes were once again their normal sky blue, alight with awareness and consternation and a touch of disbelief. He looked as conscious in death as he ever had in life.

"Fuck," the apparition said. "Are you shitting me?"

She could hear him as clearly as if he were

still alive, she realized, rattled. Profanity and all, it sounded so exactly like something he would say, it didn't seem possible that the words were coming from a phantom.

"No," she replied, forgetting the crowd around them, that they could see her talking to what to them looked like empty space, that they could hear her side of the conversation.

His eyes widened. "I'm dead?"

She nodded. "Yes."

His lips parted, and she thought he would say something more. But then he glanced around sharply, as if he heard a sound behind him. Charlie didn't know what was there — she could never see more than the apparition itself — but an emotion that looked very much like fear contorted his face.

As if he saw something coming that would drag him to hell.

The rattle of metal wheels on concrete broke the spell that kept her eyes fastened on him. Looking beyond Garland, she saw the stretcher careening around the corner at last, propelled by a pair of guards, its clatter echoing off the walls. Behind the stretcher ran Dr. Creason and a male nurse pulling a wheeled resuscitation cart. Only a split second or so passed before Charlie realized that she could see the newcomers clearly: her view was no longer obstructed by Garland.

The apparition was gone. Only Garland's corpse remained, sprawled just inches away from her bent knees. Her soaked-through coat was no impediment as the last of his blood oozed out beneath it. Charlie felt a surge of profound pity for the dead man, along with a strong sense of thankfulness that his spirit had moved on.

"Dr. Stone, are you okay?"

Large male hands dropped onto her shoulders from behind. Startled, Charlie glanced up. While the rest of the crowd focused on the oncoming stretcher, one of the FBI agents — Bartoli — leaned over her. He frowned down at her, looking concerned. It was he who clasped her shoulders, she realized with relief. And the reason she felt relief was that he was alive, and solid. A man, not a ghost.

Thank God.

All of a sudden the reality of what was happening around her, the noise, the confusion, the presence of so many people crowding into way too small a space, snapped back into sharp focus. Charlie looked over at Pugh, who was beckoning wildly at the medical team rushing toward them while yelling at them to hurry. Two of the guards were halfway up the hall as they ran to meet the would-be rescuers. As she watched, they grabbed the stretcher by the front bar and pulled. The smell of death, of blood, of sweat, of fear, assaulted her nostrils. Colors popped: the scarlet blood, Garland's orange jumpsuit, the deep blue of the guards' uniforms. Sounds were amplified. The white glow of the fluorescents overhead bathed the scene in ugly, flickering, merciless light that hid nothing. Bartoli was still staring down at her. Charlie felt suddenly self-conscious, wondering what he and any other onlookers had noticed, and, if they had noticed, what they'd made of her conversation with the dead man.

"I'm fine," she told Bartoli, who let go of her shoulders and straightened, although her answer was something less than the truth. Shaken and drained, she felt woozy, disoriented, nauseated. Garland's death in and of itself filled her with sorrow. On its own, such a sudden, violent end was terrible enough. Add to it the fact that she was seeing ghosts again and she felt almost like she had endured a physical assault. It had been a long time, a year at least, since a spirit had manifested itself to her, but still the unpleasant feeling was disturbingly familiar. Even though she had been careful to arrange her life so the opportunity for such a thing happening was limited, when she didn't see anything supernatural she had begun to hope that her unwanted ability to communicate with those who had recently, violently passed over had waned. Apparently not, but now was not the time to dwell on it, not with so many eyes to see and ears to hear in her immediate vicinity, not with her professional reputation to consider. To a lot of people, maybe even most people, the idea that anyone could see the spirits of the dead was nonsense, and any person claiming to see them was nuts. Nuts are not respected doctors, nor do they qualify for research grants from the government. Therefore, the fact that she'd just had a brief but vivid encounter with Garland's ghost was something she wasn't planning to share anytime soon. Pulling herself together required effort, but she managed it. The first order of business was not to look at Garland's body, because looking at it made her feel ill all over again. As the stretcher arrived with a noisy rattle of wheels she glanced at it instead.

"You want we should get him on the stretcher?" cried one of the perspiring guards, letting go of it as he and two more of the new arrivals made a concerted move toward the corpse without waiting for an answer.

"No! Shock him! Shock him!" Pugh shouted, waving them back, addressing the medical team as he pointed at the corpse.

"Give me the paddles," Dr. Creason yelled to the nurse, who had pushed the crash cart up beside him. He grabbed the paddles out of the nurse's hand while barking at Charlie, "Airway clear?"

"It's too late," she said in a reasonably strong voice, then repeated the words more loudly as Dr. Creason, paddles in hand, dropped to his knees beside her. To him, to them all, she announced, "He's dead."

"Ah, hell." Pugh groaned.

A shimmer in the air on the other side of Garland's body caught her eye. It was no more substantial than a heat mirage on a blistering summer's day, just as quickly there and gone. What worried her more was the sensation that assailed her seconds later, which felt exactly like a cold breeze whispering along the nape of her neck.

Whatever it was, she didn't like it.

As the warden let loose with a stream of curses and the medical team got busy verifying her words, Charlie stood up, helped at the last minute by Bartoli, who was there with a steadying grip on her elbow when she staggered a little. Ordinarily she would have shaken free of his hand, but her knees, as it turned out, were about as stable as Jell-O. Her legs shook, she felt cold all over, and her breathing was still not entirely normal. She was also, she realized as she glanced down at herself, covered with Garland's blood.

She shuddered.

"You sure you're okay?" Bartoli stayed close beside her as she carefully stepped back from the corpse. His intentions were good, she realized, but she wished he would go away. This was something best recovered from in private. There was nothing more she or anyone else could do for Garland. He would go on to a better — or in his case, quite possibly a worse — place. Anyway, what happened to him now was out of her hands, and she wanted nothing more to do with it. From the way Bartoli continued to frown at her, it was obvious some of her upset showed. Except for him, and Crane, who had moved out of the way with them, everyone else was concentrating on the dead body, which she couldn't even think of as Garland anymore because she knew that what remained was an empty husk and Garland himself was not there. His blood was already growing cold, and she realized with a frisson of horror that she knew this because it coated her hands to the wrists, and dripped from her fingertips. Watching the droplets fall to form tiny, bright red polka dots on the gray concrete floor, she felt her stomach turn inside out. Bartoli's frown deepened. "You're white as a sheet."

"Having a patient in your care die never feels good," she admitted. It was absolutely true, and perfectly explained her distress without her having to go into the whole I-see-dead-people thing.

"You did all you could." His tone was sympathetic, but the look he gave her was borderline weird.

"Probably you want to go somewhere and wash up," Crane suggested. He was giving her a weird look, too.

Charlie sighed inwardly. Okay, so they had clearly gotten a load of her little conversation with Garland's ghost and were wondering about it. At the moment, she wasn't up to creating a plausible lie to explain it away.

"Yes, I do." Charlie genuinely welcomed the suggestion, not only because getting Garland's blood off her hands had just become item number one on her agenda but also because it gave her an excuse to go off by herself until she recovered her equilibrium. Never, not once in the last fifteen years, since she had been so unnerved by what she was seeing that she reported her visions to her mother, and the police, and anybody else who would listen, in the wake of the Palmers' murders and wound up being hustled off to a psychiatrist's office for a mental evaluation, had she told anyone about her ongoing encounters with the spirits of the dead. Over time, she had figured out she didn't see all spirits, only those who had died recently, and violently, and were in her general vicinity, and then only for the typically brief period in which they still clung to earth. Shocked to find themselves dead, many of those forced out of their bodies without warning were confused, she had learned, and didn't know where to go or what to do. Usually, for about a week they hung around some person or object to which they were attached, till they had acclimated enough to their new state to move on. Her ability to see them, which she thought of as a curse rather than a gift, had first manifested itself when she was four and a childhood playmate had been hit by a car in front of the apartment building in which they lived. Her little friend had loitered about the apartments for several days missing his mother. Charlie had talked to him and played with him without fully realizing he was dead. Her mother had been perplexed at Charlie's new "imaginary friend"; Charlie supposed she had never called the boy, Sergio, by name, and thus her mother had not made the connection but that was all the notice anyone took of it at the time. Maybe she wasn't always the sharpest knife in the drawer, but Charlie had only become convinced that she could see actual dead people when first Holly's mother and then Holly herself had started appearing to her right after the horror in the Palmers' house. Even then, it had taken her a while to catch on to what was happening. Because Holly and her mother had come to her at night, the traumatized teenager that Charlie had been then had convinced herself that the terrible visions she was having were nothing more than hideously real-seeming nightmares. Mrs. Palmer had appeared first, materializing beside Charlie's bed in the middle of the night some twenty-four hours after the murders, when Charlie had still been in a safe house in the protective custody of the police. Dressed in the bloody nightgown she had been wearing when she was killed, the wound that had killed her visible as a horrifying black smile slashed across her throat,

Diane Palmer had wrung her hands while begging Charlie to please help find Holly, who at the time was the subject of a frantic police search. Holly herself had appeared a few nights later, dressed in something that she had never to Charlie's knowledge worn — a bubblegum pink, bouffant prom dress — with her long blond hair twisted into fat sausage curls that hung down her back. As Charlie lay terrified in her bed, Holly had rushed across the room toward her, crying, "I want to go home. Please let me go home," before vanishing, only to return again the next night, and the next, always the same thing, for five nights in a row, until Holly's body was found. Then the visitations, as Charlie had finally figured out they were, although she'd been offered counseling and pharmaceuticals when she had tried to convince anyone else of it, had stopped, swallowed up by the horror of reality.

After that, something in her had apparently been sensitized, because she had started seeing spirits on a regular basis. Every single time it was harrowing, heart-wrenching, and left her feeling physically sick. One of the reasons she had decided to become a psychiatrist rather than pursue another medical specialty was because psychiatrists almost never came into contact with the recently, violently dead in the course of their work. The other reason, of course, was that she wanted to see if she could find a way to identify and stop the human sharks that are serial killers. She felt she owed Holly that.

And now there was another of those sharks loose in the world, and he was about to slaughter another terrified seventeen-year-old girl unless he could somehow be stopped in time. Charlie's heart turned over just from thinking about it. Dear God, how was it possible that such evil could exist in the world?

I can help the FBI just as much from here. . . .

"Your hands," Bartoli prompted. Jolted back to the present, Charlie nodded.

There was a staff restroom nearby. Summoning every bit of willpower she possessed in an effort to mask how bad she really felt, Charlie started walking toward it, carefully averting her eyes from Garland's body and the uproar that continued to surrounded it. Still, she couldn't help glancing down the hall in the direction that Garland had looked right before he had vanished. Despite her effort not to think about it, the fear on his face lingered in her mind. What had he seen, in those first moments after his spirit had separated from his body? He had been a bad man who had done terrible things. At the moment of death, had he found himself facing divine retribution?

She didn't know. She never knew.

Evil man or not, he was still deserving of pity: she said a silent, heartfelt prayer for his soul.

"Were you talking to somebody back there?" Crane lobbed the question at her in an offhand way that was belied by the look he gave her. He and Bartoli were walking with her, like some kind of Praetorian guard. "You know, at the end, just after you had lifted your hands up away from the wound but were still kneeling down beside the convict? Because it kind of seemed like you were talking to somebody, but nobody was there."

Bartoli gave him a sharp look that said *shut up* as plainly as words could have done.

"I was saying a prayer," Charlie answered with dignity, inspired by the one she'd just sent winging skyward for Garland. Crane frowned, but with Bartoli's eyes on him, he let it drop.

"Do you want one of us to come in with you?" Bartoli asked as they reached the restroom.

Clearly, Charlie realized, she was not giving off the kind of I-got-it-together vibe she wanted to.

"No, of course not. I'm fine." This time it was almost true. She was feeling stronger, almost herself, almost normal, as she pushed through the restroom door. That is, until out of the corner of her eye she glimpsed the guards heaving Garland's body onto the stretcher. It took four of them, one latched onto each limb. His head dangled limply back in a way that simply wasn't possible in life. Blood streamed from his chest, splattering as it hit the floor.

As the door swung shut behind her, Charlie felt sick all over again. Barely making it to the toilet in time, she promptly vomited.

After flushing, the first thing she did was wash her hands, carefully averting her eyes from the dyed-red water as it swirled down the drain. Then she rinsed her mouth, and her face. Finally, she sank down fully clothed on the toilet because it was the only place in the single-user restroom to sit, closed her eyes, and dropped her head to rest between her knees.

In an effort to make the restroom stop swirling around her, she started on a series of slow, deep breaths.

You wimp, you cannot *faint in a bathroom with the FBI waiting outside. Get a grip.*

But almost as soon as she had the thought she realized that the strong smell of fresh blood she couldn't seem to escape was real, and from a still-present source, and her eyes popped open again. Seconds later she catapulted to her feet.

From her knees down, her pants were soaked with Garland's blood.

"Oh, God." Quivering with horror, she kicked off her sneakers, then stripped off her pants. Her legs, which were toned and tanned and shapely from her running regime, were smeared with blood, too. Stomach once again churning, she instantly attacked them with wet paper towels. Her sleeveless blouse was okay, she concluded as, having finished with her legs, she checked herself out front and back in the mirror, but her white ankle socks had to go: blood had leached onto them. The socks she discarded by dropping them into the wastebasket. She would have done the same with her slacks except, oh, wait, she couldn't walk out of the restroom wearing nothing but her shirt and a pair of silky pink bikini panties. So she did the only thing she could think of: she plopped her pants in the sink and rinsed the blood out of them, careful to sluice them only from the knees down. Probably there were drops of blood elsewhere on her pants, but if so they were impossible to see — and in any case, she didn't want to know. All she wanted was to get them blood-free enough so she could wear them for a brief period without having her skin crawl. As soon as she got home she would throw the pants away, never to be worn again, but for now she was stuck with them.

"Dr. Stone? You okay in there?" Bartoli called through the door.

Charlie realized she had been in the restroom for a good deal longer than just washing her hands required. She hated knowing that Bartoli and Crane were waiting right outside the door for her, wouldn't even allow herself to consider that maybe they'd heard her losing her lunch, and tried not to think about why they were waiting, and what they wanted her to do.

"I'm fine," she called back, glad that it was actually starting to be true. As long as she didn't let herself think about the corpse — or the spirit that had been so violently separated from it — that would continue to be the case, she hoped. Thank God the water in the sink was running clear. Turning off the tap, she started to wring out the legs of her pants. Forget trying to dry them with the hot air from the hand dryer: she would wear them wet until she could get rid of them.

"Doc, you gotta help me," said Garland's voice behind her.

Charlie practically jumped out of her skin. Whirling, clutching the sink for support, she found him standing in front of the toilet, looking every bit as tall and muscular and solid as he had when he was alive. The shackles were gone; so was the blood. His prison jumpsuit was zipped to about halfway up his chest, and he balanced on the balls of his feet like a man poised to run. There was something dark and hunted in his eyes as they fastened on her.

"You got to fix me. Put me back together. Quick."

Charlie took a deep breath. God, she hated this. He was *dead,* and yet here he stood crammed with her in a tiny, should-be-private bathroom, minus his restraints, which made him scary as hell, still possessing enough physicality to trap her against the sink, pinning her with his eyes, talking to her in that honeyed southern drawl, which fortunately she knew better than to trust one inch. A ruthless killer in life, she doubted he'd changed any in death. And because she was the victim of some hideous cosmic trick, she had no way to get away from him.

This whole I-see-dead-people thing totally sucks.

"I can't put you back together," she spoke as calmly and reasonably as she could. "I can't fix you. You're *dead.* You should be able to see a white light. Go toward the light."

His brows snapped together. He looked at her with disbelief. "What are you, the fucking ghost whisperer? 'Go toward the light' is the best you can do?"

Actually, never having died herself, she had no idea if there really was a white light, but she'd said it before and spirits had never taken issue with it. She'd done a lot of research into the afterlife, too, and according to it — and, yes, TV — there should absolutely be a white light.

"The light should take you to where you're supposed to go. To — to heaven." Okay, she faltered on that last bit. Heaven for Garland might be a stretch.

He snorted. "Yeah, right. I'm gonna get beamed right up to those Pearly Gates and get my angel wings and halo on. I don't think so. Look, I'm thirty-six years old. I got things to do, places to be. I fucking can't be dead. Fix me."

"I can't fix you. You're dead. Really. Go

toward the light."

Looking pissed, he crossed his arms over his chest. "News flash, Doc: there's no damned light. There's like this purple fog with *things* in it." With a quick glance around, he seemed to become aware of exactly where he was. She got a glimpse of what she thought was panic in his eyes, and just thinking about what it must take to panic somebody as big and bad as Garland gave her goose bumps. "What are you doing in a bathroom in your underpants? Why aren't you out there giving me CPR or something?"

Banging on the door, Bartoli called, "Dr. Stone, are you okay? Is somebody else in there?"

Crap, he must be able to hear her talking to Garland.

"I'm fine," she called back for what felt like the dozenth time, making no effort to disguise the irritation in her voice. "I'm on my cell phone."

Having glanced instinctively at the door when Bartoli knocked, Charlie looked back at Garland just in time to see him dissolve into a shimmer that swooshed toward the wall before vanishing.

"There has to be a light. Find it and go toward it," she whispered after him urgently.

“Nice legs, Doc.” The reply that floated back to her was no louder than a breath, but Charlie heard it. Then, even more faintly, “Forget the fucking light.”

Chapter Five

By nightfall, which in North Carolina in August happens right around ten p.m., Charlie was in the FBI's makeshift search headquarters, otherwise known as a Greyhound bus–sized RV parked in the driveway beside a pale pink beach house just outside of Kill Devil Hills. The RV was central command, the house provided parking for the RV and lodging for the agents — and Charlie, whose suitcase had already been carried up to the second floor. Not that she had been inside the house yet: she had been ushered straight into the RV. The feds had commandeered the property, which was next door to the murder scene, as their base of operations for the duration of the investigation. Having flown to this bustling beach town in a private plane with Bartoli and Crane, she was now surrounded by FBI agents — and cops, and sheriffs, and deputies, and constables, and practically every other law enforcement type known to man. Even as twilight had turned to full dark and tourists had left the wide white sand beach just beyond the dunes in favor of the town's restaurants and nightlife, more law enforcement types had swarmed the place to report in or exchange information or otherwise help in the investigation, until the RV was as busy as a Macy's just before Christmas. Seated at a desk in front of a computer in a tiny back bedroom that had been turned into a surprisingly efficient office, Charlie pushed the hard-copy files she had been studying aside to pour over the autopsy photos that had just popped up on her screen. Shaken loose from her safe haven at Wallens Ridge by the unnerving prospect of encountering Garland's ghost every time she turned around for approximately the next week, she had embraced the lesser of two evils and agreed to do what Bartoli and Crane wanted.

Now she couldn't believe she had ever hesitated. Bayley Evans' desperate need had smacked her in the face the minute she'd stepped inside the RV to join the search dedicated to finding her. Any distress Charlie might be feeling — and she was definitely feeling some distress — was nothing compared to the terrible reality of the missing girl's plight.

She's going to die if we don't find her fast.

The knowledge sat like a rock in Charlie's stomach.

"So is anything jumping out at you?" The question came from Crane, who leaned back against the wall just a few feet away, scant minutes later. Ever since the photos had appeared on-screen he'd been watching Charlie like a dog hoping for a bone. The blinds covering the narrow window beside him were closed against the night, and the overhead light in the room was giving Charlie a killer headache. Or at least, something was. If not the light, then the glow of the computer screen, or possibly the fact that all she'd had since lunch (which she'd lost) was two cups of coffee and a candy bar. Or maybe it was because she was forcing herself to concentrate really, really hard on the details of the pictures in front of her to keep from getting emotionally flattened by the gruesomeness of the whole.

The photos were horrific. And that would be because the murders had been horrific. Charlie had known the pictures would be upsetting and had steeled herself to face them. But that didn't mean they didn't bother her anyway.

I hate this. But there was nothing to do

but deal.

Setting her jaw, Charlie continued to study the picture in front of her, practically millimeter by millimeter.

Meanwhile, her headache cranked up to a whole new level of bad.

It had been a long day. But headache or no, the situation was too urgent for anything but an all-out, full-bore effort on everyone's part, including her own.

Somewhere out there, a terrified teenage girl's life was ticking down.

Just like Holly's had. While Charlie had cowered in a hospital room under police guard.

I can't think about that. If I do, I'll lose it.

"We just got those photos uploaded a few minutes ago. Give me a break," FBI Special Agent Lena Kaminsky snapped at Crane before Charlie could answer him. Late twenties, small and curvy, with a black, chin-length bob and an olive complexion, Kaminsky was pretty in a sultry, exotic kind of way that her snug-fitting navy blue skirt suit and killer high heels elevated to glamorous. Her super-feminine looks had made her aggressive personality come as something of a surprise. She'd already made clear her feelings about assisting Charlie, which were, in a nutshell, she had better things to do. At the moment, she was seated at the other desk in the room, which was catty-corner to the one Charlie was using, looking at the same images Charlie was viewing.

"Sorry." Crane held up both hands and grimaced as Kaminsky glared at him. Clearly there was some kind of history there, but Charlie had no interest in trying to figure out what it was. Every bit of her focus needed to be on the screen in front of her.

Maybe I can find something that will save this one.

As soon as she had it, Charlie banished the thought. She had to deliberately force away the sense that she had any kind of special responsibility for the victim. Emotions would only get in the way of what she needed to do. If she started reliving what had happened to Holly — which she recognized was what her mind was subconsciously attempting to do — she would no longer be objective, and thus would be no use at all to Bayley Evans.

She was the expert. As such, she had to keep her past out of this. She *would* stay in the present. This girl deserved the best she had to give.

Looking at pictures of the gruesome slash mark that had nearly decapitated Julie

Mead, Bayley Evans' mother, Charlie felt both grimly determined and ill. The wound was so eerily similar to the one that had killed Diane Palmer that it took every ounce of willpower she possessed not to close her eyes and turn away. Horrible memories tried to thrust themselves upon her consciousness, but she kept them at bay — barely — by concentrating on mundane details that kept her grounded in the here and now: the squeakiness of the office chair on which she sat, the uneven legs of the white metal desk in front of her, the glare coming off the monitor.

And if Bayley Evans reminded her irresistibly of Holly, well, that was just something she was going to have to keep from thinking about lest it cloud her judgment. Although that was difficult with a photograph of the sweet-faced blonde push-pinned to a bulletin board above the desk.

Cheerleader cute, tanned and blond, Bayley looked enough like Holly that they could have been sisters.

She also looked so young and happy and carefree that she broke Charlie's heart. Once upon a time, Charlie had looked like that herself. *Holly* had looked like that. Until they, too, had been ambushed by random evil.

Only this time, Charlie was in a position to fight back.

"I'm ready." Charlie nodded at Crane, who pushed the record button on the video camera he was holding. They had agreed that her insights would be recorded so that they could be viewed by the investigative team, which would convene again in the morning. The recording could then be replayed whenever and wherever it was needed.

"Go ahead," Crane said.

"This guy hates his mother," Charlie said into the camera. "Or his mother substitute. He was very likely raised by a single mother, probably biological but possibly adoptive or foster, middle- to upper-middle-class household. His mother or mother figure was abusive to him from a young age. Certainly physically and psychologically, possibly sexually as well."

"You can tell that from looking at a couple of autopsy pictures?" Kaminsky broke in skeptically.

Charlie glanced at her. "Yes." Turning back to the monitor, she pointed to the wound on Julie Mead's neck. Crane came around with the camera to capture what she was pointing at. "The depth and severity of this wound indicates extreme rage and hatred. Either the killer knew this victim well and hated her, or she served as a symbol of a similar figure in his own life whom he hated. We have to assume the latter, because this is the third matriarchal figure to suffer this violent of an injury, and it's very unlikely that the killer personally knew and hated all the mothers in all three of the targeted families. Therefore, she acted as a surrogate for his own."

"Okay." Crane turned the camera from the screen back to Charlie. "So why a middle- to upper-middle-class household?"

"Because of the nature of the victims. Bayley Evans' family — all three families — are middle to upper-middle class. The killer is targeting these families for a specific reason, which is most likely that they remind him in some way of the circumstances in which he himself grew up. He is in part lashing out at his past."

Kaminsky looked unconvinced. Charlie felt a flicker of annoyance.

"Anything else?" Crane asked.

"The killer is probably an only child. Or if there are siblings, they were much older and out of the house when he was growing up."

Kaminsky's brows went up. "How can you possibly tell *that* from autopsy pictures?"

Charlie kept a grip on her patience. "If

you'll call up a full body photo of each member of Bayley Evans' family, I'll show you." The vagaries of an unfamiliar computer system were the reason Kaminsky was in the room: Kaminsky knew how to operate it. Charlie was perfectly proficient with computers, and it wouldn't have taken her long to figure it out, she didn't think, but however long it took her was time Bayley Evans didn't have.

Or at least, that was how Bartoli had put it when he had ordered Kaminsky to work with Charlie on this.

A moment later autopsy pictures of Julie Mead; her husband, Thomas Mead; and their son and Bayley's half brother, Trevor Mead, appeared side by side on the screen.

Charlie tried not to notice that Trevor Mead was a cute eleven-year-old kid. The only way she was going to get through this was if she mentally objectified the victims.

"The killing wounds in both of these victims were stabs, not slashes." She pointed to the wounds on the torsos of Thomas and Trevor. "The only slashes were suffered by Julie Mead." There were slashes to the woman's arms and chest area and left cheek in addition to the fatal wound to the neck. Charlie pointed to each of them in turn. "The father and son were simply killed in the most efficient manner possible. The mother was slain with far more emotion, as the slashes clearly indicate."

"He would have to be a pretty big guy to overpower Thomas Mead, who was six foot one, weighed in at around two hundred thirty pounds, and was a former football player and current assistant high school coach, without Mead showing any signs of defensive wounds, wouldn't he?" Crane asked.

Charlie shook her head. "I can't speculate about that. I will tell you that many times serial killers exhibit what appears to be extraordinary strength, which is believed to result from the adrenaline rush they get from acting out their fantasies."

"According to the position, depth, and angle of the wounds, the perp is six foot one and approximately one hundred ninety pounds," Kaminsky said impatiently, giving Crane a look. "We got that already without any help from Dr. Stone here. What we're still working on is how he was able to take out Mead and the other adult male with such apparent ease. You'd think they would have fought like tigers."

"He used a stun gun." Having left without explanation about half an hour earlier, Bartoli was back, standing in the doorway, looking as tired and wired as Charlie felt. His eyes were bloodshot, the top button on his shirt collar was unbuttoned, and his tie was slightly askew. Stubble darkened his cheeks and chin, and his hair looked like he'd been running his fingers through it. He was still handsome, which Charlie absently noted in passing even though her thoughts were almost totally consumed with gruesome things. "We just had that confirmed a few minutes ago. The marks were right up past the hairline on the base of the neck, so they weren't immediately apparent. They were present on the other adult male, too."

The first case, which involved the slaughter of the Breyer family and the abduction and subsequent murder of their eighteen-year-old daughter, Danielle, included an adult male victim, Danielle's father, whose first name Charlie had forgotten for the moment. The second case was the Clark family, consisting of two pre-pubescent sisters and their mother, as well as the teenage victim and presumed target, seventeen-year-old Caroline. The attacks had come three weeks apart, in separate small beach towns along the North Carolina coast. The teenage girls had been determined to be the primary target. Both their bodies had been found within ten days of the murders of their families and their abduction, buried under nearby boardwalks. It was only after the third attack, which was on Bayley Evans' family, that the FBI had gotten involved, because until then no one had put the crimes together and suspected they were dealing with a serial killer, or connected the new killings to the unsolved Boardwalk Killer cases of fifteen years before. The local FBI had in turn contacted ViCAP, or the Violent Criminal Apprehension Program, a specialized group that tracked serial killers, among other particularly dangerous violent criminals. Bartoli, Crane, and Kaminsky were an elite Special Circumstances FBI unit that was sent around the country to investigate serial killers as an offshoot of ViCAP, and they were assisting local agents in this case. When Bartoli had filled her in on these facts on the plane ride down, Charlie had been impressed with how fast the FBI had worked. In not much more than twenty-four hours, every available investigative force had been mobilized.

Including herself.

"That explains a lot," Crane said, while Kaminsky threw him a triumphant look.

"And you thought they had to have been drugged. Told you that would have been way too hard to coordinate," she said.

"You like being right way too much," he retorted.

"This making any kind of sense to you?" Bartoli asked, his eyes on Charlie. She was looking at autopsy pictures of the other two adult female victims — the mothers, although she didn't like to think of them in that way — whose wounds confirmed what she already knew.

"You're looking for a Caucasian male who was raised by a single mother." Charlie swiveled her wheeled chair around to fully face Bartoli as she spoke. Crane moved to keep the camera on her. "His mother was overbearing and abusive, certainly physically and psychologically and possibly sexually. There were no siblings in the household in which he grew up. He is heterosexual, probably with an addiction to pornography. He wet the bed, most likely past the age of twelve, and was severely punished for it. As an adolescent, he would have had trouble in school and been socially isolated. Wherever he went to high school, he'll have a disciplinary record. There may be instances of fire-starting or voyeurism, or possible animal cruelty in his background, any of which might have drawn the attention of authorities, so he may have a juvenile record. I am almost certain that he either lives or works within a few mile radius of his victims, which since they are located in three separate towns means he is itinerant in some way. And there will have been a trigger event, something that precipitated the killing spree, probably within a month of the first murder. Most likely a divorce or romantic breakup, goading him to lash out against the victims, who are acting as substitutes for the female who rejected him."

Bartoli lifted his brows at her. "You work fast."

"I'm good at what I do."

Bartoli's tense face relaxed into a near smile. "That's why we wanted you."

"I would place his age at twenty-five to thirty-five, except for one thing: if he is indeed the Boardwalk Killer, then he would have to be older, forty to fifty."

"You cannot possibly tell that from those pictures." Kaminsky looked at her with palpable disbelief.

"No, I can't," Charlie agreed. "I know how old the Boardwalk Killer was because I saw him. He looked to be around thirty."

Kaminsky's eyes widened. Then she grimaced. "I forgot about that. Sorry."

"That's another reason you're here," Bartoli said imperturbably. "We've got the sketch of the unsub you assisted the police with fifteen years ago. We're having it age progressed as we speak."

"I'm not convinced it's the same man. The dormancy period has been too long." Charlie kept her voice steady, even though remembering the circumstances under which she had helped the police artist make the sketch made her palms grow damp. The artist had come to her in the hospital. Charlie had tried to stay calm, but by the time the sketch was finished she'd been shaking and crying: a mess.

And in the end, none of it had helped Holly.

I can't think about that.

"We're not one hundred percent convinced, either. It's a possibility we're exploring," Bartoli told her.

Charlie looked up at Bartoli. "He will have taken a trophy of some sort from the primary victims, like a piece of jewelry or clothing. Always the same type of object, which he will keep as a memento. Do you know what he's taking for trophies? Because that will tell you something about him."

"Not yet." Bartoli signaled to Crane to turn off the recorder, then looked at Charlie again. "You up to visiting the crime scene tonight? If you're exhausted, we could hold off until tomorrow, but . . ."

His voice trailed off. There wasn't any need to say more. Everybody in that room knew that every second counted in the race to find Bayley Evans while she was still alive.

Charlie refused to think about what she was letting herself in for. "I'm up to it."

"Let's go, then." He looked at Crane. "You can get busy pulling up the juvie records for two periods of time: twenty-five to thirty-five years ago, and seven to seventeen years ago. Whether this guy is the Boardwalk Killer or not, that should cover his teenage years. Look for what Dr. Stone said: fire-starting, animal cruelty, any kind of predatory violence. Also, run Dr. Stone's original sketch through the juvie databases to see if we can find a match."

Crane nodded. "On it."

"And you" — Bartoli's gaze shifted to Kaminsky — "start looking for someone who's been out of commission for the past fifteen years and has just resurfaced. Caucasian male of the right age who's been in prison and was just released, been out of the country, been in a hospital, you know the drill."

"Got it," Kaminsky said.

Ten minutes later, with Bartoli beside her, Charlie was heading for the Mead's rented beach house, which was pastel blue and located next door to the pink one the RV was parked beside. The pink house, she had learned, had been chosen precisely because it was the next property down from the crime scene, although the two houses were separated by a considerable expanse of sea oats–covered sand. Walking along the wooden sidewalk that wound through the dunes — Bartoli had nixed driving; he didn't want to alert the media (presently being kept at bay out front by the local cops) to their arrival — Charlie let the brisk wind blowing in from the ocean do what it could to soothe her. It smelled of salt and the sea, and lifted tendrils of her hair that had worked free of the loose knot at her nape and slid beneath the V-neckline of her sleeveless white blouse to caress her skin. Even with the breeze, the night was warm enough so that the black blazer she carried over one arm was not needed. She was once again wearing black pants — clean black pants; she had a lot of them — with heels. It was her professional but not-inside-a-prison look.

A makeshift fence composed of a line of yellow crime scene tape surrounded the house, blocking the sidewalk in front of them. Bartoli circumvented it by the simple expedient of ducking beneath it, then holding it out of the way so Charlie could follow.

Once on the other side of the tape, she took one last look at the house from the sanctuary of the beautiful summer's night. It was a large, rambling, two-story structure, with a multitude of windows and a wide gallery on the second floor. Built back-to-front, as most beach houses were, it had the main living areas facing the ocean, while the garage and lesser areas, like laundry rooms, fronted the street. The curtains were tightly drawn, but inside the house blazed with light, making the windows seem to glow. It was a sad commentary on the situation that the darkness outside seemed way preferable to what awaited within, Charlie thought. For a moment longer she stood still, drinking in the night with its starlit, black velvet sky and palely gleaming beach and rumbling waves. Then she mentally squared her shoulders and let Bartoli usher her inside the house.

It was still being processed as a crime scene: technicians were busy everywhere Charlie looked. There was a lot of activity, a lot of noise, a lot to see and hear.

"We're just going to take a look around," Bartoli told the cop who admitted them, who clearly knew who Bartoli was. The cop was young, maybe late twenties. Military-cut dark hair, tall and thin in his dark blue uniform. "This is Dr. Stone. Dr. Stone, Officer Price." Charlie nodded politely, but she didn't say anything: she was too busy bracing herself for what lie ahead.

Price nodded. "Help yourself."

"We think the perp came in through the garage," Bartoli told Charlie as the cop moved away. "The side door has a cheap lock, and there's some evidence that it may have been jimmied with a credit card."

Busy looking around, Charlie merely nodded in reply.

They had entered through French doors that opened from the deck, directly into the kitchen, which was large and modern. Bartoli had indicated a white-painted door next to the refrigerator. The door stood ajar. Beyond it, Charlie saw at a glance, was the garage. Its light was on, and a red mini-van was parked inside. Some evidence that investigators had been at work in the garage was visible, but nothing drew her. Turning her head, she surveyed the downstairs. A dining area with a glass-topped table and four chairs adjoined the kitchen, and beyond that was a living room furnished with lots of white wicker. The floors were white tile, the walls soft blue, and the cushions on the wicker sported beach-y motifs. Nothing seemed out of place.

Nothing seemed wrong.

Charlie felt her stomach tighten.

Maybe there's no one here. Maybe they've already crossed over.

"We should go upstairs first." Bartoli was beside her, steering her toward the front of the house. Charlie saw the entrance hall, saw a flight of stairs leading up, and realized why the atmosphere down here felt relatively normal even as Bartoli spelled it out for her. "The victims were found in the bedrooms."

Okay, then.

Taking a deep breath, Charlie allowed herself to be escorted to the stairs. Glancing into the front hall, she caught a glimpse of a technician dusting the doorjamb for fingerprints. As she walked up the stairs with Bartoli behind her, she could hear a TV playing somewhere on the second floor, and then as she neared the top it went silent. As they reached the upstairs landing a man of about fifty, with a salt-and-pepper crew cut and a grim expression, walked out of what she presumed was one of the bedrooms. He moved with a slight limp, and had the burly, paunchy build of a former football player gone to seed. He was wearing civilian clothes — a navy sport coat and gray slacks

— but no one would ever mistake him for anything but a cop.

"Bartoli," he greeted them with a marked lack of enthusiasm. His eyes were impossible to read behind thick, black-framed glasses. "You back?"

"Haney," Bartoli responded just as flatly. "This is Dr. Stone. Detective Lou Haney. Kill Devil Hills PD."

"I'm in charge of the investigation," Haney said. Then he shot Bartoli a look. "Or at least I was until the feds showed up."

"We're only here to help," Bartoli replied.

Charlie would have offered Haney her hand, except her palm was damp with sweat. She nodded at Haney instead. He was looking her up and down, and from his expression he wasn't real pleased with what he saw.

"This is your serial killer expert?" The look Haney shot Bartoli was scornful.

"That's right, I am," Charlie answered before Bartoli could reply. She was no stranger to having to defend her credentials. Her youth, looks, and gender tended to work against her being taken seriously, she knew. That's why she was still letting Bartoli and the others address her as Dr. Stone instead of inviting them to call her Charlie. If she wanted them to give weight to what she had to say, she first had to have their respect.

"Hell's bells," Haney said.

"Good to meet you, too." Charlie's tone was cool.

"Anything new?" Bartoli asked. As Haney's gaze shifted to him, Charlie glanced around. Her heart was picking up the pace, and she didn't know if it was in dreadful anticipation or because at some deep, fundamental level she sensed a presence she would really rather not know about.

Haney shook his head. "We're rerunning some tests. Guy had to leave something behind."

"You'd think," Bartoli replied as his hand moved to rest in the small of Charlie's back, silently urging her forward.

But Charlie didn't move, or at least not in the direction he obviously wanted her to take. She could once again hear the TV. Four doors opened off the spacious landing, and the sound was coming from the room on the far left. The one Haney had exited as she and Bartoli had reached the top of the stairs. Moving away from Bartoli's would-be guiding hand, Charlie took a couple of tentative steps toward the sound.

Every sense she possessed seemed to quicken. She felt like a bird dog on alert.

"The master bedroom is over here. That's where we probably want to start," Bartoli said behind her, but Charlie barely registered the words.

"The TV . . ." Breaking off, she headed determinedly toward the room from which the sounds were emanating. Just inside the doorway, she paused. A glance showed her marine blue walls with a sailboat-themed wallpaper border at chair rail height. Glossy hardwood floors. A pair of twin beds with dark wood, ship's wheel–style headboards, stripped of their mattresses. A matching dark wood chest with a small flat-screen TV on top of it. A tan corduroy armchair in a corner, facing the TV.

The TV was on. Some weird dragon-fantasy thing filled the screen.

A kid — the blond eleven-year-old from the autopsy photos — curled in the armchair, eyes fixed on the TV, a game controller clutched in both hands. Skinny and undersized, he was clad in soccer ball– dotted blue pajamas and had a determined expression on his face.

Charlie watched as he busily punched buttons on the controller.

"Damned TV keeps switching on by itself." Haney's voice sounded like it was coming from far away. "I don't know what the hell's wrong with it."

Even as Charlie gathered her wits enough to realize Bartoli was watching her closely, Haney brushed past her to walk over to the TV and turn it off, stabbing the button with a little more force than the action called for. The kid looked around then. His eyes widened as they fastened on something. Charlie didn't think it was any of the three of them, or anything at all that was still real and present. His gaze seemed to fix just beyond her. For a second he simply stared. Then, face contorting in fear, he cast the controller aside, leaped to his feet, and fled toward a white-painted door in the wall. A closet, clearly. He grabbed the knob. . . .

Then disappeared. Gone, just like that. Not as much as a shimmer.

Charlie didn't even have time to brace for the wave of nausea before it hit.

CHAPTER SIX

"Dr. Stone." Bartoli's hand curled around her upper arm. Charlie felt the warm strength of it against her chilled skin, glanced around to find his eyes on her face, and did her best to suck it up. So she'd seen a ghost, and now she wanted to hurl. Absent a convenient toilet and a little privacy, hurling wasn't happening. And there didn't seem to be a damned thing she could do about seeing ghosts. Sad as it was, it looked like that was her fricking fate.

What's up? Bartoli's eyes asked, but he didn't say it. Maybe because Haney was watching them. Maybe because Bartoli knew what she would reply: *Not a thing.* After all, they'd had the equivalent of this conversation before.

"This was the boy's room, right? Where was his body found?" Charlie strove to sound normal as she unobtrusively detached her arm from Bartoli's hold. Her skin was cold and clammy; her pulse was jumping. As long as Bartoli was touching her, he was privy to proof positive that something in her world wasn't all fine and dandy. It was always difficult, trying not to reveal what she saw. Which was one among a number of really excellent reasons she tried not to see anything everyone else didn't see. Glancing around, she spotted the chalk outline between the beds on the hardwood floor, and had the answer to her question even before Haney moved to the foot of the nearest bed and pointed it out.

"Trevor was found right there," Haney said.

Oh, God, I can't think of the kid as Trevor.

There were bloodstains on the floor where Trev— the kid had died.

Charlie felt cold sweat breaking out around her hairline.

"We think he was asleep when the unsub attacked him," Haney continued. "The amount of blood on the sheets leads us to believe he was stabbed in his bed, then either managed to get up before collapsing on the floor — or rolled or was pulled onto the floor, where he died."

"Defensive wounds?" Bartoli asked.

Haney shook his head. "None. Two knife wounds to the chest. Either would have been fatal."

"Where was the woman found?" Charlie asked as an excuse to turn away from the pathetically small outline on the floor, and was proud of how cool and steady her voice sounded. Inside, her stomach was roiling.

"Master bedroom," Bartoli answered. "Husband, too."

With Haney in the lead, they were all on their way out of the room when the TV came back on. A glance around told Charlie that the kid was once again ensconced in his chair, controller in hand, his thumbs as busy as the rest of him was still.

"Goddamn thing," Haney muttered, abruptly changing directions to head for the TV. This time, after he turned it off, he yanked the cord out of the wall for good measure. "Driving me crazy," he said shamefacedly as he turned to find both Charlie's and Bartoli's eyes on him.

Trev— the kid — continued to sit in the chair, his face a study in concentration as he worked the controller as avidly as if the game was still on. Which Charlie supposed it probably was, for him. The dimension he existed in was governed by an alternate reality that Charlie didn't perfectly understand, but in it she was sure the video game still played. Certainly he worked the controller as if it did. He showed no evidence whatsoever of being aware that she, Bartoli, and Haney were in the room. Just like most people didn't see ghosts, she had realized over the years that most ghosts didn't see living people. Which had its good points and its bad.

"He's just a little kid." The words escaped her throat of their own volition. Impossible not to feel something for the murdered boy, no matter how hard she tried to remain detached. *Damn it.*

"We're going to catch whoever did this," Bartoli told her as Haney once again started moving toward the door.

"Fucking sick bastard." Haney's voice was hard with agreement.

Even as she and Bartoli followed Haney from the room, the kid got that terrified look on his face, jumped from the chair, and ran toward the closet again.

A loop was what she was seeing, Charlie realized. Trevor's traumatized spirit was caught up in re-experiencing the last moments of his life over and over again.

A lump formed in Charlie's throat. Goose bumps chased themselves over her skin.

Kid shouldn't have died like that.

"The boy hid in the closet," she said as she and the men crossed the landing toward another door. Haney was slightly in front, while Bartoli stayed beside her. "He was sitting in the chair playing a video game, heard or saw something that terrified him, jumped up and ran for the closet. Probably the killer found him in there. Either the boy tried to run for it when the door was opened, or the killer pulled him out. Either way, you should check for forensic evidence in the closet."

Both men stopped walking to stare at her. The look Bartoli gave her was sharp with curiosity. Haney's face creased into a frown.

"You got some basis for thinking that?" Haney inquired.

"It's what I do," Charlie replied. "Believe me, I'm not wrong."

"I'd believe her," Bartoli advised. "She's the expert."

"Yeah." Despite the fact that his voice was heavy with skepticism, Haney turned away from them to walk to the top of the stairs. Cupping his hand around his mouth, he bellowed, "Baldwin!"

"Yeah, boss?" The reply from downstairs was faintly muffled.

"You and Rutledge get up here. Bring your stuff."

Another answer floated up, followed a moment later by the thud of ascending footsteps. Charlie realized that a pair of hazmat-suit-wearing cops lugging bags of equipment were climbing the stairs to join them, that they were talking with Haney, that they were looking hard at her and talking some more before disappearing into the kid's bedroom, but she was only peripherally aware of any of it.

That was because, through the master bedroom's open doorway, Charlie was caught up in watching Julie Mead rise up from the far side of the stripped king-sized bed, then glide around it and float across the room toward her. Transfixed, Charlie saw that the woman was drenched in fresh blood. Whatever she was wearing — some sort of sleep shirt that ended just above her knees — was wet with it. Streaks of glistening scarlet matted her badly mussed, chin-length blond hair. Her throat was cut from ear to ear. It looked to have been freshly slashed, because blood still streamed from it, pouring down over her shoulders and chest, adding to the gore on her shirt. Her mouth worked. Her eyes were wide with horror — and then they fixed on Charlie.

She knows I can see her. An electric frisson of connection ran down Charlie's spine. Her heart thumped. Her breath caught.

"You've got to help us," the woman begged, flying toward her with her hands outstretched. "Please!"

Several things happened at once: Charlie felt another onslaught of nausea slam her. A terrible flashback to Diane Palmer's murder all those years ago made her go weak at the knees. Even as she thought, *They're the same,* a wave of freezing cold air blasted her as Julie Mead's spirit reached her. The sheer force of emotion surrounding the spirit made Charlie take a couple of staggering steps backward.

She fetched up against Bartoli, who was standing behind her. His arm came around her waist.

"Are you all right?" Bartoli asked in her ear. Charlie heard him, felt the hard strength of his body, registered the steadying grip of his arm. She was able to do this because Julie Mead was no longer around to rivet her senses. As it had reached the threshold of the master bedroom, the specter had vanished into thin air.

Charlie found that she could breathe again.

"I'm going to be sick," she said, because she was. There was no holding it in this time. She could see just a glimpse of the en suite bathroom off the master bedroom. "I'm sorry, excuse me, I have to —"

Breaking off because she really couldn't

say another word, she pulled free of Bartoli's hold and darted into the master bedroom.

Closing the door behind her, she locked it, then ran for the toilet.

She barely made it in time.

When she was finished, she flushed the toilet, rinsed her mouth, then walked on shaky legs back into the bedroom. She was sweaty and weak, and her head ached like someone was pounding on her skull with a hammer. What she wanted more than anything else in the whole wide world was to turn her back on the horror into which she had been plunged, whisk herself home to her safe little house in the mountains, and do her serial-killer-analyzing from a safe distance while pretending she knew no more about what happened after this life than . . . Bartoli, for example.

Oh, grow a pair. No one else here can do what you do.

Grimacing as she faced that inexorable truth, Charlie turned to the *second* reason she had locked herself in the bedroom. Chalk outlining a shape on the hardwood floor beside the bed showed where Julie Mead's body had been found.

Knowing she didn't have much time — Bartoli wouldn't wait passively in the hall forever, and for all she knew, Haney and the others were now there, too, throwing a hissy fit because she'd locked them out — Charlie stood beside the outline and whispered, "Julie? Can you hear me? I'm here to help."

Julie Mead materialized in front of her. The blood, the gore, the gaping wound in her throat were as real-looking and gruesome as if Charlie were seeing them in life. There was no trace of the meat-locker smell usually associated with a new kill, but the blood appeared so fresh that it almost seemed to steam in the chill of the air-conditioning. When the apparition reached out its hands in an attempt to clutch at her, it was all Charlie could do not to back away. The dead hands passed right through her flesh with a sensation that felt like a cold mist making contact with her skin. Even then, when every instinct she possessed shrieked at her to draw away, the anguish in the other woman's eyes held her in place.

"My babies. Trevor. Bayley. Something terrible has happened, hasn't it? Oh, please, you have to help me!"

Charlie steeled herself against the spirit's energy. It was frantic and dark, filled with fear and horror at what had been done to her and hers. Charlie knew from experience that if she did not guard against it she would soon be overwhelmed with those emotions herself.

She kept her voice at a whisper, hoping it could not be heard beyond the door. "I'm going to do my best. You have to tell me who did this to you."

Julie Mead wet her lips. "A man — it was dark — I couldn't see. He — he hurt me. Cut me. I'm bleeding. Oh, God, I'm bleeding! Where's Tom? Oh, where are my children?"

The anguish in her voice cut Charlie to the heart. Every instinct she possessed urged her to tell Julie Mead to look for the light and go into it, because once the woman did that her spirit's suffering would be at an end. But as long as Bayley was missing, Julie Mead, in whatever form she now existed, was still needed here on earth.

"Julie," Charlie whispered the woman's name forcefully, hoping to keep her grounded in the present for long enough to provide what answers she could. "Where's Bayley? Did you see what happened to Bayley?"

Julie Mead looked bewildered. "Bayley — Bayley's asleep. Isn't she?"

The bedroom doorknob rattled as someone tried to get in . . . or was warning that her time was almost up.

"Isn't she?" Julie Mead's voice went shrill. Her eyes began to dart around, and Charlie felt a change in her energy. "She came home. She went to bed. Bayley! *Bayley!*"

"Can you describe the man who attacked you?" Charlie tried her best to keep the spirit focused. Mindful of the possibility that she might be overheard, she kept her voice so low that it was scarcely louder than a breath even while trying to project calm insistence.

"I didn't see him. I told you. He was strong. Tall. Oh, God, he has a knife!"

Her voice went shrill again on that last, and the abject fear in it told Charlie that Julie Mead was once again on the verge of getting caught up in reliving the nightmare of the attack.

"How old was he?"

"I told you I didn't see him."

"Did he say anything?"

"No. Nothing. I woke up — and he was stabbing Tom. Tom! Tom! My God, Tom's dead!" The rising hysteria in Julie Mead's voice made Charlie's chest tighten. It seemed pretty clear from the widening of her eyes and flaring of her nostrils that the spirit was re-experiencing a sighting of her husband's murdered body.

"What do you see? Anything about your attacker that might help us find him," Charlie commanded urgently.

"I tore his glove — surgical glove. He wore surgical gloves. He has a heart — a red heart — on the back of his hand." Julie Mead looked sharply around. "Oh, my God, no!" She vanished with a terrified shriek that made every tiny hair on Charlie's body catapult upright.

Left alone with Julie Mead's scream still ripping the air, which was made all the more terrible because no one else could hear it, Charlie had to take deep, steadying breaths to keep from screaming right along with her. Finally, when the last shivering note went silent, she was able to summon the fortitude to push the experience away, turn, and answer the now-determined knocking on the door.

Unlocking it, she pulled the door open to find herself practically nose to nose with Haney, whose fist was raised to pound again.

"What in the name of all that's holy was *that?*" Haney verbally pounced before she could say anything, his fist lowering as he glared down at her. "You call that professional behavior? You just compromised a major crime scene."

"I had to throw up. Would you rather I'd

done it all over the floor? *That* would have compromised the crime scene." Still battling the headache from hell, a chill that permeated her bones, and a pervasive, all-over feeling of utter bodily weakness, to say nothing of the wrenching sorrow for the victims that clawed at her heart, Charlie rallied to cover any suspicion that there was more to her bolt into the bedroom than that. She shot Haney a stick-it-where-the-sun-don't-shine look to boot as she walked past him. Bartoli was right there, arms crossed over his chest, waiting for her. As soon as he saw her his arms dropped and he moved toward her. Something in his face as he looked at her told her that he wasn't entirely satisfied with her version of what had gone down, but instead of piling on along with Haney, he shifted his eyes from her to clash with the cop's.

"Back off, Haney. She didn't compromise the crime scene any more than she would have done if we'd taken her in there." Bartoli put himself between Charlie and the cop. Ordinarily Charlie didn't need anyone springing to her defense, but at the moment she was feeling decidedly sub-par, so she appreciated any help she could get.

"She touched the knob. She touched the lock. She touched the goddamned toilet handle." Haney practically bristled with indignation. "At a minimum."

"So? If your people did their jobs, all those surfaces have been tested for fingerprints," Bartoli countered. "I know our lab's already working on the trace evidence that was recovered in there."

"A killer of this type would wear gloves. Probably surgical gloves," Charlie said, with Julie Mead's words in mind. "I doubt you'll find any fingerprints, although if the gloves were ripped it's possible."

Haney gave her a hard-eyed stare.

"Detective!" A shout-out from the kid's room interrupted before he could say anything, making them all glance that way. "You want to come in here a minute?"

"Yeah," Haney called back. With a dark look at Charlie and a glare for Bartoli, Haney growled, "She's your expert. In the future, I suggest you keep her under control," before heading that way.

"When they find forensic evidence in that closet, you can thank me," Charlie called after him.

Haney replied with a dismissive wave of his hand before disappearing into the kid's bedroom.

"Way to be tactful." Bartoli gave her a faint, wry smile.

"I don't think he likes me," Charlie said, making an effort to lighten the atmosphere.

"I doubt I top his favorite person list, either. He's one of those local cops who resent us being here. He thinks it's his investigation, and we're hijacking it. Happens sometimes. Plus, word is he suffers a lot of pain from his leg. Smashed it up pretty bad in a car accident years ago." Bartoli slid a comprehensive look over her. "You sick or something? That's the second time today that you've tossed your cookies. What's up?"

She managed what she felt was a truly commendable casual shrug. "I'm thinking I might have a touch of food poisoning. Or the flu. Hard to say, really."

"Yeah." Bartoli's eyes slid over her again. "You up to the girl's bedroom?"

No was the honest answer. But it had to be done, so Charlie braced herself and nodded.

Chapter Seven

In the end, there wasn't anything to see. Just a small bedroom with a stripped double bed. Pale blue walls, white wicker headboard and chest. No bloodstains, no sign of a struggle. Clothes and other belongings already carted away by the FBI. Since the house was a vacation rental, Charlie wouldn't have expected to find anything of Bayley Evans' personality in the room, and she didn't. What she also didn't find was Bayley Evans' spirit.

Which didn't necessarily mean that the girl was still alive, although Charlie hoped it was the case. Charlie hadn't seen Tom Mead's spirit, either, and he was definitely dead. Some souls, no matter how violently they had died, crossed over peacefully without lingering. Although it was always possible that Tom Mead's spirit was still earthbound and was just not attached to anything in the house. In her experience, spirits forcefully ripped from their bodies were unpredictable in what they attached to. She'd encountered one attached to a neighbor's cat.

"Come on, let's go," Bartoli said as they emerged from the bedroom. His eyes slid over her, the expression in them making Charlie question what she looked like. If the way she felt was any indication, she was as white as Wonder bread, huge-eyed, and covered with a fine sheen of sweat. Chalk it up to meet-the-ghosts anxiety. Although, of course, he had no way of knowing that. "Time to wrap it up for the night."

Charlie wasn't sorry to precede him down the stairs. She'd had the day from hell several times over, and right now what she needed was to put as much distance between herself and the spirit world as she could.

There was just one problem with that.

"Bayley Evans is still out there." Her voice was flat as she spoke over her shoulder to Bartoli, who followed her out the French doors. Letting herself think about what might be happening to the girl was the worst thing she could do, Charlie knew. If she did, she would devolve into a mass of quivering despair, which would do no one any good. As difficult as it was, she had to stay strong, had to stay focused, had to keep the horror at arm's length. It was the only way she could do her job.

Anything else was counterproductive.

This time, when the brisk sea breeze hit her, she shivered like it was an arctic blast. She was glad for her jacket. Sliding it on as she walked across the deck and down the steps to the walkway below, she was still freezing as she buttoned it up and had to fold her arms over her chest in an effort to get warm. Everywhere she looked, the night was dark and forbidding. The beach was deserted, the sea oats blew almost double, the tide rolled in with a crash, and the weathered planks beneath her feet seemed to stretch out endlessly into the shadows. Even the stars seemed small and cold and distant.

She was, Charlie realized, still suffering from her reaction to the gruesome visions of Julie Mead and the heartbreaking ones of her son.

God, you've got the wrong woman here. I'm not tough enough for this.

Bartoli said, "We have teams of agents working twenty-four seven to find her. You've done everything you can for today. You are officially off the clock."

Charlie sighed inwardly. She was so exhausted, so cold and queasy and headache-y, that her thought processes were affected. For the moment, coming up with a good lie to explain how she knew what she knew was probably beyond her, but still there was something that she had to tell him.

"The killer wore surgical gloves. More important, he has a red heart on the back of his hand. Maybe it's a tattoo, I'm not sure."

Bartoli had been walking beside her. He stopped. Charlie kept on going, head bent against the wind, arms folded, trudging on determinedly toward the pink house that thankfully was getting close now. It took him a few seconds to catch up with her again.

"You want to tell me how you know that?"

No, she really didn't. "I just know. It's accurate. Use it to find Bayley Evans."

"You do some kind of fancy expert analysis back there that I missed?"

"Yep."

"Want to explain your methodology?"

"Let's just say that your investigation is benefiting from my years of experience, okay?"

Bartoli said nothing for a moment. He was frowning, and Charlie could feel speculation rolling off him in waves. She kept walking. The planks ended when they reached the driveway. It was packed with official-type vehicles, and the RV was brightly lit and still as busy as a beehive at noon. It was good to know that, even if she was about to bow out for the night, the search for Bayley Evans would be proceeding at full throttle.

Realizing she was just a tiny cog in a big machine was an enormous relief.

She was going to put Bayley Evans, and her family, and the other victims, out of her mind, at least for the next few hours. What she needed to do now was rest and get her brain back up to speed. Then she would turn all her formidable resources to helping the authorities find the bastard who had done this.

Please, God, let it be enough.

"A red heart on the back of the unsub's hand. You're sure enough about that for me to add it to the official description of the individual we're looking for," Bartoli said finally. From his tone, it wasn't really a question.

"As of the night the Meads were killed, he had a red heart on the back of his hand." Charlie looked back at Bartoli as they reached the steps that led up to a wide, screened-in back porch. "I'm absolutely positive about that. I'm not sure what it is, or if it was permanent. But it was there."

"Okay. If you say so."

"I do." Charlie felt her throat tighten. She'd been battling the memory ever since Julie Mead had described the heart, but it kept thrusting itself into the forefront of her mind, and now there was no escape.

Once again she was seventeen years old, peeking around the basement door just in time to watch a killer cut Diane Palmer's throat. For the space of a terrible heartbeat, she could picture the scene as clearly as if she were there.

Stumbling on the top step, Charlie nearly fell to her knees. Only Bartoli's arm hooking her waist at the last minute saved her from a fall.

"Careful." He hauled her upright.

"Thanks." Thrusting the memory away, grateful for the steadying arm that remained around her waist as she regained her balance, she took a deep breath, then forced herself to take one more quick plunge into the past. "The Boardwalk Killer — the man I saw when I was seventeen — didn't have a heart on his hand. There was nothing on the backs of his hands, nothing at all."

"You sure?"

They were walking across the dark screened porch as they talked. When they reached the door, Bartoli's arm dropped away. Charlie was surprised by how much she missed its warm support.

"Yes. Absolutely." Trying not to shiver openly, Charlie cast a quick look around while Bartoli unlocked the door. The screened porch was darker even than the night, with inky shadows everywhere. The wind blowing off the ocean was picking up, making the fronds on the nearby palms flap with a sound like birds' wings and carrying a strong smell of salt with it.

"He could have acquired it later."

"Yes."

At least Bartoli didn't start delving into the whole how-sure-are-you-and-how-do-you-know-anyway school of questioning, and for that she was grateful. Something about the night itself was unsettling her, but she really didn't want to start trying to analyze why that should be. She was too tired, too emotionally wrung out. She already knew, because Bartoli had told her on the flight down, that she would be sharing the house with him, Crane, and Kaminsky. She was less clear on how that was going to work, exactly, and at the moment she didn't care. What she desperately needed was a couple of Tums (knowing she would probably be encountering nausea-inducing spirits, she had brought her own supply, but unfortunately the two she had taken prior to leaving her house back in Big Stone Gap had worn off by the time she encountered the dead kid in the chair), a hot shower, and bed, in that order.

Got to lie down before I fall down. Her mother used to say that a lot, when she came home drunk. Charlie couldn't believe she was hearing the familiar slurry voice echoing in her head under these very different circumstances, even if the sentiment was apt.

"You want something to eat? Might make you feel better." Bartoli pushed the door open, and gestured to her to go inside, which she did. "Unless my nose deceives me, they ordered pizza."

Like the Meads' rental, this beach house had its main rooms facing the ocean. Charlie walked into the kitchen and glanced around to discover a familiar cardboard box on the table: as Bartoli had predicted, there was pizza. With her stomach in the shape it was in, though, food was the last thing she wanted. Walking past it, trying not to breathe in the spicy aroma, she saw that the layout of this house was very similar to that of the Meads'. The main difference was that the tile floors were terra-cotta and the walls were sunshine yellow. Otherwise, kitchen, dining area, living room, entry hall, stairs: everything looked to be pretty much the same.

Charlie fought the impulse to turn and run away, screaming.

Someone was coming down the stairs from the second floor.

"I ordered pizza. Pepperoni. There's plenty left." The speaker was Kaminsky, who stopped a few steps from the bottom. Despite the hour, she was still fully dressed in her suit and heels. Her expression as she looked at Charlie was less than welcoming. "Or if you'd rather, there are some groceries in your refrigerator. Eggs, cheese, lunch meat, that kind of thing. For tonight, that's the best you're going to get."

"I'm not hungry." The mere thought of food made her stomach cramp warningly. To divert herself, Charlie latched onto something that puzzled her. "I have a refrigerator?"

"You've got the in-law suite. It's basically a self-contained apartment. Fridge included."

"If you're ready to go up, Kaminsky will show you where it is," Bartoli said.

Charlie was. More than ready. She nodded.

"Get anything?" Bartoli asked Kaminsky as Charlie started up the stairs.

"Twenty-seven men who fit the parameters living within a two-hundred-fifty-mile radius. I was working on narrowing it down when I had to stop to babysit." Kaminsky's gaze shifted to Charlie, who had almost reached her by that time. "No offense."

At the moment, Charlie was too tired to take any. She shook her head. "None taken."

"You're not babysitting, you're protecting a witness." Bartoli's voice was crisp. "There's a strong possibility that Dr. Stone has seen our unsub, remember. If he knows that, and discovers she's here helping us, there's a chance he'll come after her."

That stopped Charlie in her tracks. Her heart lurched. *There's a happy thought to top off a perfect day.* She was surprised it hadn't occurred to her. Gripping the rail hard with one hand, she turned to look at Bartoli.

"The Boardwalk Killer knows I saw him, or at least he should," she said. "He didn't see me at the time, but it was all over the news. Killers of his type tend to like to follow the investigation through the media. If this is the same man, he probably has a scrapbook or some similar physical record filled with news clippings from the killings. The authorities tried to keep my identity secret at the time, but it leaked out. I'm quite sure information about me, including my picture, will be among his artifacts."

Bartoli nodded. "If this unsub *is* the Boardwalk Killer, and that's still an if, we're hoping he doesn't find out you're here. We're doing our best to keep the fact that you're working with us confidential. Outside of the three of us, and my boss, nobody else knows who you are, and by that I mean about your association with the previous murders."

"Even if he has a picture of you, it would be of a seventeen-year-old girl, not the illustrious Dr. Charlotte Stone, serial killer expert." Kaminsky's eyes ran over her mockingly. "I'm guessing there's a pretty big difference. He probably wouldn't even recognize you if he saw you."

"It's possible he's kept track of me over the years," Charlie pointed out, although it was something she had long since forbidden herself to dwell on. For years after the attack, she had harbored the secret fear that the next time she turned around there he would be, ready to murder her just like he had the Palmers. With the help of therapy and a lot of self-talk, she'd managed to tuck that fear away into a tiny corner of her mind, where it rarely bothered her. Now it was back, impossible to ignore.

I should have stayed away.

"We'll keep you safe, don't worry," Bartoli said, making Charlie wonder what he'd seen in her face. His gaze shifted to Kaminsky, and he gave an upward jerk of his head, which Charlie translated as *Go.*

"Yeah, okay, I got this." Sounding slightly more resigned to her fate, Kaminsky started walking back up the stairs, then glanced over her shoulder to tell Charlie, "I'll be sleeping right across the hall from you, and Bartoli and Crane are crashing in bedrooms on the first floor. You can go to bed and sleep like a baby and not worry about a thing."

"Good to know." Charlie followed Kaminsky up the stairs.

"Eight a.m. good for you to get started on this again?" Bartoli called after them. Charlie knew he was speaking to her.

It wasn't a lot of decompression time — but then, the situation was beyond dire. "Yes, that's fine."

"Come downstairs. One of us will be waiting."

As she reached the top of the stairs, Charlie glanced down at him. "Okay."

"You're in here." Kaminsky opened a door to the right of the landing as, from the corner of her eye, Charlie saw Bartoli head back out the door. Presumably he was not yet ready to call it a night.

Charlie caught herself wondering if the team that had searched for Holly had been as dedicated, then forced the thought from her mind.

"By the way, a two-hundred-fifty-mile radius is too large." Charlie walked past Kaminsky into what, from her first glance around, appeared to be a decent-sized apartment that took up the entire left side of the second floor. "The killer should be living — or working — within a thirty-mile radius of the crime scene at the most. Say, a half hour's drive. Since there are three separate crime scenes, that would apply to each of them. If anyone on your list is staying in RV parks or campgrounds within that circle, I'd start there."

"Thanks for the tip." Kaminsky's voice was dry. Charlie once again got the impression that Kaminsky wasn't a fan, but at the moment she was too tired to care. "If you need anything, I'm right across the hall." She nodded toward an open door just across the landing. Charlie glimpsed a bedroom through it. "Give a shout."

Charlie nodded. Then Kaminsky left, closing the door behind her. Locking the door, beyond thankful to finally be alone, Charlie glanced around her new living quarters. She was standing in a small sitting room furnished with a yellow chintz couch, a deep green recliner, and a bentwood rocker, plus the appropriate tables and lamps. A large flat-screen TV on a bamboo console took up a corner, and on the opposite side of the room a round, glass-topped table complete with four bentwood chairs composed an eating area. A half wall to the left of the eating area provided separation from a small but modern kitchen, complete with white-painted cabinets and stainless steel appliances, including the promised refrigerator and a gas range. Beige wall-to-wall carpet covered the floor. Three of the walls were celadon green, and the same chintz that was on the couch had been made into drapes that covered the entire fourth wall. Since that was the wall facing the ocean, Charlie presumed there was a spectacular view behind the yards of gaily-patterned floral pleats, but she was too exhausted to even think about checking it out.

Lit by the round white ceramic lamps on either side of the couch, the sitting area was warmly welcoming. Charlie turned her back on it and walked through the small hallway that bypassed the kitchen, to the bedroom.

It held a queen-sized bed with a quilted spread made from that same yellow chintz, and a bamboo headboard, plus the usual nightstands and a bamboo dresser with a mirror over it. Her suitcase was on the floor beside the dresser. Swooping down on it, she extracted her toiletry kit, her white terry cloth robe, and the first nightgown that came to hand. The bottle of Tums was tucked in beside her running shoes. Opening it, she popped two chalky, mint-flavored tablets into her mouth, shook two extra-strength Excedrin out of another bottle, and then, chewing, tottered off toward the adjoining bathroom. Unpacking the rest of her stuff would have to wait for morning. She didn't have the energy to do anything except shower and fall into bed.

The bathroom was solid white: white tile, white fixtures, white towels. It had both a tub and a separate, glass-walled shower. First she swallowed the Excedrin with a handful of water in hopes of easing the headache that wouldn't quit. Then, stripping like she was being paid to get naked fast, Charlie twisted up her hair, pulled on a clear plastic shower cap, stepped into the shower, and turned on the tap. Hot water had never felt so good. Closing her eyes, Charlie let it sluice over her skin, warming her up, taking the worst of the tension out of her muscles. The soap was plain white Dove, but it smelled nice. By the time she turned the water off, she was feeling . . . not a hundred percent, but at least a hundred percent better.

At least she was until she stepped out of the shower, reached for the towel hanging nearby — and discovered a man standing just inside the closed bathroom doorway, watching her.

Chapter Eight

Every tiny hair on Charlie's body shot upright. Jumping backward, she screamed like a steam whistle.

"Jesus Christ, Doc, it's me!"

If that was supposed to make Charlie feel better, it failed miserably. Even as her heel caught on the threshold of the shower and she smacked down hard on her butt on the tile floor, she recognized him: Garland.

Correction, Garland's ghost. The orange prison jumpsuit was gone, replaced by a white tee, snug jeans, and cowboy boots, and his hair had morphed from its previous prison crop into a tawny mane that almost brushed his shoulders, but there was still no mistaking the just-about-hottest guy she had ever laid eyes on for anybody else.

Dead or alive.

His expression was almost comical. Clearly death hadn't affected his hearing any: he was wincing from the earth-shattering blast that she'd loosed even as he loomed large as Bigfoot in the claustrophobic confines of the bathroom.

Sprawled in a semi-reclining position half in and half out of the shower, Charlie realized two things at once: she was naked, and he was eyeing her just like any live human male would eye her under the circumstances. She had a good body, slim and tight and long-legged, with breasts that might have been on the small side but were perky and well shaped, and a well-groomed strip of pubic hair in the usual place. His gaze didn't skip an inch of her, and the carnal glint in his sky blue eyes as he looked sent a rush of alarmed adrenaline pumping through her veins.

"Smokin' bod, Doc," he drawled.

Bad enough that she was plagued by ghosts, but horny, homicidal ghosts? It was too much. Charlie saw red.

"Get out of my bathroom!" she snarled, outraged, and clapped the towel she'd managed to grab on the way down to her bosom. It covered her salient parts — barely — but still left way too much of her shiny wet skin exposed for her comfort.

"Hey, don't —"

But whatever he'd been going to say was interrupted by an urgent pounding on the apartment door.

"Dr. Stone? Dr. Stone, are you all right?" It was Kaminsky, and from her tone she'd be kicking down the door in another split second.

"I'm okay," Charlie yelled, scrambling to her feet while keeping the towel clutched to her front and a ferocious glare fixed on Garland. "I slipped in the shower."

"Dr. Stone? I need you to open the door. *Now.*"

"I'm coming," Charlie shouted back, upping the volume just to make sure she was heard, while frowning fiercely at the menacing-looking apparition. He seemed way more solid than any ghost had a right to and he stood between her and the door. Any way she looked at it, he posed a ginormous problem. If she tried to get out, he might stop her. If she didn't, she would have to explain to Kaminsky how it was she couldn't leave her own bathroom. Even if she did manage to get past him, if she tried to hitch the grossly inadequate towel around herself, she didn't see any way to avoid flashing him, and although he'd already seen it all she didn't want him to see it again. On the other hand, if she tried getting past him the way she was, and succeeded, he was going to get a full and unobstructed view of her bare backside. In motion.

Not happening.

"Dr. Stone!"

"I'm coming!" Charlie shrieked. No way Kaminsky didn't hear that. It was so loud it hurt her own eardrums.

"Who's that?" Garland asked. To her fury, he was starting to look amused.

"Throw me my robe," she hissed at him, because he was standing right beside it — it was hanging from the hook on the inside of the bathroom door. Glancing around, Garland obligingly reached for it — and his hand went right through the thick terry cloth without disturbing so much as a thread.

And that would be because he's dead.

"Fuck," he said, looking mildly surprised.

"Dr. Stone! I'm coming in!"

"I'm *coming,*" she yelled at Kaminsky. Then her voice dropped until it was scarcely louder than a breath, but her eyes killed as she skewered the apparition. "Get out of here. I mean it. *Go.*"

Expression fierce, she made shooing motions with her one free hand as she stomped purposefully toward him. It was pretty much the same technique she used to chase the neighbor's chickens from her garden at home.

His brows arched, but somewhat to her surprise he retreated, backing right through the closed door. Then he was gone, or at least she couldn't see him anymore. What she found herself glaring at instead was her robe hanging against a solid panel of white-painted wood. Charlie snatched her robe from the hook, managing to fumble into it without dropping the towel until the robe was on, just in case Garland was still somewhere he could see her. Then, still tying the belt around her waist, she jerked open the bathroom door. Keeping one wary eye out for Garland, who was thankfully nowhere in sight, she hurried toward the apartment door just as Kaminsky came bursting through it.

So much for kicking down the door. Charlie could see a key in the lock.

Spotting Charlie, Kaminsky stopped short just steps into the sitting room. Still fully dressed except for her heels — she was now in stocking feet — Kaminsky was flushed, breathless, her black hair ruffled, clearly on high alert. Charlie's eyes widened as she spotted the gun the other woman was two-handing.

"Is somebody else in here?" Kaminsky's

voice was sharp. Her eyes ran swiftly over Charlie.

"Cute friend," observed an appreciative male voice behind her. Charlie tensed even as she cast an automatic glance around: wherever Garland had disappeared to, he was now back. Arms crossed over his chest, leaning a broad shoulder against the hall wall, he looked as real and solid as Kaminsky. God, what had he been doing since he'd been killed? In the course of the last few hours, he'd even acquired a tan. "Think she actually knows how to use that gun?"

She's FBI, Charlie almost snapped before remembering that for all intents and purposes he was not present and she and Kaminsky were alone.

"No, of course not," she said to Kaminsky instead. The strain of not being able to reply to Garland gave her voice an edge.

"I thought you were being attacked. You're telling me you screamed like that just for fun?" Kaminsky looked pissed. She cast a suspicious glance past Charlie in the direction, Charlie realized, in which she herself had just thrown that hostile look at Garland. "You trying out your own personal version of a test of the emergency broadcast system, Dr. Stone?"

Garland grinned. Charlie tried not to

notice. "I slipped in the shower."

"And screamed like that? Most people just say *ouch.*"

"It hurt."

Kaminsky glanced past her again. "You mind if I look around?"

"Knock yourself out." Okay, Charlie realized she sounded grumpy. But the strain of ignoring a six-foot-three-inch, muscle-bound, smirking ghost with possibly evil intent was making her nerves jump. "You think I'd lie about a thing like that?"

"I don't know you well enough to know what you'd do."

"What's up with that chick?" Garland watched Kaminsky with interest as she walked swiftly through the apartment, gun held low in front of her, checking corners, closets, bathroom. Twice she walked right past Garland — who'd stepped inside the living room to give her clear passage — coming within inches of him both times without appearing to sense a thing. "She's a cop, isn't she? I can smell 'em a mile off. What, are you on some kind of house arrest now or something?" He shook his head. "Damn, Doc, what the hell did you *do?*"

Aside from a glare at him that she hoped said *Shut up,* Charlie ignored him.

"So you really made that much fuss just

because you fell in the shower," Kaminsky marveled as, search completed, she walked back into the sitting room, clearly much less wary than before. The look she gave Charlie as she tucked her gun back into the shoulder holster beneath her jacket brimmed with disgust. "If you scream like that when you fall down, what do you do when something scares the snot out of you?"

"I'd say scream louder, but I don't think you could," Garland said to Charlie, once again clearly enjoying himself. "That scream was *righteous.* Scared the hell out of me."

Kaminsky stopped right in front of him. His lids went to half mast, and Charlie was willing to bet the farm that it was because he was giving Kaminsky a thorough once-over.

Part of Charlie wanted to shriek *There's a serial killer in the room with us, right now, right behind you,* but she didn't because she knew it wouldn't do any good.

Kaminsky couldn't see him. Kaminsky wouldn't believe her. Kaminsky would think she had bats in her belfry, and the word would spread.

Besides, even if Kaminsky did believe her, what could she do?

Nothing, that's what. Couldn't arrest him, couldn't kill him.

With that, Charlie had a terrible epiphany: the only thing worse than a live serial killer was a dead serial killer.

Sad truth was, Garland was her problem, to deal with on her own.

"Sorry," Charlie managed stiffly, while exercising extreme control in keeping her gaze focused on the other woman instead of blasting Garland with a dirty look as his eyes lifted to focus on Charlie again instead of — all right, she was guessing here, but the general direction seemed right — Kaminsky's butt. "The scream kind of — popped out. Next time I fall, I'll try to remember to say 'Ouch,' instead."

"You do that." Kaminsky headed for the door. Reaching it, she looked back at Charlie. "Why don't you do us both a favor and just go to bed?"

She left before Charlie could reply.

"You sure put her panties in a twist," Garland observed as Charlie went to close and lock the door. Her spine stiffened. Turning to face him, her back to the door, she forbore snapping, I *put her panties in a twist?* You're *the one who made me scream,* in favor of a more controlled, "Why are you here?"

Remembering Kaminsky, she'd kept her voice to a whisper.

Garland shrugged. "Beats me." He, on the other hand, spoke in a perfectly normal tone. Because he wasn't concerned about being overheard. Because no one but her could hear him. Thinking about it, Charlie practically gnashed her teeth.

Why, God, why?

"That's not an answer," she growled.

"It's the best one I've got. So what's up with the cop? You had FBI agents show up for you at the Ridge right before I bit the big one. You in some kind of trouble?"

"She's not a cop. She's FBI. They came to the prison because they wanted my help."

"With what?"

Charlie knew she should have foreseen the question. The truthful answer, to help them catch a serial killer, didn't seem like the smartest thing in the world to admit under the circumstances. Not when the man — apparition, whatever — she was talking to *was* a serial killer — former serial killer? — himself. Now that the excitement of Kaminsky's would-be rescue mission was over, she remembered that she should be afraid of him. That she was, in fact, afraid of him.

He's a ghost. He can't hurt me. Can he?

She eyed him warily. "A case."

"What kind of case?"

"What do you care? It's nothing to do

with you. You're dead, remember?" Charlie moved away from the door as she spoke, heading for the bedroom. Having been plagued by the random appearance of apparitions for many years now, she'd put some effort into learning how to manage her affliction. Most of the spirits she encountered were harmless; she had never yet known one to be able to inflict physical damage on the living, but *yet,* she cautioned herself, was the operative word there. Nevertheless, some were malevolent, giving off negative energy that could adversely affect their environment and the people around them. And some, with Garland being a case in point, were downright frightening, whether she actually thought they could hurt her or not. Still others were merely stuck here on the earthly plane. Over the years, she had done enough research, and discreetly consulted with enough mediums, psychics, and clairvoyants, to know how to deal with wayward phantoms when the need arose. Knowing even as she had agreed to accompany Bartoli and Crane that the likelihood she would encounter the disembodied spirits of the newly, violently deceased was high on this excursion, she had tucked what she called her Miracle-Go kit into her suitcase. That's what she was heading for now, with, unfortunately, the very ghost she most wanted to send into eternity standing between her and her objective.

Chapter Nine

Fortunately, Garland had no clue what she had in store for him.

"I remember, all right," he said. "Piss poor job you did saving my life, by the way."

"You bled out. There was nothing I could do."

He still stood inches away from the entrance to the hallway. If she wanted to get to the bedroom and her suitcase, she had to walk right by him. If he'd been alive, she wouldn't have done it in a million years: it would have offered him way too good an opportunity to grab her. But in his current state he couldn't grab anyone — she didn't think. Remembering his failed attempt with her robe partly steadied her frazzled nerves. Keeping careful watch out of the corner of her eye for any sudden moves he might make, she marched past him with what she considered commendable aplomb, even managing not to speed it up when he turned and followed her.

"About that. You sure there's no way you could, like, hook me up to life support or something and bring me back?"

The skin between her shoulder blades prickled, and she guessed it was because his eyes were boring into her back. Then the sensation disappeared. Either he'd quit looking, or, more likely, was staring at a body part that was lower down — like her butt.

Charlie's brows snapped together.

"I'm sure. There's no way. Sorry to break it to you, but even aside from the injury you sustained, your body is by now past being able to support life."

"What does that mean?"

Sometimes, Charlie thought, you just had to spell things out. "You ever hear of decomposition?"

"Oh, shit."

"Yeah." There was a certain grim satisfaction in her tone. "You're going to have to move on, because your life as you knew it is *over.*"

"Fuck," Garland said. "That SOB Nash. I hope he rots in the hole."

Nash, Charlie remembered, was the name of the inmate who had killed him. Allegedly.

"I'm sure he will."

"Nah, they'll probably give him a medal. I was a real pain in the ass."

"Yes," Charlie agreed before she could stop herself. "You were."

"I never did one bad thing to you, Doc. You can't say I did."

Garland stopped in the bedroom doorway to watch as Charlie grabbed her suitcase and heaved it up onto the bed. In the process she caught a glimpse of herself in the mirror over the dresser. Appalled at what met her gaze, she took instant stock: barefoot, clad only in her white terry robe, she was still damp from the shower. Scrubbed free of every last trace of makeup, her face looked tired and pale. To add insult to injury, the shower cap was still on her head.

Verdict: not hot.

In quick, instinctive reaction, she pulled the shower cap off. Her hair spilled down to her shoulders, its rich chestnut color and heat-and-moisture-induced waves immediately upping her sexy quotient by, she saw with relief, a considerable degree. She was just lifting a hand to brush some wayward strands off her forehead when she met Garland's eyes in the mirror.

The carnal glint was back. His eyes were very blue now, and his mouth had taken on a sensual curve. He was watching her with what she could only describe as lust. Charlie's breath suspended. Her pulse quickened. Answering heat flamed through her veins. Then she caught herself. The guy was gorgeous, no doubt about it. Even with everything she knew about him, including the absolutely-should-have-been-chemistry-killing twin facts that he was a psychopath and *dead,* the sad truth was that she had snatched off her shower cap because she had been concerned with how she looked to *him.*

That's some serious sick, girl.

She would have plopped the shower cap back on her head again if doing so wouldn't have been absolutely ridiculous. Also, a total giveaway.

Not only would letting him know she found him attractive be embarrassing, it might also be dangerous.

She didn't know exactly what it took to trigger his urge to kill, but she did know she didn't want to find out.

Whether he still possessed the capacity to follow through or not.

"You lied about what you saw in the inkblots," she accused to distract him, and dug down deep in her suitcase, feeling around beneath her underwear and workout gear and running shoes, hunting for the only weapons she had.

"Maybe I did. Maybe I didn't. You're the expert. You figure it out." He glanced around. "Where the hell are we anyway? Is this your place?"

"This is an apartment in a beach house just outside of Kill Devil Hills, North Carolina."

"So how did we get here?"

"I flew. In an airplane. I have no idea how you got here." Having located what she needed, she scooped the items up in one hand, then with the other picked up and dropped the bottle of Tums on the floor.

"Oops," she said as it hit. Okay, that had sounded fake even to her. Well, nothing she could do about it, and he didn't appear to notice. Crouching to pick up the bottle, she used the cover provided by the bed to slip the items she needed into her robe pockets without Garland seeing what she was doing. Then she grabbed the bottle of Tums and straightened to her full height again. Ostentatiously she opened the bottle and shook two tablets into her palm. So far seeing him hadn't made her feel sick to her stomach — too much commotion surrounding the visitation, probably — but there was no point in taking any chances. Besides, she needed an excuse to go to the kitchen.

"What's that?"

"Medicine. If you'll get out of my way, I'm going to go to the kitchen to get a glass of water to wash it down." The tablets were actually chewable, but she was absolutely willing to lie about needing water to take them if it got her into the kitchen.

"Why do you need medicine?"

"Ghosts make me nauseous." Closing her fist around the Tums, she walked determinedly toward him as she spoke. She had no way of knowing for sure, but she was gambling on the supposition that the best way to manage a predator like Garland hadn't changed just because he was no longer alive. Rule one, show no fear.

"Are you telling me I make you want to puke?" He grinned as he moved out of her path, and with a silent sigh of relief Charlie made it past him. "You probably want to work on getting over that."

"What I want to work on is not seeing ghosts," she flung over her shoulder. "Present company *not* excepted."

He was following her again. This time, though, it was what she had hoped for. Even if the mere thought of how he was likely to react to what she was about to do kinda/sorta scared her to death.

"Believe me, it's better to see one than be one," he said.

"Funny."

"You see all ghosts? Or am I special?"

"I can see the spirits of people who've suffered recent, violent deaths. Sometimes."

"I got to say, you're a woman of unexpected talents, Doc. Who woulda thought the Ridge's uptight, no-nonsense, my-way-or-the-highway shrink was some kind of closet psychic?" His tone turned reflective. "Or that you looked that good naked, for that matter."

"You know what, Garland? I'd drop that line of conversation right now if I were you."

Charlie walked into the kitchen. The stove, sink, and refrigerator were all lined up against the back wall. Popping the Tums in her mouth, she chewed as she opened a cabinet, pulled out a glass, and turned on the tap.

"You don't like being told you look hot in your birthday suit, Doc? Now, me, I would've thought you'd have been pissed if I hadn't noticed."

Filling the glass partway up with water, she took a sip, swallowing like she needed it to at least kill the taste. What she wanted was to keep him off guard until she got everything in place. All she needed now was an open flame and a little resolution, and the thing was done.

"Then you would have thought wrong," she replied with bite, setting the glass down.

"Come on, Doc, tell the truth. You like having a killer bod. You like me thinking you have a killer bod."

He had been staring hard at the running water, Charlie saw as she shut off the tap and turned around. As his focus switched back to her, she felt the full impact of his presence. Close enough that she could reach out and touch him if she wanted to, he stood just inside the opening between the kitchen and sitting room, blocking the only way out. With his chiseled face and sculpted body, he oozed sex appeal — and, since she knew what he was, menace. He looked intimidatingly tall and powerful and as solid as the wall. If he were alive, he could have grabbed her in a heartbeat and almost certainly overpowered her despite any resistance she might put up.

He wasn't, but anxiety still quickened her pulse and set her stomach a-flutter.

"For your information, popping up on unsuspecting women when they're in the bathroom is just creepy," she threw at him. Gathering her courage, thankful for the heavy terry and capacious pockets of her robe that allowed for the concealment of something so substantial, she pulled out the thick white candle and set it down on the counter beside the glass. It stood sturdily upright, its wick pristine.

"You think I came looking for you deliberately? Get over yourself, Doc. Your bathroom just happened to be where I came out." He squinted at the candle.

"Came out from where?" She turned on the stove. The hiss of gas made what she was doing impossible to overlook. Not that the sound actually mattered, because he was watching her closely anyway.

"Hell if I know. That other place. And if you think I'm going back in there, you're crazy." He folded his arms over his chest as his gathering frown solidified. "What are you doing?"

"Lighting a candle. The scent helps with the nausea." In a round-about way, that actually had the advantage of being true. The scent would help with the nausea, because it would help get rid of him. As flame raced out of the pilot light and ran around the burner, igniting the gas, she took a deep breath. Her palms were damp, and her pulse raced. What she was feeling was acute anxiety, but there was more to it than that. Unbelievable to realize that she actually felt guilty about what she was getting ready to do. Picking up the candle, she felt a little bit like the ruthless murderer that she needed to keep reminding herself *he* was. "Anyway, you have to go back there. It's where you'll find the way to . . ." she hesitated ". . . the hereafter."

His eyebrows went up. "The hereafter?"

Okay, heaven she wasn't promising him. "You know, the afterlife. Eternity. Or . . . whatever."

"Whatever. Yeah, that sounds about right." His voice was dry.

Tilting the candle into the flame, she watched the wick catch fire. "There should be a white light —"

"We've been over this already. Take it from me, there is no fucking white light."

"You just haven't found it yet." Holding the candle, she turned to face him. The faintest scent of jasmine wafted upward.

"Too bad. I'm sure as hell not going looking for it."

"Why not?"

"Because it damned well isn't there. And I wouldn't trust it if it was."

As the scent of jasmine grew stronger, Charlie had to work hard to corral her guilty conscience. "So what *is* there?"

"Mist. Fog. A constant, purple twilight."

He gave her a long look. "There's things in it. People — I can't see 'em, but I can hear 'em screaming. It's like they're being hunted down or something. Whatever's hunting them — I think it's hunting me."

A flash of fear darkened his eyes. Whatever could make a man as big and bad as Garland look scared, Charlie didn't want to meet.

Then she remembered: he wasn't a man anymore. Where he'd found himself, big and bad probably didn't matter.

She had no idea what did. But none of it was her problem. The universe had been rolling along just fine for many millennia before she'd come along, and the whole Great Beyond deal had to have been fine-tuned by now. It was up to a higher power to sort things out vis-à-vis Garland. She just had to trust in the process.

"You have to go back. There's no other choice." Mentally squaring her shoulders, holding the candle carefully so that the flame wouldn't go out, she moved toward him.

He didn't budge. "Sure there is. And I just made it."

Eyes narrowing, Charlie was forced to stop because he was in her path. Theoretically, she probably could have walked right through him. Unless she had to, though, she wasn't about to make the attempt. "What do you mean?"

"I'm staying here."

"You can't."

"Sure I can."

"No, you can't. Even spirits who linger almost always move on within about a week. Uh, you want to get out of my way, please?" There was no point in arguing with him. The discussion would be moot in a couple of minutes anyway. All she had to do was position the candle behind him, and then herd him toward it. She felt a little bad about resorting to what amounted to psychic force, but in the end she had no doubt that it would be the best thing for both of them. She would be rid of a phantom serial killer, and he would be where he was supposed to be in the eternal scheme of things. "I need to set the candle down on the table. It's dripping wax."

"This helps you to not throw up?" His tone was skeptical, but he stepped aside.

"It does." Moving past him, Charlie set the candle down on the glass-topped dining table, made sure the flame was burning strongly, then headed back into the kitchen.

"You left the burner on."

"I know." She was back at the stove. No

longer blocking the door, he was all the way inside the kitchen now, watching her curiously. Not a hint of suspicion in his face. *Get thee behind me, guilt.* Pulling a slender wand of sage incense from her pocket, she held the tip of it to the flame. It caught with a crackle and a flurry of sparks.

"What the hell is that?"

"Incense," she told him over her shoulder.

Inhaling the earthy scent, Charlie waited a second to make sure that the incense was burning strongly enough to be effective before shutting off the burner and turning to face him. His eyes fastened on the smoldering stick in her hand.

"You're starting to weird me out here, Doc." Then, as the smell of sage grew stronger, and slender white tendrils of smoke rose from the tip of the stick to waft in the air, his gaze shifted to her face. "That crap stinks worse than three-day-old roadkill. Are you seriously telling me *that* stops you from throwing up?"

Waving his hand in front of his face, he tried to ward off the aroma. It was clearly bothering him, but he just as clearly had not yet figured out that anything was majorly amiss. Charlie wet her lips. Her heart thumped. What she felt was a kind of dreadful anticipation. The sage would drive him not only from the apartment, but from this earthly plane entirely, while the jasmine candle would open a portal to the other side. At least, that was how it had been explained to her by her gurus in ghostbusting, and she knew from experience that at least the sage worked. The key was to refuse to think about what eternity might be like for Garland.

This is the way it's supposed to be, she told herself defensively. But she couldn't help feeling bad for him nonetheless.

"I'm sorry, but you need to go now," she said firmly. Careful not to get too close too soon, Charlie inched toward him, taking tiny baby steps, waving the burning sage so that the smoke formed a barrier between them. "Your time here on earth is over. You have to move on."

"What the fuck?" As the smoke reached him, Garland's eyes widened. Then his face contorted. From his expression, by waving the sage at him she was assaulting him with the ghostly equivalent of mustard gas. Throwing up an arm, he started backing away from her and it. "Goddamn it, Doc, put that stuff out. You hear me? I'm not kidding."

The budding threat in his voice was clear.

It took every bit of resolution she had, but

Charlie kept going. "The light is there, waiting for you. That's the purpose of the candle, to draw it near. You should be able to find it if you look."

"Jesus Christ, this is some kind of voodoo shit you're pulling on me, isn't it?" His mouth twisted as if he were in pain even as he continued to back away. His heel caught on the threshold between the kitchen and the eating area, where tile floor turned to carpet. "Oh, *God.* Don't do this, Doc."

Her stomach clenched. "I'm really sorry, Garland, but it's for the best, I promise you."

"For you, maybe." Panic flared in his eyes as she kept coming, waving the incense, backing him inexorably through the kitchen doorway toward the table. The candle was close enough now to start pulling him in. Charlie could see the ends of his hair starting to move toward it, could almost feel the gentle suction herself. *"Ah."* He made another pained sound, and it was all she could do to close her heart to it. "Damn it to *hell,* that hurts. *Put that thing out!*"

"I'm *sorry,*" she said again, meaning it, hating that he seemed to be suffering. Garland's pained resistance was something she hadn't anticipated. But she couldn't stop now. The thought of having a ghostly serial killer, whom she had just seriously pissed off, left behind in the land of the living to wreak terrible vengeance on her was enough to keep her advancing, waving her wand even though she felt like she was running over Bambi with an eighteen-wheeler. "Look for the light."

"Don't fuck with me, Doc," he warned, flexing his wide shoulders menacingly, baring his teeth at her. The powerful muscles in his arms bunched as his hands shot out as if to grab her. Charlie jumped and almost dropped the incense as he batted thin air just inches away. When he realized he couldn't get to her, his eyes blazed with fear and fury combined. Thank God the power of the smoke was strong enough to hold him at bay! He was maybe a yard away, but he might as well have been on the wrong side of steel bars. "Don't make me do something I don't want to do."

"Are you threatening me?" she shot back, summoning every last scrap of bravado she could. Getting a glimpse of his violent side should have made her feel better about what she was doing, but it didn't. As she continued to drive him backward, she felt like a murderess. A scared murderess. Her heart thundered. Her stomach twisted. Her hand shook. Barely managing to hang on to the incense, she waved it at him; at this point there was simply nothing else she could do. Smoke swirled past him. It was being drawn toward the candle just like he was. His hair flowed backward now, as though being sucked by a vacuum. The skin on his face seemed to have tightened, so that his high cheekbones looked like blades. He looked huge, terrifying, insane. Probably because, she reminded herself grimly, he was all of those things.

Forget Bambi. Think Voldemort on steroids.

"Hell, yeah. Whatever you're doing's not going to work, and I'll . . . *Ah.*"

"Just *go,*" she almost wailed as, wincing in pain, he broke off in mid-threat. Gritting his teeth, bracing as if in resistance to the force pulling him backward, he seemed to be doing his best to battle a strong wind she couldn't feel.

"I can't believe you'd do this to . . . *Ah. Put it out. Ah.*"

Charlie's throat tightened with pity at the same time her heart lurched with fright. By this time she was so agitated she was practically jumping out of her skin. Fear, pity, regret, determination — she had no clue which emotion was strongest.

"For God's sake, stop fighting it. You're only making it worse."

He opened his mouth as if to say something, then looked sharply around behind him. Following his gaze, Charlie saw that the candle flame was almost perpendicular to the table now, blowing backward in the vortex that had been created.

"Jesus, do you hear that? Do you hear the screaming?"

"Garland, *please.*" She felt tears starting in her eyes. "Go toward the light."

"Fuck the fucking light."

He was moving again, inch by inch, clearly against his will, being pulled backward by a force too powerful to resist. Shaking, breathing hard, sick to the core at what she was doing but knowing she had no choice, she had him backed up all the way to the edge of the table — when suddenly he lunged at her, breaking through the barrier of the smoke, eyes wild, mouth twisting violently. Squeaking, Charlie jumped like a scalded cat, but retained enough presence of mind not to drop the incense, not to back off, and not to scream. He slammed into her, grabbed her, smashed her against him, which given his degree of muscularity should have felt something like being smacked hard into a stone wall. She saw him coming, saw herself being enveloped by him, knew the attack was happening as it happened. But besides a single microsecond in which she seemed to experience an uncannily real sensation of physical contact and an accompanying quick, instinctive burst of terror, all she actually for sure *felt* was a kind of electric tingle, a surge of energy, a blast of air.

"Think you're going to —" he snarled in her ear before breaking off abruptly. Letting go, whirling around, he jerked and screamed like his heart was being ripped from his body.

Even as Charlie clapped a hand over her mouth to keep herself from screaming, too, he was gone.

Just like that.

Left with nothing to see but the now perfectly ordinary-behaving candle, Charlie let her shaking hand drop and took a deep, hopefully calming breath.

It's over.

Then without warning her knees gave out, and she sank in a boneless puddle to the floor.

Chapter Ten

By eight p.m. the following day, Charlie was so tired she was drooping in her chair. Her armless, ergonomic, rolling and swiveling chair that was pulled up in front of the white plastic desk on which rested a state-of-the-art computer with a huge, merciless monitor displaying image after image of what seemed to be every male in every crowd scene that had ever gathered in connection with the murders, or who had ever paused to gape at or had even passed by one of the crime scenes, present and past. She had spent the last few hours in what she had come to think of as the War Room at Central Command (the bedroom office in the RV) poring over every bit of photo footage from newspapers, television, surveillance cameras, cell phones, previous investigation archives — all the evidence of record that had captured pictures of those who had turned up to watch the proceedings at the sites where the murders had occurred, or, later, the primary targets' — the girls' — bodies had been found.

All of which had been triggered by her own observation, to Bartoli that morning, that the killer would almost certainly return to the scene of the crime. "We should be watching the watchers," was what she'd said.

So she'd gotten to watch them until she was about ready to fall out of her chair. By now the smell of coffee and old food and stale air that permeated the small space made her feel like she couldn't breathe. Her head ached unmercifully. She was seeing purple spots in front of her eyes from staring for too long at the computer screen. Her back hurt. Her butt hurt.

The brilliant sunlight outside the one small window she could see beckoned. She longed to decompress by going for a run.

But because Bayley Evans was still out there somewhere, hopefully still alive, still with a chance, Charlie was, like the others, prepared to keep doing what she was doing for as long as it took.

"How's it coming?" Bartoli walked into the room, a welcome interruption. Blinking in an attempt to get her eyes focusing normally again, Charlie pushed back from the desk to peer up at him. He looked tired, with lines around his eyes and mouth that Charlie hadn't noticed before, and an intriguing suggestion of five o'clock shadow darkening his chin. His black hair had developed an unruly wave, his tie was slightly askew, and his mouth was tight. Entering behind him, Crane was sweaty and rosy-cheeked and suffering from a bad case of dandelion hair. He had lost his suit jacket and rolled up his sleeves in deference to the heat. Bartoli, on the other hand, still wore all parts of his charcoal suit and looked surprisingly cool despite it. They brought with them the smell of fresh sea air — something Charlie hadn't had a whiff of since Bartoli had ushered her into the RV shortly before eleven a.m. that morning, having first taken her on a quick tour of the two other current crime scenes, during which, thankfully, she had encountered no earthbound spirits, the dead having presumably passed on. She and Kaminsky, who'd been with her since Bartoli had dropped her off at the RV and at that moment sat at the adjoining desk feeding her computer images, had even eaten lunch — McDonald's, which a sheriff's deputy had gone out to get at around one — at the tiny table in the kitchen area.

"We've got nothing," Kaminsky said flatly

before Charlie could reply. Kaminsky's tone had an edge to it. She seemed to take personally Charlie's failure to recognize the Boardwalk Killer among the crowds.

"The man I saw that night at the Palmers' isn't in any of the photos I've seen." Addressing her response to Bartoli, Charlie kept a grip on her patience with an effort. Kaminsky's attitude was really starting to wear on her nerves. Reminding herself that she was operating on maybe four hours of unrestful sleep and was not perhaps at her most calm and centered was the only thing that kept her from snapping Kaminsky's head off as the agent sent photo after photo to her monitor, saying, "Really? You don't recognize *anyone?*" every time she replaced an image with another one.

"Assuming you even remember what he looks like," Kaminsky said now, casting her a dark look.

"I remember what he looks like." Charlie's reply was tart. "But after fifteen years, he'll have changed. For one thing, if it's the same guy, he'll be — wait for it — fifteen years older."

"Our age-enhancing software is pretty good. That picture up on the right-hand corner of your screen" — the age-enhanced image of the sketch made from Charlie's description of the Boardwalk Killer that night at the Palmers' was a tiny constant on the monitor — "is pretty much who you're looking for. That's why it's there."

"There's no way to be sure how accurate that is," Charlie retorted. "He might be balder. He might be fatter. He might be wearing a hat. Who knows? And it might not even be the same guy. It might be a copycat."

"Which would make this whole thing pretty useless," Kaminsky summed up.

This whole thing meant *you,* Charlie knew.

"We got a possible lead on the heart," Bartoli intervened before Charlie could respond. Probably a good thing, because her annoyance level at Kaminsky was rising dangerously. "The Sanderling holds a barbecue and dance every Friday night during the summer."

"The Meads were killed and Bayley Evans went missing on Wednesday," Kaminsky pointed out.

Bartoli held up a hand. "Let me finish." He was clearly a patient man, certainly far more patient than Charlie was at this point. Charlie decided that she liked that. In fact, she liked just about everything she'd seen of Tony Bartoli, from his dark good looks to his apparent willingness to work until he dropped to find the missing girl alive.

"When someone pays admission, the staff at the Sanderling stamps the back of the customer's hand with a red heart and the date," Bartoli continued. "We've been talking to Bayley Evans' friends, and a group of them went to the Sanderling this past Friday night, the last Friday night before the whole thing went down. The group included Bayley Evans."

"Which, since Dr. Stone thinks the unsub has a red heart on the back of his hand, means there's a strong possibility he was there as well," Crane added on a note of barely suppressed excitement.

"Is Dr. Stone ever going to clue us in on the technique she used to come up with the theory that the unsub has a red heart on the back of his hand? Because I still don't get how she could possibly know that," Kaminsky objected, darting another less-than-fond look at Charlie.

"That's the whole point of bringing in an expert," Bartoli answered before Charlie could. "To tell us things we don't know. A lead's a lead, and this seems like a solid one. That's all that interests me."

As rebukes went, it was mild, but Kaminsky definitely got the point. Her eyes darkened. Her mouth thinned and firmed.

"Today's Friday," Crane stated the obvious, and Charlie wondered if he meant to deflect attention from Kaminsky's chagrin. "There's going to be another dance tonight."

"So we're going to check it out?" Kaminsky stood up abruptly, her relief apparent. "Suits me."

Charlie knew how she felt: at this point, just about anything that would get them away from the computer and out of the tin can (RV) was a welcome development. And a dance — Charlie had a sudden flashback to Holly wearing sausage curls and puffy pink prom dress. The nightmare Holly who had come to her in the hospital all those years ago. The killer could have forced her to dress up as if she were going to a dance. . . .

Charlie's pulse picked up the pace.

"Yup." Bartoli looked at Charlie with the slightest of smiles. "You up to going on a field trip, Dr. Stone?"

"Absolutely." Far be it for her to look a gift horse in the mouth, but . . . "There's just one problem: even if the killer did come into contact with Bayley Evans at this place, he has her now. It's unlikely he's killed her yet, so he has no reason to go trolling for another victim. He shouldn't be there. He has no reason to be there."

"Unless he works there," Crane pointed out. "Or has some other reason to hang around the place."

"He won't stay with the victim all the time." Charlie mulled the possibilities over as she spoke. The image of Holly in that garish prom dress stayed stuck in her head. Of course, it wasn't anything she could share. "He'll try to go about his normal daily routine as much as possible to avoid attracting attention. So if he works at this place, you're right: he should be there."

"Then let's go." Not even trying to disguise her eagerness, Kaminsky pulled her jacket off the back of the chair and headed for the door. She wore another of her form-fitting skirt suits. This one was navy blue, with a white short-sleeved blouse bisected by her shoulder holster. Watching Crane watch Kaminsky walk past, registering his expression, Charlie wondered once again what was between them, because clearly something was. But it wasn't any of her business — and in any case, she really didn't care, Charlie concluded, standing up at last, glad for the opportunity to stretch.

"Think we could grab something to eat while we're there?" Kaminsky threw the question back over her shoulder. "I'm starving, and fast food is getting old."

"No reason why we can't," Bartoli agreed, as he waited for Charlie to precede him then followed her out into the semi-organized chaos that was the rest of Central Command. "As long as we eat fast."

The RV's main living area had been retrofitted as one large office. In it, phones rang, computers hummed, a couple of administrative assistants manned phone lines and keyboards, and various law enforcement types went about their business. Over in a corner a pair of guys in suits — local FBI agents Sy Taylor and Frank Goldberg; Charlie had been introduced to them earlier — were using a large black marker to X through gridded areas on a map.

"They're marking off search areas," Bartoli told her, seeing where her gaze lingered. "The local cops are conducting a physical search for the girl or anything that turns up that might lead us to her. Thousands of volunteers are out there combing every square inch of every neighborhood and marsh and woodland in the vicinity."

Charlie nodded. Once again, she found it comforting to realize just how huge the effort to save Bayley Evans was.

"Any leads?" Bartoli asked Taylor as the agent glanced around at them.

"So far, nothing worth mentioning, but it only takes one time to get lucky." Taylor's bulldog eyes were almost lost in the pale folds of his drooping eyelids. Shiny, bald, and bulky in the way of weight lifters, looking to be in his late forties, he was, so Kaminsky had told her earlier, a career agent with over twenty years in the local office. Goldberg, some ten years his junior, was tall and thin, with slicked-back dark brown hair and handsome, aquiline features.

"It's like she vanished into thin air." Goldberg sounded frustrated. "Where the hell does he take them?"

"That's what we've got about four days to figure out." Bartoli's grim reply reminded everyone that the clock was ticking. Taylor made a tired huffing sound as he and Goldberg turned as one back to the grid.

Kaminsky pulled open the RV's door. The slice of brilliant blue ocean and sugar white beach Charlie could see through it glittered in the sun. Waves rushed toward shore with a muted roar that blocked out the sounds coming from inside the RV. Wet and heavy, the air smelled of the sea. The sky was starting to show the striated shades of lavender that heralded the approach of night, but near the horizon it was still dotted with fluffy clouds as white as the froth that curled in on the surf.

"Just one thing, Kaminsky: before we get there, you need to lose the shoulder holster. And the attitude. If our unsub is there, we don't want him to make us as feds the minute we walk in," Bartoli said.

"You want me to go in unarmed?" Kaminsky sounded mildly outraged. She and Crane were already standing on the asphalt driveway as Charlie, eyes narrowed against the sudden brightness of the golden evening sunlight, started down the rickety metal steps of the RV. Even at this relatively late hour, the heat and humidity were intense enough to make her feel like she was stepping into a steam bath. Her sapphire shirt was sleeveless, thin silk. Nevertheless, it was too much, and immediately felt like it was clinging to her skin. With it she wore slim black slacks and low-heeled pumps, professional attire that, since she had left her jacket behind in her rooms that morning, she'd expected to be comfortably cool in. Now, walking into the wall of humidity, she felt way overdressed for the heat, and for the beach town in general. Bringing up the rear, Bartoli closed the door behind them. Glancing back at him as she stepped down onto the pavement, Charlie registered his suit jacket and long-sleeved shirt and tie and quit feeling sorry for herself. Clearly a better person than she was in that regard, Bartoli hadn't even broken a sweat.

"It's a dance, not a gunfight," Bartoli told Kaminsky dryly as he rattled down the steps. "I think you'll be fine."

"You'll have Bartoli and me for backup if you need it," Crane added. "We're armed."

"Oh, wow, I feel better now," Kaminsky retorted as Bartoli reached the ground. *"Not."*

"Think of this as an undercover operation." Bartoli started walking, and the rest of them followed toward the end of the RV. "We're tourists out for a social evening. If the unsub even begins to suspect we're there looking for him, he'll disappear like that."

He snapped his fingers.

"Special Agent Bartoli? Do you have any comment on the progress of the investigation? Or any information at all that you would care to share with our viewers?" A reporter with a microphone jumped in front of them, seemingly out of nowhere, catching them by surprise as they emerged from the alley formed by the RV and the house. Blond and willowy, she was accompanied by a camera crew that instantly zeroed in on the four of them as the reporter thrust her microphone toward Bartoli for a reply.

Chapter Eleven

Taking in the reporter's gauzy orange sundress, Charlie felt a stab of envy: in something like that, she would at least stand a chance of beating the heat.

Before Bartoli could answer the woman's question, a shout went up from somewhere to Charlie's right. Glancing in that direction, lifting a hand to shield her eyes from the blinding sunlight, Charlie saw to her dismay that a whole pack of media types was rushing toward them. Apparently the "secret" location of their imported team was no longer a secret.

"Special Agent Bartoli! Any leads on Bayley Evans?"

"Do you think she's still alive?"

"What's being done to find the victim?"

"Is this the Boardwalk Killer again?"

Reporters yelled questions as the news crews mobbed the four of them. Mobile klieg lights which were brighter than the brilliantly setting sun blinded Charlie to the point where she had to look down at the heat-softened asphalt underfoot. A shuffling wall of legs and feet surrounded her, backing away incrementally from the four of them as the cameramen jostled for position.

"I can't comment on an ongoing investigation," Bartoli responded tersely, his hand closing on Charlie's upper arm, pulling her along with him as he forced his way through the horde by, as far as Charlie could tell, sheer force of personality.

"Have there been any ransom demands?"

"Were the other girls tortured?"

"How were the victims killed?"

The shouted questions came so fast and furiously that it would have been difficult to reply even if Bartoli had wanted to, which he clearly didn't. Stone-faced, he plowed through the crowd with Charlie in tow and Kaminsky and Crane right behind them. Half blinded by the lights and wary of the cameras anyway, Charlie kept her head down and kept going.

The black SUV in which she and Bartoli and Crane had driven from the airport was parked just a few yards behind the RV. Unlocking it with a click, Bartoli pulled open the front passenger door and thrust Charlie inside. Even as she registered the suffocating heat in the interior of the vehicle, Bartoli slammed the door on her. Fortunately the windows were tinted. Charlie was fairly certain that the flashes aimed at the SUV could not penetrate them. Still, she ducked her head.

"Are our citizens safe in their homes?"

"Can you at least tell us if you've identified any suspects?"

As the vehicle's other doors were jerked open almost in unison the media's shouted questions peppered Charlie's ears like hail.

"Should we expect more murders?"

"What is it that the victims have in common?"

A moment later the other three were inside and the SUV was once again closed up tight, doors locked against the onslaught. To Charlie the scene felt surreal, as though the four of them were barricaded inside the sweltering vehicle against a mob. Bartoli, who was driving, looked over his shoulder as he backed the SUV away, slowly and carefully so as not to hit an importunate reporter. The cameras kept filming even as the vehicle broke free of the crowd at last. Still reversing toward the street, the SUV picked up speed.

"Damn." Bartoli flicked a glance at Charlie. "What are the chances they're not going to run your picture all over the eleven p.m. news?"

She grimaced. "Maybe they'll think I'm just another agent."

"We knew they were going to find out who she is sooner or later." In the backseat with Crane, Kaminsky rolled down her window to let in air despite the running, shouting, filming camera crews that were doing their best to keep up. It was so hot and airless in the vehicle that Charlie didn't blame her. Besides, the cameras were by that time too far away to capture much, and she was in the front seat, which made the chances of them getting a good shot of *her* even more remote. The sounds of all the commotion going on outside coupled with the whoosh of air coming through vents as Bartoli cranked the air-conditioning made it necessary for him to raise his voice as he replied.

"I was hoping it would take a while." Bartoli whipped the SUV out onto the road, shifted into drive, and steered around the news vans that were partially blocking the way. Flipping down the passenger visor, Charlie watched through the inset makeup mirror as the news crews broke ranks and raced for their vans to follow. "I was hoping they would focus on the local search headquarters in town and leave us alone."

"Think we'll be lucky enough that they'll just identify Dr. Stone as a noted serial killer expert we've brought in and leave it at that?"

"No." Bartoli's face registered no emotion. "So far, we haven't caught a single break in this entire investigation. No reason to think we'll catch one now."

"You think they're going to publicly identify me as the sole survivor of the original Boardwalk Killer murders?" Charlie's heart started pumping hard at the prospect. The nightmares that had haunted her for years seemed suddenly way closer to reality than she could bear to think about: ice-cold terror filled her veins as the scene at the Palmers' popped into her brain. If the killer knew she was here, knew that there was a high probability she could identify him, what would he do?

Come after me, was her immediate, visceral response. Her second thought was, *I should have stayed away.*

Panic made her chest feel tight.

I need to get out of here. I need to hide.

Then she thought of Bayley Evans, and managed to get a grip. *She needs me.*

"I'd say there's a good chance." Bartoli's tone was grim.

"You think maybe we should contact the press, explain the situation, ask them not to out her?" The last one to do so, Crane hastily fastened his seat belt with a *click* as, reaching the closest intersection, Bartoli jetted through it just as the light was changing, drawing an indignant honk from another motorist. The purpose, Charlie figured, was to lose any remaining reporters. The near miss inches from their rear bumper as the emptying-the-beach traffic resumed its stampede toward town made Charlie's lips purse. Then, looking in the mirror in time to catch the news vans screeching to a stop on the other side of the intersection, she silently gave Bartoli kudos for his maneuver.

"Tell me you're not actually naïve enough to think that would do any good." Kaminsky shot Crane a derisive look.

"I think that if they find out who Dr. Stone is, whether because we tell them or through some other means, it's way too good a story to hope they'll keep it quiet," Bartoli intervened. "If the news breaks, we'll just have to step up our protection efforts. For one thing, Kaminsky, you may need to move into Dr. Stone's suite with her."

"I don't think that would be necessary," Charlie objected hastily, appalled at the prospect.

"I'm right across the hall," Kaminsky

protested at almost the same time, sounding equally appalled. Breaking off, the two of them exchanged measuring glances in the makeup mirror.

"I feel perfectly safe with Agent Kaminsky across the hall," Charlie said. "In order to function optimally, I need sufficient rest, and I don't sleep well unless I have a certain amount of privacy."

"Anyway, the walls are thin as paper. I can hear everything that goes on in there, believe me," Kaminsky put in. Once again the two women exchanged measuring looks. Charlie was left wondering what, exactly, Kaminsky had heard. Not Garland; that would be impossible. But maybe her part of their conversation? Well, if it came up, she would just have to claim that she'd been on the phone.

"We'll see how it goes." Bartoli didn't sound convinced.

Kaminsky rolled up the window finally, as they headed south down N.C. 12, also known as Beach Road, toward Nags Head. To the left, the view was simply spectacular: sand dunes, rolling ocean, purpling sky. To the right, colorful, tightly bunched beach communities thinned into funky little clusters of houses dotted with convenience stores, gas stations, and the occasional strip mall. Toilets, showers, bathhouses, and picnic shelters lined the seventy miles of beaches. The archipelago they were traveling through narrowed the farther south they went, until it was no more than a long, curving finger of bridge-connected land, and soon they could see both Albemarle Sound on the right and the Atlantic Ocean on the left. Either the news vans weren't allowed to leave the area immediately around Kill Devil Hills or Bartoli had successfully lost them, because they weren't being followed anymore. After about twenty minutes, Charlie felt confident enough of that to relax.

"Did anybody interview those two persons of interest I found? The ones living in RVs in local campgrounds? Martin Blumenthal and D. L. Jones, who were in a mental hospital and a prison, respectively, for the last fifteen years?" Kaminsky asked. "I did," Crane said. "Neither is the right age. Plus, Jones is black, and both have alibis."

"I knew that was too easy," Kaminsky responded gloomily.

"Here we are." Bartoli pulled off into a lushly green enclave marked with a discreet sign announcing their destination: the Sanderling. It was, Charlie had learned from various bits of conversation on the way, one of North Carolina's finest resorts. Charlie flipped up the visor in order to get a better look at it. A line of cars preceded them, making their progress necessarily slow. The long drive through acres of manicured lawns was shaded by twin rows of giant oaks bearded with lashings of silvery Spanish moss. Masses of brilliantly colored flowers lay in lavish beds backed by gray stone walls. A golf course complete with players teeing off and carts zooming around the paths was visible in the distance. Charlie's eyes widened as they rounded a bend and what looked to be an eighteenth-century plantation house came within view. Arriving cars pulled beneath a canopied porte cochere, where red-jacketed valets ushered the occupants out before parking their vehicles. A steady stream of well-dressed patrons trooped up the wide steps to the wrap-around verandah and from there to the front door.

"Hope you brought your wallet, boss." Kaminsky's tone made it clear that she was getting the same sense of this-place-is-way-expensive that Charlie was. Glancing back, Charlie saw Kaminsky was using the tinted window as a makeshift mirror to smooth her hair.

"Crane's paying." Bartoli didn't crack a smile as he flicked a glance at Crane in the rearview mirror, but Charlie could still see his eyes: they twinkled.

"I'm not the one with the Bureau's Amex," Crane replied. "Or the expense account."

"Eat light," Bartoli ordered, sounding as if he was only partly joking. "I don't know if you heard, but Uncle Sam's cracking down on expense accounts these days."

"Guess I can forget about ordering that bottle of Dom Perignon, then." Kaminsky's tone was dry.

"I thought you couldn't drink alcohol," Crane said. "What with being a Scientologist and all."

"You thought wrong," Kaminsky retorted even as Charlie, upon hearing the other woman's religious affiliation, experienced an "ah-hah" moment. She was kind of fuzzy on the details, but she was pretty sure Scientologists didn't believe in psychiatry, which explained a fair amount about Kaminsky's attitude toward her. "Anyway, just because I was raised as a Scientologist doesn't make me a Scientologist now. I'm nonpracticing."

"I don't think you can do that," Crane said, as the SUV reached the head of the line at last and pulled to a stop beneath the scarlet canopy.

"You don't know anything about it," Kaminsky answered caustically. "And you're never going to."

Then the driver's door and Charlie's were opened simultaneously by a pair of solicitous valets. As Charlie slid out, she spotted an old man following the couple ahead of them up the stairs. Her eyes widened. Since the man was semi-transparent and being ignored by everyone else, Charlie felt safe in assuming that he was an apparition. She sighed inwardly. Seeing a dead man was par for the course for her, but it didn't mean she had to like it. Her stomach gave an uneasy rumble, but at least it was only a rumble: the connection was too slight to bring on full-blown nausea. As she joined Bartoli, she couldn't help but eye the old man carefully. There wasn't a mark on him that she could see, but obviously he had died in some violent fashion several days previously (recent deaths usually bore signs of the manner of it, and spirits rarely stayed earthbound for longer than a week). Either he was attached to the building itself, or to one or both of the couple walking up the stairs ahead of him. They were middle-aged, attractive, absolutely ordinary-looking in every respect: the chance that they were murderers or that he was a murder victim was remote, Charlie decided. Probably the old man had been killed in an accident or . . . who knew. In any case, this particular ghost had his back turned to her, had no idea she could see him, was in no apparent distress and did not seem to require her help. He was, therefore, no concern of hers, and the last thing she wanted was to make him her concern with so many witnesses, including the three FBI agents accompanying her, on hand. So she studiously ignored the apparition as he entered the building in the couple's wake, and looked the other way as they, their otherworldly third wheel in tow, were ushered through to what, from its dark-paneled coziness and the sounds of clinking glasses emanating from it, seemed to be a bar. By the time she again tuned in to her group's conversation, the four of them had arrived at the hostess' table and their SUV was heading for the parking lot.

A few minutes later Bartoli had paid for their admission and they all sported half-dollar-sized red hearts with the day's date stamped on the back of their hands.

Just as Julie Mead had described it, Charlie thought, looking down at hers, but of course she couldn't say that.

"I still don't see how you could know the perp had a heart stamped on the back of his hand," Kaminsky muttered in her direction as a tuxedoed waiter led them through a side door, across the verandah, and down into a patio area. There, dozens of glass-topped tables were set up in concentric rings centered on small circular flower gardens that were interspersed at regular intervals along the trio of descending brick terraces. They overlooked an emerald green expanse of marsh grass and, beyond that, the dark blue water of Albemarle Sound. A slight breeze blew in off the water, and that, coupled with the encroaching twilight, lifted the humidity and mitigated the heat to the point where it had become pleasant rather than enervating. The smell of slowly roasting meat hung in the air, courtesy of a couple of black iron roasters smoking away near a long line of buffet tables. In a gazebo near a wooden dance floor that had been laid down atop a swimming pool, a live band was tuning up.

"What can I tell you? I'm good like that," Charlie answered back. As the hostess seated them at one of the upper tables, waiters roamed the terraces lighting small votive candles in glass jars in the center of the tables. Charlie was just accepting her menu from their waiter when the tall bronze ibis sculpture in the center of the circular garden in front of them started shooting water from its beak.

"It's a fountain," she remarked in delight as the others looked at it, too.

No sooner had the words left her mouth than, on the other side of the garden, Garland materialized.

CHAPTER TWELVE

It took Charlie just a second to make sure she was really, truly seeing what she thought she was seeing. Yes, there he stood, dressed in jeans and a white tee, exactly as she had last seen him, still gorgeous enough that under any other circumstances just setting eyes on someone who looked like him would have made her heart go pitty-pat, seemingly solid as a stone wall, his booted feet planted apart, his fists clenched and his shoulders tensed as if, maybe, he was expecting to be attacked. Positioned between two tables of four almost directly opposite from where she was seated, with the lushly colored, perfumed garden between them, he glanced around, his movements edgy. He seemed to be a little disoriented, a little confused. The occupants of the tables closest to him laughed and sipped their drinks and looked at the menus they were holding, clearly oblivious to his sudden arrival. He was maybe thirty feet away, and it was getting dark and the fountain shot fine drops of silvery spray into the air between him and her, but that in no way interfered with Charlie's view. There was no mistaking Garland for anyone else.

He doesn't know I'm here.

But even as Charlie had the thought Garland's head whipped around in her direction as if — horror of horrors! — drawn by the power of her gaze.

Their eyes locked before she could gather her wits enough to try to duck behind the menu, or hide beneath the table, or *something.*

After that it was too late to do anything at all but sit there like a rabbit frozen in place by the proximity of a hound.

Of course he saw her.

Garland's eyes widened as he obviously registered her presence, his whereabouts, the whole nine yards, in an instant. Then they narrowed. His face hardened. His lips thinned. In short, he looked pissed.

Then he vanished.

Poof! Like he'd never been there.

Charlie couldn't believe it. It was the most unexpected of reprieves.

But her jittery heart didn't seem to have caught on to the fact that he was gone, because it just kept right on pounding.

Charlie only realized that she must have caught her breath and stiffened in her chair upon spotting Garland when she became aware that the others were looking at her curiously.

"Is something wrong?" Bartoli asked. He was seated beside her, as handsome and desirable a dinner companion as any sane woman could ask for, his black hair waving back from his high forehead, his well-formed features bronzed by nature and candlelight, his strong jaw showing just the beginnings of five o'clock shadow, his warm brown eyes filled with concern for her. Yet here she was, having a hard time bringing him into focus. Why? Because every atom of her being was focused on the whereabouts — or not — of Garland.

Spirit, spirit, go away. Don't come again another day.

She realized she was breathing way too fast, and tried to consciously dial down what she recognized as her body's instinctive fight-or-flight response.

Oh, God, please God, let my sighting of Garland have been an illusion, the product, maybe, of too much stress and too little sleep and food, or something similar. Then she gave an inner grimace. How sad was it that she would be thrilled to learn that she had just experienced a brief psychotic break in which she had conjured up an unwanted vision out of her imagination?

"I thought I saw a hummingbird," Charlie managed, feeling like a fool even as she uttered the lie. Her voice sounded almost normal as she made a vague gesture in the direction of a cluster of hot-pink hibiscus on the other side of the garden, in the general area in which Garland had — or had not — appeared. "It's gone now."

"You into bird-watching?" Crane looked at her with interest. "A lot of people are."

"I like hummingbirds." That much was true, so Charlie found saying it somewhat easier. Her nerves were jumping like a thousand tiny grasshoppers under her skin as she tried, and failed, by means of discreet, darting little glances all over the place, to spot any further sign of Garland. If she hadn't caught herself and consciously relaxed her hands, she would have been gripping the arms of her thickly cushioned, wrought-iron chair tightly.

"You see anything else interesting? Like our unsub?" Kaminsky's tone was caustic.

"N-no." Okay, stuttering wasn't going to cut it. Neither was looking around every which way like a thief hiding from the cops.

Whatever was going on with her sighting of Garland — and there was no way that she should have seen him, because there was no way he should have been able to return from the Great Beyond, or wherever the hell (probably literally) she'd sent him — he was gone now. She needed to focus on the here and now or risk having her companions think there was something seriously wrong with her. "Of course, I haven't really had much time to look at anyone yet."

"The unsub's more likely to be an employee than a guest," Bartoli said. "After we eat, we'll walk around, take a look at the staff."

"Think we should circulate his picture?" Crane asked.

Bartoli shook his head. "Not yet. If word gets out that we're looking for someone, we'll scare him off if he is somewhere on the premises — and maybe even scare him into killing the girl prematurely. We need to be real careful here."

"This seems like a pretty good place for a predator like our unsub to hang out." Kaminsky was glancing over the tables, which were now almost full. "Lots of families."

"He's an ephebophile, remember." Charlie was glad to concentrate again on the reason they were there instead of worrying about the possible presence of Garland. "His primary purpose in frequenting a place like this is to find and evaluate teenage girls for how well they fit his criteria. The families are just collateral damage."

"Ephebophile?" Crane looked at her over his menu.

"An ephebophile is someone who is attracted to post-pubescent children — teenagers," Kaminsky replied before Charlie could. "Come on, Crane. Keep up."

Just then the waiter arrived to take their order. Charlie realized that while her mind had been occupied elsewhere, everyone else had made their decision about what to eat.

Easy enough, she discovered: it was a buffet, so the waiter only wanted to know about drinks. Charlie could really have gone for a bourbon and Coke — or something even stronger, under the circumstances — but since the agents were on duty and thus not drinking, she settled for iced tea. While the waiter went to fetch the drinks, they hit the buffet. Getting in line, she surreptitiously swept her eyes over the men responsible for refilling the buffet dishes: no way any of them were the Boardwalk Killer. So far, in fact, none of the staff with whom she had come into contact even fit into the category of remotely possible.

Unless it was a copycat. Or unless everything she knew was wrong and science and statistics went totally out the window.

That was a world in which she couldn't function. Everything in life and death had rules that governed them, including ghosts and serial killers. Banished ghosts couldn't come back. And serial killers fit within certain parameters.

Or the universe — to say nothing of her head — had gotten seriously screwed up.

It wasn't until Charlie got within range of the heavenly smells of shrimp and grits, slow-roasted barbecue and corn on the cob, fried chicken and pecan pie — that she realized how hungry she was.

Unfortunately, with her stomach now in a knot, she was afraid to put too much in it. The flash she'd gotten of Garland had caused it to clench up. The last thing she wanted to do now was fill it and risk an attack of full-blown upchucking if another spirit — and please God, if she had to have an encounter with a spirit, let it be another spirit — should show up.

"Is that all you're going to eat?" Behind her in line, Bartoli looked down at her plate and shook his head. It held a spoonful of this and a little dab of that, because, sadly, that was all she dared attempt. "Getting to eat this well while on the job is a rare treat in our line of work. You probably want to take advantage."

"I'm dieting." Which was just one more lie she'd told him. Still, it was better than admitting the truth. He — all of them — would never believe the truth. Not for the first time, Charlie felt a surge of fierce resentment about the confining aspects of her unwanted ability. Her choices were extremely limited: lie, or tell the truth and have people think she was nuts; isolate herself, or suffer sudden-onset, flu-like bouts of debilitating illness every time she interacted with the newly, violently departed. Frequently being scared to death and grossed out by phantoms with horrific injuries were part of the package, too. To say nothing of the off chance of having a dead serial killer whom she had tried and failed to banish from this plane of existence come hunting for her, possibly with vengeance on his mind. Charlie gave an inward snort. Anyone who thought it would be fun to be able to see ghosts didn't know the half of it.

God, did you ask me if I wanted to be able to see dead people?

"You ate a Big Mac for lunch!" Kaminsky, in front of her, turned around to point out.

Instead of grinding her teeth, which was what she really felt like doing, Charlie managed a saccharine smile. "Which is why I'm dieting now."

"Better you than me." Kaminsky turned back to the buffet with a shrug.

"You're pretty slim. You should be able to handle a Big Mac *and* a decent supper," Crane told Charlie cheerfully. "Especially considering your height. Now, if you were short, you might have something to worry about."

Kaminsky's head snapped around. "Is that some kind of a dig at me, Crane?"

Crane looked as taken aback as if one of the shrimp on his plate had suddenly snapped at him. "No."

"Because if it is, you know what you can do with yourself." Well-filled plate in hand, Kaminsky turned and marched back toward their table. Crane looked at Charlie and Bartoli, who were behind him, with an expression of bewildered appeal. Its silent message was, *What did I do?*

"You dug your own grave," Bartoli told him with a shrug. "Women and weight don't belong in the same conversation."

"Holy Mother of God," Crane said in

disgust, and turned away to follow Kaminsky back to the table.

Charlie lifted her eyebrows at Bartoli. "I take it there's something going on between those two?"

"He was engaged to her sister for a while this spring. Broke it off two weeks before the wedding. Kaminsky wasn't happy, to say the least. I doubt the sister was, either, but the sister's not my problem, thank God."

He gave her a crooked smile as he said the last part. Looking up at him, Charlie registered that the top of her head just reached the base of his nose and that his shoulders were broad and his body was lean and fit in his FBI-guy suit, and felt a pleasant little tingle of attraction. Bartoli was a good-looking man who was gainfully employed, and she liked him. She'd had more than one relationship that had started off with a lot less going for it than that. Probably she ought to think about —

"Miss me, Doc?" drawled an unmistakable voice in her ear. Garland! Charlie jumped so high and so fast that her plate went flying. It landed with a wet *plop* right in the middle of a big crystal bowl full of scrumptious-looking banana pudding, spilling its contents across the creamy surface.

Yellow blobs of pudding went flying everywhere. Wide-eyed with horror, Charlie watched them land on a couple of individual ramekins of crème brûlée, a carrot cake, a plate of petits fours, and a chocolate pie.

"I am *so sorry,*" she gasped to the servers on the other side of the table, to Bartoli, to the diners around her in line. "I just — I don't know what happened." Even as she turned seven shades of red and stammered out more apologies, she glanced covertly around for Garland.

He was nowhere to be seen.

The sun was setting in a swirl of pinks and oranges over the purple waters of the Sound. Tiki torches were lit and their flames swayed in the breeze. Candles glowed like hundreds of fireflies from the centers of the white-clothed tables. Posh people in their Friday-night-out clothes were everywhere: in line at the buffet, sitting at the tier upon tier of tables, walking along the verandah and paths. The band was playing now. Charlie recognized the song: "Forever Young."

There were lots of sounds, lots of auditory and visual stimuli. Maybe she'd made a mistake.

Maybe it hadn't been Garland that she'd heard at all.

Even as she told herself that, and hoped,

desperately, she'd just imagined it — first, Garland's appearance, and second, his voice — she knew better: she didn't know how or why or where exactly, but she was now as sure as it was possible to be of anything that he was there.

Toying with her like a cat with a mouse.

CHAPTER THIRTEEN

"No worries, ma'am," one of the servers (who clearly didn't know the half of it) assured Charlie, while the other nodded his head. They whisked away the ruined pudding and got busy cleaning up the mess she'd made, while Bartoli gently pulled her away from the scene.

"I can't believe I did that," she told him, genuinely mortified, even as her gaze darted hither and yon in a fruitless search for Garland. Others in the buffet line who had witnessed her clumsiness made sympathetic faces at her as Bartoli took her back to the first buffet table and supplied her with a clean plate and silverware. "I'm not usually such a klutz."

"Anybody can have an accident. Didn't you get some of that shrimp stuff?" His tone was soothing as he pointed out a dish she'd helped herself to before. Charlie dutifully scooped up another serving. She didn't miss the speculation in his eyes when he thought she wasn't looking, however. Bartoli was wondering what was up. Well, she would be, too.

"I must have caught my foot on something." She tried really, really hard to sound rueful. "It happened so fast, it's hard to be sure."

"No harm done." He grinned as he watched her drop a spoonful of corn pudding onto her plate. "You seem to have had your share of bad luck since we met: you've tossed your cookies twice, lost your plate to a bowl of banana pudding, and Kaminsky tells me you fell down hard enough that it made you scream in the shower last night."

"Did she tell you how she came to my rescue?" It was an effort, but Charlie managed to keep her tone light as she finished restocking her plate.

"She might have said something about it."

Better to turn the conversation away from her own misadventures, Charlie thought as she led the way back to their table, than let him start really thinking about them and possibly realize the whole series of disasters had started when a certain convict had died under her ministrations. Kaminsky made a useful red herring.

"So, is Kaminsky married?" Charlie asked.

"No. None of us are."

"Why not?"

He shrugged. "We work too much. We travel too much. At least two of us are hard to get along with." That crooked smile appeared again. "And no, I'm not telling you which two."

Charlie laughed, which helped to ease some of the tension that had her shooting wary looks at every moving shadow. *Chill,* she warned herself fiercely as they reached the table and sat down. *If Garland's here, he'll show himself again soon enough, and then you're just going to have to deal. In the meantime, there's no point in making the others think there's something wrong with you.*

"We were beginning to wonder if you two got lost," Crane greeted them a little too heartily.

"I dropped my plate and had to start over."

Charlie, at least, had become immediately aware that Kaminsky and Crane had broken off an argument upon her and Bartoli's arrival. Stabbing a fork into her pulled pork and lifting it to her mouth, Kaminsky was still glowering.

"This place seems to attract an older crowd than Bayley Evans and her friends." Bartoli sounded thoughtful. He was looking around as he ate. "It's expensive, too. Not the kind of place you'd expect a group of teenage girls to want to hang out."

"Maybe they came with their families," Crane suggested.

Bartoli shook his head. "According to her friends, they came in a group. Six of them. I just assumed the venue was the attraction, but now I'm not so sure."

"Excuse me." Kaminsky summoned their waiter with a slightly raised voice and a smile. When he reached them and looked at her inquiringly, she continued, "My teenage niece was here last Friday night and said she had a wild time. This doesn't look like the kind of gathering she'd call a wild time. Was something special happening last week?"

The waiter smiled. He had introduced himself as Keith, Charlie remembered, as in *Hi, I'm Keith, and I'll be your waiter tonight.* Keith was a cute blond guy in his early twenties, maybe a college student. Young enough to have plenty in common with a pack of teenage girls, Charlie thought. Old enough that they'd probably thought he was cool. Or hot. Or whatever teenage girls thought about cute guys these days.

"Kornucopia played last Friday night," Keith said with enthusiasm. The blank looks around the table must have told him they didn't have a clue what he was talking about, because he added, "They're a boy band, real popular with the high school girls. They drew a big crowd, so management will probably do it again. Only we couldn't serve alcohol, you know, because of the age thing, so I don't know how much profit they made. If they didn't make a lot of profit, I guess it might've been a one-off."

"Tell me about them. How many guys are in the band? And how old are they?" Kaminsky asked.

"Um . . . four guys. Hank Jones, Axel Gundren, Ben Teague, and Travis Fitzpatrick. I don't know how old they are exactly. Like, twenty-five, twenty-six, most of them."

"Are they a local band? Or regional? 'Cause I've never heard of them; but then, I'm not from here." Kaminsky's tone stayed light.

"Mostly they play around this area. I guess you could call them regional."

"You seem to know quite a bit about them. You a fan?" Bartoli tried to mask the sudden keen interest in his eyes with a friendly smile, but Charlie saw it.

"When they play, the girls show up." Keith

shrugged. "What's not to like?"

Kaminsky laughed, and thanked him as another table beckoned and he hurried off.

Crane said, "Now, there's a lead."

Kaminsky looked around the table with a superior smirk. "Sometimes all you got to do is ask."

"A band." Bartoli's eyes gleamed. "Good work, Kaminsky. When we're done here, pull together information on them."

"You thinking maybe they've played somewhere near where the other two families were attacked?" Crane asked.

Bartoli shrugged. "Won't know until we check it out."

"It won't be the band members," Kaminsky asserted. "They're too young. At least, according to Dr. Phil here."

Charlie shot her a withering look, but refused to engage.

"They're only too young if this is actually the Boardwalk Killer," Charlie said. "If it's a copycat, the mid-twenties would fit the statistics."

"You don't think our guy's the Boardwalk Killer, do you?" Bartoli asked curiously.

Charlie met his eyes. The truth was, she didn't *want* to think it was the Boardwalk Killer. The idea that the predator who had stalked her nightmares for years was back, that he was nearby, that he was once again slaughtering families and preying on innocents, and might at any moment discover her presence and turn his sights on *her* was terrifying enough to make her blood run cold. But there were other, research-based reasons why it was unlikely to be him, and it was to these she clung.

"He would be too old now," she said. "It's very rare to find a serial killer older than forty. And there's the time gap: where has he been for fifteen years?"

"Both are good points," Bartoli said. "But I think we would be foolish to discount the possibility."

"It doesn't have to be the band members themselves. It could be someone connected with them," Crane mused. "If the band's traveling around, they'll have people working with them, won't they? Maybe we're looking for a roadie, or someone like that."

"I'll check out everybody connected with the band, too," Kaminsky promised. "How big an entourage could they have?"

Charlie told her, "Look for someone with a history of sex offenses against underage females at any time over the last ten years. A poor relationship with his parents. Hypochondria or other attention-seeking maladies. Probably someone working with him will have noticed that he can't take criticism, so you could ask about that."

They had all finished eating by that time.

"I'll just give them all a questionnaire to fill out, shall I?" Kaminsky responded caustically. "Let's see, I can start with, *How much do you hate your mommy and daddy?* Then, how about, *Do you get sick a lot?*"

Charlie's eyes narrowed. "You want to find this guy? Those traits are markers. Think of them as the equivalent of a trail of bread crumbs leading to a particular destination, which in this case is the killer."

Kaminsky hooted. "Oh, wow, now we're Hansel and Gretel."

"A background check should do it, coupled with a few interviews," Bartoli said to Kaminsky before Charlie could reply. "Just keep it as low profile as you can. We don't want to spook this guy. And remember, we're all on the same team here."

Kaminsky made a face. "Yeah, I know." She shot Charlie a look. "Bread crumbs. I got it."

"You up to a dance, Dr. Stone?" Bartoli asked. Charlie's gaze shifted from Kaminsky to him, and her eyes must have given away her surprise, because he smiled. "Don't look so shocked. I want to get this crowd on video. Kaminsky's going to walk around recording us dancing from one angle, Crane from another, and between them we should be able to get a picture of almost everybody who's here, including the staff, without alerting anyone to what we're really after. Then we can take the video back with us and go over every frame." He looked from Crane to Kaminsky. "Any questions?"

Crane shook his head. "Sounds like a plan."

"Should work," Kaminsky agreed.

"You brought cameras?" Charlie hadn't seen any such equipment.

"iPhones," Kaminsky replied impatiently. Then Bartoli was on his feet pulling back Charlie's chair for her. *See, he's a gentleman, too. Relationship material if I ever saw it.* She stood up, and when he held out his hand she placed hers in it. His grip was warm and strong, and he held her hand firmly as he pulled her after him toward the dance floor. Strictly business, she knew, but it felt personal.

She liked holding his hand, she discovered. *I should definitely pursue this.*

"Aren't they such a cute couple?" Kaminsky trilled behind her. Charlie knew that the comment was part of their cover, that Kaminsky had her phone out and was filming as she followed them, that it was all in service of the urgent cause of finding Bayley Evans, but still she cringed inwardly. With what felt like all eyes on her, she felt slightly uncomfortable and way too conspicuous. "Won't Aunt Bessie be excited when we show this to her? Are you getting them, Buzz?"

"Oh, yeah."

Apparently Crane was enthusiastically filming, too.

Charlie felt about as relaxed as a taxpayer undergoing an audit. She wasn't used to being in the spotlight. In fact, she had spent years deliberately avoiding it. Add to that a degree of shyness about her newly minted possible attraction to Bartoli, and her near certainty that Garland was there somewhere, and the very last thing she wanted was to be the object of attention.

But there didn't seem a whole lot she could do about it.

A moment later they were stepping onto the dance floor. There were maybe a dozen couples on it, gliding around the smooth wooden surface to the torchy strains of "We've Got Tonight." People stood around the edge of the dance floor, sipping colorful cocktails and chatting in groups and *watching.* Tightly packed tables ringed the area: more watchers. The band, the buffet line, the layers of tables on the terraces, and even a nearby parking lot that, from the looks of the vehicles in it, was reserved for the use of service trucks, were within view. Kaminsky and Crane should be able to capture almost everything going on outside with their cameras. Of course, it was dark now, but the moon hanging just above the horizon was as round and full as a glow-in-the-dark tennis ball, and between it and the garden lighting and the tiki torches, visibility wasn't really a problem.

"I warn you: I'm not much of a dancer." Bartoli smiled at her as he pulled her into his arms.

"Me neither." Smiling back at him, Charlie settled a hand on his wide shoulder, and found herself appreciating with a kind of half-amused irony the fact that what her hand was resting on was a suit jacket. *What you want is a man who goes to work every day wearing a suit,* she could almost hear her mother (who had never — that Charlie knew — taken her own advice) saying. Not that she meant to be influenced (ever) by her mother; but still, she would be the first to acknowledge that stability was a good thing in a man.

"Last time I danced like this was at my wedding," Bartoli said.

Charlie stumbled a little. Her eyes flew to his face. "I thought you weren't married."

He steadied her. This wasn't the plaster-yourself-against-the-guy-and-sway kind of dancing that she remembered from high school. This was more formal, with a few inches of space between them and one of his hands holding hers while the other rested on the small of her back. During medical school and her residency, she had attended enough formal events, including enough of her classmates' weddings, that she was familiar with the steps. Still, she had to dredge them up from deep in her memory, and pay attention, or Ms. Klutz came back. She'd been doing her best not to reinforce the too-clumsy-to-live image that the incident with the banana pudding had probably permanently solidified in his mind, but his announcement had caught her by surprise.

"I'm divorced. Married my college sweetheart when we graduated. It lasted a little over a year."

"I see. Was it a bloodbath that had you swearing off women for the rest of your life?" She was trying for light, but maybe that came off as a little flirty. For whatever reason, his hand tightened on hers.

"Not at all." There it was: the same sort of

awareness of her in his eyes that she was experiencing for him. A preliminary, maybe-this-could-go-somewhere kind of thing. "It was all over a long time ago. We were just too young."

"So who's the special woman in your life now?" *That* was subtle. Well, maybe not, but before she made up her mind whether to explore a potential romantic connection with him further, she needed to know certain essential facts.

"There isn't one." He smiled at her, and Charlie was once again struck by how good-looking he was. "What about you?"

"You two! Look this way and *smile,*" Kaminsky called before Charlie could reply. A little startled, glancing around, Charlie discovered that she and Bartoli had danced about a quarter of the way around the floor, which had brought them within close range of Kaminsky. She was smiling and waving — and filming — from the sidelines. Charlie suddenly wondered if any of what she'd been thinking about Bartoli had registered in her face, and if so, if it had been caught on film.

Just considering the possibility made her go warm with embarrassment.

"Kaminsky and Crane are having way too much fun filming us." Bartoli's tone was rueful. She got the feeling that he knew exactly what she was thinking, which didn't help. "Tomorrow, I guarantee you, when we're taking this thing apart, they'll have even more fun with the play-by-play."

With her gaze still on Kaminsky, Charlie made a face. "Let's hope we get something usable out of it."

"I'm hoping we might." There was a note in his voice — something warm and almost humorous — that drew her eyes to his face. "But we don't want to talk shop right now. Too many ears."

"I —" she began, meaning to finish with something like *couldn't agree more.* But instead of Bartoli's lean, dark features, the face she found herself looking up into as she spoke was the sex-on-the-hoof gorgeousness that was Garland.

The smile he gave her as their eyes connected chilled her blood. "New boyfriend, Doc?"

Chapter Fourteen

Of course she couldn't acknowledge that he was there.

Charlie just remembered that in the nick of time and snapped her teeth shut on the startled squeak on its way out.

Luckily, shock rendered her incapable of jumping, because she definitely would have jumped.

Go away crowded against her lips, but she swallowed it with Herculean effort.

No glaring allowed, either.

Garland had insinuated himself between her and Bartoli, so that it was Garland she was dancing with, Garland who was holding her hand, Garland who was looking down into her face, she realized with a galvanizing sense of panic. Her hand now rested on Garland's wide, white T-shirted shoulder. His powerful arm curved around her waist. She could feel him there, against her, his essence as tangible as an electric field. Her skin prickled as if lightning was about to strike in her vicinity. Her vital functions — her heart rate, her breathing — sped up.

"Cat got your tongue?" Garland's eyes mocked her. She had forgotten how tall he was, or maybe she hadn't really gotten the full effect before because this was the closest she had ever been to him. She had to look way up.

How did you get back? But she dared not say anything out loud.

"So much for voodoo, huh, Doc? I'm still here. Tough luck for you that your woo-woo stuff didn't work."

She almost jerked herself out of his arms, only she remembered at the last minute that they weren't *his* arms, but Bartoli's. It was Bartoli she was dancing with, Bartoli who was speaking to her, Bartoli who was waiting for her reply.

Oh, God, she could actually see Bartoli again, because suddenly Garland wasn't altogether solid anymore, but she couldn't *hear* him over the agitated roaring in her ears. What was he saying to her?

"Lover boy wants to know if there's anyone special in *your* life." Garland *could* hear Bartoli, apparently, and passed the message on with an undertone of malicious enjoyment.

"No," Charlie replied out loud, concentrating on the reassuringly solid features of the real, live man behind the phantom. The man she was actually dancing with and talking to.

"What, you're not going to tell him about me?" Garland's eyes swept her face. His hold on her tightened so that she could feel the power in the arm around her, feel the rock-solid muscularity of the body she was suddenly pressed tightly against. "Don't tell me you're a love cheat, Doc."

Go fuck yourself. But she managed not to say that out loud.

"I'd rather fuck you," Garland said.

She must have looked shocked, or horrified, or something pretty transparently wigged out, as much at Garland's apparent ability to read her thoughts as at his words themselves, because he laughed.

"I'll be around."

Then he shimmered and was gone.

Just like that.

The sense of being tightly held against a muscular male body was gone, too. There was space between her and Bartoli again.

Had there ever not been?

Charlie's heart pounded like a hammer.

Garland was many things (most of them

unprintable) but corporeal he definitely was not. No way should she have been able to feel him.

On the other hand, no way should he have been able to come back from wherever she'd sent him, either.

So maybe on the Highway to Hell (which was the best name she could come up with for the purple-twilighty-monster-filled place he'd described) there were a few twists and turns with which she was unfamiliar.

The thought sent tingles of alarm down her spine.

"Dr. Stone?" As if they were traveling to her from a long way off, the words Bartoli had just finished uttering finally reached her brain.

He'd said, "Is something wrong, Dr. Stone?"

"No," Charlie got out, hoping that she hadn't taken too long to reply. Her voice sounded strange to her own ears. She felt as if she were speaking to him from the bottom of a well. Then she realized that she was stiff as a poker and gripping his hand hard and digging her nails into his (dark-suited) shoulder and was probably pale and tight-lipped, too, and he must think that all that tension was somehow directed at him.

"You sure? Because it almost sounded to

me like you just told me to go fuck myself." The only saving grace was that he was looking down at her with a quizzical gleam of humor in his eyes.

Oh, God, so I did say it out loud. As she heaped a thousand curses on Garland's head, that thought was instantly followed by two others: *At least Garland can't read my mind,* and *Think fast.*

"What?" An actress she wasn't, but the surprise in her reaction was convincing because it wasn't in fact fake. It was just rechanneled from her very real surprise that the thought she'd flung at Garland had actually emerged from her mouth in spoken words. "It must be the music." Which wasn't really that loud, but still. "I'm having trouble hearing, too." She took a deep breath. "What I *said* was, I'm just like yourself." Whew. Close enough. "In being currently uninvolved, that is."

"Oh. Well. Good to know." He grinned at her with a sudden boyish charm that made her despise Garland even more. This guy was handsome and smart and decent, and if he didn't think she was at least two parts clumsy fruitcake it wasn't for want of evidence. "I thought I might have hit a nerve with something I said."

"No, of course not."

A sardonic laugh in her ear sent goose bumps racing over her skin. Garland! She couldn't see him, the SOB, but he was still nearby. Close enough to listen in. Right behind her, she guessed.

It was all she could do not to whip her head around to check.

But she couldn't, not while she was dancing with Bartoli, and Kaminsky and Crane were darting around the sidelines filming their every move. She had to ignore one more phantom one more time. She had to be calm. She had to be cool.

Where is he?

Not knowing was driving her insane. Her nerves were so on edge that she imagined every whisper of the warm breeze against her skin, every curl of gray smoke from the tiki torches, every stray snippet of conversation that reached her ears from the other couples, crowding close in around them, was just one more manifestation of *him.*

From somewhere fairly close, Crane called, "Yo, bro, can you look this way?"

Charlie and Bartoli — clearly the "bro" Crane was jokingly addressing — both glanced in the direction of Crane's voice. Sure enough, there was Crane, waving and grinning and filming from the sidelines, on the opposite side of the floor from where

Kaminsky continued to film. Charlie realized with the part of her mind that was still capable of processing anything tangential that she and Bartoli had completed almost one full circuit of the floor.

Bartoli had far more presence of mind than she did: he grinned at Crane just like a tourist mugging for the camera.

Charlie summoned a weak wave.

"Holy shit, that's the FBI guy from the Ridge you're dancing with. Tell me you're not hitting *that.*" Garland's growl in her ear made Charlie's breath catch and her lips tighten. But by the time Bartoli looked back down at her, she had regained enough command of herself to dredge up a smile.

"You should've told me you were that hard up, Doc. We could've worked something out," Garland said. "All you had to do was walk around the table in that room where you showed me your inkblots. We could have had a good time. Don't tell me you didn't fantasize about it, because I sure did."

Charlie's shoulders tensed. Her smile froze in place. She could *feel* the hostility bubbling up inside her.

Ignore him, she ordered herself.

"Probably we ought to try to engage in some general conversation," she said to Bartoli. Maybe she sounded a little stiff, a little pedantic, but, hey, she was talking and making sense, and with Garland uttering foul things in her ear, that was no mean feat. Discussing the case was out; talking about anything personal with Garland listening was out, too, although of course Bartoli wouldn't know that.

Bartoli said, "Let's see, general conversation; suppose you tell me a little bit more about yourself? I know that after . . . what happened, you and your mother moved to South Carolina and you finished high school by correspondence. I know you graduated from the University of South Carolina with a major in biology, you were top of your class at USC med school, and you did your internship and residency at Johns Hopkins. I know that both your parents are still living, but not together, and according to what you just said you are currently unattached. Any other pertinent information about your life you want to fill me in on? Pets? Food allergies? Hidden talents? We probably need to do one more circuit of the dance floor before we stop, so now would be a good time to let 'er rip."

Charlie blinked at him in surprise as he so casually reeled off the basic facts of her life. Then the answer hit her like a brick: "You did a background check on me."

"You bet your big blue eyes he did," came Garland's voice from somewhere to her right. "Don't let him snow you, Doc: he knows everything you ever did in your life. He can tell you what color panties you have on right now. Even supposing he hasn't already seen them."

Charlie refused to so much as flicker an eyelash in the direction of the voice in case Garland took it as admission that she'd heard him.

Ignore. Ignore.

"Had to," Bartoli said. "Before we asked you to come on board, we needed to know as much about you as possible. I wouldn't have been doing my job otherwise." He gave her an apologetic grimace. "If it makes you feel any better, if you've got any deep, dark secrets, the Bureau didn't find them."

"Speaking from personal experience, the Bureau couldn't find its ass with both hands," Garland said.

"I don't." Charlie kept her eyes glued to Bartoli's face. "Have any deep, dark secrets."

"You have me," Garland pointed out. She still couldn't see him, which was driving her insane. "Don't tell lies to the po-po, Doc. Don't you know you can go to jail for that?"

Go away. Charlie wanted to shriek it, but managed to smile at Bartoli instead.

"I was pretty sure of that even before the background check," Bartoli said. "In this business we get good at reading faces, and what yours says about you is that you have character and intelligence and honesty. I saw that as soon as I met you."

"This guy sucks," Garland said. "He should be telling you what a hot little body you have."

Charlie shot a lightning glance in the direction of the voice — she didn't mean to; it just happened — but since she couldn't actually see Garland, she couldn't be sure he got the whole *shut up or die* import of it.

"I appreciate that. Thank you," she told Bartoli. Okay, she did sound kind of stiff and pedantic, but she was having trouble working out how to have a real conversation with him while a demon listened in and jeered in her ear.

"I have to admit, you were a surprise," Bartoli said. "After going over your credentials, I was expecting somebody more . . . imposing."

"What he means is, he thought you were going to be butt-ugly," Garland said. "That was what I thought, when I found out the psychiatrist they were taking me to see was a woman. I mean, who sticks a babe in a men's prison?"

Concentrating on Bartoli while tuning out Garland was challenge enough without having the fact that Garland had called her a babe break loose and start worming its way into her mind, which is what, Charlie was horrified to realize, it was doing.

"You were a surprise to me, too. I mean, having the FBI show up at the prison was a surprise to me," she said, rattled. Her dilemma was maddening: if she encouraged Bartoli to go where she thought this conversation might be heading — i.e., somewhere more personal — Garland would hear everything, yet if she tried to keep Bartoli from going there, he might take it as her subtly warning him off, which was the last thing she wanted to do.

"Not a bad one, I hope." Bartoli's smile *was* personal. Her pulse would have quickened except, oh, wait, it was already racing from stress.

"Other than the whole Boardwalk Killer thing, no," Charlie replied, and smiled, too. "I wouldn't characterize it as bad."

"I wouldn't characterize it as bad," Garland mocked. "Jesus Christ, Doc, he ought to have his tongue down your throat by now. Dancing like this, you ought to be wanting

him so bad you're getting wet in your panties. Instead, there's six inches of space between you and he's *smiling* at you like you're a fricking nun. I can tell you right now, you ain't gonna have no fun in that bed."

"Is anything wrong?" Bartoli frowned down at her. Charlie realized that her face must have frozen — or something — as she'd listened to Garland. Actually, no telling what her face had done. If the way she felt was any indication, it might have gone homicidal.

Damn it — him, Garland — *to hell.*

"No," she said hastily. Then she amended her reply to, "Well, nothing much. It's just . . . my stomach's acting up again."

She hoped the explanation was enough to cover any weird behavior he might have noticed while she was trying not to react to Garland.

"You've been pretty much under the weather since we met, haven't you?" The sympathy in Bartoli's voice made Charlie want to howl. Why, just when she had met this absolutely great guy, did she have to be afflicted with the worst ghost in the history of her own particular universe?

"Seems like it, doesn't it?" She summoned a pseudo-rueful smile. Her entire body was tense as she realized she had lost track of Garland. Was he still close by, or had he, by some miracle, gone? *My luck isn't that good.* "I think maybe I have a touch of the flu."

"I'm sorry we're —" Bartoli broke off. Charlie followed his gaze, to spot Kaminsky waving them in. He looked back down at Charlie. "Looks like we've done our time." They stopped dancing, and he took her arm. "Come on, back to the salt mines."

"That was fun," Charlie said brightly as they made their way through the dancers toward where Kaminsky waited on the sidelines. A glance around told her that Crane was working his way toward the same spot. The same glance revealed no trace of Garland.

"It was," Bartoli agreed. "We ought to do it again sometime — when I'm not on duty and we're not on camera."

Charlie glanced up at him, suddenly feeling warm all over. He *was* interested. The sense that something could be beginning here hadn't been all on her side.

"I'd like that," she agreed. She and Bartoli had rejoined the crowd on the sidelines, but hadn't quite reached Kaminsky when it happened.

A derisive snort in her ear located Garland for her. She'd *known* he was still there.

"Just to give you a heads-up, Doc, he's the type that asks permission. Is that what you want? *May I put my hand on your titty, Dr. Stone?*" Garland's mocking falsetto made Charlie clench her teeth. *"Is it okay if I put my dick in your —"*

Jerking her arm from Bartoli's hold, Charlie stopped dead. Then, as Bartoli looked down at her in surprise and Charlie remembered that she was the only one who had any idea that a devil was tormenting her, she grabbed hold of her composure with both hands and held on tight.

While winging this heartfelt admonition toward Garland: *No more.*

"Um, you know, if you'll excuse me, I really need a bathroom break," she said.

Without waiting for Bartoli's reply, she turned on her heel and headed toward the ladies' room, the sign for which she could see outside a one-story, whitewashed brick outbuilding on the far side of the gazebo.

"You. Come with me," she ordered out of the side of her mouth, as certain as it was possible to be without actually seeing Garland that the rat bastard was close enough to hear her perfectly well. It was all she could do not to stalk through the crowd, but with careful self-control she managed it. Reaching the ladies' room moments later, she pushed through the swinging door, where she was greeted by a delicate floral scent and a wall of blessedly cool air-conditioning. At a glance she took in the posh lounge with its aqua leather couch and chairs and a small corridor leading into the sinks and stalls beyond, and ascertained that the restroom appeared to be empty. Marching into the center of the lounge area, she whipped around to snarl at what looked like empty space, "This. Has. Got. To. Stop."

"You sound like you're pissed at me, Doc." Just as Charlie had expected, Garland materialized right in front of her, all six-foot-three hunky golden inches of him. "Now, that's what you call a real co-inky-dink. 'Cause, see, I'm pissed at you, too."

Chapter Fifteen

"Is that right?" Charlie's eyes flashed fire. Standing scarcely more than arm's length away, Garland looked as big and bad and muscular and intimidating as ever. At that moment Charlie was just so furious she didn't care. Taking a step forward, she thrust a pugnacious finger at his chest. "Listen, you jackass: any more dirty talk in my ear, and what I do next will make that whole incense-and-candle thing look like a party game."

Garland's eyes narrowed dangerously. "You threatening me, Doc?"

"Oh, yeah," Charlie replied with relish. "Count on it."

"I wouldn't." He smiled a tigerish smile. "If I were you."

"Oh, dear, maybe you're right. Maybe I *shouldn't* threaten you." Charlie clapped both hands to her cheeks à la the *Home Alone* kid, then let them drop again as she finished by fixing him with a glare. "Maybe I should damned well *promise* you that if you don't stay away from me, bad things are going to happen. To *you.*"

"If anybody should be threatening anybody, I should be threatening you. Last night you did your damnedest to kill me."

"I did not. Nobody can kill you. You know why? Because you're *already dead.*"

"Yeah, well. Whatever. You did your best to screw me over, then. You think being sucked into that damned wind tunnel you created didn't hurt? It did. It hurt like hell."

Remembering, Charlie suffered a brief pang of conscience. "I didn't mean to hurt you. I was trying to send you to where you're supposed to be."

"You were helping me out, in fact."

"That's right, I was." Honesty compelled her to add, "Sort of."

"Let's get real, Doc: you tried to send me off to hell."

"If that's where you're supposed to be, it's not *my* fault."

"Well, you can forget it: I'm not going."

"The thing is, you don't exactly have a choice. You die, you go. So go already."

"You'd like that, wouldn't you? Too damned bad."

"You know what? I don't care. As long as

you go be a ghost somewhere else and keep your nose out of my business, I don't give a flip what you do."

"What, you didn't appreciate my heads-up about your new boyfriend? I was just trying to help you out there. Keep you from winding up with a dud in the sack."

Charlie didn't smile; she bared her teeth. "And I was just trying to help *you* out by hurrying you on your way to eternity."

"Yeah. About that: you try that woo-woo stuff on me again, I'm liable to get nasty."

"Nasty how? Are we talking popping out of dark corners going *Boo?* You're ectoplasm, remember?" The face she made at him was pure mockery. "You don't scare me, Casper."

"Casper?" He looked both surprised and affronted.

"Yeah," she said, rubbing it in.

"Just so we're clear, Doc, I ain't no fucking Casper. Mess with me again, and you're liable to find that out. The hard way."

"Oh, I'm shaking in my shoes. At least, I would be, except, guess what?" Charlie stabbed a finger at him again, only this time it sank knuckle deep into his wide chest. The electric tingle she felt at the contact was hardly noticeable. It paled in comparison to the satisfaction she got from watching his expression change as her finger penetrated what appeared to be the solid surface of his shirt, then withdrew with as little fuss and muss as if she'd been poking air. "You've got no substance. You're about as dangerous as water vapor. Except for being childishly annoying, there's absolutely nothing you can do."

"Start waving your incense at me again, and you'll wish I was only being childishly annoying."

"Oh, so there are other options? Enlighten me, why don't you? Exactly what *are* you going to do, tough guy?" She took another pugnacious step toward him. With her face tilted up now and him looming over her, they were practically nose to nose. His eyes were as brightly blue as the ocean had been earlier. He looked, in a word, alive. As vividly alive as anyone she'd ever seen, as a matter of fact, even though he absolutely was not. "Moan a little? Rattle some chains? What?"

His face hardened. "You try sending me to Spookville again, Doc, and one of two things is gonna happen: either you're not going to succeed and I'm going to make tonight's *childishly annoying* little threesome the least of your problems, or you will succeed and then I'll find my way back just like I did this time. Only next time I'll bring something with me: one of those monsters prowling through the fog, maybe, or some other poor damned soul who'll help me make your life miserable. And that'll just be for starters. I guarantee it."

"You can't bring things back with you."

"How do you know?"

"Because that's not the way it works."

"What do you know about how it works? You ever been dead? No. Let me give you a hint, Doc: you don't know shit about it."

"I —" Charlie had to break off as the door opened just then to admit an elderly, white-haired woman in a tea-length lilac dress. She was maybe seventy, medium height, thin, sweet-faced, a little stooped. As the door swung shut behind her, the newcomer looked right through Garland. Of course, she was seeing nothing but thin air.

"Oh, hello," the woman said to Charlie, who had frozen in place. It was one thing to *know* that no one besides herself could see Garland, and another to ignore the solid-to-her, rampantly male figure standing inches away from her in the middle of the ladies' room as another woman walked right past him without a clue that he was there. As she made her way toward the lavatory, the old woman smiled brightly at Charlie and added, "Beautiful night out, isn't it?"

"Y-yes indeed," Charlie stuttered. It was all she could do to get the words out. She knew her eyes had gone wide, and her expression had to be a study in alarm. There was a reason for that: the woman wasn't alone. Bursting through — literally *through* — the closed door as if the heavy metal panel didn't exist came a tall, stocky, dread-locked man in a black track suit. He was armed with a wicked-looking knife. Screaming, "Tell me where the money is," he ran toward the old woman, viciously swinging the knife at her back as soon as he was within reach of her.

Charlie's heart leaped. She started to call out a warning, clapped a hand over her mouth to stifle the words before they could escape, and hurried in the attacker's wake, only to stop stock-still on the threshold between the lounge and the restroom. With a racing pulse she watched as the knife drove harmlessly through the victim's lilac-clad back. The woman disappeared into one of the stalls, unaware.

Violence crackled in the air, potent as a thunderstorm.

"What the — ?" Garland began from behind her. But he broke off as the knife-wielding apparition — because an apparition was what it was, as Charlie had known from the first — turned on her. For a split second the apparition's eyes met hers. His were wild, crazed, terrified — and terrifying. He knew she could see him: it was there in his harsh-featured face.

As quickly as their eyes locked, he raised the knife high and charged her.

"Where's the money, bitch?" he screamed, his face contorting with fury. Except for his shriek, no other sounds accompanied the assault: no scrape of feet on tile, no rush of a body moving through air, no rustle of clothing.

Nothing. Because there was nothing physical there.

Adrenaline shot down Charlie's veins anyway. But before she could react, before she could summon up something potentially disarming to say, like *You're dead, give it up,* before she even had time to move out of the doorway or do anything except suck in air, Garland somehow stepped in front of her, planting himself between her and her would-be attacker. Charlie found herself blinking at his back. His torso was honed, V-shaped to the waist above a small, tight, athletic butt. The muscles of his legs appeared to tighten and flex as he braced himself. His arms bunched. His shoulders suddenly looked as wide and formidable as an NFL linebacker's in full gear.

"Back the fuck off," Garland roared at the other apparition, who didn't. The two of them converged, the knife slashed at Garland's chest, Garland grabbed the other man's wrist, and they both vanished.

Gone. *Poof.*

A toilet flushed.

Shaken, heart still pounding, struggling to get her suddenly roiling stomach under control, Charlie tottered a couple of steps forward then leaned against the nearest wall as the old woman emerged from the stall. With a glance and a smile for Charlie, she headed for the sink, where she turned on the faucet.

Charlie welcomed the rush of running water because she hoped it would cover the sound of her quickened breathing.

It was clear that the old woman had no clue that anything out of the ordinary had just happened.

"Is something the matter, dear?" As she soaped her hands, the woman glanced at Charlie's reflection in the mirror.

Catching sight of herself, Charlie wasn't surprised at the question. The humidity had added waves to her usually smooth chestnut hair, but still it fell in attractive profusion to her shoulders. Her sapphire blouse and black pants were maybe a little office-y for a Friday night out, but they were expensive-enough-looking for the surroundings and had the added, happy bonus of showing off both her coloring and her slim figure. No, what was wrong with the picture of herself that the mirror was throwing back at her was her face. It was rigid with tension. Her skin looked too tight, making her high cheekbones and square jaw seem way more prominent than they actually were. Despite her slenderness, her cheeks were usually a little too round, a little too rosy, which — coupled with her slender nose and full lips — tended to make her look just a tad too youthful to be taken entirely seriously. Not tonight. She was utterly white, big-eyed, shocked-looking. Before she saw and clamped her lips together to combat it, her mouth trembled. She looked like . . . she had seen a ghost.

Well, duh. Two actually.

As the thought popped into her head, Charlie was surprised into a wry inner smile. Then she got a grip.

"I know this may sound strange, but I was wondering . . . have you been involved in any kind of violent incident in the last week or so?" Charlie asked. Her upset stomach made her voice sound a little thin. "With — with a man wearing dreadlocks?"

Turning abruptly away from the sink, where the faucet still ran, the woman looked at her with sudden fear in her eyes.

"Who are you? What do you know about that?"

"Nothing. Don't be afraid, I just . . ." Charlie thought fast. ". . . thought maybe I recognized you. And him. From the papers."

"It wasn't in the papers. We kept it quiet, because we thought there might be some backlash. The police said my husband was totally right to do what he did. The man broke into our shop. He would have killed us. George had to shoot him." The woman was as white and shaken-looking as Charlie had been a moment before. "Who are you? How do you know about this?"

As she spoke, she was edging around Charlie with the clear intent of booking it back through the lounge and out of the restroom. Telling the woman that the ghost of the violent robber her husband had shot and killed had attached himself to her would not only serve no earthly purpose, it would also most likely not be believed.

Think fast again.

"That explains it, then. I must have seen the pictures in the police report," Charlie said to the woman's fleeing back. "See, I file those, and, well, I guess I saw your picture and remembered the face."

"I didn't know anyone ever took my picture." Yanking the door open, the woman looked back at Charlie. "The policemen said no charges would be filed. *My husband had no choice.*"

Then she was out the door.

"I know that," Charlie called softly after her as the door swung shut, then held her breath and waited. If the knife-wielding phantom was anywhere around, he should be materializing about now to follow the old woman. And Garland — where was he?

Could two ghosts hurt each other? Charlie had never experienced a situation like that, so she had no idea. Uneasy visions of an epic, otherworldly battle to the death (or whatever the already-dead equivalent of death was) danced through her brain; she banished them with an impatient shake of her head.

There was no point in worrying about something she could do nothing about.

As she moved toward the sink, where the water still ran, Charlie realized that Garland had said at least one true thing: she had no idea what actually happened after someone died. Once the spirits she saw left her vicinity, anything was possible.

Her stomach was still unsettled, still threatening to rebel. Cupping her hand beneath the running faucet, she scooped up a handful of cold water and swallowed it, then did it again. It seemed to help. She was reaching for the tap to turn the water off when Garland spoke behind her.

"Interesting life you lead, Doc." He sounded a little breathless. "You got any more of those deep, dark secrets your boyfriend couldn't find up your sleeve? I mean, besides me and the whole ghost whisperer gig you got going on?"

Perversely, she was almost glad he was back, Charlie realized as she shut off the tap and turned to face him. At least now she knew he hadn't been murdered — or cast into outer darkness or anything else horrible — by the maniacal knife-wielder.

She instantly dismissed the idea that she might actually have been worried about him, however briefly, however minutely.

"Don't you have anybody else you can haunt?" Her voice was sharp.

His brows went up. "Gee, Michael, thanks for keeping the bad guy with the knife from hurting me." His mocking falsetto made Charlie's eyes narrow. It — *he* — was really starting to get on her nerves. "I am *so* grateful. Really I am."

"He couldn't have hurt me, just like you can't hurt me." She was (almost) positive about this one; she'd lived in the world of ghosts-on-the-ground for too long. These rules she knew. "No substance, remember?"

"I wouldn't bet my life on it." He leaned a shoulder against the wall and folded his arms across his chest as he looked her up and down. Again, if Charlie hadn't known for sure he was dead, she wouldn't have believed it. Her stomach was even starting to settle down. "Anyway, you're welcome."

"I never said thank you."

"That was me ignoring your bad manners."

Charlie's lips compressed. "What happened to the guy with the knife?"

"He won't be back. We crashed through into Spookville right in front of a hunter. He was nabbed. Lucky for me, I'm getting pretty good at slipping out of there. Just dove right back out the same hole I came in through. What the hell was that guy doing anyway?"

"Apparently the old woman's husband shot him a few days ago. He was trying to rob their shop at the time. He just hasn't figured out he's dead yet. He's confused, and he's repeating the last few minutes of his life." Charlie shrugged. "It's what happens sometimes."

"Jesus, are you telling me you see nut-jobs like that all the time?" He regarded her with a combination of alarm and fascination.

"Oh, yeah. *All. The. Time.*" Her heavy emphasis on each word, coupled with the pointed look she gave him, implied that she included him in that number. He grinned.

"I bet it's a real joyride." He glanced around restlessly. "Damn, I've seen the inside of more ladies' bathrooms lately than I ever expected or wanted to see in my life. Don't you ever hang out anyplace fun? Bars? Nightclubs? Football games?"

"No," Charlie answered. "During the day I work. At night I go home — or when I'm not at home, like now, I go to wherever I'm staying. And I hate football. But feel free to go to all those places without me. In fact, please do. Start now. The door's that way."

She pointed.

"You act like you think I'm showing up where you are on purpose. Sorry to bust your bubble, Doc, but like I told you before, it ain't a choice. I come out where I come out. So far, it just so happens it's been in your vicinity."

Charlie stared at him with as much horror as if he'd suddenly sprouted horns and a tail. A terrible thought — no, scratch that, a terrible certainty — had just clonked her over the head. She couldn't believe she hadn't seen it before.

"Oh, my God." She started shaking her head. "Oh, no, no, no."

"What?"

Charlie took a deep breath. "I don't believe this. I think *you're* attached to *me.*"

Chapter Sixteen

Garland looked wary. "I like you and everything, Doc, but *attached* to you? I am — was — attached to my dog. And my Harley. And —"

"No," Charlie interrupted. "I see this kind of thing happen all the time. You're *attached* to me. That's the only way I know how to describe it. Just like that guy with the knife was attached to the old lady. Sometimes when people die suddenly and violently, like you did, they latch onto someone or something that's close by at the time of their death. I think it's kind of a way of not letting go, of hanging on to their lives and the earth, like throwing out a psychic anchor. I was compressing your wound when you died. You latched onto me."

Garland stared at her. After a moment his mouth twisted. "I got to say, if you'd started spouting off stuff like this a week ago, I would've said you were the one who needed to see a shrink. Bad."

Charlie had gotten used to skepticism, back when she was still trying to enlighten people about the undead in their midst, but the difference here was that Garland had to believe her, because he himself was living (?) proof. It made a nice change, she discovered.

"Yeah, well, welcome to my world."

"You mean to say I'm, like, tethered to you? Like by a psychic rubber band or something? Because you *didn't* save my life?"

"You ever hear the saying 'No good deed goes unpunished'?"

"*Didn't* was the key word there. *Didn't* save my life. So if I were you I wouldn't get too wound up congratulating yourself on your good deed."

"I don't want you attached to me," Charlie told him. "This doesn't work for me."

"You think I like it any better than you do? You're cute, Doc, but you're not exactly my idea of a rousing good time. Now, if you were a stripper, or a whore . . ."

"There, you see? You're disgusting. And crude. And a *psychopath.* Don't think I've forgotten what you are."

"And what's that?"

"You brutally murdered seven women."

"Did I?"

"The Commonwealth of Virginia says you did. They sentenced you to death for it, if you recall. What, are you going to try to tell me you're innocent?"

"Would you believe me if I did?"

"No." Charlie thought it over for as long as it took for logic to clench the matter, which wasn't very long. "And don't even bother trying to convince me otherwise. The afterlife you described to me — purple twilight, screams, the whole bit — that's not what most people experience when they die. Most people see the white light. The reason you're experiencing Spookville, as you call it, is because you're on your way to hell. And if you're on your way to hell, then I'm confident there's a good reason. Like you brutally murdered seven women."

"You always latch onto the worst in everybody, Doc? Or am I just getting lucky here?"

Charlie started to reply, realized there was no point, and shook her head. "I'm not doing this. Uh-uh."

"I hear you. But unless I'm missing something, I don't think you have a choice."

"You can always let go and embrace the afterlife. Sooner or later, that's what you're going to have to do anyway." She smiled less than sweetly at him. "I'd be glad to help you on your way."

Garland straightened away from the wall. "You try any more ju-ju on me —"

"And you'll do what, exactly? Just so we're clear, I think murder's out for you now. The spirit may still be willing, but the flesh is — oh, wait: gone."

The look he shot her said he wasn't amused. "Are you afraid of me, Doc? Is that it?"

"Afraid of the ghost of a serial killer who's following me around like a puppy on a leash? How crazy would I have to be to be afraid of something — you notice I don't say some*one* — like that?"

"You are. You got no need to be, Doc. I wouldn't hurt you."

"You *couldn't* hurt me, Casper."

"I wouldn't if I could."

"That's actually kind of rich, considering you've been threatening me practically since you died."

"If I've been threatening you, it's only been since you tried to voodoo me out of here. Don't do that again, and you and I should get along just fine."

"I don't want us to get along just fine. I want you gone. Nothing personal, but you're a complication my life doesn't need."

He arched an eyebrow at her. "Afraid I'm going to cause a speed bump in your love life, Doc?"

"Afraid you're going to be a total pain in the ass, which obviously you are."

He gave her a warning look. "You try to get rid of me again, and . . ." His voice trailed off, but his face said it all.

"And chalk up one more threat." As his eyes narrowed, Charlie held up her hands in a peacemaking gesture. "Don't worry, I won't try to get rid of you again. You know why? Because I don't have to. The good news is, the state you're in is a temporary thing. As I may have mentioned before, spirits who linger usually hang on maybe a week. It's like you need time to get your head around the idea of being dead or something, and once you do you're ready to go."

"Without anybody doing anything? I'll just . . . go?" Garland looked uneasy.

"You got it. The ones I've had experience with — one day they just disappear. According to my calculations, you've got at most — probably four or five days."

Garland looked at her. "Fuck."

"Who are you talking to?" Kaminsky's voice made Charlie jump. She'd been so caught up with Garland that she hadn't even heard the other woman enter the restroom. Now Kaminsky stood just on the other side of the threshold between the lounge and lavatory areas, staring at her. With obviously no idea that she was looking right through the hottest guy she'd probably ever seen in her life, who was large enough and vital enough, at least from Charlie's perspective, to fill the space to overflowing.

"Myself." *God, I'm getting good at lying. And sick of it.* Quickly she tried to recall the part of the conversation that Kaminsky had been most likely to overhear. "If you're here to use the facilities, you'd best get a move on. We need to get going. Bayley Evans only has about four days left."

"What's *your* name, Sugar Buns?" Garland drawled at Kaminsky, who of course didn't hear a syllable. Charlie would have been furious, except she suspected the remark had been aimed at riling her rather than hitting on Kaminsky, who he knew perfectly well couldn't hear him. "Doc here never did introduce us."

"I just came to get you," Kaminsky told her. "Bartoli was concerned because you've been in here a while."

"Ooh, Bartoli." Looking at Charlie, Garland batted his eyes like a love-struck girl. "He was *concerned.* That's touching, Doc, it really is."

"Let's go, then. Um, I'll follow you." Waiting until Kaminsky had turned her back and started for the door, Charlie cast an evil look at Garland.

"If you don't shut up, I *will* ju-ju you. First chance I get, I swear to God," she hissed, hopefully too low for Kaminsky to hear. Then, just to make a point, she marched right through him. The sensation of having plunged into an electromagnetic force field was worth it, she told herself fiercely, even with her skin tingling all over and her hair going all static-y. Even when she heard Garland laughing softly behind her.

In the SUV on the way back to Kill Devil Hills, a thought began to take root in Charlie's mind. They'd been talking about the case, about various ways they could winnow the pool of suspects — which at that point was about the size of a small town — down to a more manageable number.

"Another characteristic to look for is a history of mental illness in the family." Charlie was staring abstractedly out the windshield as she spoke. Beach Road was beautiful by night, despite the sizable volume of traffic traveling in each direction. The ocean and the sky above it were both shades of midnight blue, while, hovering just above the horizon, the moon looked as rich and round as a butterscotch candy. "Bipolar, schizophrenia, maybe ECT treatments. Probably the family member will have a record of psychiatric episodes. If not, alcoholism or drug abuse might serve as markers."

"Nearly everybody we look at is going to have one of your 'markers,' " Kaminsky objected. Charlie didn't see her roll her eyes, but from the agent's tone she figured Kaminsky probably did just that.

"Possibly, but I doubt very many in your pool will have more than one or possibly two of them," Charlie replied, glancing around at Kaminsky. She and Crane were once again riding in the back, while in the third seat, the bench seat in the very back of the vehicle, sprawled out with his boots between the bucket seats occupied by Kaminsky and Crane, sat Garland. He had his eyes closed, his arms folded across his chest, and looked like he was enjoying a nap. Not that Charlie thought he was (did spirits even sleep?), but at least he was silent — silence on his part was the best she could hope for until he disappeared for good, she figured. "By itself, each marker doesn't mean all that much. It's when they're present in multiples that it sets off alarms. When we find the man we're looking for, he'll have a long list of markers in his background, I promise you."

"Just think of yourself as a kind of human metal detector," Crane said to Kaminsky. "You come across enough hidden treasure, and your alarm should go off."

"The best lead we've got right now is the band — Kornucopia — and everyone and everything connected with it," Bartoli said. "We need to look at the musicians, the technicians, the roadies, and anyone else who travels with the band. Kaminsky, while you're compiling that list you also need to screen every name you identify as a possible suspect for their whereabouts on the nights of the murders, then cross-check them with the twenty-five remaining individuals you came up with who've been off the grid for fifteen years. Not that being off the grid is a deal-breaker, because it's possible we're dealing with a copycat, so keep that in mind. Crane, you do the background checks and evaluate every viable lead with an eye to the markers Dr. Stone has suggested. Anybody that overlaps gets put on the hit parade — bring that list to me pronto. And we have to be discreet, because if this guy stays true to his pattern, the girl is still alive and we don't want to cause him to kill her faster than he planned."

"So, who's the human metal detector now?" Kaminsky asked Crane, sotto voce.

"Beep-beep-beep." Crane approximated the sound of an alarm under his breath.

"Let's try to stay focused, guys." Bartoli frowned at them in the mirror. "Clock's ticking."

"Got it, boss," Crane said. "Background checks and markers."

"I don't suppose you want me to go around *asking* this possibly very large pool of potential suspects where they were on the nights of the murders?" Kaminsky's voice was dry.

"That'd be a little obvious, don't you think?" Bartoli looked at her in the rearview mirror. "Try checking work records, phone records, credit card records, that type of thing first. If we find the guy, we don't want him to know it until we're sure where the girl is."

"You can't just arrest him?" Charlie asked. Never having been involved in an investigation of this sort from the law enforcement angle, she'd thought that swooping up the bad guy just as soon as they knew his identity would be the way to go.

Bartoli shook his head. "The smart ones never say a word. They lawyer up. They depend on the legal system to protect them."

"Even if we arrest him, we don't have any

way of making the unsub tell us where he's got the girl stashed," Crane explained.

"See, for us, waterboarding's out," Kaminsky said. "All we can do is say 'Pretty please tell us.' "

Bartoli gave Kaminsky another of those looks in the mirror, then spoke to Charlie. "We play this wrong, we could catch the perp, absolutely get the right guy, put a halt to this particular murder spree — and still not be able to save the girl. What we want to do is identify him and watch him until something he says or does leads us to Bayley Evans. *Then* we move in."

Just thinking of the girl made Charlie's heart thump. Quickly she tried to disassociate her mind from visions of the terrified, brutalized girl that threatened to take possession of it. *We're coming,* was the thought she sent winging toward Bayley, before wrenching her brain back into the cool, impersonal mode that she knew would best serve the girl.

"So you got a murder spree and a missing girl," Garland drawled. "I'd ask you to fill me in on the details, but I'm not that interested."

Charlie tensed, but didn't otherwise react. She'd known his silence was too good to last. His presence in her life was something she had no choice but to deal with until he vanished — or until she figured out how to get rid of him for good. That being the case, she concluded, she might as well see if she could make use of him.

The idea that had been taking root in her mind grew ten feet tall and shot out flowers.

"Do you think we could stop by the crime scene on the way back?" she asked. "There's something in the boy's room I'd like to check out."

Chapter Seventeen

"That's a fucking kid," Garland said. He fixed Charlie with a flinty gaze that, once upon a time (like when he was alive) would have been intimidating. "I don't mess with kids."

The kid he was talking about was Trevor Mead. The blond eleven-year-old was curled up in the tan corduroy chair in the corner of his room, playing his flying dragon video game as if it were the most important thing in his world. As if horror and violence had never touched him or his family. As if he were still alive.

"I need you to talk to him," Charlie whispered. Not that she thought Trevor Mead could hear her, because she was almost entirely positive that he could no more hear or see her than most people could hear or see him. She kept her voice low because she didn't want to be overheard by any of the living human beings outside the closed door. The Meads' house had been locked up tight and was still sealed off with crime scene tape when they had arrived. Neither the FBI agents nor the two cops in the lone patrol car that had been left sitting in the driveway to guard the place had had a key, which meant Bartoli had to call the local police headquarters for access. Haney had shown up, along with another detective, whom he introduced as his partner, Gary Simon, and two more beat cops in a patrol car. All had come inside. Now Haney waited in the upstairs hallway along with Bartoli and Crane, Kaminsky having been dropped off at Command Central to get cracking on the various things they needed to get cracking on. Meanwhile, Charlie, who had told Bartoli that she needed to be alone in the room to try to get into the mind of the assailant, got ready to do what she'd come there to do.

Which was get Garland to see if he could glean any new information from Trevor Mead.

"What's in it for me?" Garland growled.

"Seriously?"

"You better believe it."

"You narcissistic, opportunistic *jackass.*"

"Nice vocabulary, Doc. Still ain't happening."

Charlie's lips compressed. "What do you want?"

"I want you to figure out a way to keep me here. That whole vanishing-in-five-days thing? Make it go away."

"Sorry, nothing I can do."

Garland shrugged and folded his arms over his chest. "Same here, then."

Charlie felt her temper start to sizzle. "Fine. I'll try."

On a cold day in your final destination.

He shook his head.

"Don't lie to me, Doc. Think I can't tell? I want your word." Garland's face was set and hard. He was speaking in a hushed tone, too, although his voice was gravelly with intransigence.

"You have my word I'll *try.*"

Garland looked at her measuringly.

Charlie made an exasperated sound. "If I said I could definitely do it, I would be lying. What's more, you'd know it. Anyway, maybe it won't happen. Maybe you'll be an exception. Maybe you'll be one of those spirits that hang around forever, like . . . like Abe Lincoln in the White House."

Garland looked unimpressed. "Yeah, and maybe I won't."

"The point is, you have to trust that these things always work out the way they're supposed to."

"You know what? I'm a little short on trust at the moment. You going to work some of your ju-ju to keep me here or not?"

"It's not that easy."

"So talk to the kid yourself."

"He can't hear me. A lot of spirits can't see the living, just like most of the living can't see the dead," Charlie explained impatiently. "Would you quit being such a tool and just do it? I'll *try,* okay? You have my word."

Garland seemed to reflect. Then he nodded, accepting the bargain. "So what do you want me to say?"

She could sense his continued reluctance. Because he didn't want to interact with the boy, Charlie realized. Something about the idea of talking to the spirit of a murdered child disturbed him.

"Ask him what happened." Her head hurt and her stomach churned. (If she had needed proof that the only spirit she was developing immunity to was Garland, she was getting it; she'd started feeling sick the minute she had stepped inside the boy's room.) While Bartoli had been talking to the cops about getting into the house, she filled Garland in on as much of the situation as she'd felt he needed to know, which meant she'd left out the serial killer part, along with such details as the age of the victim. "His name's Trevor. Find out anything you can. Get a description of the perpetrator if he'll give you one."

"You want me to ask a dead kid to describe the guy who sliced him and his family up." He gave her another of those flinty looks. "I don't get my kicks upsetting kids, Doc. What happens if he freaks out?"

"Just do it, would you?" She glared at him. The supper she had barely eaten was behaving badly, and she didn't know how long they (actually, she, since Bartoli et al had no idea that Garland or Trevor Mead still existed in any form, let alone were in the bedroom with her) would be left undisturbed. If Haney's hostile attitude toward her presence in the boy's room was anything to go by, not long. "And hurry up."

Before Garland could reply, Trevor cast a scared glance toward where they were standing, which was in front of the door. Both Charlie and Garland went perfectly still. The boy was starting on the loop she had observed before, the one where he saw or heard something that scared him, cast the controller down, and bolted for the closet. In other words, he was getting ready to relive some of the final, terrible minutes of his life.

Only this time, he saw Garland. Charlie knew the moment it happened: the boy's eyes focused and widened. Looking terrified, he dropped the controller and sprang to his feet.

"Hey, kid, it's cool," Garland said. "I'm not going to hurt you."

"Where is he? Is he here?" Trevor's young, high-pitched voice trembled with fear. He was referring to the killer, Charlie knew. It was also obvious that he was aware Garland was not the man who had attacked him, which, to Charlie, meant he must have gotten at least a glimpse of his killer.

"No, man. Like I told you, it's cool." Casting a hard look at Charlie, Garland moved toward the boy, who seemed poised on the verge of fleeing. "I know something bad happened to you. Can you tell me about it?"

"Who are you?"

"My name's Michael."

Trevor shivered and threw a frightened glance toward the closed bedroom door. "I think something bad happened to my mom," he said in a hushed voice. "I heard her screaming. Is she okay?"

Garland glanced at Charlie.

"Tell him his mom is safe now. Ask him

what happened after he heard her scream," Charlie whispered.

Garland did.

Trevor wet his lips. "I hid in the closet. This guy . . ." The boy shook from head to toe, then wrapped his arms around himself; in his blue soccer ball–dotted pajamas, he looked so small and thin and vulnerable, he broke Charlie's heart. ". . . he found me. He had a knife. I — I screamed and fought, but he dragged me out of the closet and threw me on the bed and . . . and . . ."

"That's okay, you don't have to tell me the rest," Garland said swiftly before Charlie could give him instructions. Weirdly enough, that's almost exactly what she would have told him to say: no need to put the child through the trauma of reliving his own death.

"Ask him to describe the perpetrator," Charlie told him.

"This guy — what did he look like? Can you remember?" Garland asked. His voice was surprisingly gentle.

Trevor's lips quivered. "He was big, like a giant. And really strong. He just picked me up and threw me. He was, like, all dressed in black, like a goth warrior or something. It was like I was in this horror movie, only for real." His voice broke. "It was real, wasn't it?"

"Yeah, kid. It was real. But it's over now. He can't hurt you anymore."

"Hair color. Eye color. Age," Charlie hissed. "Was his face round or thin?"

"What about his hair?" Garland asked. "What color was it?"

Trevor shook his head. "He had on a hat — you know, one of those ski ones. It was black, I think. Or maybe dark blue. I never saw his hair."

"Garland, hurry." Charlie watched with alarm as Trevor seemed to grow fuzzy around the edges. The child's voice had thinned as he uttered the last words, making them sound as if they were coming from farther away.

Garland's eyes were on Trevor, too. "How old was he? You see his eyes?"

"I don't know. Older than Bayley. About as old as my cousin Cory, maybe. His eyes — they were like dead black. Like zombie eyes. And, oh, yeah, there was like an eagle on his hat. It was white — or maybe yellow. Or maybe it was a hawk."

"How was his face shaped? Was it fat or thin?"

"Kinda long and thin."

"Did he say anything?" Charlie prompted urgently, because Trevor was becoming more translucent with every passing second. She wasn't quite sure what was happening, but she did know that it didn't bode well for any extended questioning. He wasn't looking at Garland any longer. His attention was all on something to his right, in the far corner of the room, although there wasn't anything there that Charlie could see.

Garland, though, seemed to see whatever it was. His big body taut with tension, he was staring hard at the same place.

"Garland," Charlie hissed. "Ask him if the perp said anything."

That seemed to rouse Garland. He shot her a quick, inscrutable glance.

"Trevor. Did the guy say anything to you?" he asked.

Trevor looked around at that. " 'Peekaboo. I see you,' in this really scary voice, like he was playing a game when he opened the closet door and saw me all scrunched back in the corner. And he yelled 'Shut up' when I started to scream. And . . ." Trevor's voice trailed off as his attention shifted from Garland to the same place he'd been looking before. "Dad? Is that you?"

Cautious hope was there in Trevor's voice. Charlie felt her skin prickle. She could see no one and nothing that hadn't been there before, but it was clear the boy could.

"Ask him if he remembers anything else." Even as she shot the instruction at Garland, she watched Trevor's face break into a joyous smile. Garland obviously saw whatever Trevor was looking at, too. He stared, narrow-eyed, at the same spot, as still as if he'd been turned to stone. If he heard Charlie, he didn't reveal it by so much as a flick of an eyelash in her direction.

"Dad!" Beaming with delight, Trevor took off running with his arms outstretched. After two bounding strides, he vanished into thin air.

For a second or two, Garland's expression was a study in bemusement as he continued to stare at the place where Trevor had vanished. Then, as if finally feeling Charlie's gaze on him, he glanced at her.

"That sucked," he said. His face went as hard as his voice as he turned his back on the place where Trevor had disappeared and walked toward her.

"What just happened?" Charlie asked. From the savage look in Garland's eyes, it had been something that he found profoundly disturbing.

"There was a man, okay? You heard the kid: his dad. The man said, 'Come on, Trev,' and held out his arms, and the kid went running. Satisfied?"

"Oh, that's wonderful." As some of the awfulness that had weighed heavy as a boulder on her heart lightened, Charlie felt a tiny easing of the grief for the boy who she had been carrying around with her. The horror of what had happened to him could not be undone, but at least Trevor was at peace now, and that provided a degree of solace. "His father came for him. Loved ones do that, you know."

"Wonderful," Garland echoed in a tone that was profoundly different from hers. "Made my night."

"You're upset, I can see." At the look on his face, Charlie instinctively went into professional mode, projecting empathy and understanding to the best of her ability. "Something obviously touched a chord." The stone-cold gaze he turned on her was not encouraging, but she persevered. "Did what you just saw remind you of anything you experienced at around eleven years old? Some kind of interaction with your father or a father figure, maybe?"

Garland's face could have been carved from granite. "Don't start your shrink shit on me, Doc. I'm not in the mood."

"Sometimes it helps to talk about things. If this bothers you —"

Garland cut her off. "You want to know

what 'chord' got touched? You want to know what kind of interaction with my 'father figure' I had when I was eleven years old? I'll tell you: I shot the bastard dead."

Shocked speechless, Charlie stared at him. Before she could regroup enough to respond in any meaningful way, he strode past her and out of the room, passing right through the closed door.

Charlie's heart did a weird little stutter. Beneath Garland's anger and truculence, she sensed a tremendous amount of buried pain.

And it touched her.

Realizing that it touched her bothered her.

Don't you ever forget what he is, she warned herself fiercely.

Left alone to stare at the solid, white-painted panel that was the closed door, she took a minute to regain her composure.

When she did, she went out into the hall. Garland was nowhere in sight. Charlie didn't know whether to be worried or relieved — but in any case, she didn't have time to think about it. Bartoli was waiting for her, leaning back against the stair rail with his arms crossed over his chest, looking cool as a cucumber, as was Haney, who was standing grim-faced in the center of the hall. Bartoli smiled when he saw her. Haney didn't.

"Anything new jump out at you?" Bartoli asked as, doing her best to allow nothing of what she had just experienced to show, Charlie walked toward him. Haney just gave her an unfriendly look.

She took a deep breath. Any residual emotions she might still be experiencing weren't for their eyes. She needed to get her game face on, and interact with these men like the professional she was.

"I'm almost sure this is a copycat." With no more than a glance at the master bedroom — Charlie recognized that she had reached her limit: she just wasn't up to dealing with another spirit's anguish right then — she headed down the stairs. To Bartoli, she would reveal everything she had learned. But while Haney listened in, Charlie wanted to be careful about what she said: the last thing in the world she wanted was for him to start in on questioning how she knew what she knew again.

Believable, off-the-cuff lies were, she feared, beyond her at the moment.

"What makes you say that?" Bartoli was right behind her, with Haney behind him. As she reached the lower steps, she could see into the pretty, beach-y living room. The other cops — four patrol officers and Haney's partner, Simon — were standing around the TV.

"This perpetrator didn't use duct tape." Charlie kept a firm grip on the banister as she glanced at Bartoli over her shoulder. Something had been bothering her about the killer's MO from the beginning. This, she had realized as she had replayed Trevor's words in her mind, was it: her memory of the duct tape over the mouths of Holly and her mother were vivid. It was an important point, and one she could have easily arrived at using only facts that she herself knew, possibly jogged by her visit to Trevor's room. So this was what she was going to give to Bartoli while Haney was within earshot. "The original Boardwalk Killer put duct tape over the mouths of his victims to keep them quiet."

The sounds of the TV had apparently masked their steps until now, but as she, Bartoli, and Haney reached the entrance hall at the bottom of the steps, a couple of the cops in the living room became aware of their presence and glanced their way.

"How the hell can you know that?" Haney demanded.

Before she could formulate a reply, or Bartoli could weigh in, the cops in the living room, who were still focused on the TV, stiffened almost as one. Then Simon, who was about Haney's age, tall and stocky with short, thick, light brown hair, let out a low whistle and looked around at his partner.

"Lou, you'll want to come here and see this," he called. "Bartoli, you and the lady, too."

As they obediently approached the group, the cops rearranged themselves a little so that the newcomers could see the TV screen. On it, in vivid color and high definition, was a picture of the Palmers' house. Charlie's heart started to pound as she realized what she was seeing: old footage of the day after the killing of the Palmer family and the kidnapping of Holly.

Everything being shown on that TV was etched into her mind and heart. Even the yellow crime scene tape fluttering in the ocean breeze was the same. She remembered the sound — *flap flap flap flap* — as she had taken the police officers around, shown them where Holly had been chained, where Mrs. Palmer had died. That night — the first night after the attack, the first full night she had spent in the hospital — it had rained and rained and rained.

The rain had smelled like worms, and death.

". . . investigation into the Boardwalk Killer serial killings that have struck terror into the residents of the Outer Banks in recent days has taken a fascinating new turn: the last victim of the previous Boardwalk Killer murders, the sole survivor of the attacks that took place in beach towns a little farther north fifteen years ago, has resurfaced," the anchorman said. "Any longtime viewers, or longtime residents of the coastal towns in the area, may remember the seventeen-year-old girl who managed to hide from the killer and thus survived the attack on the family she was visiting. That girl" — Charlie was struck dumb when a picture of her teenage self, taken from her high school yearbook, flashed on the screen — "is now Dr. Charlotte Stone, a psychiatrist and expert on serial killers. She has been recruited by the FBI to assist in identifying the Meads' killer and locating seventeen-year-old Bayley Evans, who has now been missing for almost forty-eight hours."

The footage taken earlier that day of Charlie hurrying toward the van with Bartoli holding her arm while Kaminsky and Crane brought up the rear and the media peppered them with questions filled the screen. Watching, Charlie felt her chest go tight. Her stomach dropped. Her pulse shot through the roof.

"You know what they say about the first forty-eight hours, Craig," a woman anchor intoned weightily as the camera pulled back to allow a wider view of the news desk; in the Meads' living room, the cops standing around the TV all cast covert glances at Charlie. As they looked at her, Charlie realized she was holding her breath. Her hands had clenched into impotent fists at her sides. "If a missing person is not found within that time frame, their chances of being recovered alive are cut almost in half."

Charlie forced herself to breathe. Then, seeing how Haney was looking at her, seeing the surprise on his face, she put up her chin and met his gaze.

"That's how I know," she said coolly. Turning her back on the TV, she headed for the door.

Chapter Eighteen

"I'd be apologizing for getting you involved in this, except for the fact that we have a missing girl. And I have to say, I still think you're the best hope Bayley Evans has." Bartoli followed her out onto the deck. Charlie's stomach had settled down now that she didn't have any apparitions to deal with, but she still felt shaky and a little weak-kneed. Her head hurt. She was tired, and not just physically. The distance to the house next door seemed way too far to even attempt to walk it right then, so she paused by the rail near the steps to gather her strength. She didn't bother glancing around for Garland; if he was nearby, she figured she would find out soon enough, but she didn't see him or hear him right now, so she thought maybe he wasn't. Maybe the emotions Trevor Mead had triggered in him had been enough to catapult him back into the afterlife.

I hope.

But knowing what he was facing there, did she really?

"It's all right," she said.

Bartoli had stopped behind her. "Is it?"

The sky was black now, and velvety soft–looking above a black satin sea. The moon, as palely luminous as a pearl, hung high among glittering stars. The wind blowing in from the water was warm, but strong. It smelled of salt. The rush of the waves pounded as relentlessly as her heartbeat as the tide rolled in. A few people walked the beach, as faceless as shadows. Not knowing who they were, realizing that they could be anyone at all, did make her anxious. But still . . .

"Yes, really." Charlie's fingers gripped the rough wooden rail as she stared blindly out to sea. And thankfully, even as she said it, she knew it was true: whatever personal danger joining the investigation might have placed her in, it paled into insignificance when she thought about Bayley Evans. If anything she brought to the search could help save the girl's life, it was worth it. "I'm glad I'm here. I wouldn't have been able to live with myself if I hadn't come."

"You've already helped tremendously. Somewhere amidst the reams of information that has come in, we have the fact that Bayley Evans and her friends attended a dance at the Sanderling less than a week before the attacks, but it might have been weeks, if ever, before anybody focused on it. Even then, it might not have meant much if you hadn't found out the unsub had a heart stamped on his hand."

Charlie smiled a little wryly at that, and threw a glance over her shoulder at him. Bartoli was standing close, looking tall and lean and darkly handsome. Just the kind of guy she would have wished for before all this had happened.

He's even wearing a suit. How perfect is that?

"There's more," she said. "I was able to find out more tonight. I didn't want to say anything in front of Haney."

His eyes had questions in them, but instead of asking, pushing, he glanced at the lighted windows behind them. The curtains covering the French doors weren't completely closed, and through them she could see Haney and Simon and the uniformed cops standing around in the living room. They were talking, probably about her. Having observed the same thing, Bartoli took her arm. His hand felt firm and warm as it curled around the smooth skin just above her elbow.

A strong, steady hand.

"Let's walk and talk," he said, and Charlie nodded.

When they were on the wooden path, he said, "Tell me," and Charlie did. As they walked, she told him every bit of information she — or rather, Garland — had gleaned from Trevor Mead. What she didn't tell him was how she knew it.

And he didn't ask.

"So what we've basically got is more confirmation that the unsub is a tall, strong white male, probably around six-one, one hundred ninety pounds, mid-twenties, with a long, thin face, black eyes — or any color eyes, with severely dilated pupils — who was wearing all black clothing plus a black or dark blue ski-type cap at the time of the crime," he summed up when she was finished. "That's good stuff. As soon as I get you safely tucked away back in the house, we'll start digging into it. A ski cap with an eagle or hawk — it could be a company emblem of some kind. Or a team cap." He shrugged, and his tone turned dry. "Then again, it could be something the unsub picked up on sale at the Dollar Store with no particular meaning at all."

"You understand why I think the perpetrator is almost certainly a copycat." Charlie looked out toward the ocean, but didn't really see it. The coalescing certainty, the significance of which was just now really registering with her, brought with it a lessening of the terrible fear that had gripped her ever since she had seen herself on TV and realized that the monster who had killed Holly might also be watching the newscast and thus seeing her in her grown-up incarnation of Dr. Charlotte Stone. Since then she had felt exposed, vulnerable, naked. Now she grabbed on to the lifeline Trevor's revelations had thrown her way with both hands: if the perpetrator was a copycat, he shouldn't care anything about her. Except, perhaps, as just one more investigator to outwit.

"Because of the unsub's age." Bartoli seemed to be mulling the possibilities over. Charlie had told him mid-twenties, because she vaguely remembered reading in one of the files that Julie Mead had one sibling, an older sister, with two daughters in their mid-twenties. Tomorrow she would check to be sure that one of those daughters was named Cory, and verify her age. Although Charlie hadn't told Bartoli that Trevor had described his attacker as "about my cousin Cory's age," because she didn't know how to explain that.

"The age is the clincher. If the perpetrator is in his mid-twenties, he can't possibly be the original Boardwalk Killer. But there's also the duct tape. And the missing fifteen years," she said.

They were walking almost side by side, with her slightly in front, close enough so that her shoulder and arm brushed his jacket. Charlie was glad of his nearness. With the rolling dunes and blowing sea oats between the wooden sidewalk and the beach, and a stretch of scrub ground thick with trees and other vegetation on the other side, they suddenly seemed very isolated. The spill of light from the windows of the Meads' house and the subdued glow emanating from the RV illuminated only the beginning and end of the walkway, far short of where they were. Darkness enfolded them and the sandy ground around them like a blanket.

The killer could be out here right now.

A shiver raced down Charlie's spine. She glanced covertly all around: nothing. Of course nothing. Besides the police car guarding the Meads' house, there was another one, complete with two officers, parked beside the RV. And the road in front of both houses had been closed to all but official traffic, in an effort to combat media intrusion. There was plenty of protection, she knew. But she was nevertheless suddenly very glad the man she was with carried a gun.

"You're probably right." Bartoli's voice was nearly borne away on the wind. "But still, I don't want you going anywhere alone. One of us stays with you at all times now that your connection to the old cases is known."

Charlie opened her mouth to argue, then shut it again. Reluctantly she admitted to herself that, for all her increasing certainty that the man they were after was a copycat, she was deathly afraid.

The memory of the horror that had unfolded that night in the Palmers' house was something she was never going to escape; it had established itself in her body on a cellular level. And this perpetrator, this killer, had awakened her once again to that inescapable truth.

"Just as long as Kaminsky doesn't have to stay in the apartment with me," she responded, rallying. "Across the hall is close enough."

Bartoli nodded. "Fair enough. But anywhere outside the house, one of us needs to be with you. Even a short distance like this, you make sure you tell one of us, and we'll accompany you."

"I'll go nuts," Charlie said. "I'm used to being alone. I'm a runner. I miss my runs."

"So set a time. I'll go running with you."

"You?"

"Sure. Set a time. Morning is better for me. Before work."

"Six-thirty a.m. Tomorrow." Charlie's tone made it a challenge. She glanced at him to see how he would respond.

"Done." He grinned. "I —"

Whatever he'd been going to add was lost as a man came charging out of the shadows toward them. He came from the direction of the road, and his dark form blended with the night so well that Charlie was only aware of him when he was almost on top of them.

Her heart leaped. She gasped and jumped, but had no time to do anything else because Bartoli thrust her behind him and at the same time whipped out his weapon, leveled it, and barked, "Federal agent! Freeze!"

Dear God . . .

"Whoa, whoa, whoa, it's John Price." Identifying himself, the figure stopped so suddenly that he nearly toppled over. He wasn't the only one struggling for balance, either. When Bartoli had thrust her behind him, Charlie's heel had caught on the edge of one of the planks. She stumbled and would have fallen backward into the sand dunes if she hadn't grabbed on to Bartoli's waist to steady herself.

"Price?" Bartoli questioned sharply.

"Yeah." The man's reply was sheepish. "You know, Officer Price from Kill Devil Hills PD."

"Did you want something?" There was an undertone of disgust in Bartoli's voice. As he asked the question, he slid an arm around Charlie's shoulders to help steady her. Even though her brain registered that they were not in danger after all, her heart still thundered, her pulse still raced, and her legs felt like spaghetti. Grateful for the support, she leaned into Bartoli's side as he reholstered his gun. His arm stayed around her, and she liked it being there.

"Haney sent me to tell you . . ." Price, out of breath, huffed between words. ". . . that we got a surveillance video of a car he wants you guys to look at. It's from Wednesday night . . . Thursday morning, I guess . . . about four a.m., taken off a traffic camera not far from here. The picture's blurry, but he thought you guys might be able to sharpen it up so we could get something off it."

Bartoli's eyes brightened. "Where is he?"

"In the car, out there on the road. We were heading back to town when he spotted you and Dr. Stone walking here, and he told me to bring it over to you. So here it is." Still huffing, Price pulled something from his pocket and handed it to Bartoli. "He said he'll stop by tomorrow to see what you get." He took a deep, shuddering breath. "He said he doesn't want anybody talking about it on the phone. He's paranoid that some of the reporters . . . or somebody else . . . might be listening in."

Bartoli nodded. "Tell Haney I said thanks, and we'll do our best." He pocketed what appeared to be a small DVD.

Price nodded, and turned to head back the way he'd come.

Bartoli looked after him for a minute, then glanced at Charlie. She was suddenly way too aware of her hands on his waist and his arm around her shoulders. Beneath the smooth cotton of his shirt, his waist felt firm and trim, and his arm felt warm and solid and protective curved around her shoulders. He smelled nice, too — maybe some kind of detergent or fabric softener in his clothes, she thought.

And we're this close because I almost bit the ground. Again. The realization took the this-almost-could've-been-romantic overtones out of the situation.

"Okay, I admit it: I'm a terrible klutz," she said with a sigh, and stepped away from him.

He let her go. "That's not what I was thinking about," he protested, and grinned. The grin was a dead giveaway.

"You don't have to be polite about it." Charlie started walking. Bartoli fell in beside her. "I've been falling all over myself since we met."

"If you knew me better, Dr. Stone, you'd know polite isn't exactly my strong suit."

Charlie looked up at him. He wasn't quite as tall as Garland — *not that I'm thinking about Garland* — or quite as muscular, or quite as handsome — *or comparing him to Garland in any way.* It was just that Garland was the last man (?) she had stood this close to. But Bartoli was plenty tall and muscular and handsome in his own right, and a dependable, steady man of good character besides.

"Probably it's time you started calling me Charlie."

The slow smile he gave her told her he liked that. No, it told her he liked *her.* Which was great, because she liked him, too.

"Charlie," he said. "But only if you call

me Tony."

"Tony," she repeated, and smiled back at him. This was progress. Plus, they had a date to go running together in the morning, which was something, too. Then, a little worried that she might be moving too fast, or heading in a direction she wasn't a hundred percent sure she wanted to take, she glanced away and added in her best professional tone, "I wouldn't have picked Detective Haney as the type to hand over potential evidence his department found to the FBI. He strikes me as being more territorial than that."

Bartoli — no, Tony now — seemed content to follow her lead. "Yeah, but he's got a problem: the media around here are going to crucify *him* if we don't catch this guy fast. He's the local detective in charge of the case. He's the one who'll take the heat if Bayley Evans . . ."

With a glance at her, he trailed off. But she knew what it was he wasn't saying: *if Bayley Evans dies.* And with that thought, any lingering hint of prospective romance in the air vanished. The night suddenly became a whole lot colder and darker and every bit of pleasure she'd taken in the deepening of her connection to Bartoli — Tony — was gone.

He must have felt the weight of the case on him, too, because their conversation from then until he handed her over to Kaminsky, who was in the RV with Crane, stayed strictly professional.

Seated at adjacent computers in the War Room, Crane and Kaminsky were exchanging verbal jabs about the significance of a drunk driving arrest in one of the background checks when Charlie and Tony, having made it almost unnoticed through the hustle and bustle still going on in the front part of Central Command, approached them.

"By itself, not that significant," Charlie advised, and Crane smiled triumphantly at her, while Kaminsky looked put out. Tony interrupted the budding discussion that threatened to follow with a quick description of the news report that had revealed Charlie's true identity and to tell them about Haney's disc, and then told Kaminsky to escort Charlie back to their lodging.

"And stay put. It's almost midnight. You're done for the night," he added sternly to Kaminsky.

"You and Crane —" she protested.

"Will be coming when we're done here. Go do your job, Kaminsky."

Kaminsky sulked, especially when Tony

pulled out the DVD Officer Price had given him and handed it to Crane, who inserted it into the computer.

"Go," Tony ordered over his shoulder when Kaminsky continued to show a disposition to linger.

She did, taking Charlie with her, but it was obvious she wasn't happy about it.

"So your cover got blown, huh?" Kaminsky inquired as she marched Charlie into the house, up the stairs, and into the in-law suite like a cop with a prisoner.

"Yes."

"Don't worry, we'll keep the bogeyman away."

Charlie waited as Kaminsky conducted a quick search of her rooms. She was dead tired, emotionally wrung out, and in profound need of Tums and aspirin. As a result, her patience was frayed, and Kaminsky's semi-sarcastic tone hit her the wrong way.

As Kaminsky returned to the living room, where Charlie stood by the door, Charlie snapped, "Is it me you have a problem with, or just psychiatry in general?"

Kaminsky looked about as surprised as she might have if a cat had barked. Then her eyes narrowed. "The day you explain to me how you, through some kind of psychiatric mumbo-jumbo, can tell that an unsub has a red heart stamped on his hand is the day I'll believe that psychiatry has a role to play in solving a case like this."

Kaminsky had her there. But not entirely. "Are you saying you think it's a bad lead?"

The other woman's mouth thinned. "No. But . . ."

"But nothing. I got this investigation a solid lead it wouldn't otherwise have, and I'd appreciate it if you would respect that." Charlie opened the door. The brightly lit hall beyond looked incongruously cheerful. "If you're confident the bogeyman isn't here, lying in wait for me, I'll say good-night."

Kaminsky looked at her, seemed about to add something else, then didn't, and walked out the door.

"Good-night," she said stiffly over her shoulder.

Charlie closed and locked the door.

After her own quick search of the apartment, in case Garland had shown up — he hadn't — Charlie kicked off her shoes, found the Tums and aspirin, and washed both down with a glass of water. Exhausted but too wired to just immediately fall into bed, waiting for the aspirin to kick in and take the edge off her headache and the Tums to do its thing on her stomach, worried about Garland although she hated to admit it even to herself, she took a quick shower. In the process she discovered the heart stamp was pretty much impervious to soap and water and filed the information away as something to be mentioned later. Then she pulled on her nightie and robe, grabbed her laptop, and curled up in the big green recliner in the living room.

Her avowed purpose was to do a quick check of her e-mail.

She was not waiting for Garland, who might very well have crossed the Great Divide permanently and be gone for good. She did *not* feel like the parent of a teenager who'd missed his curfew. She was not even *thinking* about Garland.

If he's gone, good riddance.

But still, after a cursory glance at her e-mail, she found herself opening Garland's file, which she had downloaded to her personal laptop for convenience when she had first acquired him as a research subject at Wallens Ridge.

You want to know what kind of interaction with my "father figure" I had when I was eleven years old? I'll tell you: I shot the bastard dead.

The savagery in Garland's voice as he'd told her that echoed in her head.

A history of violence as a youth: this mark of a serial killer was present in every single case she'd studied. It was textbook. Charlie had a hazy memory of glancing through a long list of qualifying offenses in Garland's past. At the time, she hadn't been paying that much attention. Garland had been just one more monster in a world surprisingly thick with them.

However, now he was sort of *her* monster.

So she paged impatiently through a file that, printed out, would be as thick as a brick, searching for his juvenile record. When she found it, she saw the offense right off: *subject, 11, murdered stepfather with victim's shotgun.*

The entry was recorded in a social worker's neat, sloping penmanship beside *Admitting Offense* on the form used to remand Garland to a Georgia state facility for juvenile offenders. He had stayed there until the age of fourteen, when he had run away.

The body of the entry, a single handwritten paragraph in the space allowed on the form, said:

> Subject was adopted by Stan and Susan Garland as a three-year-old, after having been in foster care from the age of seven months. Stan Garland subsequently left

the family and Susan Garland filed for divorce. Susan Garland married Barry Davies, the victim. This marriage took place when subject was seven. Police records indicate multiple domestic violence calls to house before the time of the offense. Susan Garland Davies states that the victim was "a crazy drunk" and would beat her and subject regularly. Susan Garland Davies and Barry Davies both have numerous documented instances of alcohol abuse. Susan Garland Davies states that on the night of the offense, victim had beaten her and subject and subsequently left the house. When he returned, subject shot victim with a 12-gauge shotgun victim kept for household protection. Susan Garland Davies expresses anger at subject for killing victim, and is in the process of giving up her parental rights. Susan Garland Davies states that subject is "a mean little shit" and she wants nothing further to do with him now that he has killed her husband.

Charlie was surprised to find that she had a lump in her throat as she finished reading. She was even more surprised to realize that her sorrow wasn't for the victim, but instead for the abused eleven-year-old boy whose mother described him as "a mean little shit" and deliberately gave up her rights to him. Probably, given what Charlie knew of the juvenile corrections system, just when he needed her the most.

Suddenly her own mother, difficult as her alcoholism had been to deal with, seemed worthy of mother-of-the-year honors. At least Charlie had never doubted she was loved.

Charlie was just clicking through to the next page in Garland's file when there was an urgent knock on the door.

"Dr. Stone." It was Kaminsky.

"I'm coming." Kaminsky's tone set off alarm bells in Charlie. Shoving the laptop onto the nearest table, she jumped up and hurried to answer the summons. Before she could reach the door, Charlie heard a key in the lock. Kaminsky had sounded like something was wrong, and now she was coming in without waiting for Charlie to admit her.

Whatever it is can't be good. . . .

Charlie discovered that her heart was pounding even as Kaminsky, still fully dressed, down to her shoes, burst through the doorway. Their eyes met for a pregnant instant. *Trouble,* was what Charlie read in that look, and then Kaminsky glanced around wildly.

"What?" Charlie registered Kaminsky's drawn gun and surrendered to a full-blown case of the nervous jitters.

"Did someone come in here?" The agent's voice was sharp. Shutting the door, she looked around with more care. Then, shaking her head at Charlie in a gesture that warned her to stay where she was, she started moving carefully through the living room, two-handing her gun, glancing behind the furniture and into corners before eyeing the kitchen suspiciously.

"No one's here but me," Charlie assured her.

"I saw a man in the hall right outside your door. I had just come up from the kitchen and stepped inside my room, and I caught a glimpse of him behind me out of the corner of my eye. I didn't see where he went, but there wasn't time for him to go anywhere else. I — I'm almost sure he came in here." There was the tiniest degree of hesitation in that last sentence, which told Charlie that Kaminsky was growing less sure by the second.

"You saw a man?" Charlie's eyes narrowed as a possibility occurred to her, but it wasn't anything she could share. "What did he look like?"

Having checked out the kitchen, Kaminsky was doubling back to search the bedroom. "Tall. Blond. Built. Way hot." Kaminsky cast a suspicious look at Charlie before she stuck her head inside the bathroom and glanced around. "Naked."

Charlie blinked. "Naked?"

"Starkers."

Charlie saw a shimmer moving through the air near the bathroom. Keeping a wary eye on it, she called to Kaminsky, "Believe me, there's no naked man in here."

Just as soon as she said it, the shimmer turned solid and, sure enough, there *was* a naked man in there. It was Garland, of course, in all his tanned and muscular splendor. He cast Charlie an unfriendly look and disappeared into the bathroom.

Chapter Nineteen

Kaminsky emerged from the bedroom looking confused. She held her gun in one hand, which was down by her side. An admission, via body language, that she'd been mistaken.

"There's no one here." She sounded like she hated having to say it. The look she shot Charlie was distrustful. Despite Kaminsky's continual prickliness, Charlie almost felt sorry for her.

"No," Charlie agreed, doing her best to keep her face expressionless. What could she do? Telling the truth wasn't an option.

"I know what I saw." Kaminsky looked at her hard.

Charlie shrugged. "I don't know what to tell you."

"If you snuck some guy up here for a sleepover —"

"I didn't," Charlie interrupted indignantly, her moment of feeling sorry for Kaminsky over. "Do you *see* a guy?"

"I did. I know I did." Kaminsky grimaced and strode toward the door. "He must have gone somewhere else. Let me do a quick search of the house."

"Isn't the alarm on?" Charlie asked, with the aim of saving the other woman some effort. In fact, she knew the security alarm was on, because she had watched Kaminsky reset it after they had entered.

"Yes." Kaminsky pulled open the door and walked out into the hall, where she glanced swiftly around. With one hand still on the knob, she looked back at Charlie. "Maybe he was already inside when we came in. Maybe . . . I don't know. But I have to check."

"I don't think —" Charlie began.

"Lock this door. Stay put," Kaminsky threw at her without waiting for Charlie to finish, and closed the door.

Charlie stared at the closed door for a second, concluded that there was nothing else she could do to discourage Kaminsky from wasting her time, and locked it.

Then she went in search of Garland.

He was in the bathroom. Naked. With his back to her, swiping in obvious frustration at one of the white bath towels hanging on the rack. If he was hoping to connect, he was out of luck: his hand passed right through it.

A quick, comprehensive glance was all it took to emblazon on Charlie's memory forever the absolute eye candy of his broad shoulders, corded arms, powerful back, narrow hips, tight ass, and long, strong-looking legs. Muscles upon muscles rippled as he moved. His hair was wet, slicked back from his face, curling just a little on the ends. His tan looked golden in the bathroom's bright light. *Gorgeous* wasn't quite the right word — it was too feminine to do him justice — but it was the first one that sprang to Charlie's mind.

Dangerous was the second.

"Why are you naked?" she whispered accusingly, mindful of Kaminsky out there searching the house.

"Why do you think? I just felt like stripping off." He sounded angry. He turned to glare at her. His right biceps sported a tattoo, she saw: a cobra in green and black. But she saw that only in passing, because she was too busy getting a load of his full-frontal glory: wide, smooth pecs and a pronounced six-pack and . . .

Of course he would be totally hung.

Charlie jerked her eyes elsewhere as her body reacted with a carnality that, until now, she would have said was absolutely foreign to her nature.

What's wrong with you? It's not like he's the first naked man you've ever seen, she scolded herself. Then, in an annoying, involuntary corollary, her internal dialogue concluded with, *He's just the best-looking.*

He stalked toward her, all hard-bodied and lean-hipped and rampantly male where it counted. He was looking her over. Charlie was suddenly supremely conscious of the messiness of the tousled hair that ten minutes earlier she'd shaken out of her shower cap, run a brush through, and tucked behind her ears; her scrubbed-clean face; the white robe belted around her waist; her bare calves and feet. As if in self-defense against his approach, her hands gripped the ends of the terry cloth belt and tightened it around her waist.

"You want to fuck?" His growled question as he stopped in front of her snapped her eyes into shocked collision with his.

"What? No." At least she didn't stutter like a flustered high-schooler. But she had a terrible feeling her cheeks had turned pink. Because the hideous truth was, for just a split second there, maybe she did.

His eyes were blue as a summer sky and hard as glass and as sexually charged as a lap dance.

"Then quit looking at me like that."

Charlie didn't know how she was looking at him — she didn't want to know — but fortunately anger snapped her out of it.

"How do you expect me to look at you when you show up here *naked?*" The fact that she was whispering took none of the indignation out of her tone. "And just to set the record straight, I don't think you *can* fuck anymore, Casper."

The look he gave her crackled with ill temper.

"Oh, yeah? Let's find out." Garland reached out to yank her into his arms. Charlie squeaked and jumped back and would have — well, she didn't know what she would have done, because instead of grabbing her, his hands passed right through her. She felt the electric charge of the miss clear through to her bones. Glancing down at his empty hands, Garland first looked surprised, then mad.

"See?" Feeling both smug and way safer than she had just seconds before, Charlie smiled at him. She couldn't help it; there was a taunt in there somewhere.

"Enjoying yourself, Doc?" The words were soft. Too soft. The purr in his voice and aggressive set to his jaw would have given her pause not so long ago. But now . . .

She realized she wasn't the least little bit afraid of him anymore. And it wasn't only because he'd lost the power to be a physical threat.

The sound of Kaminsky coming back through the door kept her from responding. Charlie heard the key in the lock, heard the door open, and tore herself away from the devil in her bathroom to deal with the FBI agent in her living room.

"I couldn't find anyone," Kaminsky said from the open doorway when she saw Charlie. "I came to tell you so you wouldn't worry."

Charlie almost said she wasn't worried, but bit the words back in time. If she hadn't known who the naked man was that Kaminsky had spotted outside her door, she wouldn't just have been worried, she would have been scared down to her toes.

"Maybe what you saw was a shadow. Or a reflection of some kind," she offered, simply because she felt a little guilty that Kaminsky was looking so perturbed. Out of the corner of her eye, she watched Garland walk into the living room. He was still naked. Still all rippling muscle and bad attitude.

It required what was almost a physical effort, but Charlie managed to stay focused on Kaminsky.

"Maybe." Kaminsky didn't sound like she believed it. But after all, what other explanation could there be? Charlie had been around the agent long enough to be almost certain the truth would never even occur to her.

If Kaminsky didn't believe in something as universally accepted as psychiatry, Charlie was willing to bet dollars to doughnuts she also didn't believe in things that go bump in the night.

"Don't worry, you're perfectly safe. We've been all through this place. There's nobody here but us." Tony walked up behind Kaminsky and gave Charlie a reassuring smile over the other woman's head. Charlie was surprised to see him: she hadn't realized he'd returned to the house. Immediately self-conscious about her un-made-up, tousle-haired, bathrobe-clad self, she summoned the internal fortitude to smile back, then caught a distracting glimpse of the naked man on the other side of the room looking up sharply from what he was doing — which involved her laptop, damn it — to watch.

"I must have imagined it," Kaminsky told Tony, sounding embarrassed. From the suspicious glance she shot Charlie, it was obvious she was still not totally convinced she *hadn't* seen what in fact she had. "I never would've called you guys over here if I hadn't thought there was good reason."

"Better safe than sorry," Tony replied. "We're all tired. Anybody can make a mistake."

"I blame all that wine you had with dinner," Crane called up from somewhere below. He was joking, Charlie knew, because of course Kaminsky, like the rest of them, had not had a single alcoholic drink.

Kaminsky's brows snapped together. It was clear from her expression that Crane's joke had gone over like a lead balloon. "I'm going to bed," she told Tony. Then, with another of those quick, mistrustful looks at Charlie, she turned and strode toward her room. "Hey, Buzz Cut, go soak your head," she yelled down the stairs.

"Love you, too, Lean Cuisine," Crane shot back.

"And on that totally professional note, I'll say good-night," Tony said with resignation. He looked beyond tired, with lines around his eyes and mouth that Charlie hadn't noticed before, and shadows beneath his eyes. But he also looked determined and capable. The kind of man a woman wanted on her side when a serial killer might be hunting her.

"I'm sorry your work got interrupted," Charlie said quietly.

He shook his head. "It was time to pack it in for the night anyway. We got a make and model off that surveillance shot Haney gave us, by the way. No license plate, though. At least, not yet."

"That's something."

"Yeah." He smiled at her. "Don't worry, Charlie, we'll keep you safe."

"I know you will." She smiled back at him. "Good-night, Tony." Their eyes connected in a warm and friendly way that had overtones of something more. Then the naked serial killer ghost behind her made a rude noise, and she glanced in his direction automatically, breaking eye contact with Tony, and the moment was lost.

" 'Night. Lock this door," Tony told her as he pulled it shut.

Charlie did, then turned around to glare at the problem. Fortunately, enough furniture stood between them that she could only see him from approximately the navel up. Still, that much unclothed Garland was definitely something to see.

"Charlie. Tony," he mocked. "You're making progress, Doc. Keep it up, and pretty soon he'll be asking to hold your hand."

"Put on some pants," she snapped, moving toward him with the intention of snatching her laptop, which was in front of him and thankfully in sleep mode, out of his reach.

"You got any ghost pants lying around?"

"Ghost pants?"

"Yeah, because real pants don't work for me anymore. Neither do towels. I tried."

She stopped walking, folded her arms over her chest, and regarded him quizzically. "What happened to your clothes?"

"I went for a walk on the beach. Then I decided to go swimming in the ocean. Flag's up, but it doesn't matter, because I sure as hell ain't gonna drown. What did happen was that my clothes disappeared. I'm out there, bobbing along like a cork on the waves, since I apparently have no weight anymore, and I realize I'm naked. Why? Got me. What to do about it? Got me. You have any suggestions, I'm all ears."

Charlie frowned. The problem of ghost wardrobe had never come up previously. "Where did you get the clothes in the first place?"

He shook his head. "One minute I'm in a prison uniform, next minute I'm wearing the clothes I wore when I got arrested. I've gained some muscle since then — not a whole lot to do in prison besides work out and read — but they fit fine. While I was in the water they vanished. I took off my boots before I went in. When I got out, they were gone, too."

Charlie didn't know what to make of that. "Hmm."

He gave her a disgusted look. " 'Hmm'? That's all you've got?"

"You know, I've never had a pet ghost before. I may not be totally up to speed on all the ins and outs of it."

His eyes narrowed. "I ain't no pet, Doc. If I were you, I'd keep that in mind." He looked her over. "So are you gonna clue me in on why three FBI agents are guarding you like the Crown Jewels?"

Charlie thought back to their exchange in the car. "You said you weren't interested in knowing."

"I am now."

Frowning, she considered for a moment.

"All right." If he was going to be hanging around, it was time to lay it out for him. No more glossing over the aspects that he might find disturbing — or worse. "Trevor Mead and his parents were murdered, and his half sister, Bayley, was taken, by a serial killer. The same serial killer who slaughtered two other families and kidnapped and killed two other teenage girls within the last few weeks.

This serial killer may or may not be the same one who butchered five families and kidnapped and murdered five teenage girls fifteen years ago. And the FBI is protecting me because I am of value to them, and I am of value to the FBI because I am, as you know, an expert on serial killers."

Her tone had bite, and was in the end even accusatory, because after all he was one of *them.* But something in her expression must have been a little off, because Garland looked at her more closely.

"That doesn't explain why you're holed up in here under guard, like you're a potential victim. Unless I'm missing something, this guy's target is teenage girls. You're not a teenage girl. So what's up?"

Charlie's lips pursed. Having been freshly reminded of what he was, she lost any inclination to spill her guts to him. If the human race was divided into sub-groups of predator and prey, she knew which group they each belonged in. The look she gave him was challenging. "I told you. I'm of value to the FBI."

"Ye-eah." The way he drew the word out left her in no doubt that he didn't believe that was all there was to it. "You don't want to tell me, that's fine by me. But I'm in here with you, and your boyfriend and his pals are out there. If I were you, and I was in some kind of trouble, I'd be thinking of me as your last line of defense."

"Defense?" She gave a scornful little laugh. "First, I'd have to be nuts to trust you to defend me, and second, you couldn't even if you wanted to. You can't even pick up a towel, remember?"

He was leaning over her computer again, like he'd lost interest in the conversation. But at that, he cast her a glinting look.

"You can trust me, all right, Doc. You know why? Because you're my ticket to staying here. As for not being able to defend you, I admit, you've got a point. But I'm working on it." He jabbed at the keyboard with a frustrated forefinger. To his obvious surprise — and hers, too — the screen began to glow. He'd managed to wake the thing up. "Look at that! I'm coming back."

Obviously elated, he bent back over the laptop. Charlie was galvanized by the memory of what was on the screen: the sheet describing the killing of his stepfather. Even as she scooted over there and snatched her laptop from the table — "Give me that!" — she could tell by the way he straightened and looked at her that he had seen enough to know exactly what she'd been reading.

Chapter Twenty

"Checking up on me, Doc?" Garland's eyes were hard.

Her chin came up. Shutting the laptop, she clutched it close. "Rereading your file. I didn't pay all that much attention the first time. I wanted to verify . . . what you said." She felt guilty. Why? Damn it, she refused to feel guilty for doing what was no more than her job. Or at least, what had been no more than her job. Probably the fact that he was no longer alive had taken the mandate to figure out what made him tick beyond the parameters of her grant.

He came out from behind the furniture and walked toward her, clearly not one whit bothered by the fact that he was naked. Muscles flexed. Sinews rippled. Other things . . . moved. Charlie resolutely kept her eyes on his face. It could have been carved from granite.

"You wanted to verify that I killed my

stepfather when I was that poor kid's age? I did."

"I saw."

"He deserved it."

"I'm sure you think so."

"If you're looking at me like that thinking you're going to see some of that *remorse* you were always asking me if I felt, you're shit out of luck. I don't feel any remorse. I'd blow that bastard away again right now." Near enough so that an involuntary drop of her eyes gave her a real up-close-and-personal view of his chiseled chest, to the point where she could see the faint scar that still remained over his left nipple, he exuded magnetic energy.

Jerking her eyes up, she found him looming over her, his whole manner radiating aggression.

Something unexpected happened to Charlie. Meeting the hard stare of this intimidatingly tall, powerfully built man whom she knew to be a stone-cold killer, she had an instant mental vision of the skinny little towheaded kid whose eyes had looked out at her from the snapshot clipped inside his paper file, which was still locked in the file cabinet in her office at Wallens Ridge. And her heart ached for him.

"You killed your stepfather to protect

yourself and your mother. You were a little boy, and he was violently abusive. I'm sure you felt there was nothing else you could do," she said quietly.

His eyes flickered. "Making excuses for me, Doc?"

She searched his face. "It's the truth, isn't it?"

He made an impatient sound. "I knew the first time I laid eyes on you that you were way too soft-hearted under all that ball-busting, my-way-or-the-highway crap of yours. You want to be careful about being softhearted, Doc. It can get you in bad trouble."

"So are you going to tell me what happened that night with your stepfather, or not?" she asked.

He countered, "Are you gonna tell me why you're locked up in here with three damned FBI agents standing guard over you?"

Charlie hesitated. Then she made a decision. After all, there was no real reason not to tell him, and if she revealed something of her past maybe he would open up, too. She found that she was as fascinated as ever by the prospect of understanding what had made him what he was. "Those serial killer attacks that took place fifteen years ago? I survived them. I was the only one who survived, the only eyewitness to what happened. If this is the same perpetrator, I can identify him."

He went very still. "You saw the killer?"

Charlie nodded.

Garland let out a nearly soundless whistle. "So what the hell are you doing here?"

"I told you. Tony — the FBI — came to get me because they needed my input. They thought I might be able to help them rescue Bayley Evans. And identify the killer."

"To hell with that. If *Tony* had the brains of a gerbil, he would have kept you as far away from here as possible. If this is the same guy, and he knows you saw him, and he finds out you're here, he's going to be coming after you with everything he's got." Charlie's face must have once again given something away, because Garland's gaze sharpened. "He knows you're here, doesn't he?"

"It was on the news tonight," she confessed. Remembering the broadcast caused her heart to flutter. Her chest tightened with anxiety. She wet her suddenly dry lips. "Anyway, I'm sure — almost sure — this killer is a copycat."

Garland swore. " 'Almost' can get you killed. You need to hightail it out of here.

Let *Tony* and his pals find the girl. And the killer. That's their job."

She shook her head. "I can't just leave. That girl —"

"You have to," he cut in ruthlessly. Clearly forgetting that any kind of physical gesture on his part was a waste of time, he grabbed for her arms and, of course, failed to make contact. "Damn it, Doc —"

An electric tingle accompanied his miss. Charlie involuntarily glanced down at the source. At what she saw, her eyes widened and shot to his face. He was looking down, too — at his hands, to be precise. Or, rather, his hand. His right one was missing to the wrist, which was a little fuzzy around the edges. "Fuck," he said, staring at the stump.

"Oh, dear." As soon as she said it, Charlie realized that her response was woefully inadequate. But really, what do you say to something like that?

"Ya think?" Their eyes collided. Then an expression that she could only describe as mild panic crossed his face. "You don't suppose I'm being sucked into Spookville in pieces, do you? Like, the clothes first, then the hand, then God knows what other body parts, until it's got all of me?"

She shook her head. "I have no idea."

"Me either, but I'm not taking any

chances. That voodoo stuff you promised me? I want you to do it now."

"What? No. I can't."

"What do you mean, 'No, I can't'? You gave me your word. I'm holding you to it."

"I gave you my word I'd *try.*"

"So try already."

"I've never even attempted to keep a ghost earthbound. I'm not sure I know anything that will work."

"You knew enough ju-ju to get me sucked away."

"Getting rid of ghosts I can do. The other is problematic." Charlie shot him an exasperated look. "Anyway, did it ever occur to you that maybe I don't *want* you attached to me for the next however long?"

"Yeah, well, I'm not real wild about the idea of being stuck with you, either, but when I consider the alternative, you win. By a landslide." He was staring at his truncated wrist in fascination tinged with horror. "You've got to help me out here, Doc. Please."

The *please* did it. He was right: she was way too softhearted. The last thing she wanted was to have Garland attached to her for any length of time — but then, that probably wasn't going to happen: no matter what she did, the universe had its own laws and Garland had his own fate. She would try, because she had promised, although she felt the chance she would succeed was small. But because she would have to deal with him until nature took its course, she would seize the opportunity to lay down a few ground rules for him to follow until he went away.

She told him, "For as long as you're around you have to help when I need you."

He met her gaze. "Just so we're clear, I ain't talking to any more dead kids."

Charlie discovered that there was a lot of pleasure involved in so clearly having the upper hand. "You want me to help you? Then you talk to any spirit I need you to talk to. And you keep your mouth shut when I'm trying to have a conversation with people, keep your nose out of my business, and in general stay out of my way."

The merest suggestion of humor glimmered in his eyes. "No more trying to help you with the boyfriend, huh?"

That earned him a glower. "You're blowing it here, just so you're aware."

"I was kidding."

"Well, I'm serious. Any opinions you might have about anybody I might be . . ." she hesitated ". . . with, you keep to yourself."

"Fine."

"And the rest of it."

He didn't look happy. But then, he didn't have much choice. "Agreed."

Having just had an idea of what she could do to at least temporarily keep any more of him from crossing over, if that was indeed what was happening, Charlie turned and headed toward the bedroom.

"Where are you going?"

"Wait right there," she flung over her shoulder. Somewhat to her surprise, he did.

When she came back, she was carrying the small canister of sea salt that was part of her Miracle-Go kit. Garland was sitting on the couch gripping his right wrist: his hand was back, Charlie saw at a glance. So were his clothes. She felt a rush of relief.

"I've got no idea what just happened here." Garland looked up to see her eyes on him. He let go of his wrist, flexed his fingers. "But I'm sure as hell glad it did."

Charlie didn't say, *Me too.* No point in letting him think that it made a difference to her one way or another.

"They just came back? You didn't do anything?" She took the lid off the canister.

"Not a thing. What's that?" He quit wiggling his fingers to watch as she began to sprinkle the sea salt in a thin line around the perimeter of the room. Its purpose was to create a barrier that a spirit could not cross. Charlie had first meant to use it to barricade herself in the bedroom so she could snatch a few hours of much-needed sleep without worrying that Garland might come in. Then it had occurred to her: if she could ward him out of the bedroom, she could probably use the same technique to ward him into the living room. If he couldn't pass through the barrier she put down, he wouldn't be going anywhere — not into the room where she lay sleeping, and not back to Spookville. It was the psychic equivalent of locking him in a jail cell.

"Sea salt," Charlie said. The coarse white crystals were all but disappearing into the carpet, but she didn't suppose it really mattered. The key was to not leave any openings.

"Sea salt." He sounded a little wary. "How do I know you're not going to use that to get me sucked into Spookville again?"

Charlie shrugged. "I guess you're going to have to trust me."

"Usually when people say things like *You're going to have to trust me,* you can pretty much kiss your ass good-bye. Just saying."

Charlie paused with her hand in the

canister to pucker up and make kissy sounds at him.

"Funny." He watched her moodily. "How is that supposed to work, exactly?"

"It creates a barrier. You can't get past it. In theory." She reached the couch. "You want to get up for a minute? I need to sprinkle this behind the couch."

"In theory? You got a hell of a bedside manner, Doc." He stood up, reached automatically for the couch arm to pull the heavy piece of furniture out for her, and had his hands go right through it.

"Great. You're useless." She pulled the couch away from the wall herself and dribbled sea salt behind it. "I told you I've never done this before. If it works, it works." When she glanced at him, she saw that his expression had changed. "What?"

"I think I got this thing figured out." He had his hand up and was turning it over thoughtfully, looking at it. "When I walked into the ocean, I could feel the water just like when I was alive. It was warm, and I got wet all the way up to my waist, which is how far in I walked before I started swimming. A little bit after that, I started feeling different. I told you, like I didn't have any weight. And now that I think about it, I couldn't really feel the water anymore.

That's about the time I noticed my clothes were gone. In here, when I turned your laptop on, I could feel the keyboard when I touched it. The other times when I tried to touch things, I couldn't feel them. I couldn't feel that couch just now, and my hands passed right through it." He dropped his hand and looked at her. "I think somehow, every now and again, I'm able to turn solid for a little bit. And when I do, something gets thrown out of whack. Then some part of me — my clothes, my hand, probably whatever took the brunt of what I was doing — dissolves or disperses or gets swallowed up by Spookville or something. In reaction."

Charlie finished salting behind the couch and shoved it back into place, then moved on around the room.

"It's possible," she said. "I know some spirits are able to manifest physically occasionally. Somehow their atoms kind of come together and they're tangible for very brief periods. I suspect strong emotion triggers it, and that's what's behind a lot of ghost sightings."

"That's why Sweet Cheeks was able to see me in the hall. And I paid for it by going invisible for a few minutes right after."

Charlie quit laying down salt to narrow

her eyes at him. "You know, just for your information, calling Agent Kaminsky names like 'Sweet Cheeks' and 'Sugar Buns' is disrespectful and demeaning."

His eyes brightened, then twinkled. A smile tugged at the corners of his mouth. "You don't have to worry, Doc. Your ass blows hers away. Want to know what I used to call you? Hot —"

"No," Charlie snapped, glaring as she interrupted him before he could finish. "I don't want to know. You're treading on dangerous ground here," she warned.

He held up his hands. His grin was full-blown now. "No offense meant. It's just that I'm bad with names," he said, and she snorted.

"I guess that makes us even, then, because I'm bad at keeping spirits away from divine retribution." Charlie put the lid back on the salt canister with a snap.

"Aw, come on, it was a joke." His mouth sobered, but his eyes still twinkled. "Finish up with the salt."

"No more with the demeaning nicknames," Charlie said, and he nodded solemnly. She eyed him — if penitent was the expression he was going for, he was failing miserably — then took the lid off the salt, and resumed sprinkling.

"You think there's any way I could learn to — what did you call it? manifest physically? — on purpose?" he asked after a moment.

Charlie shrugged. "How would I know?"

"Jesus Christ, Doc, you're supposed to be the expert here."

"When I see an apparition, it's usually for ten to fifteen minutes, tops. I've never been saddled with one on a full-time basis before. It's a whole new experience." She finished with the salt by creating a line across the doorway that led into the bedroom, then put the lid back on the canister again. "There you go. You're now locked in for the night. Enjoy yourself. I'm going to bed."

Even as she said it, she realized how tired she was. The adrenaline rush associated with discovering a naked Garland in her apartment had probably masked it until now.

"Wait a minute. Explain to me what you just did."

"I sealed you into this room. You — including your clothes and all your body parts, hopefully — can't get out. Tomorrow I'll see if I can come up with something better. For tonight, that's the best I can do." She headed for her bedroom.

"Doc. Wait. Come back."

He sounded like it was urgent. Charlie stopped, cast her eyes heavenward, then turned and retraced her steps, frowning at him from just beyond the line of salt. "What?"

"I was serious about what I said earlier. If there's a serial killer at work in the area who knows you can identify him, you need to be getting on out of here. Like, first thing tomorrow. He'll be coming for you, I can almost guarantee it."

Fatigue was starting to take its toll. Her shoulders drooped, the small canister of sea salt felt like it weighed a ton, and her emotions were closer to the surface than usual. Fear had started creeping through her veins from the moment she had seen herself on TV. Now it flowed freely, ice cold and thick as oil. Despite trying as hard as she could, it was all she could do to keep the terrible memories of that night at the Palmers' at bay. Given her history, it was unreal that she was standing here feeling sorry for Garland, liking Garland. A visceral reaction to her own gullibility made her snap: "And you're so sure of that because . . . ? Oh, that's right, you'd know all about serial killers, wouldn't you?"

He looked at her without speaking for the space of maybe a couple of heartbeats. "I'm gonna say this one more time, Doc, and you can believe me or not: I've done a lot of bad things. But I didn't do that."

The stupid thing was, for a moment there she trembled on the brink of maybe, kinda, sorta, halfway believing him. Then her thoughts snapped back over a combined police/FBI investigation, a trial and conviction, a textbook list of markers, a forensic file as thick as a dictionary. What was she going to believe, the preponderance of all those things, or a man who even before he died she had concluded was a psychopath, albeit a handsome, charismatic one?

The answer was clear.

"Nice try, but no cigar," she said, and as his eyes darkened she turned to once again head to the bedroom.

"Doc." His voice stopped her before she'd taken much more than a single step. She pivoted to face him.

"What?" she responded tartly. She was on guard now, armored against any type of persuasion he might try to use: *Hopelessly Naïve R-Not-Us.*

"Could you at least turn on the TV?" As she stared at him, he gave her a wry smile. "I don't sleep anymore, you know."

Why not? It was a small thing. Walking back to the coffee table, she picked up the remote and turned the TV on for him, volume down low.

"ESPN," he requested.

She found the channel.

"Thanks," he said, as without a word she put the remote on the coffee table, and clicking off the light as she passed the switch, went to the bedroom.

"Hey, Doc," he called after her.

She stopped. "What now?" she growled, without even turning around.

"Like I said, way too softhearted."

Charlie stiffened. Then, to the sound of his low laughter behind her, she stalked into the bedroom.

Chapter Twenty-One

Alone in the bedroom, Charlie could still hear the TV. It was infuriating to realize that she found the barely audible sounds of whatever game was on comforting. It was even more infuriating to realize that she found the knowledge that Garland was right there in the next room comforting.

You know your life has serious problems when having a serial killer ghost nearby makes you feel safe.

Charlie reflected sourly on the sorry state of her life as she tucked the canister of sea salt safely away in her suitcase.

Then, dropping her robe, shivering a little because the shortie nightgown and matching panties she wore beneath were thin nylon and lace and left a lot of skin available to be chilled by the air-conditioning, she scrambled into bed, clicked off the bedside lamp, and yanked the covers practically all the way over her head.

Within minutes she was asleep.

Sometime after that, Holly came to her.

Not Holly's ghost, because Holly's ghost had crossed over and didn't appear to her anymore. This was a dream, and with the small part of her brain that was still cognizant enough to recognize such things, Charlie knew it was a dream, even as she found herself caught up in it. It featured Holly as she had looked on the day her family had died, the day she had been kidnapped, Holly of the sweet smile and beach-girl tan and long blond hair.

"I love dancing, don't you?" Holly called over her shoulder to Charlie. Charlie realized that they were both dancing, each swaying around on a dance floor in a man's arms — close enough so that she could see Holly, hear Holly. And she realized that it was her present-day, thirty-two-year-old self interacting with seventeen-year-old Holly, and it didn't seem weird to either of them.

In the dream, Charlie answered, "Yes." She saw that they were on the Sanderling's dance floor, saw the glittering night sky and flaming tiki torches and other couples crowding close around them, and knew that it was a replay of the evening she had just spent, only with Holly added to the mix. That was fine, there was nothing wrong with that, and Charlie smiled as she watched Holly being happy, Holly enjoying herself, Holly young and carefree and alive — until she noticed what Holly was wearing. It was the poufy pink prom dress that Charlie had only ever seen on Holly's ghost. Something struck her as being important about that, and she frowned, but she couldn't quite put her finger on what it was. Watching Holly, struggling to clear away the foggy-mindedness of the dream for long enough to make the connection, Charlie remembered Bayley Evans. The girl had gone to a dance less than a week before she had been kidnapped. Had Holly gone to a dance in the days before she was kidnapped? Charlie didn't know. If so, Charlie hadn't been invited along, although as she had been a newcomer to the school and not a member of the popular crowd, like Holly was, that wouldn't be surprising.

Frowning in her dream, she glanced back at Holly, only to discover that her friend was being whirled off the floor. Beautiful even in that garish dress, Holly was throwing her head back to laugh up at her partner as he danced her away into the darkness. Frantic suddenly, Charlie tried to call her back, tried to see the face of the man Holly was dancing with, tried to do something to stop what she knew was going to happen next — but there was nothing she could do.

"Holly!" she cried, craning her neck in an attempt to keep the other girl in sight. Her heart pounded, her pulse raced, every muscle in her body strained to go after her friend — but she just couldn't break away. Helpless, consumed with the need to see into the darkness where Holly had disappeared, she struggled to free herself from the arms holding her even as she cried out again: *"Holly!"*

But it was so dark beyond the dance floor that she could no longer see Holly.

As she struggled more violently to break free, knowing even as she did it that she was caught up in the terrible futility that was part and parcel of the dream state, the arm around her waist suddenly hardened and tightened, and she was whirled around then caught up abruptly against her partner. The man she was dancing with was an abstract dream figure no more. He was solid and *there* as he pulled her hard against him. She could feel the unyielding strength of his body, the steely muscularity of the arm around her waist, the warmth and size of his hand gripping hers, with a vividness that had been missing before.

"You're okay. I've got you now. It was only

a bad dream."

Even through her terror for Holly and desperation to stop what she knew she couldn't stop and the mind-clouding effect of the dream, Charlie would have recognized that distinctive voice in her ear anywhere in the universe. She looked up sharply, and met Garland's sky blue eyes. His tawny head was bent over hers. His beautifully cut mouth was hard with concern. His broad shoulders blocked much of her view. It was Garland she was dancing with now, Garland whose hand held hers, Garland whose arm was tight around her waist, Garland whose rock-solid body she was pressed against.

And she realized that, in her dream, she was foolishly, ridiculously, but undeniably glad to see him.

Something of what she was feeling must have shown in her eyes, because his expression changed. His eyes narrowed on her face. Some of the tautness around his cheekbones relaxed.

"Now, ain't this a kick in the head," he drawled, and gave her what she could only describe as a wolfish smile.

Whatever he meant by that, at the moment she had bigger fish to fry than him.

"My friend — Holly," she told him in despair, neck twisting as she tried one more time to look into the darkness beyond the dance floor to where Holly had disappeared. "I need to go after her. I need to stop her."

"You were having a nightmare." Despite her attempts to get away, Garland held her fast. "I've got you safe now. Whatever you saw before wasn't real."

Charlie searched the darkness at the edge of the dance floor for a moment longer. It was impenetrable, dredged up from what seemed to be a thousand mental images of the darkest night ever. As she stared into the unnaturally stygian depths she realized that Garland was right: Holly as she had just seen her had been no more than a memory invading her sleep. Holly didn't need her; Charlie could let her go. As she accepted the truth of that, she almost imperceptibly felt herself start to relax. Idiotic to think of Garland as someone she could depend on, but for now, just for now, she apparently did. Her body softened, and in the process molded itself instinctively to Garland's wide-shouldered, lean-hipped frame. The instant reaction of her nipples to contact with his hard chest sent a flutter of pleasure scooting along her nerve endings. The pressure of his lower body against hers made her blood begin to heat. Then she realized that she could actually *feel* him, feel the solid wall of his chest against her breasts with every breath she drew, feel the brush of his jeans against her bare legs with every movement of his powerful thighs, feel the unmistakable maleness of him pressing hard against her abdomen. Feel him just as surely and acutely as if he were a living, breathing *man.*

Holding her in his arms.

Her body responded with a throbbing awareness that made her catch her breath.

Then the rest of what Garland had said registered.

She looked sharply back up at him. "Are you saying that *this* is real?"

He smiled at her, not wolfish any longer, but a slow, intimate smile that dazzled her a little. *God, he's handsome.*

"What do you think?"

"It can't be."

The square angle of his jaw was right above her eye level. He was clean-shaven, his skin firm and tan. His head was bent over hers. Her eyes wandered the flat planes of his cheeks, the high curves of his cheekbones, the thick, dark brown eyebrows, the elegantly carved nose. His glinted down at her, impossible to read. But there was something in their depths that told her he was every bit as aware of her as she was of him.

That he could feel her, too.

Her heart was beating too fast still, but not because of Holly now.

"There you go, then," he replied, and swung her around in a movement of the dance. Refusing to be distracted by an action she guessed was deliberately designed to do exactly that, she narrowed her eyes at him with quick suspicion.

"I'm dreaming this, right?"

He sighed. His hand gripped hers more firmly. She could *feel* the thickness of his palm, the slight roughness of his fingertips. She could *feel* the texture of his soft cotton T-shirt and the tensile flexing of his shoulder beneath it. She could *feel* how big and muscular he was, how absolutely, unmistakably male, and whether it was a dream or not her pulse went all tremulous and her stomach began to quiver.

Real. This feels real. He *feels real.*

"Jesus, Doc, relax for once. Go with the flow. Just dance with me," he said, which wasn't really an answer at all. But she didn't argue, because she didn't feel like arguing anymore, and because she discovered that she liked being in his arms, in a major way, and because this *had* to be a dream, which meant she could relax and enjoy it because none of it mattered. Now that she thought about it she knew for sure it was a dream, as they were still on the dance floor at the Sanderling, dancing politely while the band played. The same couples as before were dancing all around them, and the same spectators crowded the edge — and while Garland was wearing his jeans and boots and T-shirt, she was out on the dance floor, in the midst of everything, in her flimsy shortie nightgown and bare feet, which wasn't even remotely possible.

I can feel the texture of the floor beneath my feet. I can smell . . . What can I smell? Slow-roasting meat, and the citronella from the torches, and plants and flowers and a hint of perfume from the woman in the black dress who just danced by. I can smell Garland. He smells like the sea.

His hips cradled hers. His thighs moved against her thighs. She could feel the roughness of his jeans against her bare legs. She could feel the pressure of his hand splayed possessively across the small of her back.

The music was that same torchy love song that had played before, with its slow, throbbing beat.

We've got tonight. . . .

Dancing with him, swaying to the music,

the tough leather of his boots sliding alongside her bare feet, she felt her body start to pulse with that same slow, torchy rhythm.

Earlier, when she'd been dancing, first with Tony and then, for that brief, infuriating moment, with Garland, her body hadn't quickened and started to go all warm and liquid inside. It hadn't softened, and it hadn't wanted.

But this time, in Garland's arms, in her dream, it did.

"Where's Tony?" she asked, because if this was some kind of semi-skewed re-creation of her evening, Tony should be in it, too, along with Crane and Kaminsky, although she hadn't seen them yet, either.

A muscle twitched at the corner of his mouth.

"Fuck Tony," Garland replied coolly, which made Charlie smile because it sounded so exactly like something Garland would say that her dream suddenly felt way real again.

Only it wasn't, because it couldn't be.

But it felt real enough when, without warning, his thigh moved between hers, rough and solid, pressing against her, sliding hard against her silky panties. The effect was electrifying. Her body instantly tightened. It instantly burned.

"What . . ." Her eyes shot to his face in instinctive protest, but then she was distracted by the realization that there was now a ceiling above them as they danced. Dark and metallic, it glittered with a thousand brilliantly colored stars thrown by a disco ball that hung spinning high above her head. Charlie gaped at it, gaped at the crowd, which as quick as a blink had turned rougher and younger, and at the packed tables crammed in around the dance floor. The smell had changed, too: it was now popcorn and beer. Cool smooth wood lay beneath her feet. The couples dancing near them looked like bikers and their babes. The bar stretching along the far wall was packed with revelers. The vibe was low-class and raucous, the decibel level off the charts. The music was hotter, wilder, with a different, pulsing rhythm. The song — she knew that song. What was it?

Adele's wailing "Rolling in the Deep."

". . . just happened?" she finished, because the transformation was so mind-boggling she forgot that she had been meaning to conclude with a starchy ". . . do you think you're doing?"

Holding her close, swaying with her to the pounding music, moving that long, powerful thigh between her legs to devastating effect, Garland smiled into her eyes. She could feel every muscular inch of him. The combination was enough to send a fresh infusion of heat rushing through her veins.

Forget starchy. This was its opposite.

"Don't know. But this is more my kind of place."

"How did we get here?" Foolish question. How did anyone get anywhere in a dream?

"Beats me." The music was so loud that he had to speak right in her ear. "Whatever you do, don't let go of me, Doc. Wouldn't want to lose you." She felt his warm breath against her skin, and then what she thought were his lips, nuzzling the outer curve of her ear. A delicious little shiver ran along her nerve endings. She didn't pull away.

"Do you think that's possible?" The thought was faintly worrisome. He lifted his head to look down at her. Charlie frowned at him.

"Who knows? This is one screwy dream. I vote we don't test it." His voice took on a husky note. "Put your arms around my neck, Doc. Both of 'em."

CHAPTER TWENTY-TWO

Garland lifted the hand he was holding and guided it around his neck. Charlie didn't resist. Instead her arms encircled his neck while he wrapped his arms around her waist. He was holding her so tightly now that it was hard to know where she ended and he began.

Because of his height and her lack of shoes, hanging on to his neck pulled her up onto her toes. She was practically glued against the warm, taut wall of his chest while his body moved suggestively against hers. The pleasurable throb inside her intensified until it was something way hotter and more liquid.

This is sexual foreplay to music, she thought. This baddest of bad guys was heating her up. Turning her on.

He was doing it deliberately, too, she was sure, and she — face facts — was reveling in it.

"I don't know how to dance like this." She sounded faintly breathless to her own ears. Sad to realize that she had never given herself the opportunity to learn. From the time she was seventeen, her life had been all about accomplishing one goal. She hadn't played, she hadn't partied, and unless a social occasion she was attending had called for it, she hadn't danced. And even when she had, those had been country club dances. Nothing like what was going on around her now.

"Just hang on and trust me. You trust me, don't you, Doc?"

"No." She shook her head, and he laughed.

She was plastered so close against him that she was able to feel every bulge and sinew and belt buckle and zipper, moving with him like he was her lover, like he was her man. She had never in her life danced the way they were dancing now, swaying and sliding and turning and writhing in a sensuous give and take that made her feel like someone she didn't even know.

"Why am I dreaming about dancing like this with *you?*" Tinged with vexation, the words popped out of her mouth, because it had just occurred to her that if she was going to get blown away by sexy dream fantasies, the man they should be focused on was Tony, or one of her ex-boyfriends, or some great new guy she was just now imagining — or, basically, anybody but *him.*

" 'Cause you like me." Garland lifted his head from where it had been nuzzling into her hair and met her gaze. His eyes were intense, with a dark, smoldering gleam. "Come on, Doc, admit it. You know you do."

Charlie couldn't say anything. To deny it would be a lie. To admit it — she wasn't going to admit it. Not even in her dream. Not to him. Not to anyone. Not with her heart beating a mile a minute and her pulse racing and her breathing coming way too fast. When he saw she wasn't going to answer, he didn't press her. Instead his head dipped, and his lips found her throat. Hot and damp, his mouth slid down the side of her neck. Charlie shivered. She went weak at the knees. His mouth found the tender curve between her neck and shoulder, and she could feel his tongue caressing her there. She sucked in air. Her body suddenly felt boneless. His arms tightened, pulling her closer still, and her breasts swelled against his chest and her nipples tightened and yearned. His leg between hers was part of the dance, she knew that now, but the friction of it moving against that most sensitive part of her made her body quake.

She liked the quaking. She liked his lips on her skin. She liked the way he was making her feel. And yes, although she wasn't about to admit it out loud, she liked him.

Actually, *like* was too pale and puny a word. But it was as far as she was willing to go, even in her dream.

She was so tight against him by this time that every movement he made felt erotic. His hands on her lower back slid down the silky stuff of her nightgown to cup her butt. In real life, if a guy had grabbed her like that while they were dancing, she would have decked him. If real Garland had tried it, he would have been thrown in the hole for days. And if ghost Garland had ever so much as *thought* about it, she would have gone after him with her sage incense. But in her dream, feeling Garland's big hands on her butt sent excitement rocketing through her. She was practically riding his thigh now, arms locked around his neck as he turned with her and dipped her this way and that. The hot throbbing inside her intensified and concentrated on that one burning point of contact until she thought she might melt right there in his arms. Tiny scalding thrills raced along her nerve endings. Holding her close, he rocked into her as they danced, letting her feel him, leaving her in no doubt that he was aroused, turning her on to her back teeth.

"You're dancing like a pro now." Garland pressed his lips to the delicate hollow below her ear. Charlie went all shivery inside. It was a good thing he was bearing most of her weight, because she was pretty sure that at this point her legs were so rubbery she couldn't stand.

"Do you always make out with your partners on the dance floor?" she asked tartly, in pure self-defense. The hot crawl of his mouth along the underside of her jaw was thrilling her clear down to her toes. But the telling thing was, despite the bite of her words she didn't try to pull away.

"Nah." He was still kissing her neck. She could feel his quick smile against her skin. "Only with the real babes."

At his teasing, she had to smile a little, too, although her heart was going a mile a minute and her body had all but turned to putty in his hands. He was doing it on purpose, she thought with the minuscule part of her mind that was still on watchdog duty, charming her even while he made her want him times about a thousand.

Which was exactly what a charismatic

psychopath would do.

And she let herself go with it, because she liked it so much — and anyway, none of it was real.

For the first time in a long while, she was with a man who made her feel like a woman.

Probably you ought to try waking up about now.

That cool prickle of clarity came from another, more forceful stirring of the practical part of her mind, the watchdog part, the guardian. Charlie heard it. But she wasn't going to allow herself to listen to it, or think about all the reasons why feeling sexy in Garland's arms was wrong — or, worse, plain dumb. She wasn't going to think at all. She was just going to go with the flow, as he had suggested, and exist in the moment. Indulge herself a little. Let herself imagine that he was something other than what he was, and take pleasure at being in his arms. Take pleasure at the stirrings of her body, the rising sexual tension, the delicious heat. Closing her eyes, Charlie surrendered, allowing her head to rest on his wide shoulder, giving herself up to the music and him, immersing her senses in the sheer sensual delight of his mouth exploring her neck and his hands cupping her butt and everything else that was going on between them. Take pleasure in moving with him and against him, of feeling his hard masculinity against her softer, feminine self. He was a good dancer, no surprise there, such a great-looking guy would have had every opportunity to practice with a wide variety of partners. His body radiated heat, and because an unexpectedly cool breath of air feathered across her bare skin just then, she snuggled voluptuously into him. At the same time she tightened her grip on his neck and moved her head so that he could have better access to the hollow of her throat, which was where his lips were headed. She felt his breathing change, dig down a little deeper, come a little faster, as she arched into him.

Listening to the uneven cadence of his breathing, she felt almost dizzy, almost as if she'd had too much to drink and had a buzz going, although she hadn't consumed any alcohol at all. At the same time, her body pulsed and throbbed. He was taking her higher and higher. . . .

You want to be careful here.

As that cautionary thought flitted through her mind, his thigh slid out from between her legs. Charlie felt instantly bereft. She made an importunate sound. Gripping her bottom, he pulled her closer still in a single rough movement that brought them pelvis to pelvis, leaving her in no doubt that whatever had distracted him hadn't distracted him completely. As they'd danced, his big hands had by degrees worked their way up beneath the short hem of her nightgown to cup her bottom through her silky panties. Now his hands stilled and tightened, so she could feel every bit of their heat and strength as well as their broad-palmed, long-fingered shape through the fragile layer of cloth.

I love the way his hands feel on my butt.

They weren't dancing any longer. She could no longer hear the music over the drumming of her pulse in her ears.

His mouth left her skin — reluctantly, she thought. As another whisper of surprisingly cool air touched the dampness he had left behind, she felt him straighten to his full height. Her arms still circled his neck, so she had, perforce, to stretch upward with him, until she was on her tiptoes. She wanted in the worst way to go back to what they had been doing. She made that come-hither sound again. Her head fell back so that her neck was fully exposed, inviting the return of his mouth.

"What the hell are you wearing, Doc?" he asked with a touch of wry humor: not what she had expected at all. She was still all but lost in sensation, but his tone cut through the haze of desire that had been fogging her brain. Her eyes blinked open. He was looming over her, tall and blond and gorgeous, typical Garland. Before she could answer his question, his hands left her butt and slid up farther beneath her nightgown to grip her hipbones. She felt the imprint of his hands like a brand as they closed over her bare skin. He pushed her a little away from him, just far enough that cool air could circulate between them, even while he maintained his grip on her. She lost her hold on his neck; her hands slid down over his shoulders to rest flat-palmed against his chest. It felt warm and sleek and unyielding beneath his shirt, and she pressed her hands into the firm muscles there with instinctive, sensuous pleasure. As she looked up at him she saw that his eyes were gliding down her body.

Charlie looked down at herself, too.

Her nightgown was a lustrous pale blue, silky and insubstantial, with lavish trimmings of cream-colored lace. Wide lace straps hugged her shoulders, traced the deep V neckline, and edged the hem that ordinarily ended just at the very tops of her thighs, although Garland's hands underneath rucked the delicate garment up almost to her naval. The matching bikini panties, dainty in silk and lace, showed beneath, leaving the lower part of her toned midriff and her long, tanned legs bare. The material clung to her breasts, revealing their fullness and shape. Her aroused nipples were embarrassingly visible against the thin cloth. Only the thing was, realizing that Garland was seeing them that way, was seeing *her* that way, didn't embarrass her at all, Charlie discovered.

Just like being next to naked with him and having his hands up under her nightgown holding her by her hips didn't embarrass her at all.

Truth was, she liked it.

"I got to tell you, you keep surprising me." Garland's voice was slightly thick. When she looked up to meet his eyes, she saw that they were hot. Her heart revved until it was beating a mile a minute. Her blood heated to boiling as it rushed through her veins. "Back there on the Ridge, I sure didn't have you pegged as the type to go for sexy nighties."

"I like pretty things." She sounded maybe a tad defensive, because lingerie was the one area in which she could indulge her feminine side and she did. Her delicates were an antidote to the nearly androgynous professional look her work life demanded.

His eyes slid over her a second time, and by the time they met hers again there was a carnal gleam in them that made her want to start pulling her nightgown over her head and shimmying out of her panties. His lids had a sudden heaviness to them. A smile curved his mouth slightly.

"Yeah, me too."

By the way he said it she knew he meant pretty things like her, and her bones turned to water and her blood to steam.

Swaying close, she smiled into his eyes.

It was the smell penetrating the dreamy haze that had prompted her smile, and had her hands sliding sensuously over his chest, that did it. The smell was what stopped her cold. The air that wafted around them was fresher and cooler than it should be, Charlie realized at last. Instead of popcorn and beer, it smelled briny and fishy, like the sea. The surface beneath her feet was firm but gritty. Sand. A beach. Deserted, as far as she could tell. A sharp glance to her right found the ocean. Black waves tipped with silver rolled toward shore, surging to within inches of her toes. Overhead, the moon was as big as a saucer and silver, too, surrounded by giant tinsel stars that seemed close enough to touch.

Her mouth dropped open at the impossibility of it. She cast Garland a startled look. "Where are we?"

Then she remembered: this was a dream.

The negative shake of his head indicated that he had no clue.

"Romantic, though." The smallest touch of humor was in his voice, but there was an underlying rasp to it that told her all she needed to know. Looking up into his hard, handsome face, she saw the hot flare of passion in his eyes. And she saw he was teasing her a little, too.

"Why do you say it like that?" Her breathing was uneven. Her body pulsed with sexual need. It was ridiculous to feel shy of him suddenly, but she did. To cover up, she went with her suspicious side.

"It's *your* dream, Doc," he drawled, and pulled her close. "I figure that means it works out however you want it to."

Then he bent his head and kissed her mouth.

Chapter Twenty-Three

It was the kind of kiss that Charlie never in a million years would have expected from him: gentle and tender, a tasting. A testing.

Her heart lurched. Her pulse drummed in her ears. Fireworks went off somewhere deep inside. For a moment she simply stood there, not breathing, letting him kiss her, letting him learn the shape of her mouth and sample, just sample, the warm wetness between her lips. Her hands closed on the front of his T-shirt and her wide-open eyes searched his face.

The kiss should have been a nothing, should have been a throw-away on the keeper scale of kisses, and yet it set her body ablaze.

When he stopped kissing her and drew back and opened his eyes to look into her face, Charlie finally remembered to breathe. She was melting inside, liquefying, and it was the most unsettling thing she had ever felt. No way should she be reacting like this to a barely-there kiss. She had kissed her fair share of men — really kissed some of them, too — and not one of them had made her feel like this.

Not one of them had made her feel as hungry for sex as an animal in heat.

"Doc," Garland said. He looked down at her with what she recognized as a predator's unblinking gaze. His jaw was tense, his mouth unsmiling. Tall, hot, and dangerous as hell: Charlie knew it. *Knew* it.

In an instant, a thousand reasons why she didn't want to do this chased one another through her mind. And vanished, blown away by a blast of desire stronger than reason could ever be. Want didn't enter into it anymore. What she felt was pure need.

"Garland." Hands still fisted in his T-shirt, Charlie went up on tiptoes and kissed him back, a hot, tantalizing sampling of her own that made her dizzy.

"Michael," he corrected against her lips as she drew a little away.

Another thousand reasons why she needed to turn back now assaulted her brain. Calling him by his first name made it personal, signified a connection that she'd have to be crazy to form. This was the last guy on earth, or in heaven, or hell, with whom she needed to forge any kind of emotional bond. Any kind of physical bond. She knew that if she didn't call a halt now, right now, she was stepping into a quagmire from which she might never be able to extricate herself. But if the heart wants what it wants, the body equally needs what it needs. What was happening between them was pure chemistry, pure animal attraction, and it was as impossible to resist as a magnet's pull to the north. Their lips were millimeters apart now, but still she shivered, even as, deep inside, her body burned.

Maybe she still would have summoned the fortitude to turn away while she had the chance if she'd thought that what was happening between them was anything other than a dream.

His eyes held hers, waiting. The price for what she wanted was his name.

"Michael," she said obediently, in a throaty voice that she scarcely recognized as her own. His lips curved into the slightest of smiles. His eyes blazed down into hers.

"Charlie." He drew her name out like he was savoring the feel of it on his tongue. Other than that, his only response was to tighten his grip on her hips. His hold was almost hard enough to hurt, his strong fingers digging into her flesh, but she barely noticed and didn't care. Her heart hammered. Her body was on fire. He might be able to take his time, but she couldn't wait. Impatient, she let go of his shirt, slid her arms up around his neck, fitted her lips to his, and slipped her tongue inside his mouth. Molding herself to the whole long length of him, she kissed him with an urgency that was a silent testimony to the conflagration he'd lit inside her. He stayed still as stone against her, letting her coax him, letting her tantalize him into coming out to play.

Until he did.

One minute she was touching her tongue to his, and plying his lips with hers, and pressing herself ardently against him, and for all the response she got she might as well have been trying to seduce an especially hunky statue. Then he let go of her hips to slide his arms around her. They stayed underneath her nightgown, encircling her waist and back, hard as iron and warm as a furnace against her bare skin as he pulled her even more tightly against him. He seemed to pause for a second. She got the impression that he was making sure he had himself under rigid control.

"You're going to hate me for this in the morning, you know," he murmured in a rough-edged voice that made it as much a turn-on as a warning. She shook her head.

"No, I won't. Why would I?"

"I guess we'll just have to see." His eyes moved over her face, fastened on her mouth. Then his lips slanted across hers and he tipped her head back against his shoulder and took her mouth, and she was lost to everything except him, and the way he made her feel.

He kissed her with a fierce passion that made her blood sizzle and her bare toes curl into the sand. His mouth was hard and hot and demanding, taking possession, taking control.

Fire shot through her body as he explored her mouth with a voracious hunger that was greedy and domineering and completely enthralling all at the same time.

He knows his way around women, she thought, *and it shows.*

She kissed him back as if she would die if she didn't. Her senses went into instant meltdown. The hot spiral of arousal that had been building inside her for what seemed like days spun into a blazing whirlwind that threatened to consume her in the flames. As they kissed, lightning struck and thunder rolled, and Charlie felt herself being swept away by a blistering storm of passion that was like nothing she had ever experienced.

Those experts in sexual attraction, the French, have an expression: *coup de foudre.* Thunderbolt. That's what she felt. He was kissing her like he could never get enough of her mouth, and for her the heavens split and the earth shuddered, and everything she had ever thought she knew about the depth and breadth and height of her own capacity for sexual desire flew out the window.

She saw now that as far as her own sexuality was concerned, she had never had a clue. Something about *him* — his kiss, his touch, the feel of his body against hers, she didn't know — roused her to a fever pitch of excitement. He kissed her, and she burned for him. She lusted for him. She craved him.

His mouth was fierce on hers. His tongue staked bold possession. She kissed him back with abandon. She loved the taste of him, the heat of his mouth, the feel of his body against hers.

By the time she pulled her mouth from his, she was shaking. Her knees had gone weak and the hot rhythmic throbbing deep inside her body was too urgent to ignore.

"Michael. Let me go."

His eyes opened, narrowed, and he looked down at her with a frown that couldn't quite mask the hungry glint in his eyes.

"Getting cold feet, Doc?" His face was hard and tight with passion, and a faint flush rode his cheekbones as she unlocked her hands from around his neck and set her hands against his chest and pushed a little away from him. Calling her "Doc" was, she felt, an effort to distance himself from the attraction blazing between them now that he thought she was calling a halt. He didn't quite let her go — she remembered his concern about that — but he did loosen his grip enough that she could put a few inches between them. His next question was a growling taunt: "Ready to turn tail and run already?"

She shook her head. Not in a million years. "No."

Then she did what she had been meaning to do all along: grasped the hem of her nightgown and pulled it up over her head. When it was off, when she was naked except for her panties, she dropped the gossamer flutter of blue to the sand. The sea breeze caressed her skin. Glancing down, she saw that, bathed in silvery moonlight, she looked slender and pale. Her breasts stood up full and firm, with her nipples proudly erect. His hands were big and dark against the suppleness of her waist. The delicate triangle of blue clinging to her hips was the only interruption to the long slim line of her hips and legs.

If this was her dream, her sexual fantasy, she wasn't going to be half-assed about it. She would have what she wanted, and she would have it all.

His eyes were riveted on her. They were hot and dark as they roamed her body. That perfect masculine mouth of his firmed into a hard, sensuous line.

"You're beautiful." She could feel his tension in his hands gripping her waist, and see it in the bunched muscles of his powerful arms, and hear it in the guttural undertone to his voice. "I've been imagining you like this since the moment I first laid eyes on you."

Remembering the steely-eyed, honey-voiced convict chained across the table from her, she shivered, then put up her chin. "You think I didn't know?"

His mouth quirked. His eyes met hers with tender mockery. "You were a real ball-buster. Sexy as hell, though. If you knew, why didn't you run away screaming?"

Charlie gave a delicate shrug. "I wanted to psychoanalyze the heck out of you. Plus, I had a lot of faith in those shackles."

He laughed, looking like the sound was

surprised out of him. Then he pulled her toward him. Charlie's heart hammered and her breath caught and her body went up in flames.

She caught just a glimpse of his eyes, glittering with the thrilling promise of what was to come, before his arms closed around her. Then the two of them were kissing and her hands were moving up under his T-shirt to slide over the taut muscles and warm, sleek skin of his back and he was scooping her up and then sinking down with her onto the sand. It was soft and warm and faintly damp, the perfect mattress. She felt it give beneath her even as she surged against him. He rolled onto his back and pulled her on top of him, to protect her from the ground, she thought, until his mouth on hers stopped her from thinking at all. He kissed her like he was never going to get enough of her mouth. The feel of his hot, strong body beneath hers drove her wild. Then his hands closed on her rib cage and he lifted her a few inches higher. His mouth, scalding hot and hungry, slid down her throat and over the upper slopes of her breast in search of her nipple.

She waited with breathless anticipation. His lips were crawling over her skin. He was taking his time, taking it slow. Closing her lips on a groan, she buried her hands in the tawny thickness of his hair.

"I want you," he said in a voice that was like nothing she had ever heard from him before.

She wanted him, too. So much that she could no longer form words, or get them out. So much that she felt everything in the world that wasn't connected to sex and him start to spin away.

"Michael," she breathed, writhing against him shamelessly as every single inhibition she had ever possessed fell away. She needed him to hurry, needed him to . . .

A sound jolted her. It was loud. Shrill. Intrusive. Charlie's eyes snapped open as abruptly as if someone had slapped her in the face. For a moment she simply lay there, blinking dazedly into the dark, not knowing quite where she was or what was happening. She was breathing in ragged little gasps. Her legs moved restlessly, and her body burned. She felt hot all over, like she had a fever. Her lips felt swollen and tingly. So did her breasts. Deep inside, she felt a desperate wanting. She throbbed. She quaked.

Oh, God, Michael's — no, *Garland's* — mouth had been just about to close over her nipple. Even now, awake, she wanted it there so badly that her back was arching up as if to offer it to him.

Where is he?

A long shudder racked her, along with a surge of searing heat. *I want you* was what he had said. Well, she wanted him, too.

Now. Hot and hard and . . .

Charlie took a deep, shuddering breath. She diagnosed her problem at just about the same time she realized the darkness she was staring up into hid a plain white ceiling and not a night sky full of an improbably large moon and millions of stars. The surface she lay on was a bed, not a beach. What was twisted around her were the covers, not Garland's gorgeous body. What she smelled wasn't sea air, but a hint of fabric softener combined with bleach.

Her problem was that she was consumed with lust. Suffering from a bad case of near coitus interruptus. Turned on to her back teeth. Horny. Aching for a man.

Face it, you're aching for Garland.

And she had reached that sorry state of affairs because she'd had a bad — okay, bad and really, really sexy — dream.

Even as Charlie recognized the truth of that, even as she recoiled in dismay from the path her wayward subconscious had led her down, she was startled into motion by the blare of the alarm clock on the bedside table. In a flash she knew where she was: in her bed in the in-law suite of the FBI's rented beach house. Apparently the clock's ring was what had jolted her out of her dream, and, still groggy, she'd hit snooze, and the thing was going off again. Turning a disbelieving eye toward the clock, she saw that it was 6:05 a.m. As she grimly smacked the off button, she remembered right before she had fallen asleep sitting up and setting the alarm clock for her scheduled run with Tony.

For a moment, as she lay there trying not to think about the still urgent clamoring of her body, Charlie debated: exhaustion plus the sudden disinclination to go messing up her love life any further by dragging a perfectly nice man into it argued with canceling out by staying in bed. Mental confusion, a sexed-up body that needed to be cooled by about several hundred degrees, and the need to give herself a guy to think about besides Garland weighed in on the side of the run.

What sealed the deal was the thought of Garland in the next room. The TV was still on; she could hear it. Given the time frame, and the salt, he was almost certainly in there, no convenient vanishing in the middle of the night for him. The knowledge made her tense. It made her nervous. It made her insides take on the approximate consistency of melted butter. It made her — well, she refused to acknowledge it, but the bottom line was that she badly needed to clear her head before she had any kind of significant interaction with Garland. The last thing in the world she wanted was for him to get some kind of an inkling of the role he had so recently played in her dream. And the way she was feeling right now, he might pick up on it.

As aroused as she was, she was probably giving out massive vibes screaming *Do me.*

That did it: the run won.

Stifling a groan, Charlie clicked on the lamp, tossed back the covers, swung her legs over the side of the bed, stood up, and headed for her suitcase. Padding across the carpet, she yawned hugely.

I feel like I didn't get any sleep at all.

On the heels of that thought came another, horrifying one: what if her little interlude with Garland hadn't been a dream? Her pulse kicked into overdrive at the mere possibility. A quick glance down at herself was reassuring: her blue nightgown was definitely on. Definitely the same one she had gone to sleep in. Her panties were intact, too. In other words, she was still as completely dressed as she had been when she had tumbled into bed the night before. Anyway, he was about as substantial as water vapor, remember? No way they could have . . .

Wincing as vivid images of herself pulling her nightgown over her head replayed themselves in her mind, Charlie shucked her sleep-wear — not so much as a single grain of sand in it — and quickly checked herself out in the mirror over the dresser. No swollen lips, no love bites. No telltale signs of a passionate interlude on a starry beach. Letting out a breath she hadn't realized she'd been holding, she pulled on her running gear, brushed her hair back into a ponytail, and headed for the bathroom. Moments later, face washed, teeth brushed, moisturizer-cum-sunblock in place, she was ready to race out the door.

Only she had to get past Garland first.

The last thing you want is to let him sense fear.

She remembered thinking that about him back at Wallens Ridge. When he'd been nothing to her but a dangerously handsome serial killer she'd been studying — who was having, according to what he'd told her in her dream, a high old time imagining her naked. Now she had the same thought about not letting him sense her fear — albeit fear of a totally different kind.

What was scaring her now was that he would somehow divine how badly she wanted to have sex with him.

A predator was a predator, and she knew how to deal with those. But a spectral predator whose bones she wanted to jump? That was new.

Get a grip, she thought. Then, back straight, chin up, she strode into the living room.

CHAPTER TWENTY-FOUR

Garland lay sprawled on the couch with one arm bent behind his head, watching some kind of sports show. The living room was dark except for the glow from the TV, so she didn't get the details, but she could see that he was staring at the screen with a less-than-enthralled expression on his face. His big body took up practically the entire piece of furniture and was as solid-looking as her own. He'd taken off his boots: his feet were encased in white athletic socks. He looked so completely normal, so alive, so much the typical, couch potato, sports-watching male that for a moment, as he turned his head and looked at her, Charlie was thrown off her game.

Was his expression appraising? Broody? Or, God forbid, *knowing?*

Say good morning and get out. That had been the plan.

But just looking at him made her heart

pick up the pace, and her breathing quicken, and her blood heat. Panicking a little as his eyes slid over her — it absolutely had to have been a dream, so there was no point in letting herself even begin to imagine otherwise — she felt her body tightening deep inside.

Thank God it was dark.

If the warmth in her cheeks was any indication, she was blushing. The man — ghost — whatever — was not a fool. Given a reasonable degree of light, a blush he would see. That, coupled with her expression, which she guessed was something less than cool indifference, would be easy for him to interpret.

Probably as a sadly misguided case of the hots for him.

Crap. Leave. Fast.

Jerking her eyes away from him, not saying a word, Charlie kept on moving, heading for the door even as Garland frowned and sat up.

"Where are you going?" His eyes tracked her.

"For a run," she answered, and was out the door before he could say anything else.

She ran lightly down the stairs. Like her rooms, the house was dark, shadowy, because all the window coverings were drawn.

She was just thinking that if Tony wasn't up she had a problem, because she didn't know which of the downstairs bedrooms was his, when she saw movement in the little alcove off the kitchen. Her heart gave an automatic lurch a split second before Tony's black hair and tall form registered. He was up, then, dressed in running gear, and doing a series of stretches as he waited for her.

"You're early," she said.

"I heard your alarm go off." He grinned as her eyes widened fractionally. "My bedroom's right below yours." Charlie barely had time to wonder what else he might have heard when he added, "So, you ready?"

She nodded.

"Security alarm's already off," he said as she started toward the keypad, so she turned back and waited for him. What she really wanted — no, needed — at the moment was to be alone. Usually her runs were her time to think her own thoughts, sort through things, clear her head. But being alone right now wasn't smart; and if she couldn't run alone, she would just as soon have Tony with her as anyone else. No, sooner, actually. She liked him a lot, and she certainly wouldn't have to worry about the Boardwalk Killer with him beside her, which, she discovered as he followed her out the door into the pale morning light and the fresh ocean-scented air hit her in the face, was a bigger relief than she would have thought. With the rustle of the sea oats and the roar of the tide loud enough to drown out any noise up to, possibly, a siren, and the dunes to provide concealment if someone wished to hide, Charlie realized that, alone, she would have been feeling pretty vulnerable as she set out down the narrow wooden walkway toward the beach. With Tony only a couple of steps behind her, though, she did not.

That was the thing about a man with a gun.

"If you'd told me you were going with your boyfriend, I wouldn't have busted my ass breaking through your ju-ju walls to get out here," a growly voice said in her ear. It was so unexpected that Charlie almost stumbled on one of the weathered gray boards underfoot as Garland materialized beside her, looking disagreeable as all get-out. He was bleary-eyed, with stubble on his jaw, and if ever a ghost could look like the morning after the night before, he did.

"Go away," Charlie muttered out of the side of her mouth.

"Cramping your style, Doc?" But to Charlie's relief, he vanished as suddenly as he had shown up.

She was left to deal with a jumble of emotions, none of which were pleasant and all of which it was necessary to hide as she reached the beach and Tony caught up with her.

"Beautiful morning," Tony observed, smiling at her. With his chiseled features, dark eyes, quick smile, and tall, well-built frame, he was good-looking enough to make any woman take notice. Charlie noticed, but, unfortunately, she was not in the mood to appreciate. She nodded, and set out.

The beach was perfect for running: firm and flat, a wide, white sand surface that she refused to compare to the soft, crumbly texture of the beach she'd visited in her dreams, although that comparison — *was this the beach?* — was what immediately popped into her head. Dismissing the memory with an inner snarl, she picked up her pace. To paraphrase *South Pacific,* she was going to run that . . . whatever he was, right out of her hair. To that end, she put one foot in front of the other and concentrated on the here and now. She deliberately didn't look at the Meads' house as she passed it, although all she was actually able to see of it from the beach was the second story, which had its own terrible connotations that she wasn't going to allow herself to think about. As it was, she could almost feel Julie Mead's anguish rolling out in waves from the master bedroom. As long as she kept going and kept her eyes turned toward the ocean, though, she could cope.

The view was spectacular. The sun was just rising above the eastern horizon in an orange and purple and pink blaze of glory. Rainbow-colored breakers rolled toward shore. The temperature verged on hot — probably low eighties — but it was not yet humid, and a nice breeze blew in off the ocean. Only a few others — a couple of joggers, a wader or two — had ventured out so early in the morning, so she and Tony practically had the beach to themselves.

"You usually do five miles, right?" Tony asked. He was between her and the dunes and the houses, Charlie noted, and wondered if he'd done that deliberately, positioning himself to act as a buffer for her against the most likely source of potential danger, sort of like a certain kind of man automatically walked on the outside of the sidewalk to protect the woman with him from runaway cars.

It was a nice gesture, but again, she wasn't in the mood to really appreciate it.

Damn Garland anyway. Last night he'd

invaded her dreams. Now he was invading her run.

"You found out I usually do five miles from the background check you ran on me, right?" Charlie asked with resignation.

"Yes." He kept pace with her easily, although she was kicking it up because she really, really needed the endorphins. A sideways glance told her that he wasn't even breathing hard yet. Athletic, which considering his build wasn't really a surprise. Probably played some kind of sport in high school or college. Plenty muscular, although he was less so than — anyway, he was muscular, and from the way he'd had his gear with him and his current lack of difficulty catching his breath although she was setting a mean pace, she guessed he must run regularly to keep fit, too.

Here's the guy I should be dreaming about, she thought sourly, and scowled.

"Like I said before, I was just doing my job," Tony said, clearly misinterpreting her expression. Since it was impossible to explain how cosmically unfair it felt that she had found this great guy at the same time as she had been saddled with the ghost from hell who unfortunately seemed to possess the ability to invade her dreams and make her wild with lust, she changed the subject.

"Any luck identifying the car from the surveillance film Officer Price gave you?" she asked.

He shrugged. "It's a gray Avalon. Right place, right time to be of interest. No visible license plate or identifying marks. Driver impossible to see."

"Hmm. So how helpful is that?"

"We're having a DMV check run to identify all local owners of gray Avalons. I imagine we're talking a fairly substantial number. Will our guy be among them? Who knows? It's one more puzzle piece."

"That's what you do, isn't it? Put the puzzle pieces together."

"We have to find them first." Tony gestured at a banana yellow shingle house a little farther up the beach. "If you're going for five miles, that's the halfway mark. We probably want to turn around there."

Charlie glanced at him. He was breathing a little harder, and there was sweat beading his brow. Well, she was breathing a little harder and sweating, too. Usually she ran at a more deliberate pace, but this morning she'd felt the need to clean out as many cobwebs as she could.

"How do you know?" she asked.

"I try to run every day. Keeps me sane."

Charlie gave the cosmos a mental kick. The thought of seizing the day and suggesting they run together regularly in the future occurred, only to be immediately dismissed. Later she might count it as an opportunity lost, but for now she just was not in the mood to pursue this particular romantic path.

She had a ghost to deal with first.

They reached the house Tony had indicated and turned around. Despite her best efforts, Charlie had another flashback to that thrice-damned dream. Only as she forcibly rejected it did her mind's eye focus on the other key player beside herself and Garland: Holly.

Holly in that pink prom dress.

The connection hit her like a baseball bat to the head. The only possible excuse she could make for not having seen it before was that she had been preoccupied with Garland.

"You know, I think the dance connection is key." She was huffing a little as she spoke now, which was good. Despite certain unwelcome mental intrusions, she was already feeling much less tense. "Last night I . . ." *Dreamed* was what she didn't say. ". . . had kind of an epiphany about Holly

Palmer — my friend who was murdered." Tony nodded to indicate he knew who she was talking about. "I think she might have gone to a dance in the days before she died, too. I wonder if all those girls did."

"I'll have it checked out, although I don't remember reading anything about the victims going to dances in the original files." His breathing was coming a little harder than it had been, too, as he frowned at her. "You realize that if it turns out the girls who were killed fifteen years ago also attended dances in the days before they died, it makes it more likely that we're dealing with the original Boardwalk Killer than a copycat."

Charlie nodded. "I thought of that. But it's also possible that this guy is a copycat who is intimately familiar with details of the original case, details that didn't really register on law enforcement's radar at the time. If he's a copycat, he would be obsessed with the original. You've heard the saying 'Imitation is the sincerest form of flattery'? This guy will be trying to slavishly re-create the original murders down to the smallest details."

"That the current killer possibly finds his victims at dances is something that's not out there in the media. Even the local agents are unaware. We just started to look in that direction ourselves." Tony sounded like he was thinking out loud. "So if this is a copycat, he must be basing his actions off the original files, assuming this information is in there somewhere. How would he have access to them?"

Charlie shook her head. "Maybe it's not the files. Maybe at the time of the original murders there was speculation in the media that the Boardwalk Killer might be trolling dances for victims. Or maybe he has some kind of tie to the original killer, so he knows how the victims were selected."

"All possibilities." Tony's face was a study in concentration as he kept pace beside her. "We've gone over the original Boardwalk Killer investigation with a fine-tooth comb. There's no mention of dances in there, unless we just plain missed it, which I don't think we did."

Charlie stopped as she reached the point opposite the rented beach house where they'd started their run. Having finished with a flat-out sprint, she was panting. Tony stopped beside her, and she saw that he was panting, too.

She felt one hundred percent better.

"Look, I know you're banking on this being a copycat. But at this point that's not something we can be totally sure about."

Tony gave her an unsmiling look as they stood there catching their breath.

Charlie knew he was right. Still, she had to argue, and she knew why: to do anything else was to admit the possibility that the bogeyman who had stalked her nightmares for years was back. "This guy's not using duct tape. And the original Boardwalk Killer definitely wasn't subduing any of his victims with a stun gun."

"So maybe he's evolved." Tony sounded impatient. "Charlie, I know this is hard for you. But you've got to keep an open mind. For your own safety, and for the investigation. Fixating on the idea that this is a copycat might cause you to miss something that's important."

Tony was right, of course. Charlie knew it. The idea that the vicious animal who had killed the Palmers was slaughtering new victims and possibly now setting his sights on her terrified her to such an extreme that she was doing her best to reject it at every level. She recognized that, and also recognized the possibility did indeed exist. The last thing she wanted to do was miss something that might assist in the search for Bayley Evans.

They had maybe four days left to find her alive.

"I'll keep an open mind, I promise," she said, and headed for the house.

"Good." He followed her. Once inside, he asked, "Can you be ready to go in half an hour?" and she nodded.

After bracing herself to encounter him, Charlie felt a degree of letdown as she walked into her rooms and discovered Garland was nowhere to be seen. The TV was still on, but there was no other sign of him. She clicked the TV off, then considered. Having somehow gotten out of the cage she'd created to keep him safe, had he not been able to get back in, sort of like a dog with an invisible fence, which, having breached the shock barrier to get out is then stuck on the outside? That and a dozen other possibilities occurred to her as she quickly showered and dressed in order to get back downstairs at the appointed time. She had half expected Garland to materialize while she was in the shower — the salt barrier clearly wasn't working, and that would be just like him — but he didn't. By the time she was ready to leave, she was sufficiently concerned to use a DustBuster on enough of the salt crystals that he could get back in if that was what was keeping him out.

The possibility that something might have

happened to him — like, say, he'd been whisked off without warning to the Great Beyond to answer for his sins — bothered her more than she cared to admit, even to herself.

Of course, there was always the possibility that he was here and just keeping himself invisible to mess with her.

Finally, as she was getting ready to exit the room, she couldn't stand it any longer.

"Garland, are you in here?" Although she was careful to keep her voice to a near whisper, impatience sharpened it as she glared around at thin air. "I don't have time to play games this morning. If you're in here, kindly cut the crap and let me know."

Chapter Twenty-Five

Nothing. Not even a shimmer. A knock on the door seconds later was the only reply. And it wasn't Garland on the other side, Charlie knew.

"If you think you're worrying me, you're wrong," she hissed, and opened the door.

"Are you sure there isn't anyone else in here?" Kaminsky cast a suspicious look past her. "I heard you talking to somebody."

"Oh, my God, are you still stuck on the idea that I've got some kind of naked sex god tucked away in here?" If Charlie sounded a little annoyed, there was good reason: annoyed was exactly how she felt. The really annoying thing about it was, the naked sex god in question had very annoyingly disappeared. "If you heard me talking, it was to myself."

Kaminsky eyed her with something very close to out-and-out dislike as, closing the door behind her and casting a surreptitious look around the upstairs hallway for Garland, Charlie joined her on the landing. Kaminsky was in another of her body-hugging suits. This one was charcoal gray pinstripes. The blouse was pale gray, the shoes killer. In her own signature look of utilitarian black pants, sleeveless blouse — this one was coral — and sensible shoes, with her hair coiled into a loose bun at her nape in deference to the heat, Charlie felt frumpy in comparison.

She didn't like the feeling.

My clothes serve their purpose, she thought defensively. Which was to look professional, not sexy. But at the time she'd put her wardrobe together, the population of men around to observe it had been such that her purpose was to obscure her femininity rather than play up her looks. *But maybe it's time I shopped for a few new outfits. For when I'm not working.*

"I've been thinking about it: I know I saw what I saw last night." Kaminsky gave her a piercing look. "A tall, blond, hot, naked guy was on the landing. The only place he could have gone was into your room."

Kaminsky was exactly right, but there was no way Charlie was ever going to admit it.

"Ever think you might be projecting your own obsession with the opposite sex onto me?" Charlie parried, taking the war to the enemy camp as she preceded Kaminsky down the stairs.

"My obsession with the opposite sex?"

"It's obvious you have one."

"That's total bull."

"Is it? Examine how you've reacted to my inclusion in your group: you've been antagonistic from the beginning, and it's quite possible that you're having that reaction because you view me, another female, as a rival for the two males on your team. More specifically, as a rival for Agent Crane, who seems to be your primary focus. You two bicker endlessly, and that's a classic sign of attraction. It's understandable that you would resent another female, who you fear might start to encroach on your territory."

"My territory . . ." Kaminsky was so outraged she sputtered. Gathering herself, she tried again. "If that's an example of a psychiatrist at work, then I see why so many people, myself included, think psychiatry is total crap. If I've been antagonistic to you, it's because Bartoli inviting you to tag along with us makes me feel like a babysitter. It takes me out of the field, when I'm needed there the most. And as for Crane, you don't know what you're talking about. I am not attracted to him, and I certainly don't see you as a rival for him."

"You even have pet names for each other." Charlie reached the bottom of the stairs and turned to look at Kaminsky, who was a few steps behind, glaring at Charlie. As a means of distracting Kaminsky from Garland, her ploy had hit the jackpot. As a means of making a friend of Kaminsky, probably not so much.

Can't have everything.

"Pet names?"

"Buzz Cut. Lean Cuisine."

"Oh." Reaching the bottom of the stairs, Kaminsky looked briefly self-conscious. "Not that it's any of your business, but we went to the same high school. He and my older sister — well, we all knew each other. I call him Buzz Cut because that's what people call him sometimes, because he always had one. That's where he got his nickname. His real name's Eric. And as for him calling me Lean Cuisine, I gained forty pounds in college. I lost it by eating a lot of Lean Cuisine. My sister started calling me that instead of Lena. Buzz — Crane — picked it up. Until I told him I hated it, and he stopped. Mostly."

Charlie could see from Kaminsky's face that her emotions where Crane was concerned were all over the place.

"He's obviously attracted to you," Charlie said softly. In response, Kaminsky's eyes showed the first sign of vulnerability that Charlie had ever seen her exhibit. Then her lips pursed tightly together and she frowned.

"I don't want to —"

"Care for breakfast, ladies?"

Kaminsky broke off what she'd been saying as Crane emerged from the kitchen to toss them both a protein bar. Catching hers, Kaminsky immediately shot Charlie, who had caught hers, too, a drop-the-subject-or-die look. "We can grab coffee over at the RV. Bartoli's already there, hard at work."

After that, the day got busy. With Kaminsky researching Kornucopia and its associates at an adjacent desk, and having confirmed first thing that Trevor Mead's cousin Cory's age was twenty-six, Charlie sat in front of one of the oversized monitors in the War Room going over images of the crowd at the previous night's dance. Facial recognition software had zeroed in on nineteen faces that met the broad criteria of the sketches and descriptions, but none of those identified struck a chord of recognition with Charlie. Crane was busy checking out those individuals and comparing them with the parameters they'd established. Charlie's job in reviewing the previous night's footage was to look for body language that didn't fit the environment.

"So, you catch anybody scratching his nose inappropriately yet?" Kaminsky asked. Charlie had been so keyed in to what she was doing, she hadn't realized the other woman had come to stand behind her.

Charlie glanced over her shoulder. "Body language is much harder to fake than facial expressions. Most people aren't aware of how much their bodies reveal, and don't try to police it."

"I see what you mean." Kaminsky reached around Charlie to tap the monitor. The central image, the one that Charlie hadn't been looking at because it was her job to concentrate on the crowd, was her and Tony dancing. "I don't know what Bartoli's saying to you, but you're sure blowing hot and cold on him. Look at that. First you're making bedroom eyes at him, and the next second you look like you want to rip his throat out."

The sequence they were watching was the one where Garland had shown up and inserted himself into the dance. Of course, there was no sign of Garland on the monitor. Watching, Charlie had to admit her reactions looked more than slightly schizophrenic.

"You know, I'm no psychiatrist, but from watching you two together like that, my analysis would be that your feelings for the boss are romantic, but highly conflicted." There was way too much suppressed glee in Kaminsky's tone. "Would that be one of your classic signs of attraction, Dr. Stone?"

Careful to keep the frown that wanted to snap her brows together at bay, Charlie rolled the cursor over a (okay, random) male face in the crowd so it was immediately enlarged enough to cover most of the image of her and Bartoli dancing.

"You get anything?" Tony's voice behind them was so unexpected that it almost made Charlie jump. Glancing around at him, glad to be saved from the necessity to reply to Kaminsky, she shook her head.

Kaminsky said, "The bad news is, Kornucopia hasn't played in any venues this summer within easy driving distance of the Breyer or Clark homes."

If the two families who had been slaughtered prior to the attack on the Meads had no connection to the band, then there had to be something else there, Charlie thought. She let the computer go into sleep mode (the last thing she wanted was for Tony to start studying the image of the two of them dancing) and turned around in her chair to face the others.

"You say that like there's some good news," Tony replied before she could comment, crossing his arms over his chest and lifting his eyebrows at Kaminsky. He was once again in agent mode, in a dark suit, white shirt, and power tie, and Charlie was once again conscious of how perfect he seemed to be for her. One day, maybe, she might actually get a chance to explore the possibilities where he was concerned, but for now he had murders to solve and a missing girl to find and she, too, was preoccupied with those matters, along with — other things.

Like a possibly missing ghost.

Breaking into a wide smile, Kaminsky nodded. "Two members of Kornucopia also play in another regional band, the Sock Monkeys. It performed within twenty miles of the Breyer and Clark residences. Both the week before each family was attacked."

Tony's arms dropped to his sides. His eyes instantly looked as refreshed as if he had just chugged twenty cups of coffee. "Good job, Kaminsky. Which two?"

"Axel Gundren and Ben Teague." Kaminsky walked to her computer, bent over, typed in a couple of commands, and the faces of two young men popped up. The photos appeared to be taken from their driver's licenses, and they showed that Axel had a shock of near-white hair and blue eyes, while Ben had a biscuit-colored, Justin Bieber–style bowl cut. Both faces could have been considered long and thin, which would match Trevor Mead's description of the killer. "Ages twenty-five and twenty-six."

Kaminsky glanced over her shoulder at Tony, who nodded. Then she typed in something else and stood back as what looked like a Venn diagram filled the screen. The three overlapping circles contained dozens of names, with dozens more lining the screen on the outside of the circles. "Both are approximately the right age, height, and weight." She tapped a portion of the diagram with a well-manicured forefinger. "That puts them here. We know they were at the Sanderling on the same night as Bayley Evans, so that also puts them here." She tapped a smaller portion of the Venn diagram. "Axel has a juvenile record — for drug possession, which I'm not sure is really relevant, but it puts him here as well." Another tap. "Unfortunately, except for that, neither has any of Dr. Stone's markers. Axel lives in the basement of his parents' house in Greenville. Ben lives in an apartment in the same town. Both have multiple siblings. Neither owns or has access to a gray Avalon, as far as I can tell. According to their cell phone records, neither was anywhere near Bayley Evans' house on the night of the murders."

"So it's looking like neither one is our guy," Tony summed up flatly. The sudden flare of interest had gone out of his eyes.

"That's pretty much it," Kaminsky agreed. She tapped the center of the circles of the Venn diagram, a tiny area that was the only place on the screen empty of any names. "Anyone who fits all the criteria we've established will end up *here*. When we get a name there, he's going to be our guy."

"Keep working on it, Kaminsky," Tony said.

Kaminsky nodded.

Tony looked at Charlie. "I want you to help me interview the five girls who went to the Sanderling with Bayley Evans last week."

"When?"

"Now."

"Didn't we already talk to them?" Kaminsky asked as Charlie obediently stood up.

Tony nodded. "Yes, but the four of them here on vacation are heading back home to Winston-Salem tomorrow. The Meads are from Winston-Salem, too, and the funeral for the parents and the little boy is scheduled for Monday, so I'm guessing the girls and their families want to be there for that. I want to talk to them again before they go."

"You really think you'll get some new information out of them?" Kaminsky asked.

Tony shrugged. "I don't know. At the time of the previous interview I didn't realize the significance of that dance. I want to talk to them again with that in mind, and I want Charlie with me to see if she can pick up on anything I might be missing." Charlie caught the slightly surprised look Kaminsky cast her way upon hearing Tony call her by her first name, but of course the other woman didn't comment out loud in his presence. That, Charlie judged, would come in the nature of a zinger later. "Meanwhile, find out if there are any other people the two bands have in common — support staff, maybe an agent or a manager, anything that might tie them together, would you?"

Kaminsky nodded. "I'm on it."

As she turned back to her computer, Tony stood aside for Charlie to precede him out the door. The buzz of activity in Central Command was so loud that she had to wonder if the War Room was soundproofed, because until now she hadn't been aware of any of it. Phones rang. Volunteers manned the tip lines. A couple of sheriff's deputies in orange vests — which meant they were part of the search party that was still combing the area for any sign of Bayley Evans — stood in front of the search grid that hung on the wall talking to Agent Taylor. Most of the squares had been X'd through by this time, and even as she watched, Taylor drew a big X through another section. Charlie must have made some sound, because he glanced at her as she and Tony passed. His beady little bulldog eyes were grim.

"I hope you're having better luck than we are," he said to Tony, who shrugged noncommittally. Charlie could feel Taylor's eyes following them out the door.

The interviews took place in a plush condominium farther down the beach, where four of the girls had been staying with their mothers on what had been intended to be a two-week-long getaway before school started. The fifth girl, Hannah Beckett, who was also from Winston-Salem, was in Kill Devil Hills for the entire summer as a result of a custody arrangement between her recently divorced parents that required her to spend school vacations with her father and new stepmother. Like the others, she would be a senior in the fall at Winston-Salem's Lowell High School. She was also Bayley Evans' cousin.

"I feel so bad," Hannah told Tony, tears welling in her blue eyes. Her long hair was a darker shade of blond than Bayley's — more honey than platinum — but otherwise her resemblance to her cousin was strong. All the girls, in fact, were the same pretty, popular, cheerleader type. "Bayley — everybody — came here because of me. None of this would've happened if my parents hadn't gotten divorced." She shot a poisonous look at her stepmother, who sat with the other mothers on the two long, white-slipcovered couches that flanked the giant flat-screen TV. Along with Tony and Charlie, the girls huddled around the glass-topped dining table in the eating area of the combination living/ dining room in front of floor-to-ceiling windows looking out over the beach. It was not a happy gathering. With the notable exception of Hannah's new stepmother, who was a decade younger than the other women and dressed more like the teens in short white shorts and a black tee in contrast to the older womens' country club chic, the mothers were somber and at the same time fiercely protective of their daughters. Sipping from tall glasses of iced tea, they talked quietly among themselves while watching the conversation at the table with nearly identical gimlet gazes. Every single one of the girls had, at one point or another during the questioning, started to cry, which had earned Tony and Charlie multiple glares.

"It's not your fault, Hannah," Laurie Cole, who was sitting beside Hannah, reached out to clasp her friend's hand where it rested on the table. The thinnest, tannest, and most athletic-looking of the girls, Laurie had long, seal-brown hair sleeked back into a ponytail. "All of us wanted to come. Bayley too."

"So besides the two boys whose names you already gave us, did anyone else pay any of you particular attention?" Tony asked. According to what the girls had already told them, the boys he was referring to had met the girls at the Sanderling, danced with them, gotten the phone numbers of Laurie Cole and Grace Rafferty, a doe-eyed, pigtailed brunette who was sitting across the table from Hannah, and subsequently called them. They would be checked out, but Charlie was almost sure they would be cleared — unless the girls were mistaken about their ages, those boys were too young.

"It was dark and everybody was dancing with everybody," Monica James said. The only one of the girls with short hair and no tan, she was a redhead with delicate bones.

"Guys would just come up to us and start dancing. Bayley" — her voice caught a little on the name — "Bayley was out there in the middle of it just like the rest of us. But I can't remember anyone she danced with in particular."

"What about that waiter?" Jen Merrick asked. She was petite, with inky black curls and blue eyes. "Remember, the really cute one? When we were leaving, Bayley forgot her purse. He came running after us to bring it to her."

All the girls nodded.

"His name was Andrew," Kristen Henry volunteered. Probably the least attractive of the girls, Kristen was tall, with a sturdy frame, nut-brown hair that hung in a long braid over one shoulder and slightly coarse features. When the other girls looked at her, she shrugged. "Hey, so I remember. Like Jen said, he was really cute."

Charlie could tell from Tony's expression that he was making a mental note of the name.

"Has any male you don't know well attempted to talk to you about Bayley since her disappearance?" Charlie asked. As she had told Tony on the way over, the killer would have tried to insert himself into the investigation in any way he could. Reaching out to Bayley's friends in an attempt to vicariously experience their grief and horror was absolutely something he would have done.

"We've talked to you." Laurie's nod indicated Tony. "And the FBI agent who came with you the last time. And the police. And a couple of reporters tried to talk to Kristen and Jen when they went to the grocery store with their moms the other day."

"Nobody else?" Charlie asked.

They all shook their heads. "Except for Jen and me going to the store that one time, we haven't been outside," Kristen said. "You know, because that guy's still out there."

Several of the girls visibly shuddered. Charlie knew exactly how they felt.

"Do you think Bayley's still alive?" Hannah asked in a tiny voice.

"I think so," Tony answered, while Charlie felt her heart constrict. If she let herself dwell to any extent on Bayley, she started feeling physically sick.

After a few more questions, Tony ended the interview. He and Charlie then talked to the mothers, who knew no more than their daughters. The mothers took the opportunity to pepper them with questions, which Charlie left Tony to answer. He responded with a patience and empathy she truly admired. At the same time he made it clear that he couldn't actually discuss an ongoing investigation and subtly steered her toward the door.

The man has tact. Chalk up another plus.

"I wouldn't be at all surprised to find that the perpetrator has tried to make contact with these girls or their families." Charlie glanced over at Tony as they rode the elevator down toward the lot out front, where the SUV was parked. "If there's some way to keep tabs on the men they come into contact with . . ."

Her voice trailed off as Tony shook his head. "Neither us nor the local police force have the manpower to stay with them twenty-four seven." As the elevator stopped and they emerged into the spacious, tile-floored lobby, he looked up and around, then frowned thoughtfully. "I guess it wouldn't hurt to check the security cameras, but I don't expect to get much out of it. Speaking for myself, if I were him and wanted to make contact with any of those families, I wouldn't do it in a place where I was so obviously being recorded."

Following the direction his gaze had taken, Charlie saw the security cameras mounted high in every corner. As their purpose was obviously to deter crime, they were impossible to miss.

"Good point," she responded.

"It's suppertime," he said. "And I'm starving. I'd ask you out to dinner, but until we find Bayley Evans, I can't spare the time. How do you feel about grabbing some carryout on the way back to the house?"

Charlie smiled at him. She liked the idea that he wanted to take her to dinner. If he had asked, she would have said yes. One day, she was going to. "Are we talking McDonald's, KFC, or Arby's?" Those were the three fast-food outlets between the condo and their rental.

He grinned back at her as he pulled the building's heavy glass door open so she could walk on through. "Tough call. You make it."

She never got the chance to — stepping out into the bright sunlight and baking heat of the parking lot, they were swarmed by a crowd of shouting, microphone-and-camera-wielding reporters.

Charlie blinked in surprise. Her hand automatically went up to shield her eyes from the sun, then stayed in place to hide her face from the cameras. A police cordon had successfully kept the media away from their house, as well as Central Command and the crime scene area — except for yesterday's one breach, which meant that they, or at least Charlie, hadn't had to deal with an onslaught like this since. But here the media was again, surrounding them in a shoving, shouting ambush.

Tony's arm wrapped around her waist and he pulled her protectively close as they made their way through the pack. Charlie appreciated the gesture, and not just because she was rattled by the aggressive tactics of the media. At some point, she thought, this relationship might have some real potential. All it needed was a chance.

"Agent Bartoli, any fresh leads?"

"How are Bayley's friends holding up?"

"Can you give us an update on the status of the investigation?"

"Does this feel like déjà vu all over again to you, Dr. Stone?"

The last question, yelled by a male reporter, made Charlie drop her hand from in front of her face and look at him sharply. Something about it struck her as wrong. Watching her avidly, thrusting his microphone in her direction, the reporter surged forward until he was just feet away. He was fifty-ish, portly, with a bad toupee and a shark's smile. The right age . . .

A shiver ran down her spine.

Dear God, am I starting to see the Board-

walk Killer in every age-appropriate male?

"Any identity on the body yet, Agent Bartoli?"

Tony's arm around her tightened. Charlie could feel the sudden snap of tension in his body. He frowned at the reporter who'd asked the question even as he continued to propel her toward the SUV, which was now only a few parking spaces away.

"What body are we talking about?" Tony called back warily.

"The one found about half an hour ago out at Jockey's Ridge. Jesus, didn't you hear? Security's tighter out there than at the White House, and nobody's saying anything, but I sure thought they'd let the FBI know."

Another reporter yelled, "Can you confirm it's Bayley Evans?"

Chapter Twenty-Six

Jockey's Ridge is the tallest natural sand dune on the East Coast. Located in Nags Head, the park surrounding it comprises 426 acres. Part of it is maritime forest. Except for some tall grass and a few scrubby bushes, the rest is rolling waves of white sand that reminded Charlie, as she stood near the end of the weathered, 384-foot-long boardwalk, of a picture she had once seen of the Sahara. It was evening by that time, past nine p.m., which meant the sun was hanging low in the west and long shadows stretched out everywhere, but the temperature was still so hot that even the wind blowing off Roanoke Sound felt suffocating.

The sand was thirty degrees hotter.

A young woman's body was buried in that sand, in the shadows beneath the raised end of the boardwalk, beside one of the sturdy pillars that elevated the decklike platform into a scenic overlook providing a clear view of the dunes and the choppy blue waters of the Sound below. Charlie stood near enough to the burial site to smell the chemicals that were being used to preserve the more perishable bits of trace evidence being painstakingly lifted from the sand. She could see the shape of the body being revealed by the sand's slow removal. She could see the horrible brown discoloration that clumped the once-white sand together in places so that it resembled coffee grounds.

Just thinking about what had caused that brown discoloration made Charlie's chest feel tight. Blood, of course, although she tried not to let herself picture what terrible injuries the victim must have suffered to have lost so much. If she did, if she let herself dwell on what lay beneath that sand, she would have to leave the scene, and there was still too much for her to do. Determined to combat the physical symptoms of PTMD (Post-traumatic Murder Disorder, a too-cute label for a potentially disabling, way personal syndrome she had just identified in herself and named), which were threatening to make themselves an issue, Charlie took a sip from the bottle of water someone had handed her not long after she and Tony had arrived at the crime scene. The water, which was tepid, unfortunately didn't help. Whether the heat and thick humidity were to blame, or whether it was something else, Charlie was finding it hard to catch her breath as she watched the North Carolina Bureau of Investigation (NCBI) crime scene analysts at work. They were carefully removing the sand from a grave-sized area above and around the body and depositing it and anything they found in it in plastic bags for later laboratory analysis. The crime scene had already been measured, photographed, video-recorded, and visually searched by every group of investigators on the scene, from the NCBI to the local Nags Head police. Tony, Crane, and Kaminsky had made their own record. Now everyone waited for enough of the sand to be removed that the body could be lifted from the ground.

Official identification had not yet been made — the body had not yet been completely uncovered — but Charlie, and the others, had little doubt it was Bayley Evans.

Strands of the victim's long blond hair were mixed with the sand. The color and length matched Bayley Evans'. A blood-stained hand and arm up to the elbow were just visible beneath the thin layer of sand that remained on the corpse's right side. Clearly they belonged to a teenage girl. Apparently a handful of her hair had gotten pulled up through the sand somehow as she was being buried, so the ends had been lying on the surface. The hair had been spotted by a woman with a dog, which had led to a little digging and a horrified call to the police.

Now here they all were. So many law enforcement types were on the scene that Charlie had long since given up trying to distinguish one group from another. NCBI investigators, Sy Taylor and the other local FBI agents, the FBI Special Circumstances team of Tony, Crane, and Kaminsky, the medical examiner and his team, the local Nags Head police department, Haney and the cops from Kill Devil Hills, the Dare County sheriff and his deputies, and numerous other officials who Charlie couldn't even begin to identify all milled around doing whatever it was that they were supposed to do. It was a crowd scene of investigators, nobody was happy about the presence of the others, and to the obvious chagrin of everyone else, NCBI currently had jurisdiction.

The shocked-looking woman who'd found the body now huddled with two friends just inside the barrier of uniformed officers and crime scene tape that was holding the growing crowd of gawkers at bay. The media was out in full force, with their reporters and camera crews set up as close as they were allowed, all broadcasting the proceedings as the on-camera talent gave real-time updates to the viewers at home. Overhead, a news helicopter circled, the sound of its beating rotors punctuating the jumble of voices and equipment and other ground noise with a steady *thump-thump.* The parking lot at the far end of the boardwalk was packed with vehicles, from police cruisers to an ambulance to the TV stations' satellite-sporting vans. Even as Charlie glanced in that direction, she saw the medical examiner's van bumping over the firm-packed sand beside the boardwalk, toward the grave. Charlie was almost sure that meant the body would soon be lifted out of the ground.

So far, Bayley Evans' phantom had not appeared to her. Charlie hoped and prayed that it was because her soul had already found its way to eternity and was at peace.

Please, God, help her spirit find its way.

The thought that they had failed to save her was shattering.

"Looks like they're getting ready to bring her up," Crane said, confirming Charlie's conjecture. Perspiring, his cap of curls frizzing in the humidity, his suit coat laid aside and his shirtsleeves rolled up, he stood beside Charlie, carefully filming the crowd at her instruction. The killer was present. Charlie not only knew it objectively, from everything she had ever learned about narcissistic serial killers who invariably returned to the scene of the crime, but she could feel it in her bones.

She could feel him watching her.

Her heart pounded in a slow, steady rhythm that throbbed all the way down to her fingertips and toes. Dread prickled over her skin like wave after wave of goose bumps. Glancing sharply around at the faces, she caught no one looking at her. Every eye appeared to be focused somewhere else.

But the sense that she was being watched with malevolent intent was strong.

She had been scanning the growing crowd ever since she'd gotten her wits together enough to realize that the killer wouldn't be able to resist the opportunity to watch what was happening, but so far she'd seen nothing amiss.

He was being careful. Anonymous. Just one more face in the crowd. But he was there.

Who are you? Where are you?

"Anything?" Still thin-lipped with anger at the local cops for not having immediately notified him about the discovery of the body, at the NCBI for winning jurisdiction, and at the situation in general, Tony stopped beside her. Since he knew she'd been watching the crowd, she had no trouble interpreting his question.

Charlie shook her head. "But he wants to be part of the process. He's here somewhere." She kept her voice low. An island in the midst of barely controlled chaos, they were surrounded by investigators, and she didn't want to be overheard.

"Unless he's smart enough to stay home and just watch what's happening on TV," Kaminsky added tartly. Like Tony and Crane, and Charlie, she was taking the death of Bayley Evans personally, and the chip she always seemed to have on her shoulder bristled larger than ever. She had shed her suit jacket in deference to the heat, and tucked her hair behind her ears. Since Crane had been assigned to Charlie, Kaminsky had been with Tony from the time they had arrived. She stopped on Charlie's other side now, and from the woman's teetering movements, Charlie realized that Kaminsky was having trouble with her high heels sinking into the sand. As hot as the sand was, though, removing her shoes and going barefoot was not an option, so Kaminsky had no choice but to deal.

"It's possible that for some reason he can't be here. But if there's any way he can, he's here at the scene. This type of killer is compulsive that way," Charlie responded.

"Get the license plate numbers of every vehicle here," Tony ordered Kaminsky. To Crane, who was still filming the crowd, he said, "Don't miss a single face. We're going to get this bastard before he kills anybody else."

"If this is Bayley Evans —" Kaminsky began.

"It is," Tony said grimly. "There's not a doubt in my mind."

Kaminsky concluded, "— then we should have almost a three-week window before he goes after another family. I know we're getting close. Damn it, if we'd just had a few more days . . ."

"We'll get him," Crane said.

"When?" Kaminsky snapped. "Before or after he kills somebody else?"

Nobody replied directly, because of course there wasn't any answer to that.

"Don't count on the time frame holding. He had this girl for less than four days. He's escalating." Voice tight, Tony cast one more raking look around the site, then strode off in the wake of the medical examiner's van as it rolled by them to park within a few yards of the grave. With Tony gone, Kaminsky said to Crane, "Maybe something happened that made him kill this girl before he wanted to."

Crane looked at her. "Like what?"

"How the hell should I know?" She looked at Charlie. "You're supposed to be the expert at what makes loony tunes like this tick. What do you think?"

"You could be right. Something might have happened that threw him off his game," Charlie replied. "I have no idea what."

"I guess we'll never know, will we?" Kaminsky's tone was savage. "Because we didn't get to her in time, and now it's too damned late."

With an impartial glare for both Charlie and Crane, she turned and strode off toward the parking lot, her gait made unsteady by her heels sinking into the sand.

"I keep telling her she's got to maintain some distance or she's going to burn out," Crane said accusingly as he watched her leave. "Of course, she keeps telling me to soak my head." He glanced at Charlie. "I need to get some footage of the way the body is situated before they lift it out of the grave. And we have strict instructions that you're not to be left alone. So if you don't mind . . ."

Charlie nodded and followed him. The last thing she wanted at this moment was to be left alone: the sense of a malignant gaze watching her was too strong. As a gurney was removed from the back of the ME's van and placed beside the grave, Charlie cast another long, fruitless look around the crowd. She stood beside Crane, who was filming from graveside . . . and made the mistake of looking down into the partially excavated hole at the body. Two dark jump-suited, white-surgical-gloved coroner's assistants climbed in beside it and grasped it by the shoulders and ankles as she watched. As much as she wanted to, Charlie couldn't look away as the body was handed up to another pair of assistants, and was then lifted completely out of the grave. Charlie's stomach knotted as the stench of decay reached her nostrils. The last of the sand that had remained on the body fell away in a golden shower. During this process, the corpse remained stiff as a plastic mannequin. Rigor mortis had obviously set in. The only part of the victim that moved was her long blond hair, which was ruffled by the breeze. Matted with sand and blood, it rippled like a particularly gruesome banner. One arm lay frozen across her body. The other was clamped to her side as firmly as if it had been carved from wood.

Charlie caught her breath as she watched what remained of Bayley Evans being laid out on the gurney.

The girl was fully dressed, in what Charlie was almost certain were the clothes she'd been wearing when she'd been taken.

Her eyes were closed. Her lashes were crusted with sand. She was the color of death, her skin grayish, with lividity already having set in. Her once delicate features were bruised and misshapen, as if she'd been beaten. A clump of black-colored sand that looked like coffee grounds clung to the left side of her mouth. More coffee-grounds-looking sand was caked in the gaping wound in her throat, which was cut from ear to ear. Her shirt — the upper half of pink summer pajamas — and her arms were brown with dried blood and frosted with sand. The blood had been wet when the body was put into the grave. Charlie knew this because of the coffee-grounds look of the sand, which was the result of it having been saturated with blood and then clumping as it dried.

Pray for us now and at the hour of our

death. . . .

Holly had died the same way: she had been beaten, and her throat had been slit. Charlie had never wanted to know the details of what her friend had suffered in those days before she'd been killed, but somehow, over the years, that much had seeped past the defenses she had erected.

Looking at what had once been Bayley Evans, Charlie felt the horror of it hit her like a tsunami. Shaken and sick at heart, she was assaulted by a wave of dizziness. The sight of the girl's lifeless body was almost more than she could bear. It brought it all back, Holly, the rest of the Palmer family, the others. Unwillingly remembering the moment when she had connected with Diane Palmer's eyes, Charlie shuddered. The water bottle dropped from her suddenly nerveless fingers. As if it were happening in slow motion, she watched it fall. The splash of water spilling from the plastic container as it tumbled to the ground sounded abnormally loud to her ears. The bottle hit with a *thud,* tipped over, and disgorged what was left of its contents into the sand. Charlie feared she might soon hit the ground in just that way. Her knees wobbled. Her chest tightened. Her throat worked. Desperate, she glanced around, then took a few thankful steps backward to sink down on a large plastic cooler that probably belonged to the crime scene technicians. She was still in the shadow of the boardwalk, but far enough away from the crew working on the body that she was no longer breathing in the scent of decomposition, or confronted with the terrible reality of the corpse. Crane was close enough that she could call out to him if she needed to. He was too busy to notice that she was no longer beside him, and since she was outside the bustle of activity around the body, no one else paid her the least bit of attention.

For now, for just the few moments until she got her stuff together, that was what she needed.

She was hot, so hot. Her blouse clung to her sweat-dampened skin. With one hand she brushed away little tendrils of hair that had escaped the knot at her nape and threatened to stick to her face.

How unprofessional would it be if she were to keel over in a dead faint?

Charlie concentrated on her breathing as the world continued to spin around her. When she felt like she might topple sideways off the cooler, she quit worrying about looking unprofessional, folded her arms on her knees and rested her head on them.

"You faint, there's not much I can do." Garland's familiar drawling voice was unmistakable. "Me trying to catch you before you hit the dirt probably ain't going to work out so well."

Chapter Twenty-Seven

Charlie's eyes popped open. Garland crouched beside her, his mouth twisted into the slightest of wry smiles, his eyes focused watchfully on her face. He had appeared out of nowhere, and for an instant, the tiniest sliver of time, she was intensely glad to see him. But even as she registered that she felt stronger and safer and, yes, *comforted* by his presence, she remembered what he was. A member of the same vicious, conscienceless, sub-human fraternity that had done this to Bayley Evans, to Holly, to countless others over countless years. Had she actually been starting to care about him? Had she really been worried that he might have been whisked away to a well-deserved hell? Charlie scourged him with a look, and turned her face away.

"Not over the whole hating-me-in-the-morning thing yet, hmm?"

That snapped her eyes open and brought

her head back around in a hurry. Appalled, she stared at him.

"What are you talking about?" Conscious of the people all around her, she mouthed the words rather than spoke them.

His smile widened, turned mocking. "Forgot what I told you right before you took your nightie off for me?"

Charlie sucked in air. No, she hadn't forgotten. She remembered it as vividly as if the scene were branded into her memory cells.

He'd said, "You're going to hate me for this in the morning, you know," and then kissed her mindless. Right before she'd taken off her nightgown.

Oh, God, it wasn't a dream.

As that horrified realization slammed home, she sat bolt upright. It was only as she saw the satisfied gleam in his eyes that she realized she'd forgotten all about being dizzy and sick.

Her lips thinned. Her eyes narrowed.

"You okay?" Tony loomed over her. Charlie hadn't even realized that he was nearby. Garland's eyes darkened, but that was all she noticed about his reaction because she jerked her gaze away from him and looked up at Tony instead.

Focused on the real, live, good guy with

long-term potential versus the ghost of a murderous psychopath who just happened, through some strange cosmic alchemy that she was never going to understand, to turn her on to her back teeth.

At least the adrenaline rush from the shock of Garland's revelation had knocked out most of her physical symptoms. Was that what he had intended? Or had he, as usual, just wanted to be as annoying as possible?

"A little the worse for the heat, maybe," she said, prevaricating only slightly. Garland stood up to his full height beside her, looking at Tony as if he didn't like him very much. Charlie ignored him. Where Garland was concerned, she was a mess, and this was not the time or place to start sorting out anything to do with their hell-born relationship. Not quite ready to trust her legs yet, she kept her seat on the cooler as she spoke to Tony. "Listen, I think we really need to concentrate on why the perpetrator does what he does. The dance — he is most likely re-enacting something that actually occurred in his past, a real dance, a girl who rejected him. She would have been blond and pretty, a popular girl, and they both would have been teenagers. Bayley, the other girls, are substitutes for the original blond teenager who hurt him. He's abducting these girls to give himself a do-over, and when his victim doesn't behave according to the script in his head, he beats her because what she is doing spoils the fantasy. Eventually the fantasy is irretrievably destroyed and that's when he kills her."

Tony said, "Unless it's a copycat."

"If it's a copycat, and I believe it is, he's re-creating the pattern set by the original killer. The motivation that set off the murders would remain the same."

"So we'll find our unsub at one of these dances."

"So what are we going to do, stake out every single dance up and down the southern half of the Eastern Seaboard over the next few weeks?" Kaminsky's question dripped sarcasm. She had arrived in time to hear Charlie's assessment of the killer's motivation. "Do you know how many dances we're talking about? To begin with, we don't have the manpower."

"You need to go back and look at every bit of video footage you can find of any dances the three primary victims attended within a week of the attack on their families. The killer is there, interacting in some way with blond girls who fit the victim profile. He's here today, watching," Charlie said. "I'm sure of it."

"So you keep your ass with the group, Doc," Garland told her. "No more sitting on coolers off by your lonesome."

Charlie didn't even glance his way.

"We've been through the crowds," Kaminsky said. "If he's here, we're missing him."

"He's here," Charlie repeated with certainty.

"We need to cross-reference," Tony said. "Kaminsky, when we get back —"

"I'm on it," Kaminsky said before he could finish.

Crane joined them. "According to the victim's body temperature, the ME estimates time of death at around four a.m."

Charlie knew that after death the human body cooled by about one degree per hour. Of course, the heat of the sand would have complicated the calculation, but any competent ME would have taken that into account.

"She wasn't killed here, which means that after four a.m. the unsub transported the body here. Then he had to bury it without anyone seeing him. It would have taken him at least half an hour to dig that hole, and he would have done it while it was still dark," Tony said.

Kaminsky whipped out her iPhone and pressed a button. A moment later she had what she wanted. "The sun rose at five thirty-seven this morning." She looked at Tony. "Wherever he killed her had to have been within about a half an hour's drive of here."

"He not only had to bury the body before dawn, but he had to be near enough to get back here quickly when the body was discovered, without knowing precisely when that would be." Charlie's mind raced. "So he has some sort of a shelter within about half an hour's drive, and I'm guessing that's where he keeps the victims. Something in an RV park, maybe, or a campground. Something mobile."

"I'll have the local guys get a list of nearby facilities." Tony picked up his cell phone and started texting.

"You want my two cents, I'd say he's listening to a police radio or scanner," Garland said.

Charlie looked at him, momentarily surprised that he'd even felt motivated to contribute, much less that the contribution had been useful. Then she remembered that she was the only one who could see or hear him, dragged her eyes away, and repeated the observation to the others.

Kaminsky frowned at her. "You saying you think it's a cop?"

"Anybody can have a police scanner," Tony reminded them. He had finished with his text, and Charlie presumed that local FBI agents were now scrambling to identify any RV parks or campgrounds in the vicinity, and check them out.

"He's a narcissist. He's watching what we're doing right now. He's been following the investigation through the media. It makes sense that he'd have a police scanner. He shows up whenever the bodies are discovered, and that's how he knows." Charlie was thinking aloud. "And so far nobody has noticed him. He *could* be a cop. Or a reporter." She grimaced. "Or just an ambulance chaser. But whoever he is, he's here, and he blends in." Even as she spoke, she swept another look around. He *was* there, she could feel it, and yet she couldn't spot him.

The knowledge was both frustrating and terrifying.

"We're wasting time here. Let's get going." Tony held a hand down to Charlie. "Need some help?"

"He's here," she said one more time, scanning as much of the crowd as she could see. "Right here with us."

"Since we don't know who we're looking for, the best thing we can do is go back and compare today's video with video from the dances." The very reasonableness of Tony's voice told Charlie that he was feeling the frustration of it, too. "Whoever is in all those places makes our suspect hit parade."

It made sense, and Charlie knew it. Still, knowing the killer was there and not being able to identify him was a bitter pill that she was finding hard to swallow. Taking Tony's hand, she let him pull her to her feet, then smiled her thanks at him. All the while, she was supremely conscious of Garland's narrowed eyes on them. It was obvious he didn't much like what he was seeing. Charlie was mad at herself because she even noticed.

What do I care what he thinks anyway?

Answer: I don't. This is not a relationship, and he is not a man. And even if he were a man this wouldn't be a relationship.

They were moving away toward the parking lot when Charlie glanced around again and saw that the coroner's assistants were pushing the gurney with Bayley Evans' body on it toward the van. The procession was almost abreast of them. Nobody had yet covered the girl with a sheet.

Charlie knew this because she looked. It was automatic, instinctive, and a mistake. Her heart lurched. Her chest tightened and her throat ached.

"Jesus," Garland muttered. Charlie realized that he was beside her and staring at Bayley Evans' body, too. Serial killers did not have the right to look sickened at another serial killer's atrocity, she thought with a sudden burst of fury, and shot him a look of loathing.

"What?" He caught her look. It took him only a second to correctly interpret it. His face tightened. "You really think I'd do something like that to a woman?"

Charlie didn't answer. There were too many people around.

But if she had answered, the only thing she could have said was *Yes.*

Because there was no way she was foolish enough to let her heart override what she knew.

Sometime before they reached the SUV, she realized that Garland had disappeared.

On the way back to Kill Devil Hills, everybody was out of sorts and snappy, Charlie included. The local FBI called back: two camp-grounds and an RV park existed near Jockey's Ridge, but a search had yielded nothing suspicious. After that, nobody felt like eating; Crane ordered a pizza anyway. While he and Kaminsky went into the house to wait for the delivery person to arrive, Charlie reluctantly told Tony that she needed to go back to the Meads' for just a minute. It was after ten p.m., they were all exhausted, disheartened, and weighed down with failure and sorrow for Bayley Evans, but there was something she needed to do and she wasn't about to go out in the dark alone. Tony gave her a long look, but didn't ask questions, which was one of the things she truly liked about him. Instead, he escorted her over to the Meads' house.

This time, one of the two cops in the car out front had a key. She'd already told Tony that she needed to go upstairs alone, so he waited in the living room with the officers while she trudged up the stairs.

Now that there was no more need for Julie Mead to cling to earth, Charlie meant to help her go home.

However, when she reached the master bedroom, Julie Mead was not there. Charlie called her, softly, but got no answer. She also didn't feel the least bit sick to her stomach, which was what finally convinced her that the spirit was truly gone.

A glance in Trevor's bedroom told her that it was empty, too. What Garland had said he'd seen — Trevor's father coming for him — apparently was true.

Not that she didn't trust Garland's word, but for Trevor's sake she'd wanted to make sure.

I hope Bayley and her family are all together somewhere.

The deep sadness she felt for them was oppressive. Her heart ached. And the worst part about it was, this dubious gift she had been given hadn't changed a thing.

"So when were you planning to tell me that you've got some psychic ability?" As Tony escorted her back over the boardwalk between the two houses, he asked the question in such a casual tone, it took Charlie a second to process what he was saying.

Then she stopped dead, which meant he had to stop walking, too. He was beside her, and her hand was tucked companionably into his elbow. They were close enough so that when she looked sharply up at him, she should have been able to read his expression. But it was very dark, with the moon and stars almost completely obscured by a bank of heavy black clouds that had blown in over the last hour. The air smelled of rain to come, and the crash of the waves hitting the shore promised a storm.

She couldn't tell what he was thinking, because his face was deep in shadow.

But all of a sudden she knew where that

question had come from, and she pulled her hand free of his arm.

"You got that from the background check, right?" She couldn't believe she hadn't seen it earlier: of course that's why he'd never really questioned how she knew what she knew.

"Yes."

"Why didn't you ask me about it before?"

"I was waiting for you to tell me."

"What, that I see dead people?" Angry, she resumed walking toward the house.

He fell in beside her. "Do you?"

She jerked a look up at him. "Yes. Sometimes. Not that it ever does anybody any good."

He caught her arm, pulled her to a stop. "It's not your fault we weren't able to save Bayley Evans."

She gave a bitter little laugh. "Isn't it?"

"No."

Then, to Charlie's surprise, he bent his head and kissed her. It was a hard kiss, thorough, plenty of tongue. After the first moment of shock, she slid her hand behind his head and kissed him back. Her body reacted with a tingling warmth that told her there absolutely was promise in there somewhere.

What her body didn't do was melt or

burn. No fireworks went off against her closed lids. Her world did not rock. All her preconceptions about herself and men did not shatter.

But still, it was a very nice kiss.

When he lifted his head, though, Charlie was annoyed to discover she was feeling a tad cranky.

"So what was that about?" she asked, striving to keep the crankiness out of her tone.

She thought he was studying her face, but again, it was too dark to really be sure. "I wanted to get it out of the way."

Okay, cranky was definitely happening. Nothing she could do. "Oh, goody. I like your motivation. You want to tell me *why* you wanted to get it out of the way?" She pulled free and started walking again.

He laughed, and caught up. "You came to us on a temporary basis. I want to make it permanent."

Whatever she had been expecting, that was not it. "What?"

"I'm offering you a job. Come be a permanent part of our team. Between the psychological insights and the psychic stuff, you're unique. You'll give us a weapon in this war against the monsters out there that we've never had before."

Charlie frowned at him. "Which means you kissed me because . . . ?"

"I wanted to, and I don't kiss people I work with. If you accept the job, and I'm hoping you will, our relationship is strictly professional from here on out."

"That's certainly an incentive." She couldn't quite keep the tartness out of her voice.

He grinned. "Ouch." Then his tone turned serious. "This is life-and-death work we're doing, Charlie. You could be a vital part of it."

They had almost reached the house. Through the gentle veil of the screening on the porch, Charlie could see Kaminsky standing in the lighted doorway holding a pizza box. The red-shirted delivery guy was just leaving. She watched him walk around the side of the house until the RV blocked him from her view.

"You three are based out of Quantico, right? I'd have to relocate." Charlie thought of her house in the mountains.

"You'd probably find it more convenient."

"And I'd have to give up my research."

"On the upside, you'd help catch a lot of bad guys. Which would save a lot of lives."

That was something, she had to admit. "I have to think about it," she said, and he nodded.

They walked inside in time to hear Kaminsky say, "When a person dies, it's like they just drop their bodies. Then they step into a new one."

"When a person *dies,*" Crane replied, sounding like he was talking through his teeth and making Charlie think the discussion had been going on for some time, "they enter into eternal rest. Until Judgment Day."

"You are so —" Kaminsky began witheringly, only to break off as she spotted Charlie and Tony. *"Pizza,"* she said to them in a different, brighter tone.

Charlie shook her head. "Thanks, but I think I'll just go on up to bed."

Tony followed her to the foot of the stairs. "Let me know, okay?"

Looking past him to where Kaminsky and Crane were both regarding them with identical speculative looks, Charlie gave him a wry smile. "I will."

Then she went upstairs. As soon as she stepped through the door to her darkened apartment, she noticed two things: the TV was on, although she had left it turned off, and Garland was there, big as life and looking just as substantial, standing in the doorway between the living room and the bedroom. As she closed and locked the door behind her, he propped one broad shoulder against the wall and folded his arms over his chest.

From the straight set of his mouth and the glint in his eyes, Charlie realized that she was looking at one pissy ghost.

Chapter Twenty-Eight

Charlie's immediate thought was that Garland must have witnessed Tony's kiss, and not liked what he had seen. That straightened her spine and made her pissy, too. She didn't owe him any explanations, and he had absolutely no right to object to anything she chose to do.

No right to spy on her, either.

She wanted, badly, to blast him for it. What stopped her was the fact that she was not one hundred percent sure he had seen her kissing Tony, and that kissing in general was not a subject she wanted to discuss with him at the moment.

The knowledge that what had happened between them last night hadn't been a dream was still fresh enough to make her squirm.

"If you'll get out of my way, I'm going to bed" is what she said. Her tone was icy. She had a feeling her eyes were hostile, but it was dark except for the bluish light emanating from the TV, which meant he probably couldn't tell.

He straightened, and stepped out of the hallway into the living room so that she could walk past him.

She did, ignoring him ostentatiously. Of course he followed her.

She whipped around, pointed a finger at him. "Stop right there."

He stopped. He was still in the hall. She was at the threshold of the bedroom. The room behind her was as dark as a cave. Because of the light behind him, he was a tall, broad-shouldered, should-have-been-intimidating silhouette.

Only she wasn't intimidated one bit.

"For the rest of the time you're here, the bedroom is off-limits," she informed him tightly. "The bathroom, too. They're mine. You can use the living room."

"Ain't that a treat." His low voice had a growly quality. "You owe me some ju-ju, Doc."

She knew what he was talking about: something to keep him here.

"I don't owe you anything. I told you I'd try, and I did. If the sea salt didn't work, you're shit out of luck." Turning her back on him, she marched into the bedroom and turned on the bedside lamp. As soon as her eyes landed on the bed, still rumpled from the restless night she had passed, she realized that heading to the bedroom had probably been a mistake, because it instantly brought to mind last night's dream-that-wasn't.

"Does kissing somebody always make you this bitchy?"

She whipped around again, bristling with temper. He was standing inside her bedroom looking like he was spoiling for a fight. His eyes were narrowed, his face hard, and dark energy rolled off him in waves.

The problem with having this particular fight was that she wasn't completely sure which kiss he was referring to, the one she had shared with Tony or the one — all right, many — she had shared with him. Come to think of it, though, it didn't really matter. She didn't want to talk about any of them.

"Get out of my bedroom," she snapped. "Right now."

He smiled. It wasn't a nice smile. In fact, there was a time when she would have said it was downright dangerous.

Now it just made her mad.

"Make me," he said, and because she knew she couldn't, except by using the sage and the candle and she wasn't going to try that again even if she could get it set up and get him in position for it, which she knew wasn't going to happen ever again in this eternity, she picked up a pillow from her bed and heaved it at him.

The thing about it was she was a dead shot. She hit him smack in the chest. And it went right through him, to land on the floor behind him.

He gave her a taunting look. It made her so mad she threw the second pillow at him, with the same result.

He laughed. Then he said, very softly, "Maybe you ought to try calling *Tony* for help," and she knew he had indeed seen the kiss.

The look she shot him should have singed his eyeballs. "You have no business spying on me."

"I was keeping an eye on you. Because it doesn't suit my plans for you to get your pretty throat slit. Who knew you and your boyfriend would start going at it out there in the dark? Next time, give me a heads-up, and I'll make myself scarce."

"You won't be around next time. Because in about three days or less, you'll be gone. *Poof.* Bye-bye." She said that last with defiant relish and a little wave.

His eyes narrowed. His voice mocked.

"Didn't look like *Tony* turned you on all that much. Want me to give him some pointers?"

Charlie could feel her face starting to heat. "Go to hell," she snarled.

He smiled at her. "Not if I can help it."

Then he turned and walked out of the bedroom. Past fury, she hurled the last remaining pillow, a round decorative one, after him. It bounced off the hall wall.

From somewhere in the vicinity of the living room, he laughed.

Seething, Charlie took a shower and went to bed. The shower was an awkward affair, because the last thing she wanted was to be caught naked by him, and she certainly wouldn't put it past the rat bastard to pop up at the most embarrassing possible moment. She had to maneuver with towels, her robe, etc., so that she was nude for as brief a period as possible. Then she practically yanked a nightgown over her head and jumped into bed. In the end, of course, probably simply because she was prepared for him not to, he left her alone.

Turning off the lamp, she settled down onto the pillows she had been infuriatingly forced to retrieve and closed her eyes. Her emotions were in so much turmoil that she was afraid she would lie awake for hours. It didn't help that she could hear the TV, which since she now associated the sound with Garland meant it was impossible to banish him from the forefront of her mind.

If last night wasn't a dream, what was it?

She decided she didn't want to know. In fact, she was too tired to think about it. Just like she was too tired to think about Tony, or Bayley Evans, or ways to find the monster who had murdered those three girls. She was too tired to think, period.

She had barely closed her eyes when she fell fathoms deep asleep.

Her dreams were a jumble of terrifying images. Charlie found herself looking down at Bayley Evans' body on the gurney again, in all its horrific detail. Only, in her dream, the girl's eyes suddenly popped open and she started to scream, soundlessly because her vocal cords had been cut along with her throat.

No . . .

Charlie's own eyes popped open, to nothing but a whole lot of dark. She was, she discovered, as she lay there trying to make sense of where she was, gasping for breath and making soft whimpering sounds. Thrashing around in her bed in the FBI's rented beach house, mourning a dead girl. A dead girl she hadn't been able to save.

Dear God, I can't do this.

"You're safe, Doc. I'm right here." That voice, coming to her out of the dark, instantly shut her up. It froze her in place, widened her eyes, and then practically gave her whiplash as she snapped a look in the direction from which it had come.

Garland crouched by the side of the bed. She couldn't really see much more than his outline and the gleam of his eyes: it was too dark. But she knew without a doubt that it was him.

Her heart, which the dream had set pounding, slowed. Her too-fast breathing steadied. The tension in her muscles eased.

The ridiculous, horrible, impossible-to-process thing about it was, having him there actually made her feel safe.

His hand rested on the bed near her shoulder. She could see the dark shape of it against the white sheet. Just to make sure, just to test whether this was a dream or real or, third alternative, whatever the previous night had been, she put her hand on his.

It sank right through to the sheet, leaving her to experience no more of him than an electric tingle. No warm flesh or solid muscle and bone. Nothing substantial at all.

Her ghost remained a ghost.

He yanked his hand away.

"What was that?" He sounded wary.

"I'm awake, and this is real," Charlie said, although not with complete conviction.

"Yes to both."

Charlie rallied enough to frown at him. "So what are you doing in my bedroom? What part of *off-limits* didn't you get?"

"The noise you were making was interfering with my enjoyment of *Sports Center.* I came in to shut you up."

She was immediately self-conscious. "I was having a nightmare."

"I know. Just like you did last night. I came in to shut you up then, too."

Charlie sighed and bit. It was bugging her to death, and she had to know. What was more, he knew it. If this was reality and in this reality he was nothing more than magnetic energy to the touch, and if her dreams, where she could have imagined he was a living man, were hers alone, which meant that he shouldn't have had the first clue what went on in them, then what, exactly, had last night been? Embarrassing and infuriating and unsettling as having this conversation was sure to be, she needed to have it for her own peace of mind.

"So you want to explain last night to me?" If her question was slightly gruff, it was because she still really didn't want to go where this conversation would lead.

She could just barely see his slow, curling smile. "Short answer is, looks like I'm your dream man, Doc."

If hitting him with her pillow could do any good, she would have done it. As it was, she went with what was practically her only option: ignoring it. "I'm serious. What happened last night?"

His smile widened into a wicked grin. "Well, let's see: we danced, and we made out, and we got each other hot, and then you —"

"You know what I mean," she snapped, before he could get to the part where she had started stripping.

He said nothing for a moment, and she wasn't sure he was going to answer. Hitching herself up on the pillows, she folded her arms over her chest and glared at him.

"Garland. Stop being a jackass, and tell me how you ended up in my dream."

"Try calling me Michael," he suggested. "And I wouldn't say no to a *please*."

Remembering the circumstances under which she had called him by his first name made her heart beat faster. It was all she could do to keep her breathing from quickening.

She could feel him waiting.

"Michael." She said it reluctantly, and thought she saw a flicker of something in his eyes. Despite her best efforts, she felt her blood begin to heat. The next word was several degrees less difficult: "Please."

He smiled at her, slow and almost sweet. "Now, how hard was that?" He then eased into a sitting position on the floor beside the bed, with his back against the wall and an arm on his bent knee. Her eyes had adjusted enough to the gloom so that she could actually see him a little now. They were at right angles to each other, close enough that she caught what looked like a quick, wry smile. "Since in my present state climbing into bed with you and making us both feel real good isn't looking like it's an option, I guess talking's all there is to do." Charlie was just drawing a breath at the image this planted in her brain when he added, "Like I said, you had a nightmare last night. I got through your salt barrier — went right out through the ceiling — and came in to see what was up. There was this girl in your room. Dead girl — see, I recognize the type right off now." Humor just touched his voice. "You were asleep, but you seemed real agitated, tossing and turning and moaning. I was just coming around the corner of the bed, trying to get between you and the girl in case she had bad intentions or something, when she saw me and started to turn away. Then — here's the good part, Doc — you rose right up and tried to go after her. Not your body — it stayed where it was, in this bed. But *you.* Your spirit, I guess, if that's what you want to call it. You went flying after that girl, who vanished right out through the wall. And if I hadn't caught you around the waist and hung on, you would have gone after her. But I did catch you, and it was the damnedest thing. We were both the same, both as solid and alive as you are now and I used to be. I could hold you, Doc, and feel you. It surprised the hell out of me, let me tell you. So I grabbed on tight, and then we got whisked back to that dance where we were earlier, and I figured that must be where you were in your dream. Only me grabbing on to you took me with you." His brow furrowed. "You got any explanation for any of that?"

Charlie's eyes had widened as she listened. Everything he had said was a revelation, and while her mind pondered the ramifications she answered his question almost absently. "It had to be a form of astral projection. I don't think I've ever done it before. In fact,

I didn't know I *could* do it."

"You lost me, Doc."

"Many people believe the soul can leave the body for brief periods while the body is still alive, especially while sleeping or under conditions of extreme emotion or duress. There's actually a lot of literature backing it up."

"Ye-ah." Obviously dubious, he drew the word out. "So your soul and my soul met in the sky."

His tone earned him a sharp look. "I don't know why you sound so skeptical. You're the one who's dead and still walking and talking and causing problems."

His grimace conceded the point. " 'There are more things in heaven and earth, Horatio, than are dreamt of in your philosophy,' huh?"

She blinked at him, genuinely surprised. "That's Shakespeare."

"Believe it or not, I know that. I can read, Doc. Like I said, there wasn't a whole lot to do in prison."

At another time she might have marveled a little more, but just then her thoughts were finally coalescing to pinpoint the most important part of what he'd told her.

"The girl — the one you said you saw — what did she look like?"

"Blond. Pretty. A kid — maybe seventeen, eighteen. In a puffy pink dress."

Holly.

There was no one else it could have been.

Charlie's heart started to pound.

"You actually saw her?"

"Clear as I'm seeing you now. She was coming toward you, saying something, but when she saw me she vamoosed."

Charlie sucked in air. "What did she say?"

He shook his head. "I didn't quite catch it all. Something about a bag. 'It's in the bag,' maybe, or 'where's my bag,' or something like that. Like I said, when she saw me she shut up and got out of here."

Charlie was desperately turning the words over in her mind. Although she had dreamed of Holly a few times, she had not actually had a visitation from her since right around the time of her death. Which made sense, because she only saw the *recently* violently departed. Had Holly been trying to get in touch with her all this time, to tell her something? Or had this new string of deaths somehow brought Holly to her again? The only explanation Charlie could come up with for either was that Holly must have a message for her.

But what?

"Are you sure that's all she said?" Charlie

asked anxiously.

"That's all I heard. The only part I got real clearly was *bag.* The rest could have gone a lot of ways."

"Oh, my God, you can see her." As that part finally sank in, Charlie regarded him with sudden excitement. "If she comes again, you can talk to her. Ask her what she wants."

"You know, I've got just about zero hankering to play telephone with stray spooks."

"But you can talk to her. I can't." Frantic to get him to do what she wanted, she tried to think of a way to persuade him; finally, she hit on a possiblity and took a deep breath. "There's one more thing I can try to keep you here. I'll do it, if you'll help me."

He looked at her without speaking for a moment. Then he nodded, a barely perceptible inclination of his head. "Now you're talking my lingo."

"If she comes back — her name is Holly — if she comes back, ask her what she wants. Tell her you'll take a message to me. Tell her —"

"Whoa. Slow down. Suppose you tell me who she is first."

Charlie looked at him, hesitating. She never willingly talked about that night to anyone — even unwillingly, she hadn't so much as mentioned it for years. Forgetting it had been one of the goals of her life. But if Garland was to understand how important his questioning Holly was, then he needed to know who she was, and what had happened to her.

So she told him. And found, when she had finished, that she was glad he knew. It was almost as if a weight she had not realized she was carrying around with her had eased. As if in the telling she had shifted some of the burden of it onto his broad shoulders.

For a moment he just sat there looking at her. Finally he spoke.

"You're something, Doc, you know that? That's the kind of experience that would turn most people into basket cases, but you — look at you. Dr. Charlotte Stone. Right after they first took me in to see you, and I discovered to my amazement that you were hot, I looked up all your degrees and credentials just to make sure I was getting quality service. I got to tell you, they impressed the hell out of me. Now they impress me even more. You took what happened and used it to make something of yourself. You should be proud," he said, sounding uncharacteristically serious.

His words made what almost felt like a

lump rise up in her throat. Charlie realized that this was the first time anyone had ever recognized and acknowledged what she had done, and for some idiotic, ridiculous reason it touched her to the core. Worn out and depleted from reliving those long-ago events and emotions, not wanting to speak until she was sure her voice wouldn't sound croaky, she lay back limply against the pillows without replying, her eyes on him. Her breathing was slightly uneven, but she believed it was the only outward sign of distress she showed. However, he — she realized that although he had stayed perfectly still throughout her pitiful little recital, his face had gone tight and his shoulders were tense and his hands had clenched into fists by the time she had finished. The anger and pain and protectiveness he felt on her behalf were there in his expression, in his body language. She could read it plainly. It comforted her to a surprising degree — more than anything had comforted her in a long time.

"You're not sitting over there crying on me, are you, Doc?" He peered at her, frowning.

That banished the maudlins in a hurry.

"No, I certainly am not." She summoned the strength to refute it strongly. One thing she prided herself on was, she never cried. Not once since those terrible days fifteen years ago. And she had absolutely no intention of starting now, with him.

"Good, because if you are, with me like this there isn't a damned thing I can do about it."

"Of course I'm not crying. I never cry. And if I were, and you were alive, just what do you think you could do about it anyway?" She adopted a slightly astringent tone, because allowing herself to be moved by him was a dangerous mistake, as she absolutely knew, and the last thing she wanted was for him to realize how he had affected her. "Pat me on the back a couple of times and say, *There, there, don't cry?*"

"I'd make you feel better."

"Oh? How?"

"If I were myself again, I'd crawl up there in bed with you and fuck all the bad memories right out of your head. Then I'd fuck you to sleep. I'd fuck you when you woke up in the morning, too."

At that, Charlie's breathing suspended. Her heart drummed. Her senses caught fire. Her whole body responded with a fierceness that caught her by surprise. Their eyes connected through the darkness, and there was no mistaking the heat in his.

This is bad. She wanted him to do what he had described so intensely that she was shaky with it. The sad truth was, the only thing stopping her from going into his arms and doing anything he asked was that sex with him simply wasn't possible.

But just the thought of it made her dizzy and hot and so aroused she burned for him. Which was stupid. And self-destructive. And stupid all over again. Because not only was sex with Garland something she was never going to have, it was something she never *should* have. Never should *want.*

Her chin went up. "What makes you think I'd let you?"

A smile just touched his mouth. "Oh, you'd let me, Doc. We both know that."

Charlie could feel her bones melting. For a moment she was mute, so turned on and rattled because of it, she could think of nothing to say. Because the truth was — and he knew it, too — he was right.

Some long-buried instinct for self-preservation kept her from admitting it.

"I guess we'll never know, will we?" She strove to inject some crispness into her tone — and even from her own perspective, failed miserably.

"I guess we won't, at least not unless you want to try the astral thing again."

She shook her head. The regret and sense of loss she felt at acknowledging that a brief, hot affair with her impossible ghost was something that was just not going to happen was way more intense than it should have been, she realized. "It's not something I can do intentionally. I wouldn't know where to begin."

"Yeah." He got to his feet, and for the briefest of moments stood looking down at her. Whatever he was thinking, his face was shrouded enough in shadow that she couldn't tell. But his mouth thinned out and his jaw hardened, and when he spoke again it was in a totally different tone. "What about that ju-ju, Doc?"

That sounded more like him.

"Meet me in the kitchen," she told him. She really didn't want to get out of bed and have him ogling her in her nightgown, which was just as feminine and skimpy as the one she'd taken off for him the previous night, because those were pretty much the only kind of nightgowns she owned.

If he somehow managed to stick around for more than the next few days, she was investing in heavy flannel.

He nodded, and headed for the door.

Charlie rose, snatched up her robe, put it on, and belted it tightly, then followed him.

The ingredients she found in the cabinets; the delivery system, under the sink.

The mixture of honey and oil she sprayed him with to ground him to the earth was an old Middle Eastern trick she had read about but never before had occasion to use. When he saw her pouring it into a plant mister and found out what she meant to do, his skepticism abounded — but as she pointed out, beggars couldn't be choosers. She made him stand fully clothed in the shower for it, not wanting to get the gooey mixture on anything in the apartment. Since he wasn't actually solid no matter how solid he looked, the spray passed right through him, coating the shower walls and floor but leaving him untouched. When it was done, she ordered him out and turned on the shower to clean up the mess. Then she went to bed.

He went with her.

This time, instead of sitting on the floor, he took the other side of the bed. As she burrowed under the covers, ostentatiously turning her back to him, she did her level best not to think about his big body stretched out beside her, except on top of the bedspread. His purpose, of course, was to keep a watch out for Holly.

Hers was to sleep. Not that she expected to, with him taking up way more than his fair share of the bed.

But by then it was close to four a.m. — and despite everything, she was so exhausted that sleep she did, almost as soon as her head hit the pillow.

If she had any dreams, she didn't remember them. According to Garland, she didn't do anything more exciting than switch positions once or twice. And Holly didn't show.

But Charlie did wake up knowing what Holly had meant.

Chapter Twenty-Nine

By early afternoon of the next day, Charlie was back in her own house in Big Stone Gap. Situated a little way down the mountain from the prison on the top of the ridge, Big Stone Gap was a coal mining town of about five thousand residents that had been devastated by a rash of recent layoffs from the coal company that, along with the prison, was the area's primary employer. Despite the hard times, Big Stone Gap was as friendly as the prison was forbidding, and she loved it. Her house, which she rented from her next-door neighbors, was a classic two-story white clapboard farmhouse with an old-fashioned front porch and lots of gingerbread trim. It sat on a quiet street near the edge of town, with the wooded mountainside sloping up behind it and an acre backyard complete with a sunflower patch that was a constant draw for the aforesaid neighbor's chickens. Not that

Charlie minded, really. She had spent many an early morning before heading in to work sipping coffee at her kitchen table at the back of the house and watching through the window as the birds scratched around in her flowers for seeds and bugs. Watching them was both calming and amusing.

"Tell me this hasn't been a total waste of time." Kaminsky gave Charlie a disgusted look as Charlie sorted through the items she had laid out on the kitchen table one more time. At Kaminsky's suggestion — Charlie was so focused on the need to find whatever it was that Holly had been referring to that she wouldn't have thought of it — Charlie was wearing rubber gloves, so as not to taint the items just in case one of them should prove to be important. Dressed in her usual black pants and sleeveless blouse — today's was a soft mint green — Charlie was at least comfortable. While Kaminsky in her power suit — today's was black — and sky-high heels looked hot, cross, and way too sophisticated for the country-style kitchen. On Tony's directive, Kaminsky had accompanied her on the short flight back to Big Stone Gap to recover whatever item significant to the investigation might be found in "the bag." Feeling her time could be better spent in other ways, Kaminsky wasn't too happy about it.

"No more so than following any other lead," Charlie replied, frowning as she touched each item in turn. She had been sure that "the bag" Holly had been referring to could only have been the sealed plastic bag full of Charlie's belongings that had been returned to her by the hospital, where she had stayed after Holly's murder. But in going through it, Charlie was coming up empty-handed. A brown fluffy teddy bear the hospital had given her; a manila envelope stuffed with get-well cards, all of which she had looked over and none of which seemed to contain a clue; a never-opened dental care kit containing a new toothbrush and travel-sized toothpaste wrapped in plastic; a tube of chapstick; a bottle of pale pink nail polish; a hairbrush; and a scrunchie offered not the slightest insight into the murders, as far as she could tell. Some of her clothes were there, too. Just looking at the yellow T-shirt and the jeans and sandals, the pretty flowered bra and pink bikini panties, made her skin crawl.

They were the clothes she had been wearing the night the Palmers had been murdered. Although the hospital had given her the bag about ten days later, she had never once opened it. She had not looked at those clothes from that day to this.

Instead of getting sick every time she looked at them, she forced herself to ask, *What am I missing here?*

Something had to be of significance, but she had no idea what it was. However, since this was the only bag she possessed that had any connection at all to the murders, this almost certainly had to be the bag Holly had been talking about — assuming that Garland had correctly reported what Holly had said. Having had no permanent home in the last fifteen years, Charlie had carted the bag around with her, stuffed into a blue steamer trunk with a few other longtime possessions that she didn't know what to do with but couldn't quite bear to dispose of.

She would have thrown the bag out long ago, except she'd always felt it was kind of a last connection with Holly. A way of not letting her friend go.

Apparently Holly had known.

"The only thing to do is pack these things up and take them back with us. Maybe there's microscopic blood splatter on the clothes or something," Kaminsky said impatiently. "Turn the stuff over to the lab, and let them sort it out."

Since Charlie couldn't think of a better

idea, she shrugged and started to put everything back into the bag. The only saving grace was, she didn't have to actually touch them. The gloves were useful for more than avoiding fingerprints.

When the items were packed up again and thus safely out of sight, Charlie felt better. Even though she hadn't touched anything, after she stripped off the rubber gloves she washed her hands in the kitchen sink. And that made her feel better, too.

"Nice house, Doc."

Charlie didn't even jump as Garland strolled into her kitchen. Since replying was out of the question, she flicked him a look and kept on with what she was doing, finishing up by drying her hands on the nearby paper towels. She hadn't realized he was with them, hadn't set eyes on him since she'd woken up to find him in the living room and he'd informed her that his Holly-watching had been a waste of time. He'd been terse and unsmiling, but she'd been in such a hurry to get downstairs to inform Tony that she needed to make a quick trip back home, she had barely noticed. She didn't know why she was surprised to see him now, but she was. She was also, she was slightly chagrined to discover, glad.

"Is there anything else you want to bring?

I'll go grab it." Kaminsky had made no secret of the fact that she was chomping at the bit to get back to the investigation. Imagining the other woman's reaction if she had any inkling that the hot blond naked guy she'd been chasing the other night was right there in the kitchen with them, albeit fully clothed, Charlie smiled. Trying not to watch as Garland took in the view out the wide kitchen window, Charlie said, "I already put everything else I need in a carry-on in the hall."

"Everything else" being a few extra clothes and some toiletries.

"So are we ready?"

"Let me do a quick walk-through, and then yes."

Kaminsky stayed in the kitchen as Charlie checked her spotless living and dining rooms, then went upstairs to her bedroom to look rather wistfully around. *I miss this place.* Like the rest of the house, her bedroom was very simply decorated, with polished wood floors and a lot of neutral colors, which she found peaceful. The centerpiece of the room was a big brass bed dressed in layers of white. A lot of light poured through two tall windows that looked out onto the backyard and the mountain. A fireplace with a painting of a waterfall in a woody glen hanging above it was positioned between the windows. The adjoining bathroom was made special by the big, claw-footed tub that took pride of place. Charlie was normally a shower person, but she loved taking a bath in that tub.

The truth was, she loved the house. She'd selected the furniture and decorated it herself, and it was the closest thing to a real home she'd ever had.

If I accept Tony's offer, I'll have to leave it.

Silly to let that hold weight with her, she thought. It was only a temporary home, after all. Just for as long as her work at the Ridge lasted, which once she got back shouldn't be much more than another eighteen months or so. Then she would be moving on again, in the same way that she'd been moving on for her entire life.

"So this is home, hmm?" Garland looked up from what seemed to be a concentrated study of her bed as she walked out of the bathroom, to find him standing in her bedroom doorway. "I always used to try to imagine what kind of place you lived in."

"Apparently you used to imagine a whole lot of things." Her reply, no less tart for being said under her breath, emerged before she could stop it.

No surprise: he grinned. "I did."

She shot him a glance as she crossed to her dresser to retrieve a watch she'd left on it. "Have you been with us the entire time?"

He shook his head. "I figured you were safe enough on the plane. Then I heard the sound of running water, and here I am."

Strapping the watch onto her wrist, she frowned at him. "Running water?"

"I've discovered that it yanks my rubber band, at least when you're around it. Combine you with an open faucet, and if I'm off exploring, I get pulled back to wherever you are real quick."

"You go exploring?"

He nodded. "Spookville's an interesting place." She got the impression from the look on his face he didn't much want to talk about it. That impression intensified when he changed the subject by asking, "Find what you came here after?"

She shrugged. "I found the bag I think Holly was talking about. So far, though, I'm not seeing its connection to the case."

He was looking at a photograph of her and her mother on a small chest beside the door. "You got family, friends, here in town?"

Deciding to shelve the "exploring" conversation she was dying to have for another day, when they had more time, Charlie walked toward him. "Some friends. That picture you're looking at is of me with my mother. She's my only real family. She lives in Wilmington with her third husband. Would you mind moving? I need to get back downstairs."

He obligingly stepped out of the doorway. "Your dad alive?"

Charlie snorted and shrugged as she walked past him into the hall. "Last I heard. I haven't seen him since I was seven."

"Brothers? Sisters?" He followed her.

"A couple of half siblings from my father, possibly. It's only a rumor, and if they exist I've never met them." She stopped on the upstairs landing to give him a quelling look. "Is there a reason you want to know?"

"I'm interested."

Down below, Kaminsky stepped into the entry hall, catching Charlie's eye, but thankfully not yet looking up herself.

"Would you go away? I can't talk to you now," she hissed at Garland. Then Kaminsky turned and spotted her on the landing and Charlie headed down the stairs.

Kaminsky frowned. "Were you talking to somebody up there?"

"Myself," Charlie replied as she reached the downstairs hall, relieved to discover that Garland had apparently acceded to her request and vanished. For an instant she wondered if Kaminsky, like Tony, knew about her "psychic abilities," but she didn't think so. Tony struck her as the type to keep what he had learned as the result of a background investigation private — and anyway, she was pretty sure Kaminsky wouldn't be able to restrain herself if she had access to a gold mine of potential digs like that. "It's a bad habit. Are you ready to go?"

"One hundred percent," Kaminsky replied with feeling. Moments later, Kaminsky was heading down the short flight of wooden steps at the front of the house. Behind her, wheeling the carry-on, holding the plastic bag she'd come all this way to fetch, Charlie was just stepping through the front door when Kaminsky appeared to miss a step and went sprawling into the grass.

"Are you hurt?" Charlie rushed to her side. Kaminsky was already sitting up by the time Charlie reached her. Fortunately, she'd missed the paving stones that led from the steps to the gravel driveway, which was where the car that had been waiting for them at Lonesome Pine Airport when they arrived two hours ago was currently parked.

"Damn it, I broke my heel." Apparently otherwise unharmed, Kaminsky pulled the damaged black stiletto, which hung precariously from her toes, the rest of the way off. Its narrow four-inch heel was, indeed, broken off at the sole. She glared first at the ruined shoe, then at Charlie. "Your stupid steps have a crack in the middle of them."

As each of the steps was made from two boards nailed to a trio of two-by-fours and painted, they did indeed have, by design, an inch or so space running down the middle.

"They're supposed to. If you didn't wear such ridiculously high heels, the 'stupid steps' wouldn't have tripped you," Charlie retorted as she helped Kaminsky to her feet.

"If you were five foot two, you'd wear ridiculously high heels, too. You know how hard it is to be taken seriously in a job like mine when you're short and curvy?" Kaminsky snapped at her.

Suddenly the other woman's shoes made sense. Looking at the ruined shoe dangling from Kaminsky's hand, Charlie could relate. She'd spent most of her working life in a male-dominated world, too.

"Really hard, I imagine." Charlie's reply held an undertone of fellow-feeling. "I always wear long pants and sensible shoes for the same reason."

"Yeah, I noticed the black pants and low-heeled pumps. It's your uniform, isn't it? Just like my suits and heels." Kaminsky's eyes had a rueful cast as they met Charlie's. "Sucks, doesn't it? You think Bartoli or Crane — or any guy, for that matter — ever has to worry about what they need to wear in order to be taken seriously?"

Charlie had to smile at the very idea of it even as she shook her head. "No. Listen, I have some shoes you can borrow."

"I wear a size five." Kaminsky was looking skeptically at Charlie's feet, which were long, narrow size eights.

"Flip-flops," Charlie specified. Kaminsky grimaced, but nodded. Charlie went in to fetch them and returned to find Kaminsky sitting on the steps, both shoes off and her bare toes wriggling in the grass. "Here." She handed over the shoes, then as Kaminsky slipped them on turned back to lock the door.

"At least now my feet are comfortable," Kaminsky said as they headed for the car. Charlie laughed, and Kaminsky looked over her shoulder at her. "So are you going to accept Bartoli's offer?"

Charlie glanced at Kaminsky in surprise as they got into the car. With Kaminsky behind the wheel, they reversed out of the driveway and headed through the relatively affluent residential area toward the single, two-lane road that led down the mountain.

"He told you about that?" Charlie asked.

"He got Crane's and my opinion. We're a team. Things like this, we'll discuss. For the record, I was opposed."

"Thanks." Charlie's voice was dry. "Care to tell me why?"

Already they were in the central business district, which consisted of maybe a dozen shabby brick buildings, which included a bank, a courthouse, a hardware store, and a couple of restaurants. Towering above them on the top of the ridge, the prison looked like a gray stone fortress. More mountains stretched away into the distance, as far as the eye could see, some so tall they were obscured by the gray rain-clouds that were currently starting to blow in from the east. It had been raining a little when they'd left Kill Devil Hills that morning, and it looked like the weather was following them, although it hadn't quite caught up yet.

"That whole Tony and Charlie thing you two have going on? It's divisive on a team like ours."

"Wait a minute. First of all, there's absolutely nothing except for professional respect between Tony" — Charlie refused to signify guilt by reverting to calling him *Bartoli* simply because Kaminsky was making her feel self-conscious — "and me. And second, what about you and Crane?"

"There's nothing between Crane and me. *Nothing.*"

Charlie was just opening her mouth to point out the various reasons nobody with half a brain could ever be expected to believe *that* when something unexpected caught her eye.

The First Baptist Church was a small, white-painted brick building with one highly prized stained-glass window and a steeple. It was so old the masonry around the bricks was crumbling, and the steeple listed just a little to the left. Charlie was familiar with it, because her next-door neighbor attended that church and had brought her along to a couple of potlucks. A small graveyard off to the side served as a final resting place for a number of the town's citizens. An even smaller section of that graveyard had been reserved for Wallens Ridge inmates who had no family to claim them and, in death, nowhere to go.

The church was situated on a corner of the intersection where Kaminsky had just slowed to turn left.

"Stop the car." Charlie was already fumbling at the door handle. Kaminsky, with a startled glance at her, hit the brakes.

Charlie was out of the car before it had

stopped shuddering. Heart in her throat, she hurried over to a single, freshly dug grave in the inmate section.

A simple white wooden cross had been stuck in the ground at its head.

M. A. Garland had been painted on it in crude black letters, along with *RIP* and the date.

Chapter Thirty

A coal truck rattled up behind the car. Its determined honking forced Kaminsky to drive on through the intersection.

"I'll circle the block," she yelled out the window, but Charlie barely heard her.

The grave was mounded dirt, ugly and raw. No attempt had been made to smooth it out or cover it with sod or improve its appearance in any way. There was not a flower in sight.

Charlie's heart lurched. Her stomach knotted. Her chest felt so tight she could hardly catch her breath.

Garland's human remains lay six feet down, almost certainly in the cheapest pine coffin the local undertaker could provide.

And no one cared.

Had there been a funeral service? A religious ceremony? Had he been buried in the bloody prison jumpsuit? Probably, because if he was buried here, in this pariah's grave, no one would have cared enough to provide him with something as dignified as a suit.

Charlie felt as if she were suffocating.

A hedge of six-foot-tall viburnum bushes edged the far side of the little cemetery. Charlie walked jerkily toward them, and began breaking cluster after cluster of the rhododendron-like white flowers from their woody stalks. The sweet smell of the plant hung like perfume in the humid air. When her arms were full, she turned back toward the grave.

Garland was standing there, looking down at his own grave.

Charlie's step faltered. Her heart turned over. Her throat ached so that she didn't think she could speak.

Steadying herself, she walked to the grave, bent, and lay the flowers at the foot of the small white cross.

When she straightened, he was looking at her instead of the raw mound.

"Crying for me, Doc?"

That was the first time she realized tears were running down her face.

What could she say? There was no denying it. She wasn't even sure she wanted to.

"Yes." Defiantly dashing at the wetness with her fingers, she met his gaze. His eyes were very blue, very intent on her face.

There was nothing she could do to stop the gushing tears, or the quivering of her lips. It was ridiculous to feel so shattered. She knew it, and felt shattered anyway. She had known he was dead, had seen him die, and was staring right at his hale-and-hearty-looking ghost.

But she couldn't help it. The grave seemed so lonely. So forlorn.

Unloved.

She sniffled. Then her breath caught on a sob. Finally she did the only thing she could, and gave up. Sinking to her knees because her perfidious legs would no longer support her, she covered her face with her hands and cried.

"I'm right here, you know." He was crouching beside her now. Charlie would have turned into his arms except, oh, wait, that wasn't an option. "There you go with that soft heart of yours again. I'm not worth a single one of your tears."

That was almost certainly true, and it didn't make an iota of difference.

She lifted her head to glare at him. His face was close, bent toward hers. His eyes were dark with concern.

"You think I don't know that?" she asked him fiercely, then despite her best efforts sobbed again, felt more tears gushing, and dropped her face to her hands.

"You're breaking my heart here." His voice was low and rough. "Darlin', please don't cry."

Charlie fought for control, but couldn't seem to stem the tears even when she heard, rather than saw, Kaminsky slap-slapping through the grass toward her.

She looked up, met Garland's eyes, registered the pain for her in them, then glanced around just to verify that the person coming up on them was indeed Kaminsky. When she looked back, Garland was gone.

"What the hell?" Kaminsky stopped beside her, looking from her to the grave. "This somebody you know?"

"Yes, of course." Charlie made a mighty effort. Her pride was at stake. She sucked in air, wiped her cheeks with her fingers, and forced herself to stand up.

"You're a mess," Kaminsky said with more honesty than tact as she stared into Charlie's face. "Somebody close?"

"Just somebody I knew." Moving with an effort, Charlie deliberately turned away from the grave and started walking toward the car. Weeping like a fool did no one any good, Garland least of all. Kaminsky fell in beside her. "It was a shock, is all."

Kaminsky responded, but Charlie was

never sure what she said. They got back in the car, and drove away. By the time they reached the airport and took off for Kill Devil Hills, it was raining. It was raining when they landed, too, big fat drops of water exploding all over them as they ran for the waiting car, but they made it back to the beach house before the worst of the storm broke.

And in all that time, the only thing Charlie could really focus on was trying not to think about that lonely grave turning to mud in the rain.

Central Command was still surrounded with cars and buzzing with activity, although it was after nine p.m. and rain was pouring down. As tired as Charlie was, as much as she wanted to call it a night, she knew there was too much at stake and no time to waste. If there was one sure thing, it was that unless he was stopped, the killer would strike again, soon. So she forced herself to get a grip, and walked into the RV with Kaminsky, both of them shaking off water droplets and shivering as the air-conditioning hit them, to find that the place was hopping. Tony and Crane were in the War Room, with Crane sitting in Kaminsky's chair and Tony standing behind him. They were both focused on whatever was being displayed on the computer monitor. Charlie vaguely remembered Kaminsky calling Tony from the car to tell him they were back, and now as they entered both men looked at them without surprise.

"Any problems?" Tony asked, peering closely at Charlie as she stopped beside him. She had washed her face on the plane, and renewed her makeup, and in general made sure no trace of her tears remained visible. But still, to judge from the way Tony was looking at her, and then, questioningly, at Kaminsky, something about her expression must still be a little off.

Okay, so maybe I don't have such a good poker face, Charlie thought wryly, shaking her head at Tony while waiting with resignation for Kaminsky to rat her out.

But Kaminsky didn't say anything. Hoping to ward off any revelations, Charlie stepped into the breach.

"I'm almost positive there's something in this bag that's important to the investigation," Charlie said. Having with Kaminsky's help wrapped it in several layers of garbage bags earlier to protect it from the rain, Charlie handed the swaddled shopping bag to Tony. "I don't know what it is, though."

"We're thinking maybe microscopic blood splatter on the clothes," Kaminsky added.

The look she flicked Charlie, combined with the fact that she had passed up the chance to tattle to Tony, made Charlie feel that Kaminsky was going to keep quiet about her meltdown in the cemetery. It was a woman-to-woman thing, a solidarity that was unexpected. Charlie recognized and appreciated it for what it was, and acknowledged it with a barely perceptible nod of thanks at Kaminsky. "Maybe it's something from the unsub. Maybe he cut himself. Or . . . who knows? Probably everything in there ought to be gone over with a fine-tooth comb in the lab."

Tony agreed, and disappeared with the bag. Kaminsky looked at Crane.

"So, did I miss anything?"

"Lots of stuff. You wearing flip-flops?" He frowned as he stared at Kaminsky's feet. They looked small, pale, and a little plump in Charlie's too-large flip-flops. Kaminsky had a nice pedicure, though.

"I broke a heel. These belong to Dr. Stone."

Charlie sighed. She'd had a long day, she'd disgraced herself by crying like a little girl, she was damp and hungry and heartsick on so many levels she couldn't even bring herself to try to count them all, and she was, at least for the moment, tired of being Dr. Stone.

"You know, you guys can call me *Charlie.*"

Kaminsky shot her a look. Forget solidarity. The attitude was back. "No, we can't."

Frowning, Charlie reflected attitude right back at her. "Why not?"

" 'Cause then you'll call me *Lena,* and him *Buzz,* and since you and Bartoli already have the Tony and Charlie thing going on, we'll all be just too tight for words, and it will be unprofessional."

"You know, I've been thinking for a while that the way you call me *Crane* and I call you *Kaminsky* is idiotic," Crane said before Charlie could reply. "I've known you since you had braces. Lena."

"And I've known you since you first started chasing after my sister, *Crane.* Which is at least one really good reason why neither one of us wants to go there."

"Oh, for God's sake. I —"

Crane broke off as Tony walked back into the room.

"Taylor's running that bag over to the lab. If there's anything useful in it, they'll find it." Tony must have felt a charge in the atmosphere, because he looked from Crane to Kaminsky to Charlie with a frown. "Something up?"

"No," Kaminsky said. "Crane was just getting ready to show us something on the computer."

Crane's face darkened, but he swung around to face the monitor. "This." He tapped it.

Tony shot Charlie a look. She shrugged, and then as Kaminsky leaned forward to look at the screen and ask, "What is it?" Charlie focused on it as well.

"All three primary victims attended a dance or a concert where there was dancing within a week of their deaths, just as *Charlie* predicted." Crane's shot across Kaminsky's bow did not go unnoticed by Tony, who looked at Charlie with raised brows. Behind the others' backs, she shook her head at him: *Don't ask.* "This is all the video footage we've been able to obtain from those dances. Right now I'm cross-checking to see who turns up in all three places."

"You get any hits, *Crane?*" Kaminsky was dead tired, Charlie knew, but the way she said his name had real bite.

"So far, we've got seventeen males who were at all three dances." Crane tapped a button and the screen filled with rows of tiny faces that looked like they had been culled from driver's licenses. "Two of the band members, eight members of the security staff — who work for a company called Frigate Protection Services — three members of the audience, the lighting guy, the sound guy, a waiter, and a bartender. We're running checks on all of them as we speak, but we're concentrating especially on the security staff."

"Why?" Kaminsky asked.

"Show them," Tony directed. Crane did something with the mouse that caused the faces to disappear from the computer and a picture of a black, short-sleeved uniform to appear on the screen instead.

"Zoom in," Tony said. Crane did, until the uniform's breast pocket filled the screen.

Charlie caught her breath.

Embroidered on it in bright yellow thread was a logo: a bird in flight above the company name.

"It's a frigate bird," Tony said with satisfaction. "I don't know for sure yet, but I'd say there's a good possibility that the logo is on other items of clothing, too, like maybe a watch cap."

"Oh, my God." That was the best news Charlie had had for a while. "Did you try matching the men against the physical description and other parameters?"

"Working on it," Crane said.

"We're going to get him." Tony's smile was

grim. "Hopefully before he can hurt anybody else."

"Have you had a chance to cross-check these guys against the video that was shot at Jockey's Ridge?" Charlie felt a shot of excitement. She *knew* the killer had been there, as surely as she knew anything.

"I've been over all the Jockey's Ridge video, and I've run it through the facial recognition software," Crane said. "None of them turn up."

Charlie gave a quick frown. "Let me see."

Tony intervened. "Tomorrow. I'm pulling the plug on you and Kaminsky for tonight."

"What about me?" Crane groaned.

"Not you. You're not done with the license plate checks."

Kaminsky straightened and looked first at Tony, then at Charlie, to whom her subsequent remark was addressed. "Doesn't sending the women off to bed while the men stay and work strike you as being just a little bit sexist?"

"A little bit," Charlie agreed.

"Fine." Tony threw up his hands. "You two want to stick around and help Crane? Have at it."

The license plate checks turned up nothing that even smacked of being a smoking gun, and by the time they were finished with them, it was nearly eleven. Charlie, for one, was drooping with fatigue. The rain had turned into a full-blown thunderstorm as she, Kaminsky, and Crane — Tony had headed off to confer with Haney about something — dashed for the house, garbage bags held over their heads. Damp and exhausted, Charlie left Kaminsky and Crane to bicker in private as soon as they were inside, eager to get upstairs, shower, and fall into bed. But as she reached the door to her rooms, she hesitated, then acknowledged the truth: she had butterflies in her stomach.

Why? Because after her display in the graveyard, she was nervous as all get out at the prospect of coming face-to-face with Garland again.

But he wasn't in the apartment. That was both a relief and a worry. She didn't have to see him right away, which gave her time to further build up her defenses; but on the other hand, the thought that he might already have been sucked away into eternity without either of them having so much as the chance to say good-bye was a prospect that, to her consternation, filled her with dismay.

You're worried you won't have the chance to say good-bye to Garland? This isn't good.

As she showered and then deliberately pulled on what was probably her least sexy sleepwear — silky pink pajama pants and a matching camisole, which at least covered her legs — in anticipation of Garland's showing up eventually, Charlie reluctantly did what she absolutely hated to do: she turned all her years of education and training inward and psychoanalyzed herself.

Because she had Daddy issues as a result of having the opposite-gender parent absent for almost her entire life, and because she had trust issues as a result of having an alcoholic and totally unreliable primary parental figure, she somewhere deep inside believed herself unworthy of being loved. Therefore, she chose to enter into relationships that were programmed from their outset to fail. She sabotaged them herself, subconsciously but consistently, by choosing a male partner who for some reason or another was incapable of forming a stable and lasting partnership bond.

Doing a quick mental review of every halfway-serious romantic relationship she had ever had, Charlie saw that her analysis was right on the money: she set herself up for failure every time by choosing to fall for an unavailable male.

And here she was, doing it again in spades:

on the one hand there was Tony, who seemed to be ideal boyfriend/lover/husband material; while on the other, there was Garland, who, for so many reasons she wasn't even going to take the time to mentally list them, was anything but.

So which one was she desperately attracted to?

Garland, naturally.

Why? Because he was the ultimate unavailable male.

Diagnosis: *You are one screwed-up chick.*

Diagnosis of the diagnosis: *Very professional.*

Thoroughly out of patience with herself, Charlie got into bed, turned off the light, closed her eyes, lay there in the dark, and waited for exhaustion to kick in. She found herself listening for the TV. Opening her eyes in annoyance, she searched the shadows for the faintest shimmer that might indicate a ghostly presence. Shutting them again, she tossed, she turned, she cursed under her breath.

Then she got up.

Where is he?

She walked through the apartment, turning on lights as she went, and much as she hated herself for doing it, even tried very softly calling his name.

Nothing.

Remembering what he had said about being yanked back to her by the sound of running water, she tried calling his name while turning on the kitchen faucet.

Nothing.

Finally she tried calling not *Garland,* but *Michael,* while turning on the kitchen faucet.

Still nothing.

You are nuts.

She stomped back to bed. But even as she threw herself on the mattress and started to yank the covers over her head, a terrible thought had her sitting bolt upright again.

What if he's here, but I can't see him any longer?

Holly's spirit had visited her, but she hadn't been able to see it. She only had been able to see Holly in her dreams.

The spirits she saw were the *recently* violently departed.

Garland's death wasn't all that recent. He was getting close to the time when the Great Beyond tended to claim its own. *He was getting close to the time when she probably wasn't going to be able to see him anymore.*

Her heart lurched. Her stomach twisted into a knot. Her palms went damp.

Charlie hated to even try to put a name to the emotion she was experiencing, but finally she did: panic.

Panic at the thought that, even if she had managed to bind him to the earth, even if he avoided being swept away into Spookville, soon she might never see Garland again.

She was shaken at how deep was her sense of loss.

How could I have let this happen? she asked herself, appalled.

Charlie got out of bed, roamed the apartment, ate some ice cream, watched some TV, and finally, when there was still no sign of him, got out her laptop and called up his file.

Need a reminder of why *you shouldn't be falling for this guy?*

It was all there, exactly as she remembered: unmarried, no known children, next of kin Jasmine Lipsitz, no relationship specified; eight years as a marine, honorable discharge, military record otherwise inaccessible; in civilian life, work as a mechanic, owned his own garage at the time of his arrest; an adult criminal record that consisted of a public intoxication charge, an assault and battery that was the result of a bar brawl, and seven hideous murders of young women.

Their pictures were part of the file.

Charlie couldn't do more than glance at them. The faces sickened her. They made her go cold all over, made her shiver. She had to turn off her laptop.

How can I feel anything except loathing for their murderer?

You really think I'd do something like that to a woman? Charlie could almost hear Garland saying it. She could picture the revulsion in his face as he had looked down at Bayley Evans' mutilated body.

He was a charismatic psychopath whose charm was his stock in trade. He was convincing, compelling, and calculating. A stone-cold killer. A monster who lured women to their deaths with his good looks.

Or else he was not.

The evidence of his guilt was overwhelming. It was all there in his file, ranging from the circumstantial to that absolute clincher, DNA. She would have to be the biggest fool on the planet to disregard it all.

I've done a lot of bad things, Doc. But I didn't do that.

What was he going to do, admit it? Charlie demanded of herself with asperity. Of course he would deny everything. That's what psychopaths do.

The thing was, she just couldn't picture him killing those women.

But the sad truth was, that was probably because she didn't want to.

Because she liked him. No, get real: because she burned for him.

If she never saw him again, she would be sorry for the rest of her life.

Where is he?

There was no answer to that. There was no answer to anything where he was concerned.

Eventually, Charlie fell asleep on the couch.

She was dreaming that she was fleeing desperately through a terrifying purple fog, when she saw Holly in that awful pink prom dress running ahead of her.

"Holly!" Charlie screamed, trying to catch up, but Holly, after a quick glance over her shoulder, disappeared into the mist.

"Holly, wait!"

Charlie sprinted after her, but the purple mist started to rise and swirl, disorienting her, wrapping her in creeping tendrils of cold and damp.

Where am I?

"Holly!" she cried again, heart racing as she caught glimpses of things barely hidden. Something was chasing her, she could hear it behind her, hear its labored breathing and echoing footsteps. Glancing over her shoulder, she saw — *Dear God, what was it?* Something so horrible that she screamed. Then, still screaming, racing away as fast as she could, she ran headlong into something solid in the fog.

Chapter Thirty-One

"I've got you. Hold tight." It was Garland, Charlie realized. She caught just a glimpse of his hard eyes and taut jaw as he grabbed her and pulled her against him. Her arms wrapped around his waist like she never meant to let go. Shuddering, she buried her face in his chest as whatever was chasing her let out a monstrous roar and Garland said urgently, "It's your dream. Think of somewhere you want to be, quick."

His strong arms held her close as the mist swirled and rose and parted, and then was gone. Almost afraid to look, Charlie lifted her head warily and registered a whole lot of dark.

"It's all right. We're out of there," Garland said. Looking around again, Charlie saw to her surprise that they were in her house in Big Stone Gap — *somewhere you want to be* — and they were safe.

It was only then that she realized that her

heart was pounding and her pulse was racing and she was breathing like she'd been running from a monster that had been chasing her through a fog. Why? Oh, because she had been.

That had been a dream, though, she was pretty sure. This wasn't.

This time there was no mistake. The floorboards beneath her bare feet were smooth wood. The cool breath of the air-conditioning whispered over her skin. Outside it was raining hard. Storming. She could hear the drumming of the deluge hitting her metal roof, hear the rumble of thunder, smell the indefinable scent of the rain. Bright flashes of lightning streaking across the sky glowed through the windows, illuminating the entry hall to the point where Charlie could at least see where they were, which was right inside her front door.

Garland's arms around her were muscular and hard. When she had rested her cheek against his chest, it had been warm and unyielding. Every inch of his big body felt as substantial against hers as any living, breathing human male's. And she knew that was almost certainly because she'd gone running after Holly again, done the astral-projection thing again, and Garland had found her and now here they were.

This is real.

"You went chasing after your friend?" Garland's hold on her wasn't quite as tight now, but he wasn't letting her go. Which was fine with her. She wasn't letting him go, either. For the moment, all she wanted to do was lean against him and breathe.

I'm so glad to see you. Of course, she had absolutely no intention of ever saying that to him out loud.

Instead she said, "You didn't see her?"

He shook his head. "No."

She sagged a little with disappointment. "Holly. Her name is Holly. I was lost in a purple fog and I saw her."

"That purple fog was Spookville, and it's no place you want to be. Lucky I heard you screaming. How the hell did you manage to dream yourself in there?"

She'd been waiting for him. She'd fallen asleep. Charlie's brows snapped together as she remembered. Her eyes jerked up to meet his.

"Probably because you've been filling my head with all kinds of horrible images of purple fog and scary monsters ever since you died," she said tartly, and he smiled. Remembering the last time she had seen him — when she had been crying her eyes out over his grave — sent a rush of embarrassment shooting through her. Then she remembered more, remembered exactly why she had been thinking so hard about Spookville when sleep had finally claimed her, and that smile drove her around the bend. Flattening her hands against his chest, she pushed almost all the way out of his arms — she wasn't about to pull completely free, just in case one or the other of them should go spinning off somewhere — then punched him not all that gently in the ribs. "Where have you *been?*"

"Ow." He winced, grimacing. But the remnants of that infuriating smile remained as he looked down at her. "Been worried about me, Doc?"

She wasn't about to answer that. Instead she glared at him. "Well?"

He shrugged. "I went up to the Ridge. Looked around. Nothing had changed. Ran across that piece of shit Nash — Johnson and one of the other guards were just getting him out of the hole. I was pissed off about being dead and . . . a lot of things . . . so I'm guessing I had a pretty good energy buzz going on. I didn't realize anybody could see me until Nash screamed and Johnson whirled around and grabbed for his gun. Just about as soon as I figured out I was solid I got hit with what felt like an atomic blast that kicked me straight into Spookville. Only this time, I couldn't find a way out. I thought maybe that was it. Then I heard you scream. I busted my ass to get to you before something else did. You stay out of Spookville, Doc. You don't want to mess with what's in there."

"I didn't go there on purpose, believe me," Charlie said with feeling. "Anyway, I think it was just a nightmare. I don't think anything could have actually hurt me."

"Yeah, well, when I grabbed you, you felt real enough to me. As real as you feel right now. I don't think you can count on being safe in there."

"That place is horrible." Charlie shuddered just thinking about the things she'd glimpsed in the fog. The most horrible was realizing that Spookville was where he inevitably was going to wind up, probably on his way to somewhere even worse. Remembering the epiphany she'd had about his imminent disappearance from *her* world, she no longer felt even remotely like punching him. Her hands clenched on his shirtfront as her heart swelled with sorrow. The muscles beneath the soft cotton felt taut and warm and *real.* He felt alive under her hands. But he wasn't, and she was hideously, horribly afraid he couldn't stay. Charlie suddenly had trouble catching her breath. "One of these days, you're not going to be able to get out of there."

"I know." His eyes were dark and unreadable. But even through the shadows that lay all around, she could see the sudden grim set to his mouth. "Doc, look. When — if — that happens, I don't want you to worry about me. I'll be all right."

Charlie felt a lump forming in her throat. They both knew it was probably *when* rather than *if. Oh, God, until this afternoon I hadn't cried in years and now I'm about to do it again.* Then she swallowed hard. *Get a grip.* The last thing on earth she wanted was to let Garland know how confused her emotions were where he was concerned.

Like he doesn't already have a pretty good idea. Well, she didn't have to break down and spell it out for him.

She took a deep breath, and lifted her chin challengingly. "Why would I worry about *you?*"

That infuriating little smile was back. "Oh, I don't know. Maybe for the same reason you were crying your eyes out over my grave."

Charlie stiffened. "If you're implying that I . . ." She stumbled trying to find the appropriate term; they'd definitely gone way beyond *like,* ". . . care about you —"

"Care. Now, there's a word, Doc," he interjected softly. His eyes were intent on her face.

Charlie's breathing sped up. They were heading into territory she had absolutely no wish to explore.

"I hate to burst your bubble, but it's more like I feel responsible for you."

"Oh, yeah? So what you're telling me is, you were crying like that over me because you've got the whole save-a-life-and-you're-responsible-for-it-forever thing going on?"

Charlie narrowed her eyes at him, and chose the safe route. "I didn't save your life."

"No, you didn't." His voice turned husky. "What you did was, you saved my soul."

Charlie's heart lurched. The lump in her throat swelled, making it almost impossible for her to speak. She looked at him, at his chiseled, handsome features, afraid of what he might read in her eyes, praying that it was too dark for him to see.

A piece of her heart was in there somewhere.

"I hated seeing you cry," he said.

"Garland." Her voice sounded choked to her own ears. His fingers dug into her waist in response. His eyes glinted down at her, watchful as a bird of prey's, and she knew what he wanted to hear instead. She took a deep breath. "Michael."

"Charlie." Her name was the merest whisper of sound, uttered as he pulled her tight against him and his head bent toward hers. But that whisper wrapped itself around something deep inside her, and she knew, as she went up on tiptoe and slid her arms around his neck, that after this, after *him,* her life would never be the same.

She also knew that there would be an "after him." She was alive and he was not. It was only by the most random of chances that they had connected at all. But she knew ghosts. Ghosts were ephemeral. Ghosts didn't stay.

She kissed him anyway. Kissed him like she would die if she didn't, like every dream of a happily ever after she'd had was right there in his arms, like there was no yesterday and no tomorrow and no world beyond that moment and the two of them.

She kissed him like she was crazy in love with him.

Just for tonight . . .

Drawing back, taking a breath, she looked up at him, only to discover that he was looking at her, too. For a moment, as his warm breath feathered her lips, their eyes met and held. Charlie absorbed every detail of his to-die-for good looks, of the sculpted planes and angles of his face, of his height and the width of his shoulders and the sensuous line of his mouth. His pupils had dilated until his eyes looked almost black. A dark flush rode high on his cheekbones.

"Tonight's all we're ever going to have, isn't it?" Until the words were out of her mouth, Charlie hadn't realized she was going to say them aloud.

His eyes flickered. His lips tightened and his jaw went hard.

"I want you." His voice was low and gravelly.

Charlie went all soft and shivery inside. All her common sense, all her instincts for self-preservation, vanished in that instant. "I want you, too."

He smiled at her, a slow, sexy smile that thrilled her clear down to her toes. Then he bent his head, and Charlie quit thinking entirely as his lips found hers again. Her eyes closed, her lips parted, and then she tightened her arms around his neck and put her tongue in his mouth and kissed him back like he was the embodiment of every erotic dream she'd ever had.

Oh, wait, he was.

His mouth was hard and hungry. Possessive. Demanding. His hands slid down her back, the size and warmth of them sensuous through the silkiness of her pajamas, tracing the arch of her body, molding her to him, making her tremble, making her cling. Heat radiated through his clothes. The urgency of his arousal was impossible to mistake. The sexual charge he gave off was as electric as the lightning that flashed through the night outside. It sizzled between them, igniting the air. Suddenly dizzy, Charlie pressed even closer and kissed him back just as fiercely as he was kissing her, abandoning herself to the moment, to the darkness, to the way he was making her feel. He kissed her breathless, kissed her stupid, kissed her until her heart pounded and her blood raced and her body melted.

"We're in your house, right?" he asked in a husky murmur as his mouth left hers to press burning kisses across her cheek.

"Mmm." So turned on she could hardly think, Charlie managed a nod.

"Ah." It was a sound of satisfaction, uttered as he bent her over his arm and dragged his mouth down the sensitive side of her neck. His hand found her breast through the thin camisole, and her knees practically gave way right there. She made an involuntary sound of pleasure as her nipple puckered instantly and her breast surged against the hardness of his palm. His hand tightened, caressed, and then was gone, leaving fire in its wake.

Bereft at the sudden withdrawal, Charlie opened her eyes in protest as he scooped her up in his arms and started walking.

"What? Where . . . ?" Her voice failed her. She was so bedazzled by lust, by the steam the two of them were generating, she couldn't get the rest of the question out.

But he knew what she was asking. His eyes gleamed down at her, dark and hot. "Upstairs."

Knowing what his answer meant, knowing where he was taking her, Charlie felt an explosion of desire so intense, so hot and clamorous, that it raced through her in undulating waves. Her heart pounded. Deep inside, her body pulsed with need.

He reached the bottom of the wide, old-fashioned staircase and started up.

"I can —" she began with determination, battling to keep from losing her head completely, meaning to protest that she could walk, because the idea of him carrying her up a steep flight of stairs with an eye to screwing her senseless at the top had way too many Neanderthal-esque connotations for her, but he stopped her voice with his mouth. The point that she had meant to make, that she was a grown woman, absolutely responsible for her own sexual pleasure, and certainly not the type who ever needed or wanted to be swept off her feet, was lost in the torrid eroticism of that kiss. It was drugging in its sensuality, in its promise of unspeakable pleasures to come, of dark, erotic vistas waiting to be explored.

Dry-mouthed, Charlie gave up on trying to take back her personal power and tightened her arms around his neck and kissed him back. He climbed the stairs with her easily, like she weighed nothing at all, kissing her all the while. As primitive of her as she knew it was, she reveled in his strength.

God, he excites me.

Clinging to his broad shoulders, made dizzy by the fierce possession of his mouth and the skyrocketing of her own desire, Charlie was startled enough by a clap of thunder to pull her mouth from his. Even as she registered what the sound had been, she realized that he had reached the landing at the top of the stairs. There she had one final moment of clarity.

This is a mistake.

She absolutely knew it. Knew some kind of cosmic line was being crossed, and there would be no going back from what she was about to do. The thing was, though, she decided as he walked into her bedroom with her in his arms, right at that moment she simply didn't care.

She wanted him so badly, she would have walked over hot coals for this.

Lightning flashed, and by its brief burst of light she drank in the fierce masculine beauty of his face, the hot glitter in his eyes as they met hers, the passionate curve of his mouth.

"I've been having fantasies about this bed all day." His voice was hoarse, almost unrecognizable. His lips slid down her neck and across her shoulder as he set her on her feet beside her bed. With its pure white coverings and the subtle gleam of the brass headboard, it was visible even in the darkness between lightning flashes.

Turning into his arms, she slipped her hands under his T-shirt, moving them up over the flexing muscles of his back, dislodging his shirt in the process. His skin was warm and smooth. She stroked it, loving the hard masculine contours. His reaction was instantaneous. His eyes flamed at her. He went tense, perfectly still, while heat radiated from him in waves. Then in a single fluid movement he pulled his T-shirt off over his head.

"You've really been having fantasies about

my bed?" The question was meant to be coolly teasing, to keep him from realizing how very turned on she was. It was not. In the end, Charlie just tried not to sound as breathless as she felt. But now that he was stripped to the waist, there was nothing she could do. He was so sex-on-the-hoof gorgeous she could barely look away. Merely the sight of the powerful-looking expanse of his shoulders, his broad chest, the corded muscles in his arms, his sinewy abs above the low waistband of his jeans, made her heart pound. Her hands lay flat against the firm flesh right above his hip bones. She slid them sensuously upward to settle on his chest, loving the feel of the warm, smooth skin overlying sleek muscle, loving the fact that he was hers to do with as she would.

Just for tonight.

His jaw turned to granite as his hands came up to tilt her face to his, smooth her hair back from her cheeks. She met his eyes then, and shivered at the hot blaze of passion for her she saw in their depths. Electricity leaped between them, so raw and powerful that it put the lightning streaking the night sky outside to shame.

Her arms went around his neck as his mouth found hers again. The kiss was fierce and deep and dazzling, and when he broke it off Charlie was shaking.

"I've been thinking about *you* in your bed," he clarified in a rough whisper as he pressed tiny, burning kisses along the base of her neck. "About everything I would do to you if I ever got you here."

Charlie's breathing went hopelessly erratic as his hands slid under the hem of her camisole. It was a loose, filmy garment of silk and lace, with spaghetti straps and tiny, useless silk-covered buttons marching down the front.

He pushed it upward, his hands stroking over her rib cage, over her back, after he bared her breasts. He lifted his head and looked down at her then, at the full round globes with their dark, eager tips, and his face tightened and his eyes burned. Her breasts swelled and lifted, yearning for his touch, but his hands didn't go where she wanted them. Instead he pulled the camisole off over her head and let it drop to the floor. She was still sucking in air from that when he found the satiny drawstring that secured her pants at the waist, and with unerring accuracy tugged on the end that loosened its bow. As quick as that, her pants slithered down her body to the floor.

She was naked. And his eyes were touching her everywhere.

Charlie made a little sound deep in her throat. Her bones melted. Her knees went weak. She swayed against him, and was instantly dazzled by the feel of them skin to skin, by the softness of her breasts against the wall of his chest, by his warmth and solid strength. Moving against him voluptuously, she pressed her lips to the sturdy column of his neck, then opened them to taste him with her tongue. His skin was hot and tasted of salt.

"You're beautiful." Trailing fire in their wake, his hands slid down her back to cup her ass.

The feel of his big hands on her curves made her quake inside. She gave a slight shake of her head. "That would be you."

She thought she saw the slightest of smiles touch his mouth. It vanished as she found his belt buckle. Unfastening it, she reached for the button on his jeans and undid that, too. Then she unzipped his pants. It was a small sound, but erotic enough to make her pulse pound and her fingers unsteady.

He had gone very still. Against her breasts, she felt his muscles turn to iron. The sudden diamond-hard glitter in his eyes was enough to curl her toes.

"You're just what I always wanted, Doc."

His voice was thick and hot. He tilted her face up to his, pressed a quick hard kiss to her mouth. "I'm going to make you come for me all night long."

Then he picked her up and laid her on her bed and came down on top of her.

Chapter Thirty-Two

Stretching her arms above her head, Garland pinned her beneath him, kissing her like he would never get enough of the taste of her mouth. Charlie had a brief uneasy instant in which she realized that in this position she was almost entirely helpless against a man of his size and strength. A glimmer of caution, a glimmer of doubt — what if sex was the trigger that brought out the monster in him? — was swamped by a wave of fierce need. She could feel the whole long length of him pressing her into the thick softness of her comforter, feel the pressure of his muscled chest against her breasts and the hair-roughened rasp of his powerful thighs as they settled between hers and the burning weight of his manhood brushing her skin. He was big, and heavy, all rippling sinew and hot sleek skin, and the feel of him against her drove her wild. When his mouth left hers, it trailed down her neck to find her breast. Hungry and wet, it closed over one nipple, kissing her, licking her, and then moved on to the other. Shivery with arousal, Charlie arched her back and closed her eyes and gave herself to the darkness and the heat. When he shifted his grip so that one hand shackled her wrists and the other was free to slide between her legs, she quivered and moaned and moved for him and let him play. When he finally let her wrists go, when he kissed his way down her body to lick into the delicate cleft his fingers had explored, she cried out and came for him.

After that, when he stretched back over her and started to fit his body to hers, she was warm and pliant and still pleasantly floating. Holding himself a little above her with his elbows taking most of his weight, he pushed into her slowly, letting her feel him, and her eyes fluttered open with interest as he entered that first little bit. He felt huge, long and thick and hard, all velvet over scalding steel. Sated though she was, she made a little sound of surprise and pleasure as her body got with the program again and began to clench and burn around him. His mouth was set, his eyes open and so dark they were almost black as he watched her face change, as he watched her register what he was doing to her and how it felt. She knew she must be flushed, knew her eyes must be heavy-lidded and slumberous, knew her lips were parted with anticipation and swollen from his kisses. She could sense the tremendous control he was exercising as he pushed inside her inch by deliberate inch, until she couldn't stand it anymore, until she closed her eyes and clenched her teeth and started to move, rocking up against him, trying to draw him in deeper, digging her fingernails into his back, gasping at the sheer pleasure of it, wanting more.

"You want me to fuck you, ask me." The low growl in her ear made her suck in air.

Charlie's eyes opened to find that he was watching her still. The hot, fierce gleam in his eyes made her go all liquid inside. She was moving beneath him, she couldn't help it, he was making her wild, she was on fire from wanting him. Never in her life had she been this sexually aroused. What had sprung to life between them was pure chemistry, a kind of sexual magic, an erotic intensity so potent that it sizzled in the air.

"Michael," she begged.

At the sound of his name on her lips, his eyes blazed. Charlie saw the clenching of his jaw, felt the slight tremor in the arms braced on either side of her, heard the hoarse sound he made.

Then he kissed her, a hot lush kiss, and pushed all the way inside her. Charlie cried out, clung, writhing at the sheer fierce pleasure of it. He pulled back, then pushed in again, hard and deep, and she cried out once more. He kept going, fast now, driving into her, his movements almost savage, kissing her all the while. On fire, Charlie wrapped her arms around his neck and her legs around his waist and moved with him, matching him stroke for stroke and kiss for kiss with passionate abandon, giving herself over to the hot dark wildfire he had ignited inside her until, *"Michael,"* she gasped at last, and came in a shattering climax that rocked her world.

He came, too, then, shuddering, driving deep and holding himself inside her shaking body and groaning with the intensity of his release.

For a long moment afterward neither of them moved. He was hot and damp with sweat and heavy as a slab of concrete on top of her. His arms were locked around her, holding her tight. His head had dropped to rest in the tender curve between her neck and shoulder.

I love the way he feels.

Charlie was just having that thought, just resurfacing from the aftermath of the explosions that had detonated inside her, just becoming aware of how boneless she felt and how violently the storm still raged outside and how warm and cozy her bed was with him in it, when he shifted position. Her eyes snapped open as he rolled onto his back and pulled her with him so that she ended up lying on top of his chest. Folding an arm beneath his head, splaying a possessive hand over her ass, he looked at her.

Okay, so meeting his gaze was embarrassing. So was lying naked on top of him in a tangle of bedclothes while he casually fondled her bottom. Come to think of it, so was just about everything they'd done.

"So?" he asked, his eyes crinkling at her.

Charlie knew what he was asking. Her breath caught: *The earth moved.*

"Very nice," she answered repressively, and felt her heart speed up as he gave her a broad smile.

"Don't mess with . . . ," he began, but Charlie didn't hear the rest of it because, out of nowhere, she felt a hand on her shoulder.

"Charlie." A man was speaking to her urgently. It was Tony's voice, and he . . .

Charlie's eyes widened. *"Michael."* As she realized what was happening, she clutched at him urgently, but it was already too late. He and the bed and her house and everything else dissolved around her, and then her eyes opened to find Tony leaning over her. His hand was on her shoulder, shaking her awake. Behind him were Kaminsky and Crane. All three were fully dressed, frowning, and Crane and Kaminsky were talking to each other while Tony concentrated on waking her.

After a horrifying moment in which she thought she might be naked and rosy with sex, Charlie realized it wasn't so. She was once again wearing the pink pajamas that Michael had so recently taken off her. Lying curled up on the couch where she had fallen asleep. With a single lamp burning, and her laptop lying on the floor beside her.

Even as Tony withdrew his hand and Charlie blinked and sat up, she was aware of the most profound sense of loss.

Michael.

"What is it?" she snapped, shaking her hair back from her face, glaring up at Tony like it was all his fault and then impartially at the other two, knowing that she sounded irritable and not able to help it. With every ounce of her being she longed to be back in the tumbled bed she had just left.

That was a one-time deal, you know. Don't you even begin to let yourself think it's ever likely to happen again.

The thought made her heart bleed.

"I tried to wake you up." Kaminsky sounded as cranky as Charlie felt. "I knocked, I came in, I shook you. You didn't stir. I had to call the guys. Did you take a sleeping pill or something?"

"No." Doing her best to push her recent sexfest out of her mind, Charlie took a deep breath as her head continued to clear. She brushed her hair out of her face with both hands, glanced around. The digital numbers on the cable box below the TV read 4:22 a.m. Out here in the real world, something — something major — was clearly up. "What's happened?"

"There's another victim." Tony's face was grim. "We've got to go. Get dressed."

Charlie's pulse started to pound in her ears. "Another victim? You mean — another family's been attacked?"

"Bayley Evans' cousin. Hannah Beckett. Her father and step-mother — Philip and Rosalie Beckett — are dead. Hannah's missing." Tony turned and walked out of the room, motioning to Crane and Kaminsky to follow him. He glanced back at Charlie over his shoulder. "You've got ten minutes. We'll meet you downstairs."

Left alone, Charlie dressed fast, then took a precious moment to do a quick walk-through search of the apartment, even turning on the kitchen tap. Nothing.

"Michael," she called softly. She heard the urgency in her voice, and it stopped her cold. If she was going to survive this, she needed to start backtracking, fast. To begin with, he couldn't be "Michael" to her. Not here in the real world, from which he might even now be gone. For her own sake, she had to do her best to keep what distance she could between them. Because if she didn't, her heart was going to get way too involved, and the hard truth was that he wasn't among the living anymore, and he couldn't stay.

There was no sign of *Garland* anywhere. Facing the fact that there was nothing she could do about it and that she was out of time anyway, Charlie succumbed to one last temptation, and sent a hurried prayer winging skyward asking God to keep him safe. Then she went downstairs.

The crime scene was a largish brick ranch house at the very end of a cul-de-sac not too far from Kill Devil Hills' small central business district. Very modern, lots of glass.

The property was approximately an acre, with lavish landscaping, including a privacy barrier of loblolly pines, which meant the neighbors, whom the local police were already interviewing, had not seen or heard a thing.

When Charlie and the team arrived, making their way past an already established police perimeter and an army of arriving media, the bodies were still inside. The first gray fingers of dawn were just creeping up over the eastern sky as they entered the house. Immediately they were asked to safeguard the still-fresh forensic evidence by suiting up in paper jumpsuits, booties, and rubber gloves, which they did.

"Let them in," Haney barked at the uniformed officer who tried to block their access to the master bedroom, where Haney and his partner and various crime scene technicians seemed to be taking care to hug the walls as they worked. As soon as Charlie got a glimpse of the room, she saw why: the body closest to the door lay sprawled in a veritable lake of blood that had soaked into the once-plush beige carpet and turned it a hideous shade of brown. Blood splatter covered the bed, the walls, every available surface that she could see. It looked like an abattoir. The raw meat smell of fresh carnage hung heavy in the air. Charlie felt her stomach start to churn. As the cop guarding the door moved aside and Tony led the way into the bedroom, with all of them stepping carefully so as to avoid the blood, Charlie had just enough time to identify Hannah's stepmother's blond, bird-boned body crumpled near the foot of the bed before nausea hit her hard. The rest of the room seemed to recede as her eyes flew to a tall, slender man in a pair of blood-drenched blue pajamas who came walking out of the en suite bathroom to stare down in disbelief at something on the floor in front of him. Charlie stopped cold, told herself fiercely to breathe, and followed his gaze to the floor. With the bed blocking her view, all she saw of what was transfixing his attention was a man's long, narrow bare foot and an ankle sticking out of blue pajama pants identical to the ones the man wore. The body to which the foot and ankle belonged lay on the floor on the other side of the bed. Charlie knew that what she was seeing was the spirit looking down at his own recently murdered corpse. Then the man apparently felt her gaze on him. His head came up and he looked at her. Even as he realized she could see him, Charlie recognized him from a set of pictures of the latest victims the team had been looking at on the way over. He was Hannah's father, Phil Beckett, now deceased.

"There's been a murder." Beckett's voice was croaky but surprisingly controlled under the circumstances, and Charlie remembered that he was — had been — a lawyer. Still, his eyes were wide with shock as they met hers. "It's me. And Rosalie. A man . . . broke in. We've been killed."

He came toward her, passing right through the solid structure of the bed, and as he drew near Charlie saw that he was hideously wounded. The front of his pajama shirt was in tatters, baring most of a thin chest laid open with long, vertical slashes that were scarlet with blood and gore. Half of his right sleeve was missing, and the flesh of his forearm had been sliced to ribbons. An inches-long gash across his right cheekbone went right down to the bone.

"Hannah — it's the same thing that happened to Bayley, isn't it? God in heaven, look what he did to Rosalie!"

Charlie took an involuntary step backward as he stopped a few feet away, his eyes riveted on the body of his dead wife, and swallowed hard in an attempt to combat her rising nausea. Up close, the horror of what had been done to him was impossible to miss.

"I fought. I tried to protect them. I landed some punches. I think I broke his damned front tooth." Anguish was plain in his eyes as he looked again at Charlie. "My wife . . . my daughter . . ." His face contorted with anger and grief. His voice rose. "That bastard has my daughter, doesn't he? Oh, God, what can I do?" Turning, he dropped to his knees beside his wife, and tried to touch her with a hesitant hand. "Rosalie? Rosalie!"

Remembering where she was, knowing that she was surrounded by possible witnesses, Charlie didn't say a word. Under the circumstances, there was nothing she could do to comfort him, so she didn't try. Instead she turned on her heel and left the room. Her stomach was in full revolt, and she was afraid she was going to vomit where she stood if she didn't get out of there. Blindly she strode down the hall that led to the bedrooms, meaning to rush outside and get some fresh air. But there were cops in the living room, and through the glass pane in the top of the front door she could see the bright glow of klieg lights that could only belong to the media stationed out front. Hanging a sharp right, she walked through the kitchen and found herself on the adjoining screened-in porch.

It was dark, shadowy, alive with the sound of insects and water dripping off trees from the recent rain. Fake grass carpeted the floor. Charlie knew, because she dropped to her knees on the bristly stuff and, lowering her head, took in great gulps of air.

The horror of what she had just seen stayed with her.

"Charlie?" Tony banged through the door behind her.

Charlie pushed to her feet. She turned to look at him, but discovered speech was beyond her for the moment. Her stomach heaved. Her head reeled.

"Hey. You okay? I know that was bad in there."

His arm came around her shoulders as he peered into her face. Charlie made a wordless sound, and he pulled her against him, wrapping her in a steadying hug.

Charlie leaned against him as the only sturdy thing available, grateful for his presence. He was a good guy, handsome and strong, capable and genuinely nice, and she had a serious screw loose in her psyche to prefer the darkness to the light.

"Phil Beckett fought. He may have broken the killer's front tooth." Her words were breathy and rushed, but she was lucky to have gotten them out at all. The nausea was bad. Having spoken, she dropped her head down onto his shoulder and concentrated on not losing the coffee and power bar she'd half consumed in the car on the way over.

"What? How do you know that?"

Charlie wasn't up to even attempting to answer at the moment. She just shook her head.

"Charlie?" Tony's arms tightened around her. She took another deep breath. Then she felt something — call it a disturbance in the force — that made her look up. There, standing in the dark a few feet away, looking as solid as the man whose arms were wrapped around her but bigger and a whole lot badder, was Garland. His booted feet were planted apart, his arms were folded over his chest, and his expression as his gaze fixed on her oozed displeasure.

Chapter Thirty-Three

Just looking at him made her heart beat a little faster. Charlie gathered from the way he was eyeing the two of them that he didn't much care for finding her in Tony's arms . . . and was glad to see him anyway. Something inside her she hadn't even realized was tense with worry eased.

Not good. In fact, bad. Then she had a corollary thought. If I'm not careful, this — whatever he is — is going to break my heart.

"Charlie. How sure are you about the broken tooth?" Tony's tone was urgent.

Ignoring Garland, Charlie pushed out of Tony's arms, took a few unsteady steps toward one of the three plastic lawn chairs on the porch, and sank down on it. It was still dark, but more the charcoal of awakening dawn than the pitch-black of night. There was a warm breeze blowing in through the screen. It carried the scent of rain and wet grass on it. Her stomach was settling down a little bit, and she thought the fresh air might be helping.

"Fairly sure."

"You have some kind of psychic experience in there?" His tone was slightly cautious.

Charlie sighed. She didn't like people knowing even a little bit about her ability, for all sorts of reasons, but Tony wasn't exactly people, and anyway, he knew enough to at least take what she said semi-seriously, so what was she going to do, deny it?

"Phil Beckett spoke to me. That's where I got the information."

She could see from his expression that he was curious, that he wanted to know more, and resigned herself to an interrogation. But what he said was, "Okay," and then, "Sit tight, I'll be right back" as he turned and strode back into the house.

Charlie didn't even look up at Garland as he came to stand beside her. She stared out at the night, at the swaying pines, black and tall, at the far end of the yard, at the hammock moving with the breeze closer at hand, at the lightening sky.

"You know, I'm starting to not like that guy," he said reflectively, and at that Charlie did flick a look up at him.

"You sound like you're jealous." She was

deliberately cool, deliberately off-hand, deliberately creating as much distance between them as she could, because she was horribly afraid that the alternative was going to make her life unbearable one day soon.

She could feel him studying her. "Except for being dead, I'm a pretty normal guy, and I just fucked you to Sunday and back. So, yeah." He hunkered down beside her. "You want to tell me what's with the attitude?"

There were flowers growing over by the garage. She tried to decide what kind. "What attitude?"

"Charlie."

He was right beside her, gorgeous as always — but unbelievably, achingly dear now, too. And that's what was twisting her heart, Charlie realized. Almost unwillingly, she met his gaze. Even through the shadows, his eyes were heartstoppingly blue.

"Look, we both know that . . . what happened . . . was a onetime thing," she said. "I don't regret it, precisely, but I have to move on. So do you."

His eyes held hers for a moment, and Charlie watched as his hardened and cooled.

"FBI guy what you're planning to move on to?"

"Maybe. We'll have to see how things work out."

"After I'm out of the picture, hmm?"

"Yes."

He stood up abruptly. Charlie looked at him. His face was unreadable now. "You're a smart lady, Doc. I always did think so."

Whatever she might have replied to that was lost as Kaminsky came bursting through the door. "Bartoli sent me to get you. Come on, we're on the move."

By the time she finished speaking, Garland was gone.

"He's escalating." Tony was staring at the computer monitor in the War Room at Command Central. Kaminsky was seated in front of it, having called up the pictures of the seventeen most viable suspects, which were staring out at them from the screen. In Charlie's usual seat in front of the other computer, Crane was running checks on credit card, phone, and work records that should provide at least some of these so-called "persons of interest" with an alibi for the previous night. It was not quite seven a.m., and Charlie had already drunk so much coffee she was wired. Any thought that wasn't centered on finding Hannah Beckett she had blocked out of her mind.

"Big-time," Charlie agreed. "Also, the attack was more savage. In the other murders, only the mothers bore more than one or two stab wounds. With everyone else, it was just enough to kill them and no more. Nothing egregious. But Phil Beckett was slashed to pieces. That's a sign that the killer was very angry."

"Why?" Tony stared at the screen as if the answer was right there, if only he looked hard enough. "*Why* was he so angry?"

"Something must have interrupted his routine. For whatever reason, he didn't get to play his fantasy out to the end," Charlie said.

"Are you thinking he killed Bayley Evans before he meant to?" Kaminsky glanced back over her shoulder at them.

"Before he wanted to," Charlie corrected. "Something must have gone wrong."

"What?" Kaminsky asked.

"Once we figure that out, I'm pretty sure we'll have our killer," Tony answered.

"With Hannah, there wasn't a dance," Charlie said slowly. She looked at Tony. "I think that after he killed Bayley, he went looking for a substitute to take her place. To finish out the fantasy. If, as we're assuming, he spotted Bayley at the Sanderling, he would have seen Hannah there at the same time. He's continuing the fantasy with her, not starting anew. But it's not the same. It's throwing him off. He's frustrated. And, like I said, angry."

Tony's hands were so tight on the back of Kaminsky's chair that his knuckles showed white. "Which means we may have even less time than we thought. Instead of a week, maybe two days, you think? If he's using her to take Bayley's place."

"There's no way to be sure." Charlie massaged her temples. Her earlier nausea had morphed into a killer headache. "Now that he's off his routine, there's no way to judge it."

"Okay, eight of these guys are definitely out. I've got records placing them somewhere else at the time the Beckett family was attacked," Crane said.

His tie didn't match his shirt — one blue-striped, the other green plaid — Charlie noticed. Of course, pulling on your clothes at four a.m., which was the approximate time the call had come in, was the equivalent of dressing in the dark. She glanced down at herself, just to be sure: white blouse, black pants. The good thing about an unofficial uniform was it was hard to go wrong. She'd pulled her hair into a ponytail. Charlie looked at Kaminsky, who was wearing her usual suit and high heels: no mistakes for her, either.

"I'm sending you the info," Crane said. "Take 'em off the grid."

Kaminsky nodded. A moment later an icon flashed on her monitor. A click of a button, and their prime suspect list was down to nine.

"Still too many. Who else can we eliminate?" Tony looked at Charlie.

"Pets. He won't have pets," Charlie said.

Tony shot a sideways glance at Crane.

"On it," Crane said. "Pet licenses."

"A lot of people have pets without licenses," Kaminsky pointed out.

"But if they do have a pet with a license, they're out," Crane retorted.

"Younger siblings," Charlie prompted, just as Crane whooped in triumph.

"Two with pet licenses. See there, *Lena,* some people are law-abiding."

"Seven." Kaminsky's tone was sour. "And stuff it, *Crane.*"

"Both of you stuff it," Tony snapped, then looked at Crane again. "Younger siblings," he said.

"Three with younger siblings." Crane smacked a hand on the desk beside his computer with enthusiasm. "We're getting somewhere."

"Four left," Kaminsky announced. "Always supposing Dr. Phil knows what she's talking about."

Charlie didn't even bother to shoot her a look.

"Anything else?" Tony cast an inquiring glance at Charlie. Staring at the faces left on the screen, hoping for inspiration, she had a painful throbbing at her temples and a dry mouth and nothing else.

She shook her head. "That's all I can come up with right this minute. Sorry."

"Good enough." Tony straightened. She could see his tension in the restless gleam of his eyes, in the tightness of his jaw and mouth. Shadows beneath his eyes made it clear he hadn't slept properly in a while. Like the rest of them, he was jacked up on coffee and adrenaline. Unlike Crane's, his shirt (white) and tie (blue) matched. In fact, if it hadn't been for the five o'clock shadow already darkening his jaw, he would have looked as if today was nothing more than business as usual. "Names and addresses, Kaminsky, and if there's any place besides home they're likely to be at this time in the morning, I want to know it."

"We going to go bring them in?" Crane

sounded surprised. Charlie remembered what Tony had said about the need to find the girl before arresting even the most viable suspect.

"We're going to go look at them. For a broken front tooth." Tony glanced at Kaminsky as the printer started to hum, and she said, "Got it."

"Then let's go." Tony was already on his way out the door.

Early as it was, Central Command was packed. The electricity in the air was palpable. Phones rang nonstop, every computer was occupied, and two orange-vested deputies were huddled with what looked like a civilian volunteer in front of a new search grid that had been hung on the wall. A cop talked earnestly with Sy Taylor, who perked up as he spotted the four of them coming toward him.

"Agent Bartoli, can you hang on a minute? I've got a question for you," Taylor called.

Tony waved a hand at him. "Later."

Then they were out the door.

Outside was a circus. The cops were doing a good job holding the perimeter, which was cordoned off with sawhorses strung with crime scene tape, but beyond that a sea of media stretched in all directions. White vans with satellite dishes attached were everywhere. Charlie saw from some of the logos on the vans that the coverage had gone national: CNN and MSNBC caught her eye in particular. Reporters with camera crews and microphones rushed the barrier as soon as the four of them came into view. So many questions were shouted their way that Charlie couldn't understand any of them. Part of that, she was sure, was because the drone of the helicopters circling overhead drowned everything else out.

Tony opened the passenger-side door of the SUV for her, and she got in. The door slamming shut behind her cut off the worst of the din, and moments later they were on the move. Only instead of trying to go through the frenzy, Tony reversed, and to Charlie's surprise they went bumping over the beach.

"Way to avoid the media, boss," Crane said from the backseat with approval.

"I don't want them following us." Tony seemed oblivious to the surprised looks of a couple of joggers and a man wading in the shallows with a bucket, apparently digging for clams. The sky was a bright clear blue with scarcely a cloud in it, and the ocean was as smooth as glass. The sun was the pale yellow-white of a scoop of lemon sorbet. It was going to be another hot one, Charlie could tell already, but so far the heat was bearable and the humidity wasn't too bad.

"Driving on the beach is illegal, and we're probably going to get stuck in the sand," Kaminsky pointed out. She sounded grumpy. It had been a hellacious day so far, and it was only just getting started, so Charlie was with her on that. Glancing back, Charlie saw that Kaminsky was riffling through the papers on her lap. They were the pages she'd just grabbed from the printer.

Tony shook his head. "Four-wheel drive."

They didn't get stuck, and when they drove up the public access boat ramp and out onto the road, no one was following them, prompting Charlie to give Tony a mental thumbs-up.

"Where are we going, Kaminsky?" Tony glanced at her in the rearview mirror.

"I've tried to arrange them nearest to farthest," Kaminsky replied. "But it's hard, because I don't have any way to be absolutely sure any of them will be where they're supposed to be, and —"

"Kaminsky," Tony said.

"Hampton Moore. He lives out in the county, but right now he should be opening the Blue Wave Coffee Shop on Seventeenth Street." She gave the street address, which

Tony punched in to the SUV's GPS. "He's twenty-six years old, six-one, hundred eighty-five pounds, a local. He works at the coffee shop mornings and for Frigate nights and weekends. He was at all three dances."

"Um, did you say we're going to go look at these guys to check for a broken tooth?" Crane asked. He did not add *Why?* but it was there in his voice.

"Beckett fought the unsub, who may have sustained a broken front tooth," Tony said. "The only way to keep all four of these guys under constant surveillance is to get the locals involved, and once we do that, the potential for leaks goes up astronomically. We spook this guy, let him know we're coming, he's going to kill Hannah Beckett. If we find one of them has a broken tooth, we're going to watch him ourselves, see where he goes."

"What if none of them has a broken tooth?" Crane asked.

"Then we're going to have to go to Haney, give him these names, and try to persuade him to keep them under surveillance for twenty-four hours. If we've got nothing by that time, there's no way I'm going to be able to stop him from moving in on them. Hell, we'll have to move in on them."

"We might have a problem, leak-wise,"

Kaminsky said. "Suspect number three, bartender Eric Duncan, is the first cousin of Kill Devil Hills Police Officer John Price."

A moment of silence greeted that. Then Tony said, "Damn small towns, everybody's related," half under his breath, and with that they reached the Blue Wave Coffee Shop.

Crane went in, and minutes later came back out carrying a blue plastic bag.

"You buy something?" Kaminsky asked as Crane got back in the car.

"What, did you want me to just walk in there and say 'Let me see your teeth'? I bought doughnuts. From Hampton Moore, who goes by Ham, by the way, who was working the counter. He smiled at me. His teeth are fine. No sign of facial or any other kind of injuries, either." Crane paused. "That's six dollars and two cents on the expense account, boss. Anybody want a doughnut?"

Charlie shuddered at the thought.

"Keep your receipt." Tony pulled away from the curb, sticking his hand into the backseat with a silent waggle that Crane interpreted, dropping a glazed doughnut into it. "Who's next, Kaminsky?"

"Terry Kingston. A used car salesman who also delivers pizzas at night. He, too, works part-time for Frigate Security. Unless you want to wait until after ten, we're going to his home."

"We're going to his home, then." Tony washed the doughnut down with a slug of his coffee, which they all had, in white Styrofoam cups nestled in the cupholders.

Kaminsky gave the address.

Crane asked, "Uh, what excuse are we going to give for showing up at his house and peering closely at his teeth?"

"Can't think of one," Tony said cheerfully.

"He's trying to sell a used motorcycle. I've got a copy of the ad right here." Kaminsky looked up from her papers. "Crane, you could knock on his door and say you're interested in buying it."

"Why me?"

"Because Bartoli looks like a fed, Dr. Stone looks like she's never ridden a motorcycle in her life, and I'm wearing a skirt," Kaminsky snapped. "Lose the jacket, take off that hideous tie, and go with it."

"Good plan," Bartoli said approvingly, while Crane muttered, "My tie is not hideous." A pause. "Is it?"

"Pretty hid—" Kaminsky began, only to break off as a fire truck came screaming up behind them, then swerved into the opposite lane to pass. A minute later, a volunteer fire department car, siren blaring, did the same thing. “Looks like somebody else is not having a good morning,” she said.

The road they were driving down was rural — two-lane blacktop, with piney woods on one side and farmland on the other. Only a few miles out of town, the houses were already starting to be widely spaced.

“Something’s burning,” Crane agreed.

Charlie could see the dense column of gray smoke rising ahead.

“Shit,” Tony said as they topped a rise and Charlie, along with the others, got a first glimpse of the fire. It was a house, small and off by itself . . . and totally engulfed in flames. “If I’m not mistaken, that’s our destination.”

“You’re right,” Kaminsky said.

Three fire trucks were parked in front of it. It was — or had been — a single-story white-frame house, Charlie saw as they got nearer. Orange flames now belched from it, reaching for the sky, spewing sparks like a fountain, while gray smoke poured into the air. The sulfurous burning smell penetrated even the closed windows of the SUV. Suited-up firefighters worked frantically in an attempt to save it, and as the SUV drew closer Charlie saw that they were pointing hoses at the worst of the flames. An ambulance, a couple of police cars, plus maybe a dozen other vehicles lined the road out front. Civilians whom Charlie took for neighbors stood in clumps near the edge of the action and in the field across the road, watching and talking among themselves.

"What are the chances of this guy's house burning down *today?*" Having reached the lineup of cars, Tony was already looking for a place to park. His tone was savage.

"You think Hannah Beckett might be in there?" Kaminsky's voice was sharp with alarm.

"I'm not a big believer in coincidence." Tony pulled the SUV right onto the edge of the lawn, behind the first fire truck, shoved it into park, shut off the engine, and jumped out. "Come on, let's go see if there's any chance somebody could be in there and still be alive."

They all piled out of the SUV. Tony, Kaminsky, and Crane ran toward the house, while Charlie hung back, not wanting to get in the way. The roar of the fire was truly terrible. Combined with the shouts of the firefighters, the hiss of the water shooting from the hoses, and the various clangs and pops and thuds coming from the collapsing structure, it was overwhelming.

Another fire truck arrived, siren blaring,

and Charlie hurried to get out of the way. She was watching Tony, with a cop on one side and a firefighter on the other, gesture forcefully at what seemed to be the house's basement when something flashing in her peripheral vision made her turn.

She wasn't sure, but she thought she'd seen a blond teenage girl slide between two vehicles parked across the street.

Her first thought was that it was Hannah's ghost, and she had just died in the fire. Heart in her throat, Charlie hurried across the street to check. Her second was that maybe it had been Hannah, alive, and she had somehow escaped the fire. Her third was that maybe it wasn't Hannah at all.

Of course, the girl was gone when she got across the street.

Charlie hesitated, looking around. It was bright daylight, lots of people, all kinds of activity everywhere. But really there was no place that the girl could have disappeared to, so . . .

Eyes looking at her from behind the tinted window of the small van her left side was practically pressed against caught her attention, had her looking back. There was the girl she had seen, inside the van, turning away from the glass now.

Charlie's heart started to pound.

"Hannah?" Charlie knocked sharply on the window, peering through the glass. The girl looked at her.

Charlie just had time to realize she wasn't looking at Hannah at all, but at Bayley Evans, when she heard a footstep behind her and started to turn.

Then something that felt like a mule's kick hit her in the side.

Chapter Thirty-Four

"Goddamn it, Doc, wake the hell up!"

The first thing Charlie heard as she regained consciousness was that roar. Even at top volume, which she figured it had to be close to, she would recognize that honey-dipped voice anywhere in the universe.

She smiled a little as her eyes blinked open. Garland was the first thing she saw. He was leaning over her, his big body seeming way too overwhelming for the enclosed space they were in. Then she got a good look at his face. It was flushed. His eyes were wild. His mouth was grim.

"You awake? You with me?" He bent closer, reaching for her, meaning to shake her or gather her close — or what, Charlie didn't know. Of course his hands passed right through her body. An electric tingle was all she felt.

She smiled at him. His face contorted. "Damn it, Charlie. Are you hearing me?"

Even as she started to feel the first real niggles of alarm, she registered that she was lying on a narrow twin bed with her left arm up in the air. Her arm was in the air because, she saw as she looked at it, her wrist was handcuffed to a metal ring affixed to a wood-paneled wall. The bed was covered with a rough-textured blue blanket, and smelled of damp, of mildew. Then a whisper of movement redirected her attention, and even as her stomach started to churn she saw that Bayley Evans was present. The spirit of the pretty blond teen knelt practically at Garland's feet, folded into the narrow space on the floor between the two beds. Bayley's eyes were closed, and she seemed to be crying silently, tears that appeared shiny wet pouring down her cheeks. On the other bed, apparently unconscious, lay Hannah Beckett. Unlike Bayley, Hannah was, Charlie ascertained as she saw the girl's chest rise and fall, alive.

Hannah was wearing a neon green sequined mini-dress, hiked high around her thighs, with black stilettos. Traces of what appeared to be bright red lipstick smeared the ratty white washcloth that had been used to gag her, and sparkly green eye shadow covered her lids. While Charlie's only restraint seemed to be the handcuffs,

Hannah's ankles and knees were tightly bound with what looked like clothesline. Both wrists had been cuffed together before being secured by a second set of handcuffs to a ring in the wall identical to the one above Charlie's bed.

"Oh, my God," Charlie breathed as the true horror of the situation burst upon her. It was clear to her that the killer they'd been seeking had seen her looking into the back window of the RV she was now in, had assumed she had seen Hannah, and then somehow rendered her unconscious and snatched her away. Remembering his affinity for stun guns, she guessed that was what he had used on her. The fact that she was not gagged or otherwise secured except for the handcuffs told her that it had been a spur-of-the-moment thing.

Her mouth went dry. Her pulse started to pound.

"Be quiet. He's right there. If he hears you, he's liable to come back here sooner rather than later." Garland's face was tight with fear and frustration. For him to look afraid for her, Charlie realized that the situation must be dire. She could feel the van's motion, and knew that they were en route somewhere, that they were no longer anywhere near Tony and the others. None of them, no one, knew where she was. A radio crackled, not with music, but with static and voices. She couldn't make out the words, but she looked instinctively toward the sound. That took her gaze forward, toward the front of the van, through a narrow opening between what looked like a tiny kitchen counter and a closet. Water was dripping loudly in the sink. A handheld police scanner was propped against the dashboard, and she realized that the chatter over it was the other sound she was hearing and remembered Garland's prediction that the killer would have one. She could see the gray bucket seat where the driver sat. She could see the back of his head, with its short, toast-brown hair. She could see his right leg. He was wearing black pants and black sneakers. She could see part of a black jacket lying across the passenger seat. He was young. A copycat, as she had thought, which, ridiculously, came as a relief. Why she should feel relieved she didn't know, because that certainly didn't make him any less of a threat. Even if this wasn't the man who had killed Holly and her family, he was still a vicious killer who got his jollies slashing young girls and their families to death.

Charlie pictured how Bayley's body had looked in death, and her blood ran cold.

"He's going to kill her." Brimming with tears, Bayley's eyes were open. Still on her knees, she was talking to Garland, with her head tilted back so that she could see his face. The hideous injuries she had suffered, that Charlie remembered from Jockey's Ridge and had just seen again in her mind, were no longer in evidence. Bayley was wearing a pale blue, summery, go-to-church dress, and Charlie wondered if that was what her family was burying her in. "He's going to kill them both. He hurt me so much. He is *evil.*"

Garland's nostrils flared. His jaw clenched.

"I'm not going to let that happen," he said to Charlie. His tone was very calm now, very even. He was trying to reassure her, Charlie knew, but she saw the truth in his eyes: as big and bad as he had been in life, he had no substance in death, and there was nothing he could do. "Look, I'm going to see if I can't get your FBI boyfriend here. I'll be back as quick as I can. You stay quiet."

With that he was gone.

"He's going to hurt Hannah." Bayley was looking at Charlie now. Her big blue eyes still rained tears. Her voice shook. "Just like he did me."

Charlie felt the upsurge of nausea that a

close-at-hand spirit always provoked. Her heart ached for Bayley and she longed to offer comfort, but with Garland's warning fresh in her mind, she didn't answer. She was getting a handle on the true danger of her position. Whatever this madman wanted from Hannah, he didn't want the same from her.

She wasn't part of his fantasy. She was *interfering* with it. If she knew anything of how killers of this type worked, he was in a rage right now because of it. He'd kill her as soon as he could.

Please, God, let me figure a way out of this.

Being very careful not to make a sound, Charlie adjusted her position enough to allow her to tug at the metal ring. Yanking it out of the wall probably wasn't going to happen: she wasn't all that physically strong, and it had been solidly installed. Careful not to make the chain rattle, she felt the bracelet around her wrist and each metal link that secured her to the wall.

Not going to be able to break it.

Charlie realized that she was breathing way too fast, and had to force herself to slow it down.

Stay calm.

"He made me call him *Terrybear,*" Bayley wept. "He said if I was a good girl he would let me go home."

Terry Kingston. Charlie remembered the suspect's name.

The van slowed and then turned left. Bright sunlight poured through the front windshield. The windows in the back were lined with a tinted film that from the outside would make them almost impossible to see through. If Bayley had been alive, Charlie realized, she never would have been able to see her inside the van. But the dead had their own way of making their presence felt, and Bayley had been trying to bring help to Hannah.

Instead of helping her, I'm probably going to die with her.

Cold sweat prickled to life around her hairline. Try as she might, Charlie could see no way of freeing herself. She was as trapped and helpless as Hannah. As Bayley and the other girls had been. As Holly had been.

Please, God, help us. Please.

"But he didn't let me go. He killed me." Bayley's voice shook. "He cut me. I screamed and screamed and then . . ."

She bent double with the force of her sobs.

Charlie felt desperately sorry for her, and sick to her stomach, and terrified all at the same time.

The van was stopping. Brakes squeaked,

and the vehicle lurched slightly as it came to a halt.

Charlie's breath caught. A fresh burst of fear shot through her.

Here we go.

"He kept telling me I could go home. He *promised.* But —" Bayley looked up, and her sobbing voice broke off. Her eyes went wide. "He's got his knife," she added in a very different tone. She sounded scared.

Charlie instantly saw why. Having shoved the transmission into park, the driver rolled to his feet and headed straight toward the back. No hesitation whatsoever. In such a cramped space, three strides brought him to the foot of her bed. A wickedly sharp-looking, silver-bladed hunting knife was in his hand. Charlie's breath stopped as her eyes fixed on the knife for one terrified instant. Then she looked up at his face, and her heart started to thump like it was trying to beat its way out of her chest.

She'd seen that expression in the eyes of any number of the men she had studied: he was in full serial killer mode now, primed for murder, hungry for the kill.

"You shoulda stayed away from my van," he said, his tone brutally casual as their eyes connected. Charlie saw that along with a puffy right eye he did, indeed, have a broken front tooth.

Even as Charlie spotted it, Bayley was screaming and jumping to her feet. She was right under his nose, but of course he could neither see nor hear her. Only Charlie could. The scream rattled her a little. Didn't faze him at all.

"I did everything you said. I did! You told me you'd let me go," Bayley cried to her murderer. He couldn't hear her, but his hand tightened on the knife.

A scream of her own burbled into Charlie's throat. If she let loose with it, she knew he'd fall upon her and she would die right there and then. Scrambling into a crouch on the bed because she just couldn't stand to lie there so helplessly, tethered by that hopelessly short chain, Charlie had one hideous instant to swallow the scream. Her heart pounded so hard she thought it might explode.

"Stop, Terrybear." Charlie did her best to make her voice both authoritative and calm. She met his widening eyes. *Show no fear.* "We need to talk about why you didn't keep your promise to Bayley."

He froze, knife suspended. "Why did you call me that?"

" 'Terrybear'? Bayley told me that's what you like to be called." Charlie was having to work to keep her breathing under control. Icy shivers of terror raced over her skin. She was crouched in the far corner of the bed now, as far away from him as she could get, which wasn't very far. One lunge and she would be done for. There was nowhere else she could go: she could feel the wall at her back; the damned chain kept her prisoner. "She said you promised to let her go, but you didn't. You broke your promise. She wants to know why."

"How did you talk to Bayley?" His voice was sharp. Something — suspicion? fear? — flickered behind the killing light in his eyes. The physical description they'd been working with fit: he was tall, rangy, with a long, thin, moderately good-looking face. Twenty-five or twenty-six years old. Kaminsky had said that besides working for Frigate Security, he was a used car salesman who delivered pizzas. Charlie recognized him now: he had delivered a pizza to the beach house the night Tony had kissed her. She had seen him leaving.

If only I had known.

"Bayley is here with us right now," Charlie said. "I can see the dead, you know. She's right in front of you. She wants to know why you broke your promise to let her go."

"Tell him I hate him," Bayley said. "He

made me say I loved him, but I hated him the whole time."

"She lied to me." The left corner of Terry Kingston's mouth started to twitch. "She said she loved me, but she didn't."

"That's the way to do it, Doc. Keep him talking. They're looking for you all over the place." Garland was back, radiating aggression and fear. Looking solid as a rock, he stood balanced on the balls of his feet in the space between the beds, close enough so that she could have touched him if there had actually been anything physical there for her to touch. "They're going to find you. Play for time."

"How do you know she didn't love you?" Allowing herself to be distracted could prove to be a fatal error, Charlie knew. She had to keep Kingston engaged. Instead of looking at Garland, at Bayley, Charlie kept her eyes fixed on his face.

He said, "I didn't want to kill her. I gave her a chance. I was good to her, got her pretty things, made sure she had what she needed. She kept saying she loved me, and for a little while I was stupid and believed her. Then I asked her if she wanted to go home, and she said she did. After all I'd done for her, she wanted to leave me and go home! I knew then that the bitch had been lying, I knew then that she was just like the others, that she didn't love me, so I killed her."

His face twisted, and the terrifying intensity returned to his eyes. Charlie shivered, and immediately tried to get a grip. She only hoped he didn't notice the trembling that she couldn't quite control.

"You took away my life," Bayley screamed at him. "I *was* lying the whole time. You made me sick every time you came near me. I hope you burn in hell for what you did!"

"Bayley is upset that you killed her," Charlie said steadily. From the corner of her eye, she saw that Hannah's eyes were open now. Glassy with horror, they were fixed on Terry Kingston's knife.

"You're full of shit," Kingston growled. His fingers flexed around the knife, but at least he hadn't sprung at her yet.

"No, I'm not." Charlie was sweating bullets. Her pulse pounded. Her heart raced. She felt shaky, jittery, scared to death, but she didn't dare let any of it show, just like she didn't dare to pull her eyes away from his face. "Bayley, did he get you a pretty dress like Hannah is wearing? What color was it?"

"Blue," Bayley said. Her tears were gone now. She looked at Kingston with loathing.

"Only it wasn't pretty. It was ugly and I hated it."

"Bayley's dress was blue," Charlie said. Kingston's eyes flickered. He cast a quick, apprehensive look around the room. Then his gaze returned to Charlie. There was an ugly expression on his face. He was breathing hard, his hand was tight around the knife, and he once again looked on the verge of jumping at her. Charlie's throat threatened to close up.

"How do you know that?" he demanded.

"I told you. Bayley is right here with us. Right in front of you. She told me."

"You're lying!"

"Two other girls are here. They say he killed them, too." Garland's voice was hoarse. Being unable to do anything physical to help her was causing him to practically vibrate with tension. Charlie could feel it coming off him in waves. "Caroline Clark and Danielle Breyer. Caroline says the dress he got her was red with a big full skirt."

"Caroline says the dress you got her was red with a big full skirt," Charlie repeated. Of course she couldn't see the other two girls — they had been dead too long. Thank God Garland could! If she could just keep Kingston off balance . . .

"Caroline's here, too?" Casting another

harried glance around the space, Kingston took a step back. He actually looked a little afraid.

"Her ghost," Charlie said, knowing the terrifying connotation the word had for most people. If she could scare him enough, maybe he'd . . . What? Turn tail and run? Her heart pounded so hard it hurt as she realized that rescue was her and Hannah's only hope. *Keep talking.* "The ghosts of Caroline and Danielle and Bayley are all here."

"You're lying!"

"Danielle says her dress was yellow and had a big bow in back." Garland's hands were clenched into fists. From the corner of her eye, Charlie could see the bunching of the muscles in his arms and shoulders. She could feel the violence in him. "She says she cut her hand and this little punk-ass bastard put a Band-Aid on it."

"Danielle says her dress was yellow with a bow in the back. She cut her hand and you put a Band-Aid on it," Charlie said.

"How are you doing this?" Kingston was breathing hard. For the moment at least it seemed he had forgotten the knife in his hand.

Bayley stood right in front of Kingston now. Charlie could only see her back. It was straight as a poker. Her long blond hair hung down her back in an Alice-in-Wonderland fall.

"You killed my mom and my brother. You want me to prove I'm here? You took Trevor's video game. You were playing it, at your house." Fury seethed through Bayley's every word. "You had an argument with some guy right before you killed me. Then you came and asked me if I wanted to go home, and when I said I did you told me to close my eyes and pray" — Bayley's voice broke; it was shaking as she finished — "and you cut my throat."

"Bayley says you took her little brother's video game. She says you were playing it at your house," Charlie told him. "She says you had an argument with another man, and you told her to close her eyes and pray before you cut her throat."

Kingston's head snapped back as if she'd hit him. "This is some kind of trick, isn't it? It's a setup." He looked wildly around. "You're playing me. There's no such thing as ghosts."

"Doc, your friend is here. Holly. She's telling me this piece of shit watched when she was killed. She says he was a little kid, and he watched."

Charlie's eyes jerked toward Garland at

that. "What?"

"Jesus, keep your attention on him!" The harshness of his tone sprang from fear for her, Charlie knew. "Holly says that he was hiding in a closet and he watched."

"Who the hell are you talking to?" A nerve near Kingston's eye jumped. His voice was louder now, and shriller. The knife moved threateningly, and it was all Charlie could do not to focus on it instead of his face. "And don't you go telling me it's some damned ghost."

"It is a ghost. This one is named Holly. She was murdered a long time ago, fifteen years. She says you watched as she was killed. She says you hid in a closet."

Kingston's mouth fell open. His face whitened. He visibly shuddered. As his eyes darted around again, Charlie saw that he was starting to sweat. *"Who's telling you this?"*

"The killer was his dad," Garland supplied.

"Holly's telling me. She says it was your father who killed her."

"What the *fuck?*" He wet his lips as he shot a fearful glance in Garland's direction. Charlie guessed he'd been able to tell that whatever she was purportedly talking to was about right there. Then his eyes fixed on Charlie again. They brimmed with rage and fear. "You're not doing this to me. I'm not buying it, you bitch," he snarled, and Charlie saw in the flash of his eyes that time was up: he meant to spring at her.

"God*damn it.*" Garland made an abortive movement that brought him closer to her as Charlie's heart leaped into her throat and Kingston seemed to gather himself.

Bayley screamed out, "No!"

With a loud *thud,* someone kicked open the van's door. The flimsy-looking metal panel crashed back on its hinges.

"What the fuck?" Kingston whirled, still holding the knife.

A gun blasted, just as quick as that. Charlie screamed like a steam whistle as the sound of the explosion blasted her eardrums and the back of Kingston's head blew off. Blood sprayed the small compartment. She felt the warmth of the splatter hitting her as Kingston's body dropped like a felled tree. The impact as it hit the floor shook the van.

"Is everybody all right in here?" Haney asked. Never in her life had Charlie expected to be glad to see him, but she absolutely was.

"Jesus H. Christ," Garland growled as he dropped down into a crouch beside her. She could feel the intensity of his relief. "You ever think that messing with serial killers might not be the smartest move, Doc?"

"F-fine." She ignored Garland in favor of replying to Haney, only to discover that her teeth were chattering and it was an effort to get even that one word out. Bayley was gone. Charlie could only suppose it was because her killer was now dead. Hannah's body was tense and her eyes were screwed tightly shut. Charlie experienced a quiver of fellow feeling for what she knew must be the terror the girl was experiencing. Her own body was shaking with fright and reaction, and she would have turned into Garland's arms except, oh, wait, that wasn't possible. As the realization that it was over — that she and Hannah were safe — started to sink in, she took a deep breath and sagged a bit, still trapped by that damned chain. Haney filled the little area between the counter and closet, looking from Charlie to Hannah, a pistol in his hand, a grim expression on his face.

Then he tucked his pistol away in his shoulder holster, stepped over Kingston's corpse, bent, and picked up his knife.

"Should've killed that little pissant long ago," Haney said. "Just like I should have come after you fifteen years ago once I found out you were there in the Palmers' house that night." Then he lunged at Charlie with the knife.

Chapter Thirty-Five

Charlie shrieked and threw herself back against the wall.

"Son of a bitch," Garland roared, flinging himself between her and Haney. She could feel him, she realized, feel his weight and the heat of his body and the solid steely strength of him just as if he were alive, and she guessed that the extremity of her need must have triggered him to materialize physically. His hands wrapped around the chain holding her, and he yanked the ring it was fastened to right out of the wall.

"Who the hell?" Haney yelled as Garland grabbed him and threw him down on the bed.

"Run," Garland bellowed at Charlie, who did, leaping over the pair of them like a gazelle and darting for the door because she realized that she only had seconds before Garland was mist again and Haney was free to come after her. Leaving Hannah was

wrenching, but her escape was the only hope either of them had. As she burst out into what she saw in that first instantaneous glance was a clearing in the midst of a piney woods, the image that was busy branding itself into her mind was what she had seen as she had jumped over Garland and Haney entwined: the handle of that wicked-looking knife sticking out of Garland's broad back.

He'd taken the killing blow that had been meant for her.

You can't kill a dead man, Charlie reminded herself savagely, and ran like her life depended on it, which it did. Hannah's, too. Charlie had no doubt whatsoever that once he had finished with her, Haney would turn back and slaughter the girl.

A string of curses made Charlie glance behind her. Haney leaped from the van, looked around for her. He no longer had Kingston's knife in his hand. He had his gun instead.

Charlie's heart exploded with terror. Every tiny hair on her body catapulted upright. She wanted to scream her lungs out. But she swallowed the urge, knowing it would only serve to pinpoint her location for him, and instead ran like a rabbit with the hounds after it.

You really think you can outrun a gun?

Kingston had driven up a dirt track, which he'd clearly turned onto from the road. Keeping to the track would be suicide, no cover there. Charlie had realized that in an instant, as soon as she'd escaped the van, so she was already plunging through the woods. The scent of pine filled her nostrils as she barreled past low-hanging limbs. Even this early in the morning, the heat was intense. Luckily it was summer, though, and the mulch underfoot was green and didn't crack and snap with her every desperate footfall. The sounds of birds and insects and rustling branches would mask the noise of her flight to some degree, she hoped. The pines were thick with needles, which might keep Haney from spotting her right away. But there was no point in trying to fool herself: it wouldn't take him long.

Charlie fled, racing through the woods parallel to the track, knowing that her only hope was to get to the road, flag down a car, get to some other human being who could help her before Haney got a clear shot at her.

He means to make it look like Kingston killed Hannah and me.

That much was clear. Horror took over at the realization, clouding her thought processes, causing her to go all light-headed and fuzzy-brained. Haney was the man who'd slit Diane Palmer's throat, the man who'd murdered Holly, the original Boardwalk Killer. It had been *him* whom she'd sensed at Jockey's Ridge. She hadn't recognized him — just like she'd been afraid all along she wouldn't recognize him when he came.

And he had come. It was her worst nightmare: *He's come back for me.*

Garland must have been kicked back into Spookville, or he would be with her now. It was doubly terrifying to know she was completely on her own.

Please, God, help. . . .

"There you are," Haney called with satisfaction, and knowing that she was close enough that she could hear him sent a fresh jolt of terror through her. Glancing fearfully back as she ran, she saw that he'd plunged into the woods about a hundred yards behind her, and that he could indeed see her, just as she could see him.

It took maybe another split second for her to realize he wasn't chasing her.

He was standing still and snapping up his gun.

To shoot her.

Terror sent goose bumps racing over her skin. Dread slid like ice down her spine.

With all need for subterfuge past, Charlie screamed like a siren and threw herself to the left and kept running. A bullet smacked into a tree trunk just a few feet in front of where she had been.

Please, God, please . . .

Now Haney was chasing her. She could hear him, cursing and crashing through the branches behind her. How long would it be before he had the chance at another clear shot?

Her skin tingled. She could almost feel a bullet burying itself in her back. Oh, God, would it hurt?

Please . . .

Then she saw it, through the trees. The black SUV. It was bumping up the dirt track, traveling fast.

Screaming, she bolted toward it. They must have spotted her, because it jerked to a halt.

Charlie burst through the trees just as all three of them leaped from the van, running toward her, guns out and aimed at something behind her.

"Haney, freeze!" Tony yelled. *"Drop your weapon."*

Then Charlie reached them, or they reached her. Kaminsky and Crane ran on past, and a single glance over her shoulder told her that Haney was just yards behind her. He stood still, no longer holding his gun, and she guessed he must have dropped it on Tony's command. His hands were in the air.

Her strength gave out, and she would have fallen to her knees if Tony hadn't wrapped an arm around her and pulled her against his side.

"It's okay," he said. "You're safe now."

"Hannah Beckett's up there in an RV. She's alive," Charlie gasped. Then, panting, resting against him, finally allowing herself to believe it was over, Charlie closed her eyes.

A little later, after Hannah was freed and whisked off to a hospital and Haney had been taken away and an obliging cop had removed the dangling handcuff from her wrist, Charlie sat on a fallen log not too far away from the van. Police and FBI were already swarming around, and the medical examiner was said to be on the way. She knew the media wouldn't be far behind.

She had just watched the Meads come for Bayley. Julie, Tom, and Trevor had all appeared together, not too far from where she sat. Bayley had come running from the direction of the van, and gone right into Julie's outstretched arms. Then the four of them had done the group-hug thing and gone walking off together, arm in arm, before disappearing.

Charlie liked to think they'd gone into the white light.

Tony had been in the van for a while. Now he came out to join her, sitting down on the log next to her, offering her a bottle of water.

Charlie accepted it with a nod of thanks, unscrewed the lid, and took a long drink. Until that moment, she hadn't realized just how dry her throat was.

"I have a question for you," he said. "Haney and Hannah both said something about an instant appearance and disappearance of a big blond guy."

Charlie shrugged. She wasn't about to try to explain Garland to him.

The merest suggestion of a smile touched Tony's mouth. "I don't want to know, huh?"

Charlie shook her head.

"Fair enough."

"I have a question for you," she said. "How did you find me?"

"We were looking for you everywhere when I got a call from the lab. It was the damned ChapStick. In that bundle of stuff you gave me, seems there were two of them. One was still in the pocket of your jeans. The other one had Haney's DNA on it. Apparently it was his. All we can figure is that he dropped it the night he killed the Palmers, and it somehow got caught up in your clothes. Soon as I heard that, I had the Bureau put a trace on his cell phone. It didn't take them long to find him, but it seemed like a lifetime to me."

The way he was looking at her, Charlie could see that her disappearance had scared him. She appreciated that. It was actually something she could build on.

Maybe.

One day.

Depending on how things went.

Chapter Thirty-Six

Four days later, Tony was taking Charlie home. It was around ten p.m., and twilight had just turned the corner into full dark. They were in Big Stone Gap, driving up her street in a dark blue Lincoln sedan that had been waiting for them when the plane had touched down at Lonesome Pine Airport some three hours before. They'd had dinner at the Mountain Laurel Restaurant — that dinner he'd owed her. After he dropped her off he would be returning to the airport and winging away to Quantico, where Kaminsky and Crane awaited him. Until another serial killer hit their radar, they were working at headquarters.

Charlie had already told Tony that she wouldn't be taking him up on his offer to join their team.

"I'll consult," she had promised. "Call whenever you need me."

But her home, and her work, were in Big

Stone Gap.

To say nothing of a certain lonely grave.

She hadn't seen Garland since he'd saved her from Haney.

She was hideously afraid that she might never see him again.

Either he'd been kicked into eternity and was unable to get out, or he was around and she just couldn't see him.

What both scenarios left her with was a raw and aching heart. She'd let herself get too close to him, and now she was paying the price. She already could tell that it was going to take her some time to heal.

"So Haney's claiming total innocence?" Charlie said, continuing the conversation she and Tony had been having. "How can he do that? To begin with, he tried to kill me."

"He's lawyered up, and he's twisting the facts. He's saying that he only realized that his son was the killer we were looking for when he found the three of you in that travel van. That he shot his own son to save you and Hannah Beckett. That you freaked out and ran when the shooting started, and imagined the rest."

"The liar," Charlie said indignantly.

"Yeah, I know."

"Aside from everything else, he shot

Kingston the moment he stepped inside that van. He never even saw Hannah and me until after Kingston was dead. He must have known all along his son was the killer."

"Not all along." Tony shook his head. "We don't think Haney knew the copycat was his son until a convenience store owner drew his attention to a surveillance shot of a gray Dodge Charger at the right time and place to be involved in the attack at the Meads'. Kingston has a gray Dodge Charger. When he saw the car, Haney must have recognized it and instantly started to suspect Kingston. We know this because he substituted surveillance footage of another gray car — remember the DVD of the gray Avalon he had Officer Price give me? — for the footage of the Charger. He must have made the substitution in case the convenience store owner mentioned the surveillance shot to anyone else. Anyway, we've got both shots now: the original of the Charger, and the substitute one of the Avalon Haney passed on to me, trying to throw the investigation off track. It's actually a pretty damning piece of evidence against him."

Charlie considered, then frowned. "He gave that surveillance footage to you on the night before —"

She broke off. Following the thought to its conclusion was just too horrible.

Tony finished it for her. "Bayley Evans' body was found. Yeah. After seeing the footage of the Charger, Haney went straight over to Kingston's house. He found Bayley Evans there, tied up in the basement, and had it out with Kingston. During the course of what went down that night, Kingston revealed he knew that Haney was the Boardwalk Killer, and told him that he had found one of the girls Haney had kidnapped. Apparently Haney kept them out in a detached garage behind the house. After that, when little kid Kingston was visiting his dad, he'd check to see if Haney had a girl back there. If he did, Kingston would slip into a closet and watch as his father tortured and killed her."

"My God," Charlie breathed. "How do you know all this?"

"Kingston had a webcam trained on Bayley Evans — on each of the girls, when he had them. Recording everything, so that he could relive the experience later. The argument Kingston and Haney had that night took place in the basement, right where he was keeping Bayley Evans. It got picked up by the webcam, and it's still on Kingston's computer."

"Tony." Charlie's heart had started to thump. "Did the webcam catch Bayley's murder?"

Tony's mouth twisted. "Yeah. It caught that, too."

For a moment Charlie could hardly breathe. "Did Kingston do it? Or . . ."

"Kingston. He didn't want to, but Haney ordered him to kill her right there and then and warned him to stop with the murders. When Kingston didn't — well, that's when the rest of it went down."

"Serial killers can't stop," Charlie said. "It's a compulsion. They have to kill until they are caught or something stops them."

"Like Haney's car accident stopped him," Tony said. "No telling how many more victims there would have been in the original group if that hadn't happened."

They had discovered that right after the Palmer murders, Haney's car had been hit by a drunk driver. He'd been ejected through the windshield, spent almost a year in the hospital and another year in rehab, and had extensive plastic surgery to repair his facial injuries. This knowledge made Charlie feel a little better about not recognizing him.

"That's why Kingston took Hannah so soon after he was forced to kill Bayley,"

Charlie said. "He couldn't stop. He had to play out his fantasy to the end."

"Haney must have been going out of his mind," Tony said. "We know that as soon as he left the Becketts' house, he went searching for his son. He expected Kingston would have taken Hannah to his house, just like he did Bayley and the others, but Kingston was too smart for that, since Haney had found him there the last time and made him get rid of Bayley. When Haney got there, the house was empty."

"How do you know?" Charlie asked. "Was that caught on Kingston's webcam, too?"

Tony shook his head. "Kingston had his computer with him in the van, up in the passenger seat. I'm guessing he meant to turn it on Hannah, but just hadn't gotten the chance yet. What we've got is the GPS from Haney's police car showing us where Haney went that night."

"Ah," Charlie said. "So Haney set fire to Kingston's house to make sure he couldn't take Hannah back there and finish his fantasy with her?"

Tony nodded. "Also to get rid of all the evidence. Haney knew Kingston was on our short list of suspects. He knew that there was a good chance we were going to bring him in sooner or later. I'm sure he was afraid that if we arrested Kingston, his son would spill the beans on him, too. After he set fire to Kingston's house, he waited around nearby for him to come home."

"He was actually taking a big risk." Charlie closed her eyes for a moment as she realized how differently things could have worked out. When she opened them again, it was to discover Tony watching her with concern. She gave him a small, reassuring smile: *I'm fine.* "Kingston could have gone anywhere in that van. Given that Haney had already surprised him in the house with Bayley, it's a wonder that Kingston didn't just take off with Hannah."

Tony smiled back. "But, see, Haney knew Kingston had a police scanner. He knew Kingston listened to it all the time, and that he would hear over it that his house was on fire, and come to check it out. All he had to do was wait."

"I see." Charlie nodded. "Haney was right about that, too."

"Haney was right about a lot. Having burned Kingston's house, if he had found and killed Kingston and made it look like Kingston had killed Hannah, he would have been home free." Tony's gaze was steady on her face. "What he didn't expect to find in that van was you. But ever since he'd learned who you are, that you were the girl who had survived the original Boardwalk Killer murders and had actually seen him, he'd been afraid of you, afraid you'd recognize him. Finding you there, getting the chance to finally silence you, knowing that if you and Hannah were killed he could pin the blame on Kingston and take the credit for stopping the new Boardwalk Killer was just too good an opportunity for him to pass up. And it almost worked."

Charlie remembered Holly's claim that Kingston had witnessed her being murdered, and shivered. "Haney really didn't know that his son had watched him kill?"

"I don't think so," Tony replied. "We know that Haney and Kingston were estranged, that apart from maybe a year's court-ordered visitation they hadn't really had much interaction at all since Kingston's mother, Haney's first wife, divorced him fifteen years ago. You were on the money with that one, too, by the way. Haney and Kingston's mother met at a dance, and we're working on the assumption that their divorce was what triggered the original Boardwalk Killer murders. Apparently the mother was afraid of Haney and tried to keep her son away from him. We do know that Kingston — and he's Terry Kingston instead of Terry Haney because his mother married Ron Kingston, and Terry was later adopted by his stepfather and took his name, which is why the fact that Haney is his biological father never turned up in any of our computer searches — was still visiting his father regularly right after the divorce, which is when the original Boardwalk Killer murders occurred."

"I've always wondered about the nature versus nurture element in the evolution of a serial killer," Charlie said. Detaching emotionally by reverting to her researcher persona was the best way to keep too-painful emotions at bay, she had learned. "Did Terry Kingston inherit an as-yet-unidentified serial killer gene from his father, or was his urge to kill sparked by watching his father murder those poor girls?"

"Fascinating question, Dr. Stone." Tony's face relaxed into a teasing grin as he pulled into her driveway. Except for the porch light, her house was dark, but still she felt like it was welcoming her home. "I'm sure you'll ponder it endlessly."

"Yes, I will," Charlie replied with dignity. "Because I'm a researcher, and that's what we researchers do." She took a deep breath as he braked and put the car into park. She was glad to be home, but she was just realizing how much she was going to miss Tony, and Kaminsky and Crane, too. "Let me ask you something: are you sure there's enough evidence to absolutely convict Haney?"

Tony's hand was on the ignition, but he didn't shut off the motor. Charlie got the feeling he was a little reluctant to say goodbye to her, too.

"I'm sure." Tony looked at her through the dark. "You don't have to worry that he'll ever get out and come after you again. We've got him dead to rights, even without going back to the original Boardwalk Killer murders." Tony cocked an eyebrow at her. "So, you ready to tell me about the blond mystery guy yet?"

Charlie shook her head. She absolutely was not. She doubted that she ever would be. "It's one of those I-see-dead-people things, okay? Sometimes spirits flash in and out."

To put a period to the subject, she opened the door and slid out into the night.

Tony shut off the engine and got out, too. They walked up the flagstone path together. Close. Their bodies brushing.

It was a beautiful summer's night. All kinds of stars twinkling in the sky. The moon as white and round as a golf ball. Cicadas whirring. Fireflies twinkling. Nary a neighbor in sight.

If she'd been in the mood for romance, the perfect candidate had his hand curled around her elbow. Charlie looked up at him, at his good-guy smile and dark good looks, and realized that she wasn't. Not tonight.

Maybe not for a while.

"You sure you won't change your mind and come to work for us?" Tony asked as they climbed the steps to her small front porch. Charlie already had her keys in her hand. She shook her head as she unlocked the door, then turned to smile at him.

"I'm sure," she said.

"At least there's an upside to it," he said philosophically.

When Charlie looked a question at him, he bent his head and kissed her.

Charlie kissed him back. It was, she considered, a kiss with possibilities. Warm and sweet, with a nice level of heat. Maybe one day it would even be right.

"You could ask me in," he suggested when he lifted his head. Charlie was already shaking hers at him when a sound caught her attention.

Someone's TV was playing, very loud. Eyes widening, she realized that it was her

TV, the one in her living room.

"Did you leave your TV on?" Tony frowned in the direction of the sound.

Charlie had already recognized the channel: ESPN.

"It's on a timer," she lied. Her pulse began to pick up pace. She looked at Tony, smiling at him because she really liked him a lot, even though her insides were curling into anticipatory knots and her heart was starting to flutter with hope. "I've got to go in now. Call me if you need something."

"I will," he said. "Good-night."

Charlie was already moving away from him, letting herself into her house, which hadn't had anybody in it for days, where her TV was blaring angrily.

Just like it might be if, for example, a pissy ghost who had learned to work the remote had just watched her kiss another man.

"See you," she said to Tony.

Heart hammering, smiling like an idiot, Charlie shut the door on him. Then she turned and walked into the dark.

ABOUT THE AUTHOR

Karen Robards is the *New York Times* and *USA Today* bestselling author of forty books and one novella. The mother of three boys, she lives in her hometown of Louisville, Kentucky.

The employees of Thorndike Press hope you have enjoyed this Large Print book. All our Thorndike, Wheeler, and Kennebec Large Print titles are designed for easy reading, and all our books are made to last. Other Thorndike Press Large Print books are available at your library, through selected bookstores, or directly from us.

For information about titles, please call:
(800) 223-1244

or visit our Web site at:
http://gale.cengage.com/thorndike

To share your comments, please write:
Publisher
Thorndike Press
10 Water St., Suite 310
Waterville, ME 04901